Cadence to Glory

A Novel of the American Revolution

Mary Beth Dearmon, MD
©2008

Copyright © 2014 Mary Beth Dearmon, MD
All rights reserved.

ISBN: 1502768615
ISBN 13: 9781502768612
Library of Congress Control Number: 2014918215
CreateSpace Independent Publishing Platform
North Charleston, South Carolina

Table of Contents

Part I

Chapter 1 – The Family	3
Chapter 2 – The Acquaintance	12
Chapter 3 – The Tea	20
Chapter 4 – The Idealist	23
Chapter 5 – The Gift	29
Chapter 6 – The Promise	32
Chapter 7 – The Garden	39
Chapter 8 – The Announcement	44
Chapter 9 – The Outburst	49
Chapter 10 – The Prediction	54
Chapter 11 – The Eccentrics	58
Chapter 12 – The Marriage	62
Chapter 13 – The Guests	65
Chapter 14 – The Suitor	71
Chapter 15 – The Conspiracy	77
Chapter 16 – The Interview	80
Chapter 17 – The Ball	84

Part II

Chapter 18 – The Defiance	99
Chapter 19 – The Incident	105
Chapter 20 – The Illness	110
Chapter 21 – The Excursion	118

Chapter 22 – The Plantation	125
Chapter 23 – The Letters	130
Chapter 24 – The Visitors	136
Chapter 25 – The Rendezvous	141
Chapter 26 – The Confession	150
Chapter 27 – The Return	155
Chapter 28 – The Engagement	160
Chapter 29 – The Birth	165
Chapter 30 – The Widower	173

Part III

Chapter 31 – The Warning	179
Chapter 32 – The Confrontation	188
Chapter 33 – The Unmasking	192
Chapter 34 – The Holiday	197
Chapter 35 – The Remonstration	203
Chapter 36 – The Riot	210
Chapter 37 – The Decision	216
Chapter 38 – The Departure	229
Chapter 39 – The Remembrance	234
Chapter 40 – The Confiscation	243
Chapter 41 – The Repudiation	248
Chapter 42 – The March	252

Part IV

Chapter 43 – The Scholar	257
Chapter 44 – The Physician	265
Chapter 45 – The Inheritance	276
Chapter 46 – The Prisoner	279
Chapter 47 – The Intrigue	289
Chapter 48 – The Declaration	295
Chapter 49 – The Accident	300
Chapter 50 – The Englishmen	307

Cadence to Glory

Part V

Chapter 51 – The Widow 313
Chapter 52 – The Revolutionary 318
Chapter 53 – The Passing 322
Chapter 54 – The Spy 327
Chapter 55 – The Journey 333
Chapter 56 – The Soldier 338
Chapter 57 – The Nation 342

Dedicated to my beloved parents,
Dr. Alice Smith Dearmon
and the late Dr. V. Lamar Dearmon,
to whom I owe so much,
to my late grandmother, Margie Smith,
for her encouragement in the formative stages of this work,
And to Christ, Who bestowed the gift

*"O thou that sendest out the man
To rule by land and sea,
Strong mother of a Lion-line,
Be proud of those strong sons of thine
Who wrench'd their rights from thee!"*

- Tennyson, from "England and America in 1782"

Part I

Chapter 1

The Family

In the year of our Lord 1773, all was well in Williamsburg, although a certain turbulence ruled the colonies as a whole.

The town, however, erupted with activity on such a bright August morning.

Today is market.

Amidst the clamor of negotiation, a manservant for the Parr household had been sent early to seize an advantage for the highest-quality goods.

Seventeen-year-old Priscilla Parr, fixated by the present bustle, sat in the front parlor of her family's stately brick home. Clutching a book, she surveyed the street. A smile unfolded upon her face, and her spirits soared. Priscilla soon closed her volume since the engaging hum of the town accompanied by the picturesque weather prevented literary immersion. She turned her thoughts to a conflict that had lately disturbed her privileged existence.

The ratification of the Tea Act in May had provoked the upheaval at hand. Priscilla had heard the debates for weeks now. The act had been received with profuse praise by her family but had evoked blistering resentment in others. She was perplexed that the families of some of her dearest friends remained opposed to it. Her own father grew livid when confronted by even a whisper of hostility toward the Crown. Her embarrassment, however, became suffocating when she heard him defending Parliament so stridently in company or at a public gathering.

The depth of her father's sentiments was nevertheless scarcely a surprise. The Parr family had been Loyalist for years. At dinner the previous night, her father and brother—rebuking the rebels, discussing new tidings of riots, and forgetting the presence of ladies in general—had resurrected the odious topic. Mrs. Parr and Priscilla's two sisters had glanced downward. Priscilla, however, had listened to all. In the privacy of the Parr household, she suffered no shame to absorb her father's zealous ramblings—and to ponder their implications.

Priscilla's present reverie was disrupted by the maidservant's bell, which heralded a visit by her closest friend, Miss Katherine Lee.

"Dearest Kate, I received your note early this morning!" Priscilla rose to greet her friend as the latter was shown into the parlor. "What is your news?"

Katherine's cherubic gray eyes glittered as she settled upon the sofa opposite Priscilla. "I have it on good authority that a new family is to arrive soon in Williamsburg."

"Are they Virginians?"

"Yes, of course—from Richmond, I believe."

"And what is their status?" Clutching the arm of her chair, Priscilla leaned forward. "Are they of the first gentry?"

"The very first! The family is prosperous indeed. They once lived in Williamsburg, but 'twas eight years ago. I speak of none other than the Eton family! Surely you remember them?"

Priscilla indeed remembered them.

Eight years ago, the Parrs and the Etons had frequented the same echelon of Williamsburg society. Mr. Eton, once a thriving attorney in the town, had been a dear friend of her father's, but a sterner man could not be imagined. Priscilla recollected Mrs. Eton's demeanor more fondly as that of a gracious, well-bred gentlewoman. The Eton children had consisted of an elder son, a daughter, and a younger son. Priscilla recalled the youngest son most vividly of all. She smiled at sudden thoughts of him, which returned in rapid succession on the present occasion.

Thomas Eton and Priscilla Parr had been inseparable playfellows as children. These tidings evoked memories of endless frolicking upon the Palace Green in the cool mornings of long ago. The children of affluence, they had basked in happy indolence. Priscilla sighed at these remembrances and yearned for the reunion.

"How soon are they to come, Kate?"

"They arrive on Monday. They have purchased the old Princeton home."

"I had wondered when the place would be sold. They arrive on Monday! I seem to be the last person to receive such news," laughed Priscilla.

"It might console you that few knew of it until today. Their advent has been sudden. The Etons, you remember, always were a peculiar and secretive sort of family."

Priscilla raised her eyebrows. "A characteristic most likely due to *Mr.* Eton, I should think. Dreadful man!" She suddenly broke into a soft succession of giggles. "Do you remember how he used to frighten us, Kate?"

Katherine shuddered. "My sisters and I always hid ourselves within the draperies and behind the furniture whenever Mr. Eton called upon Father."

"Yes, for he always wore the forbidding look of a miser!" Priscilla mimicked the stern expression of Richard Eton, much to the enjoyment of her friend. "His own children feared him, I fancy. Poor Thomas! And yet, my father and Mr. Eton were very close in those days." Priscilla's thoughts returned to the matter at hand as she ventured further into Katherine's intelligence. "Mr. Eton will shift his law firm back, I presume?"

"Yes, of course." Only partly recovered from the fit of laughter provoked by Priscilla's imitation, Katherine continued to dab tears of merriment from her eyes. "William, his eldest son, will join him in the practice. He was admitted to the Virginia bar a few years past."

Retrieving the book she had only moments before cast aside, Priscilla slowly fingered its worn pages. "Are any of the young Etons married yet?"

"None. None at all." A palpitation of joy seemed to dance about Katherine's small scarlet mouth—or so Priscilla imagined.

"I should have at least thought William to be settled with a wife." Priscilla clasped her hands. "These old friends shall bring us a great deal of excitement in the coming months. How I long to see them again!"

Monday brought a drizzle, which killed Priscilla's hope to glimpse the arriving Eton family. In a flurry of anticipation, she planted herself beside the window of the front parlor for the most advantageous view. Instead, the only sight afforded her consisted of a grandiose carriage rumbling through the street, mud splashing as it met the wheels.

The sour weather continued past Wednesday but cleared on Thursday afternoon. Priscilla, who had not ventured forth since church services on Sunday, welcomed the sunshine. Her principal excitement of the day occurred at dinner when her father announced that the entire family had been invited to the Eton home.

"The invitation is for next Friday. The Etons have requested the presence of all their old friends—as well as new ones," he continued. The gasp that escaped Priscilla's lips following this declaration appeared to stoke his curiosity. "Did you not know of their return to Williamsburg?"

"Yes, Father; I was aware of it."

"Then why do you look so astonished?" Mr. Parr studied her face with amusement.

"It is a sudden event." Priscilla found expression for her swirling thoughts while she toyed with the knife resting next to her porcelain plate. "One would think it better for them to become settled in their new abode before hosting such festivities."

"Yes, I thought it odd myself." Mr. Parr snapped out the linen napkin and laid it across his lap. "Men are quick to parade their wealth before society. Still, I myself am no exception to this, and the Etons' new home is a fine one. I shall be glad to see them again. You are all well aware, of course, that Richard Eton was like a brother to me when my family was first established in Williamsburg."

Priscilla's heart soared to ponder the tale he had long recounted with pride. Phillip Parr's father, as the second son of a grand English landowner, had received only a modest sum for his inheritance. Seeking the notoriety his birth had denied him, he had journeyed to the American Colonies with his sister Mary, his wife, and his only surviving son. The old man, however, had succumbed to dropsy shortly after the family settled in Williamsburg.

As a youth, Phillip had long striven to redeem his late father's hopes. Gifted with a quick mind for economics, he had invested the small English inheritance in trade. His livelihood had thus multiplied, and many a ship that docked in the great northeastern harbors bore the Parr fortune in addition to its wares. Likewise, he had achieved fame for his service during the war against the French and their Indian allies a decade ago.

Priscilla blushed with pride to recall her father's victories over adversity and surmised that anyone, including Richard Eton, who had befriended him during such a dark hour of his life would always hold a rigid claim upon his goodwill. "What could account for the Etons' abrupt return?" Priscilla, her imagination provoked, eagerly awaited a response.

"It is whispered that young William desires a wife," Mrs. Parr said, veiling her smile behind a lace handkerchief.

"Were there not enough women in Richmond to please him?" Priscilla did not even attempt to conceal the mischief flavoring her voice.

"And yet, there are more than enough in this house to satisfy him—if he so chooses!" Ben's roaring chuckle rattled the crystal chandelier that hung above the oaken table. Flashing a wink in her direction, he said, "I wager that Priscilla will turn his heart—and perhaps break it!"

Priscilla's smile masked discomfort. "You flatter me, Ben—though I am no keeper of hearts, much less a cruel mistress of the same."

Though moved by her brother's jovial affection, Priscilla found herself accosted by a mystery with which she had long grappled. From her earliest memory, she had been recognized as a beauty by her elders. Yet, whenever curiosity had driven Priscilla to examine her own image upon the looking glass in recent years, she had glimpsed a pale oval face, punctuated by incisive green eyes and somewhat overwhelmed by the chestnut-hued ringlets cascading past her waist. In Priscilla's judgment, hers was a countenance deepened by a lifetime of thought and perhaps marred by traces of cynicism…a visage unworthy to obscure the brilliance of her mind and the fierceness of her spirit.

"You address Priscilla too hastily, Brother." Ivy Parr turned upon Ben suddenly as a bright gleam leapt in her eye. "Do not forget that, as the eldest, my favor has more value should William bestow his attentions."

Priscilla struggled to suppress the irritation her elder sister aroused. Ivy, however, resumed dining in such a nonchalant manner that Priscilla wondered if the remark had indeed carried an insult.

A plain-looking awkward creature with reddish-brown locks and dull blue eyes, Ivy was not favored by nature. Likewise, an upturned nose and prominent cheekbones did nothing to enhance her appearance. Comparisons in beauty of the two eldest Parr sisters often reflected poorly upon Ivy, and several remarks, made innocently enough by friends of the family while both girls were still young, had formed an impression. Ivy, openly embittered by the scrutiny, had always made it plain that she intended to make a brilliant match to eclipse the glory of Priscilla, her sister and rival.

Ivy thus kept her own counsel, and Priscilla was accustomed to her subtle attacks. Still, neither pity nor familiarity with Ivy's sour temper succeeded in softening the blow. Priscilla parted her lips to issue a fiery rejoinder when Mr. Parr rose to her defense.

"Come, come, Ivy! No slight was intended for you." Mr. Parr, ignoring the embarrassment that reddened Ivy's cheeks, winked at Priscilla.

Touched by her father's timely interference, Priscilla silently noted that he had influenced her opinions in all matters, particularly regarding politics. Phillip Parr had been delighted with his daughter's forthrightness when she was a child. Furthermore, he had often encouraged her to spout political theories before company. While these antics had

Cadence to Glory

once enchanted their acquaintants, Priscilla's frank manner, including her penchant for political thought, had attracted criticism as womanhood broke upon her. Most were bound to the general opinion, emblematic of the age, that the affairs of state were hardly matters for discussion by a true lady of consequence. Her acumen also intimidated potential suitors. Still, Mr. Parr encouraged her to nurture a fearless and independent mind. Only his elderly widowed aunt, who lived in an even grander home down the street and forever boasted that her favorite niece would eventually marry beyond all expectations, so prized her outspokenness.

"Might I wear your fine necklace to the Etons' home?" Priscilla's younger sister Frances suddenly applied to Mrs. Parr.

Priscilla could only smile at Frances's enthusiasm. The auburn-haired child claimed little outward splendor, but she nevertheless possessed an innocent comeliness that often endeared her to strangers. Fourteen-year-old Frances had always admired Priscilla's lively delivery of thoughts and opinions even though her own tongue lacked boldness. Still, Priscilla detected a strength of mind lurking beneath the girl's smooth brow.

"Which necklace, my dear?" Mrs. Parr searched Frances's countenance for meaning.

"The one in your portrait!"

Priscilla cringed.

Frances, she realized, had reopened a wound in Elizabeth Parr's past.

In the central hall of the Parr house hung a portrait of their mother at the age of sixteen. In the depiction, her rippling auburn locks were swept into a graceful arrangement. She donned an emerald silk gown that boasted a plunging neckline. The mesmerizing diamond necklace Frances had referenced adorned her bosom. Elizabeth's skin, white and delicate, remained untarnished by the cares of life. In the painting, her lips struggled to suppress a mischievous smile and her blue eyes seemed to pierce the observer's soul.

Priscilla's mother had often blushed at the portrait after her marriage, particularly following the birth of her children, and had once suggested its removal. Phillip Parr had forbidden such an action, for, as he had once informed his wife in Priscilla's hearing, it recalled the untamed beauty who had captured his heart many years ago—and reminded him that he had succeeded where so many others had failed. Mr. Parr had once noticed Priscilla staring at her mother's portrait. He had grinned and followed her rapt gaze. Then, the sunburst of a thousand memories fleeting across his eyes, he had placed his hand upon her shoulder and declared, "Aye, *that* was your mother!"

The portrait served as an everlasting fascination, a relic of a vanished Elizabeth wrapped in the past and never to return. It was rumored that she had been a matchless beauty in her prime—a trait which, friends often observed, had passed to her daughter Priscilla—and that she had once drawn countless admirers. In the days of her youth, Elizabeth's glory had left no head unturned, no heart untouched, and no hopes intact. After her marriage, however, she had devoted herself to Phillip Parr.

Priscilla had deduced her mother's infamous history in fragments. Hints had followed her like shadows. As Priscilla's younger brother Charles had lain dying of consumption seven years earlier, Mrs. Parr had wailed, "The sins of my girlhood are heaped upon this child's head!" At the time, this declaration had meant little to Priscilla. Throughout her childhood, however, a single phrase, whispered time and again by acquaintances when they seemed to believe her mother's back was turned, had gradually acquired a darker meaning in her mind.

Fallen woman.

It was therefore scarcely a surprise to Priscilla when Mrs. Parr's features paled following Frances's request. Priscilla noticed that her mother's lower lip began to tremble. Frances's eyes pleaded with Priscilla for guidance. Only when Mr. Parr enclosed his wife's hand within his own did she recover her composure. Mrs. Parr's eyes still glistened with tears when she replied at last, "You are rather young for that bauble, Frances."

To Priscilla's relief, her brother steered the conversation toward calmer waters.

"I never liked William Eton." Ben's fingers slid through his flaming red hair as he laughed. "When we were both lads, I always defeated him at arm wrestling!"

"And I suppose mastery of that skill has become the measure of a man's soul?" Priscilla playfully mocked him. "How boorish of you."

Ben shrugged his broad shoulders. "It was only in jest." He then leaned forward in a manner which both astonished Priscilla in its solemnity and touched her by its gentleness. "Still, in earnest, I would not like it if one of my sisters caught his fancy. I never trusted him. He was never one to seek friends. I hope that young Thomas has not grown cold like his brother."

This observation startled Priscilla, and she resolved to remember his warning in the future.

Nevertheless, these misgivings were soon overwhelmed by a swelling eagerness to renew her familiarity with this family whose history had once been so intimately connected to her own.

Chapter 2

The Acquaintance

The gathering planned for the twenty-ninth of August finally crept into existence.

Music and mirth permeated the lantern-lit street as the Parr family ascended the steps of the Eton home and entered to claim their share of its merriment. Her pulse thrumming with expectations, Priscilla smoothed the silk taffeta of her gown. Upon crossing the threshold, they were received by Mrs. Eton.

"A regal young lady you have here, Elizabeth!" Mrs. Eton smiled at Mrs. Parr after surveying Priscilla from head to toe. "She has become quite the little beauty. Do you not think so, Richard?"

Priscilla watched closely as Mrs. Eton called her husband, who stood several paces behind her at the drawing room door and whose attention was engaged in scanning the room's occupants. As he turned, a shiver of apprehension swept through Priscilla's frame to discern his hard features, small black eyes, and tremendous height, an attribute which dwarfed his guests. His thick dark eyebrows offered contrast to his thinning white hair. Glancing down at them all over a high-bridged nose, Richard Eton murmured grudging assent. Nevertheless, his countenance softened as his gaze settled upon Mr. Parr.

Striding forward, Mr. Eton grasped his old friend's hand. "It has been a long time, Phillip."

Priscilla saw tears in her father's eyes as he quietly replied, "Far too long, I fear."

Cadence to Glory

The two men walked together into the drawing room. Mr. Eton thus deserted his wife at her greeting post.

After such a mixed welcome, Priscilla glided into the drawing room to meet the ringing melody of the harpsichord, punctuated by boisterous conversation. She soon spotted Katherine, who was seated upon a nearby chair while speaking with Harriet Adams.

These observations were interrupted by a tug upon her sleeve.

"An attentive host, was he not?" asked Ben, who glanced around the drawing room with a smirk. "This party exhausts me already."

"Mr. Eton is horrid as ever, no doubt. Yet, do not lose your temper this evening, Ben—as you are like to do." Laughing, Priscilla tapped her sealed fan upon his arm to emphasize each word.

"Of course not—only when my favorite sister is affronted." Ben winked at her as he walked away. "Moreover, it is *Father* who excels at making scenes..."

The following moment, Priscilla's attention was arrested by formidable voices. She turned to glimpse her father, who was surrounded by a host of other distinguished gentlemen, including Mr. Eton. They were conducting a political "discussion," rousing events which had, of late, escalated in both frequency and intensity. Startled by the fractious timbre of their discourse and amused that her father had already become embroiled in political discord, she edged toward them. Warmed by the dense throng, she snapped open her fan in a flourish and proceeded to listen.

"It will all come to nothing. Of course they shall protest, but their groans fall upon deaf ears," Mr. Parr argued.

"Parr is right. This season of grievance shall pass. It is the way in these colonies. How often in the past five years have we heard the same stale threats?" another voice reasoned.

"The times are changing, gentlemen." Mr. Eton drew up his shoulders. "Parliament has turned most perverse with this latest atrocity—this *Tea Act*! Our rights must be defended! If we do not guard them, who shall? Why does Parliament refuse to give us representatives if their aim be not to enslave us? Are the colonies alone to finance the excesses of this empire?"

That remark only resulted in further dispute. Priscilla viewed this business with the mother country as a grave matter. *Yet, how I yearn to spar with these men, to measure my wits against theirs, to chart the future of these colonies as they have resources to do,* she silently lamented. She soon recognized that she was not the only youth in the room who seemed to harbor such ambitions.

Her eyes fell upon a figure partly veiled in shadow that she had hitherto failed to notice. The form, upon closer inspection, proved to be that of a young man standing beside the ornate fireplace with his arms folded. Suddenly learning forward to listen more intently, he emerged into the candlelight and Priscilla was afforded a clearer view of his person.

His gaze, directed toward the circle of quarreling men, never wavered. She tried to read his sentiments, but he betrayed none. Every moment or so, a gleam of high passion leapt in his eyes — and then vanished.

Priscilla's curiosity stirred. She marveled at the boy's fleeting emotion as well as the force which checked it. Both his countenance and form were pleasing to the eye. His great height alone distinguished him amongst those gathered. Although lean, his figure was well muscled. The face, framed by light brown locks of neither dark nor golden hue, was furnished with character by the bewildering expression that adorned it. These features surpassed the common quality but could not compete with the power of his eyes. Those sapphire pools inspired fright and wonder in Priscilla as they blazed with concentration.

His gaze lit upon her.

She widened her eyes and froze. Shame seized her for having been caught in such a scrutiny, but he did not share her awkwardness. In fact, he flashed a smile so winsome, so befriending, and so genuine that she returned it without another thought. He strolled over to her, but before he could utter a syllable, Priscilla said, "I see that you also take interest in a matter that concerns me greatly."

"It has transfixed me for some time, in fact. Yet *this* is a novelty!" He smiled with amusement. "Never would I have imagined the topic to intrigue a young lady."

"I am peculiar, they say."

The young man laughed heartily. "Still, you are wise to consider these troubles of state, and my admiration is not a thing easily won."

"And *you* do not care for trifles! Your peers in this room indulge in shallow chat, which leads to nothing. By contrast, I have found you fixated by a crisis that will affect your future—and mine as well!"

He studied her with his head cocked to one side. "You are grave for one so young."

"I am seventeen!"

"Ah! Our ages are the same. At seventeen, what is your verdict for the debate a moment ago?"

"You will understand—the gentleman there is my father, standing beside Mr. Adams. But I suppose that—"

"Mr. Parr is your father?" His countenance slackened.

"Yes, of course!"

His blue eyes fastened upon her own. "Your name?"

Curious at this change of discussion, she surveyed him suspiciously. "Priscilla. And yours?"

"Priscilla!" An infectious grin convulsed his features. "Is my visage so altered that you do not know me, old friend that I am?"

Bewildered by his enthusiasm, she swiftly closed her fan and ignored the embarrassment trickling through her veins. "I do not understand. I have never seen you before in my life!"

"My name is Thomas—Thomas Eton!"

Her heart leapt in recognition. *"Tom!"* Priscilla instantly recalled the plump, freckled youngster she had known but eight years ago. She noted the extensive changes that had transformed his appearance for the better. "Is it truly you? You are much changed!"

"Aye, no doubt." His twinkling eye seemed to travel to years past.

"You were such a rough, freckled little boy. You have acquired much—" she struggled for the proper compliment "—dignity."

"But you have changed little. Time has only sharpened your wits, which I remember well since they often bested me." The praise rippled through his words into the shimmering blue pools.

A blush singed her cheeks. "Thank you," she laughed. "Your flattery is welcome, of course, but you know perfectly well that I was always the skinniest tot in Williamsburg."

"Well, I cannot deny you *there*!"

"Come now, where are your other family members?"

Thomas divulged in a lowered voice, "My brother William…there he stands."

Priscilla glanced in the direction of Thomas's turned face. Ivy, sitting a few feet from William, gazed at him with curiosity while a troop of young ladies hovered around the towering man. His dark hair, heavily lidded eyes, and solemn visage were most prominent. His audience, a bevy of worshipful ladies, struggled to extract some word from him. Priscilla realized at once that she had spied him earlier in the evening without guessing his identity.

"How they smother him!" Priscilla remarked scornfully. "Like desperate dogs, they await his crumbs! Does he never part his lips? There is something secretive about him."

"Yes, my brother is reserved." Thomas arched his eyebrows. "He is the sort of man who never shows great sentiment—in public or in private."

They had small opportunity to say more, for Katherine Lee joined their party.

"Kate, find a chair quickly. You will faint once you learn this young man's name!" Priscilla warmly gestured toward him.

"I have already spoken with Thomas." Katherine nodded in his direction with a smile. "But Priscilla, you still have not spoken with his sister. If you wish, I can introduce you."

"Of course." Priscilla excused herself, and Thomas bowed toward them both.

Katherine ushered her friend to the opposite corner of the room. They soon approached a young lady who was fingering music books near the harpsichord.

"Priscilla, may I present Miss Rachel Eton. Rachel, this is Miss Priscilla Parr. You must remember one another!" Katherine smiled, apparently pleased with her introduction.

Rachel Eton's dark curls bounced as she turned toward them. She was tall like the rest of her kindred. Staring down at Priscilla with lustrous blue eyes as if expecting the girl to shrink from her, Rachel appeared piqued by this intrusion into her solitary employment.

"What a pleasure," Rachel suddenly cried. "Yes, Katherine, I remember this girl. Thomas's little playfellow! Tell me, child, what is your age?"

Child indeed! Priscilla tamed the fire on her tongue and managed a civil answer. "I am seventeen."

"Ha!" Rachel broke into a shrill ripple of giggles. "Still quite the baby. My brother spoke of you often enough in the old days. I remember your dirty frocks. How you liked to play with the boys."

"Yes, I defeated them in many a contest of strength." Silently daring Rachel to say more, Priscilla returned her glare.

"If you will excuse me." Rachel sniffed and turned her back to them without another word.

Katherine reddened as Rachel retreated to another quarter of the room. Priscilla's pride, injured by these taunts, rose up in contempt and conceived an enmity. *How dare Rachel slight me so openly! Indeed, for what purpose had she done it?* Priscilla marveled that such an insolent young woman had sprung from the same stock as Thomas Eton.

"Her manners do not impress." Priscilla slid her hand through Katherine's arm and steered her away.

"I am ashamed of her discourtesy," Katherine said. "I am sorry to have brought you. Perhaps the rumors are true."

"I have not heard those rumors. Tell me!"

"Some have called her mad; there is talk of it, you know."

"Is she ill?" Priscilla shuddered with surprise.

"I think not...at least, *not now.*" Katherine sighed as they wove through the crowd. "She has strange fits of temper, it is rumored. But enough of unpleasant things! Is her brother similarly inclined? Your conversation with him was longer than mine."

"Not at all!" Priscilla said. "He is affable."

"And his intellect?"

"His mind is well formed, but wholesome. That is to say, he is no cynic like myself."

"I thought him good looking."

"Indeed." Priscilla glanced toward Thomas, who was engaged in conversation with Mr. Parr on the opposite side of the room.

"I believe, however, that his brother William is even more handsome."

"And yet, whatever charms *he* might have are spoiled by that sour look." Priscilla feigned outrage, whereupon the two girls burst into fits of laughter.

Before too many moments had passed, Priscilla was greeted again by Thomas. While the guests awaited dinner, the pair spoke of old times as children.

"Do you pine for Richmond yet?" Priscilla teased him.

"Never!" Thomas plopped down next to her on the settee. "I am determined to rise in the world. Where else to launch a career than the capital? That is not all. The years in Williamsburg were the happiest of my life." Leaning closer toward her, his voice sank into a whisper. "I have thought of you often, Priscilla."

"Why would you think of me?" Though Priscilla addressed him crisply, a warm flush accompanied this discovery of her new importance. "I have thought little of you…though am much pleased with your company at this moment."

"How could I not remember?" He scowled slightly before recovering his sunny demeanor. "You were my dearest friend of all. Do you not recall our antics during old Mr. Princeton's ball—in this very house? It was only a week before my family left for Richmond."

Priscilla turned toward him as memories raced through her mind. "We slid down the banisters all evening! I sprained my ankle on what was to be the final attempt."

"Then I had the impudence to kiss you. The blow you dealt me still smarts." The settee rocked with Thomas's laugh.

"All shall be as before." Priscilla rested her fingers upon his sleeve in merry supplication. "We are inseparable once again."

"Unfortunately, all is not the same—no matter how much we desire it." Thomas slowly covered her hand as if he had been offered an unexpected gift, but his brow furrowed. "As we have heard tonight, trials—great happenings, rather—cannot fail to sway us."

The firm touch of his hand, along with the assurance voiced by those steady eyes, struck her with the realization that she had recovered an item of infinite value: a friend with whom a kinship of hearts and minds might be forged. In her own mind, this young man from her childhood—a figure once so familiar and yet now so mysterious—represented the hope of a camaraderie with which she had only rarely met before.

Sustained by such thoughts, Priscilla returned his unblinking gaze. "I am glad that you have returned, Thomas Eton. I feel that I might speak my soul, and you would never mock me."

Their exchange was curtailed by the sudden appearance of Mrs. Eton at the entrance to the drawing room. Dinner was promptly announced, and guests began to file out of the room. As both rose to follow the throng, Thomas whispered a single admonition: "We shall talk more of these matters—*soon*."

Chapter 3

The Tea

Among the sophisticated circles of Williamsburg, a constant, though not always reliable, channel of communication existed. Many tidings discovered a home there and were likewise dispensed to receptive ears.

Phillip Parr detested the destruction it often wrought. "So much for newspapers!" he hotly declared, particularly when groundless rumors concerning his family were circulated as fact. "*Virginia Gazette?* Ha! Who needs a newspaper with all this nonsense?"

Despite her father's objections, Priscilla remained active in that very circle. Twice (and occasionally thrice) a week, the Parr girls attended teas hosted by their privileged peers. Other participants included Katherine Lee as well as her younger sisters, Rosamund and Margaret. In addition, Jane and Harriet Adams attended with regularity and enthusiasm.

During one such tea hosted at the Lee home, a certain name surfaced and quickened the young ladies to distraction.

"I have heard that Thomas Eton shall be off to the College in two years," Harriet Adams sighed mournfully.

"Prefer Thomas if you wish." Ivy plucked off her white gloves. "He is not half so handsome as William. Furthermore, Thomas is only seventeen—still educated by tutors and preparing for the College. He is in no position to marry at all."

"William also has secure employment at his father's law office." Rosamund nodded thoughtfully. "As the eldest son, he will receive the more generous bargain upon his father's death. I hope he seeks my hand for a dance at the Christmas Ball."

Harriet's eyes danced. "Thomas would suit *me.*"

Her sister Jane giggled. "Any man would suit *you.*"

"That is not true! Only a wealthy man would suit me!" Harriet sailed to the window in a huff.

Thirteen-year-old Margaret lifted her chin. "I thought William behaved strangely at the Palace yesterday."

"What do you suppose was his business there?" Jane reached for the porcelain teacup placed before her.

"I do not know! But Father said the man scarcely spoke to him."

"He is a man of few words." Katherine gave her sister a reproving look. "Pray, be lenient!"

"Oh, perhaps." Margaret waved her small hand in dismissal. "I can scarcely excuse his behavior at his father's party. I cannot mention it without feeling vexed! It was most insulting, and he should not have ignored us all so."

Priscilla only narrowly checked a laugh. "His sister is far worse—if you can believe it. Though he *never* speaks, *she* speaks overmuch!"

"Aye, Miss Eton is quite odd," Rosamund said. "Margaret and I greeted her after church services last Sunday. We asked after her health, but before we could move on to the weather, she cut us off, turned on her heel, and burst into tears!"

"I, for one, was not surprised." The saucer clattered as Margaret planted her teacup there, tea splashing onto the tablecloth. "She thinks herself above the rest of us. Why else would she reject our invitation to be here today?"

Harriet Adams, still standing before the drapes and peering through the Venetian blinds, motioned for them all to join her there. "Quickly, quickly! Look!"

In a frenzied whirlwind of petticoats, the young ladies rushed to the window.

A line of courtly houses had long flanked each side of the Palace Green. Among these genteel residences stood the Lee home, from which the girls spied the tall, graceful form of Rachel Eton. Her face partly shaded by a wide-brimmed cream silk hat, she walked across the Green on the arm of a gentleman. Their heads often bent close together, the pair appeared deep in conversation. As they approached one of the catalpa trees which bordered the Green, the young man paused and turned to face her. He brought her hand to his lips.

The girls at the window squealed with disbelief.

Priscilla recoiled from the sight in horror.

Rachel's suitor was Benjamin Parr.

Chapter 4

The Idealist

Autumn in the capital of Virginia always proved to be its most engaging season. The transformation of leaves to hues of golden and scarlet accompanied a flush of general cheer among the inhabitants of Williamsburg. The fragrance-laden breeze likewise awakened the senses.

Thus enlivened on a Tuesday morning in mid-September, Priscilla resolved to stroll about the streets and bask in the glories of the season. A tender wind blew softly against her cheeks, and she slowed her pace. No cloud marred the pale sunlit sky. Priscilla mused that, against such scenery, one might easily believe that sorrow itself was an illusion.

Such a happy delusion shattered as Priscilla approached the Magazine. This octagonal brick tower, rising in the center of town, served as a stern reminder of the unrest that brewed ever steadily beneath the tranquil-seeming veneer of Williamsburg society. The Magazine had long housed arms for the citizens' defense, particularly against those threats posed by Indians and pirates. As Priscilla passed beneath its shadow, she inferred that this building consequently embodied the rights of the people. *While the Magazine stands*, she concluded, *no honest man in Williamsburg can accuse Britain of trampling upon our rights.*

As she turned the corner of the street, Thomas Eton attained it also.

A glow of astonishment and pleasure colored the young man's fair cheeks, and his lips quivered for an instant. "Priscilla!"

"Tom!" Those warm feelings of friendship, such as she had experienced at the Etons' party, revived at the sight of him.

His bright blue eyes glinted in the sunlight. "What errand summons you into this divine weather?"

"The air, I suppose, as well as the exercise."

"I wish I had a more honorable excuse."

"And what is your excuse?"

"I slipped away to escape Percy."

"Percy?"

"My tutor, of course." He shrugged. "Well, there you have it. He arrives each morning at nine, and today I was determined to be late."

Startled by his frankness, Priscilla laughed. His eyes danced with good humor, and she could not help but notice the symmetry of his features. *It almost seems as if the world has never etched its cares upon his brow*, she inwardly marveled.

"Shall we walk some distance together?" He offered his arm and an infectious smile.

Priscilla accepted his extended arm and resumed the conversation as they slowly advanced down the street. "I hear that you are preparing to attend the College in two years. What an exciting prospect!"

"Yet, such study will produce some degree of annoyance, as study often does. Nevertheless, my father has not yet promised me a place in his practice. I must work for my own livelihood."

"Ah, but you are one of the fortunate sex. *I* am forbidden to attempt such feats!" Priscilla huffed, glancing at the swaying leaves of an old oak. "As an attorney, one can acquire skill as an orator. Fine speech is a great asset to politicians. Do you aspire to public office?"

His lips parted with a sharp intake of breath, and he gazed down at her with his head cocked to one side—whether in amusement or admiration, Priscilla could not determine. "Yes."

At that moment, they approached the Palace Green and their steps drew to a halt. Children skipped across the lush expanse while their voices rang like bells in the idle morning. The sun illumined their bouncing curls as poignant recollections of childhood swept over Priscilla.

"Remember the many times we played our games here?" Thomas whispered.

"Those are my happiest memories. Dearest Kate and Rosamund! Henry and Jane and Harriet! Our hearts bore no burdens *then*. Life was our theater, and we bent its drama to our will," she said softly.

"No more." Thomas's voice hardened as his gaze became dark.

Priscilla imbibed the bittersweet draught of the past for a few moments in silence. When such recollections had passed, they moved forward once more.

The sight of the Green conjured unpleasant memories as well. "Your sister, I hear," Priscilla probed, thinking of Ben, "is an object of general admiration. Does she have a favorite?"

"I cannot know for certain. Little do I know of her thoughts. Rachel's heart is not to be read. It is closed to me—and to most others."

Priscilla studied her friend. She was surprised to discern the similar workings of their minds, even concerning his sister. The cloud that passed over his countenance at the mention of Rachel did not escape Priscilla, who further explored his intelligence. "Why did your family return to Williamsburg?"

"The firm floundered in Richmond, but that was not all. Will had demanded that we return for months. Father pressed him for a reason, and my brother said he wanted a bride."

"He is not searching; he barely speaks!" mused Priscilla, suppressing a giggle. "If ever a stuffed boar was seen, it is *he*!"

Thomas threw his head backward with a loud guffaw. "I cannot deny it! But Father had other reasons to humor him."

"What do you mean?" Priscilla examined his countenance, which became somber as rapidly as it had brightened.

"Will had taken up with a certain set of which Father did not approve."

"What were their offenses?"

"They were Loyalists!"

"Yet, I belong to a Loyalist family." Laughing, Priscilla pressed his arm. "You do not shun *me*!"

"Are *you* a Loyalist, Priscilla?" Thomas gravely asked her.

"Yes, I—I suppose," Priscilla stammered, unnerved by his serious expression. "My thoughts are not solid in this matter."

"You are not a fiery Tory, then?"

"My sympathies, although not zealous, are inclined in that direction." Why did he speak as if Tories were no better than heathens?

They ambled forward in silence. Priscilla pondered his words. His probing queries endangered her calm. Something of the gravity that clothed his political persuasions, so foreign to his jovial manner, both frightened and intrigued her. She was tempted to draw back from him in bewildered awe.

During this interval, she distinguished familiar faces in a coach rambling past them. They also passed an elderly gentleman of their acquaintance as he descended the front steps of his home. The pair greeted him, and he returned the salute with a tip of his hat.

Thomas broke the ensuing hush with a request. "Of course you will allow me to solicit your hand for a turn at the Christmas Ball."

"Oh, Tom, do be serious! That is several months away yet."

"And why must not old playmates share a dance? I expect every man there to ask you." He winked at her. "I wish to reserve my place."

"I shall not be so admired as you expect," she said with a laugh. "My opinions alarm suitors—I watch them squirm in my presence. *To fear a lady!* It is piteous."

"Imagine that!"

Their tread slowed as they stepped upon her front lawn. As she neared the front door of her home, she released his arm and turned to observe him evenly. One moment, he teased her like the reckless boy she had once known. The next, he searched her eyes as if to unearth every thought. Whether he found wisdom or folly therein, she could not tell.

Thomas's eyebrows arched in surprise. "Priscilla, why do you stare at me in that manner?"

She swiftly withdrew her gaze. "I am not altogether certain," she replied, baffled. "You are not as you appear. You jest...and yet I feel that you *joust* with me!"

Without a word, he grinned, kissed her hand, and strode once more onto the cobblestone street.

Priscilla's eyes followed Thomas's figure for some time until, at length, he disappeared around the street corner. Her old friend had metamorphosed into an enigma, the unmasking of which she anticipated with a sudden smile. In a mere two meetings, he had awakened a storm of doubt and wonder within Priscilla, a vast and perilous chamber within her mind upon which she had never dared look. She was discomfited by their conversations yet drawn to the paradox of his nature—a whimsical manner which seemed to mask such strange and uncompromising notions.

Pondering these mysteries as she turned to enter the Parr House, Priscilla suddenly collided with her brother, who had emerged from the doorway whistling a lively tune.

"Forgive me!" Ben assisted Priscilla to her feet with haste. "What a clumsy oaf I am! You are injured, dear?"

Straightening the lace ruffles that trimmed her sleeves, Priscilla smiled at his repeated attempts to rectify his own part in the accident. "Not in the least. The fault is mine, Ben!"

As she watched him brush the soil from his waistcoat, however, her lips slackened into a frown. With a slight gasp, she realized that he had donned his finest suit of clothes, attire which might not be disparaged in Church—or even at one of the Palace balls. She guessed his destination at once.

Mounting consternation sharpened her voice more than she would have liked. "You are to call upon a young lady this morning?"

Ben's gaze swung to her face as a flush overspread his features. "How did you...who informed you..." His voice faltered for a moment before he shrugged his shoulders and his countenance relaxed into its customary grin. "What have I to conceal? It is true. The young lady is an angel."

Priscilla groaned. The memory of Rachel's odd taunts resurfaced in her mind. Desperation unchained Priscilla's tongue as she lowered her voice to a fierce whisper. "She is mad, they say. Oh, Ben, for the sake of those who love you, *leave her be*! I fear she will ruin you."

Shaking his head, Ben held up his hand as if to silence her. "She is no more a lunatic than yourself—and no less a woman of judgment." He ground his fist into his palm in a paroxysm of anger. "Who spreads these vicious lies? They must be stopped. Tell me, Priscilla. I will not have her name blackened!"

Unwilling to draw Katherine, the source of her information, into his wrath, Priscilla bit her lip in a rare moment of reticence. "It is spoken of quite generally."

"Ah, then it is only hearsay." He leaned toward her as his grin returned. "You have always been a clever girl, never one to heed such tales. Let us not quarrel today, Priscilla." Gazing past her face in seemingly profound reflection, Ben's voice softened. "You can never understand that woman's hold upon me."

Tipping his hat, he hurried past Priscilla and sauntered toward the street before she could part her lips in reply. A sense of futility paralyzed any further effort to detain him. She had no heart to arouse the anger of a brother she loved so deeply. Nevertheless, foreboding still gnawed at her soul like a small but persistent maggot intent upon its prey.

Priscilla's distrust of Rachel grew, even as her fascination with Thomas flourished.

Chapter 5

The Gift

Less than a month following the Etons' party, Priscilla's secret pursuit was almost discovered.

On this occasion, she dabbled in the paints at the corner of the drawing room. The task was a difficult one, for it required her to capture the precise shade of Frances's hair. Red, brown, and golden pigments were intermingled by her brush in shifting quantities as the remainder of the Parr family watched her every movement.

Priscilla had long been trained in all the arts expected of a well-bred lady. She had submitted to the disciplines, but her heart warmed to a particular exercise. From her earliest years, she had exhibited a flair for painting. Her restless soul consistently found a channel in this skill. Indeed, her portraits had invited much acclaim.

Whenever a visitor passed a season with her family, Priscilla had often been obliged to produce countless likenesses of the individual from every conceivable angle. Her lines were considered coarse by some who detested candor in such depictions. Most, however, readily acknowledging the proficiency with which she executed these honest portrayals, valued her efforts. Priscilla's gift remained the pride of her father and the joy of her mother.

Nonetheless, Priscilla had often tired of producing portraits. She preferred free artistic forms to more confining exercises. Her portraits were carefully stored within the bureau in her bedchamber. Within the same article of furniture, however, she stashed a very different series of illustrations. Her second set of sketches included wild flights of fancy. These works often reflected her fluctuating temper. Melancholy resulted in the image of a dark manor battered by the winds upon a forbidding hilltop. Enthusiasm was often embodied by a vision of mythical sprites fluttering within the secret folds of luxuriant foliage. Anticipating her father's disapproval, she had often designed these works furtively.

Such thoughts brooded in her mind as she now blended the paints. Gazing at her palette and then at Frances, who clutched a bulky lace-fringed fan and posed on a green armchair, Priscilla at last approved a combination of colors. She dipped the brush into the mixture and smeared it upon the canvas.

An uproar promptly ensued.

"Frances's hair is not so golden!" Ben waved his hand in protest.

Ivy tapped her foot impatiently. "I disagree; you have made it much too auburn, Priscilla."

"It calls for a deeper shade of brown, I should think." Mrs. Parr studied the half-completed portrait with narrowed eyes.

Frances, who had maintained her pose for an hour, began to shift listlessly. "May I stir now?"

Pricilla seethed with frustration. "I cannot satisfy *everyone!*"

For this reason, I detest portraits, she thought.

Her attention, however, was soon riveted to a motion in the periphery of her vision. Mr. Parr strolled over to the writing desk whereupon her preliminary sketches for the portrait rested. Her hand faltered as she resumed painting, for some of her most recent whimsical creations, which she had neglected to hide, were clustered at the base of the pile.

Her heart fluttered as he lifted the thick collection of drawings. He retrieved his spectacles and raised them before his eyes. Inspecting the foremost sketch, he beamed—then shuffled to the next one. As he cleared his throat upon viewing the second illustration, Priscilla cast another sidelong glance toward him. Brushstrokes ceased as she considered his impending reaction.

Suddenly, he returned the drawings to their former place.

"You have a gift for these likenesses, my girl." Mr. Parr gestured toward the sketches he had relinquished. "Never bend your hand to flights of fancy. Your skill is too fine for the baser tendencies of artistic talent."

Priscilla scrutinized the lines of his countenance. Had he espied her imaginative works? The broad grin, which animated his features, soon led her to conclude that he had not.

She thus continued to accumulate these fanciful compositions in silence. Nevertheless, her secrecy did not signify. As on past occasions, she still left her clandestine treasures more forlornly than she had begun them. Her heart ached with a nameless dissatisfaction. Every unfinished work inflicted a more violent disappointment, and each time she was compelled to disguise this pursuit and cling instead to the portraits, greater pangs of shame and self-loathing throbbed within her breast.

Chapter 6

The Promise

"They are drunkards and ingrates—the whole lot of them!" Phillip Parr's impassioned voice echoed from his study down the central hall.

Both Priscilla and Frances sat quietly in the adjoining drawing room and overheard his piercing cry. They gazed upward from their sewing, and their conversation ceased. Ivy, who was perched upon the sofa opposite them, lifted her passive eyes. Priscilla rose and crept toward the door of the drawing room in order to hear their words with greater clarity.

"Parr, that is powerful language. It is no matter likely to be settled in a few days. Such differences may not be reconciled in months—perhaps years!" rejoined the voice of Dr. Lee.

"Surely they are not senseless enough to openly contradict the Crown."

"They have already done so. Their resolve daily proves both violent and reckless."

"Their quibbling could never boast a chance against the mother country—and all her strength!"

"It is no mere 'quibbling.' This is rapidly becoming a sophisticated enterprise. They are not only radicals, but *organized* radicals. The movement is now carried upon the shoulders of intellectuals like Jefferson, and their complaints are not to be taken lightly."

"You must see that, although they resent the authority which governs them, they have no effective weapon against it. What a great joke it would be if a ruffian militia defied the forces of Britannia!"

Dr. Lee lowered his voice to such a degree that Priscilla was nearly unable to hear his remark. "You underestimate the power of such dissension. Boston stands upon the verge of popular rebellion—*even as we speak.*"

"Boston has always been a den of rabble-rousers! That is common knowledge."

"Open your eyes, Parr! The discontent in that colony has corrupted others as well. I hear it everywhere! A soft murmur, a word in passing on the street, furtive grievances...the traitor's venom has many manifestations."

Priscilla's thoughts froze at the terrifying words. A strange emotion gripped her heart like a murderer grips his victim. What was this fresh dread? *Discontent?* What sort of talk was this? Was the world around her infested with dreams of revolt? Were plans for a general mutiny alive in the houses down the street, in the hearts of her oldest acquaintances, or perhaps in the blank faces of the populace she often observed from her window?

She was unable to quiet this new fright. Perhaps her family was despised for their allegiance to the Crown. But no! Most of the Williamsburg gentry disapproved of the riots and lawlessness. A few dissenters existed among Virginia's elite, most notably the erudite Thomas Jefferson, the fiery Patrick Henry, and the imposing Mr. Washington.

How could she forget their treason? Her father spoke such violence against them every hour as to make her fear them. But what of the plebeians? The ordinary humble folk? How could common souls contemplate such daring deeds?

Having suffered her own judgment, Priscilla cast a sideways glance at her younger sister. Frances became ashen but did not tremble. Priscilla could not discern the girl's thoughts. Ivy's countenance remained cold as a stone. Whether she concealed any secret alarm or did not comprehend the import of the quarrel remained unclear. Ivy resumed her former occupation with ease.

Mr. Parr's irritated cry penetrated the walls once more. "Lee, I weary of this bickering. Good day to you, sir!"

"You cannot confront the truth?"

"Aye, and more than any man alive!"

Priscilla winced at his outburst. Oh, how dear a father he was to her despite all his flaws! How could his nature be so inconsistent? Alas! What had begun as a social call by one of his eldest friends had escalated into a quarrel. Priscilla recalled that this was not the first instance in which her father had recklessly alienated a cherished friend by way of a political "discussion."

Mr. Parr pressed his argument. "This matter shall conclude soon enough. Logic sets invincible odds against the rebels. You are blind to its simplicity."

"Simplicity? Conspiracies such as these are far from simple."

"And shall be stifled! Only a few poor, impractical souls feed these rumors. Be gone now, Lee! You are my old friend. Let us not differ thus."

"I do not differ. Do not fancy *me* drawn into the traitor's scheme! I only sense the birth of something more terrible than either of us have hitherto imagined."

Priscilla was drowning in her own feelings. She turned to Frances and noted that tears had gathered in her sister's eyes.

The bewildered girl asked, "What is to happen? Is the rebellion as dangerous as Dr. Lee believes?"

Priscilla considered revealing the horrid truth to Frances. Only truth, not indulgence, would instill strength in her sister. Having formed such a determination, Priscilla parted her lips to execute it. Her purpose froze, however, as she glimpsed Frances's pure expression.

Why mar such innocence? Would not her sister be rudely enough acquainted with the conflict as time passed? Priscilla pondered these things and more. In the end, unwilling to crush Frances's false peace, she lied.

"Do not fret. All will shortly be reconciled."

Ivy, evidently disapproving of the falsehood, glared at Priscilla, who returned a stare equally as silencing. Ivy coldly withdrew her eye and resumed her needlework. Frances's tears dissolved, and a relieved smile soon reillumined her delicate features.

So many uncertainties lie ahead, Priscilla thought, struggling to justify her action. *I cannot tear from her the happy ignorance of youth! Who knows when trials may introduce her to the world with all its grief?*

For an hour, Priscilla had striven in vain to finish a volume by the Greek historian Herodotus.

She could not, despite a vigorous attempt, expunge her father's quarrel with Dr. Lee from her mind. Her inner turmoil reached a particularly intolerable pitch, and she finally tossed the book aside in frustration. Staring absently at the heavy silk panels adorning the window, she struggled to believe her father's arguments. Surely the king would smother such an uprising! Still, the same doubts haunted her.

"Priscilla."

Startled, she glanced over her shoulder to her mother, who had noiselessly glided into the room.

"Your father would like to speak with you. He is in his study."

Even at the mature age of forty-eight, Elizabeth Parr formed a magnificent vision. Her rippling auburn hair had scarcely silvered with age, and she still walked with an almost queenly bearing. Priscilla, however, had always detected a deep well of sadness within her mother's eyes, which had become more prominent in the years since little Charles's death. Even now, as Mrs. Parr stood silently in the doorway of the drawing room, Priscilla noticed that it hung like a fixed shadow across her features.

"What is the meaning of it, Mother?" Priscilla rose to her feet immediately.

"I cannot say." Mrs. Parr briskly gestured for Priscilla to obey the summons. "He intends it for your ears alone, I believe."

Without another word, Priscilla lifted the hem of her dress and strode down the hall. As she advanced toward her father's study, however, old fears seized her, and she hesitated.

None of the family entered the study unless Mr. Parr was absent from it. Even then, he did not warm to the thought of anyone troubling his precious books and records. Priscilla had only penetrated the mystery-cloaked room once before. Her childish mind had often speculated concerning what occupied Father for so many long hours. She had once furtively stolen into the study while he was in Philadelphia on business. Priscilla had been disappointed in her discovery but had enjoyed the room's sunny radiance. Still, that quarter of the house remained a forbidden domain. None dared intrude. The purpose of the present audience, Priscilla thus reasoned, must be one of great import.

Summoning courage, she raised her chin and turned the doorknob.

The study housed a vast library within the sturdy shelves lining the walls. A sizeable window, which bathed the room with rich sunlight, dominated the wall opposite the doorway. Upon entering the spacious room, she noticed her father bending over a mountain of scholastic tomes upon his mahogany desk. His spectacles balanced upon the end of his nose, he glanced upward from his work at the sound of her shuffling skirts.

"You sent for me, Father?" she murmured.

"Yes." He pulled off his spectacles. "I did. Take a seat, if you please, my dear."

She lifted the edge of her skirts and settled upon the cushioned chair opposite her father's desk. He leaned back leisurely into his chair and intertwined his fingers on the curvature of his belly. He always glared at her in this manner prior to a grave, lengthy address.

"As you know," he began at last, "our colonies have, over the years, been a breeding ground for various radical notions."

She nodded.

"Do you recall the Sons of Liberty?"

"How could I forget?" Priscilla said with a groan.

When she was an impressionable child of nine, a wave of fury had rippled through the colonies. Such upheaval had erupted after certain protestors, the "Sons of Liberty," began to raid the stampmasters' homes and to tar and feather the helpless inhabitants. These atrocities they committed in protest against the Stamp Act. A boycott had been swiftly organized in the colonies. British exporters lost valuable business and pressured Parliament to revoke the divisive decision.

During that period, Priscilla's father first began to host "debates" with his fellow gentlemen—often within the Parr home. She particularly remembered that he and several government officials once convened at the Parr House to "discuss" the great dilemma. She had listened at the door all night and heard the men raise their voices whenever referring to the despised dissidents. As the evening progressed, tempers flared. Some were humiliated by the entire affair while others claimed a personal interest in the incidents. Parliament was ultimately forced to repeal the notorious act, yet it soon issued the Declaratory Act in an attempt to compensate for the mortification.

"You understand, of course, that such agitators remain," her father continued, breaking her train of thought. "They are senseless rebels. As for the colonies, but for England alone do they exist at all!"

He shook his fist with unbridled passion, and his face flushed crimson. His eyes blazed as he resumed his speech.

"They abuse their country's honor in more ways than one. Their treachery is like that of an ungrateful child striking its provider...the source of its nourishment. They are seditionists who deserve to be trampled beneath the lion heels of Britannia!"

Priscilla still could not discern the purpose of the interview. Why did he lecture her when their views on this subject were similar? She wondered anxiously if some fresh political scandal had erupted.

Her curiosity did not remain long unsatisfied.

In a deeper, steadier voice, with a small smile playing across his lips, Mr. Parr said, "You are a pretty maiden, Priscilla. I mean to caution you. Many eligible young men hail from families that profess an undying devotion to the Crown. It is better that your expectations be spent upon them."

Priscilla shook her head. "Father, I have no suitor at present. Let your heart rest at ease."

He did not yield to her entreaties. "They may resist your honest manner. Men, however, will be men and shall arrive at your door someday. When that day comes, remember this counsel."

Mr. Parr rose and slowly approached her. Tenderness flooding his eyes, he cupped her face. "You have always claimed a special place in my heart. Some seditionist may very well weasel his way into your affections. You must avoid him like the plague—like death itself. The lady's heart is a thing easily beset. I would rather die this day—this moment even—than witness my daughter, *my* Priscilla, cast her lot with the likes of that, that rebel trash!"

Such an oration failed to draw tears from Priscilla, but she was greatly moved by her father's affection.

As his shining eyes pierced her own, he further advised her, "Do not betray your family, your friends, every love you have ever known. Most of all, dear girl, never betray England! Always remember that you are British. Remain true to the empire, and you shall forever stand proud!"

"I promise, Father!" The blood of her ancestors surged through her veins as she uttered this pledge.

Her soul, overwhelmed by the passion of his address, burned with all the ferocity of Britannia herself. She was Priscilla Parr, child of the Crown and daughter of an Englishman. She yearned for the glory of England, and, through this, the glory of her beloved colonies.

Past doubts had vanished.

Chapter 7

The Garden

Clutching her wide-brimmed straw hat, which was threatened by a rising breeze, Priscilla fingered lavender foxglove blossoms with her other hand. Glancing up from the sprawling vines, she closed her eyes and basked in the afternoon sun's soft warmth.

The delights of the Parr garden were considerable. For many years, Mr. and Mrs. Parr, united in their passion for horticultural pursuits, had cultivated a little paradise, the reputation of which was spread by each visitor to their home. Priscilla could ill remember a time when her father was not often found working amongst his prized melons, peas, cucumbers, and onions on one side of the garden with her mother tending well-ordered rows of tulips, violets, and roses on the other. Her mother persisted in a fondness for rosemary—despite Phillip Parr's resentment of its symbolic associations—which she had sculpted into large elegant topiaries in the far corner of the garden. A small white arbor provided an area of repose in the center and thus served as a focal point for the entire space.

In true Georgian fashion, symmetry and order characterized the primary scheme for the garden's design. The separate spheres ruled by Mr. and Mrs. Parr were bisected by a narrow lane constructed of red brick and further subdivided by more intimate pathways. Only two entrances disrupted the integrity of the enclosure: a gate that faced the back of the house, through which the Parrs normally entered the garden, and a similar exit leading to the lawn upon which the dairy, kitchen, stable, and coach house were situated.

Rising from the foxgloves, Priscilla ambled slowly down the central walkway. Her fingers swept the hedge tops while she advanced. Priscilla allowed the anxieties of recent days to vanish from her mind. A sense of serenity pervaded her frame as the lyrical humming of a mandolin, which Frances strummed in the shade afforded by the garden's sole tree, sweetened the air like a chorus of silver bells. Even Ivy, who devoted herself to a book within the arbor, dealt no insolence to mar the afternoon's tranquility.

At that very instant, the clamor of footsteps drew Priscilla's attention toward the front garden gate, which one of the gardeners opened to admit a tall, lanky young man with tousled hair and a broad, tooth-baring grin.

"*Tom?*" Priscilla's skirts rustled as she rushed to meet him with a laugh.

"There you are!" Thomas, bending over her extended hand, bestowed the obligatory kiss before breaking into his familiar grin once more. "Mr. Parr invited me to see his garden whilst he talks with Father for a few moments."

Frances paused her playing, but only long enough to send a hearty wave in his direction, which he returned with manifest joy. Ivy's posture stiffened at the sight of Thomas as her cool blue eyes peered at him from beneath the arbor. After studying him from afar for several tense moments, she nodded and, without changing her expression, resumed her reading.

Priscilla could barely contain her enthusiasm for this unexpected visit of her restored ally. "How were you permitted to come, considering your rigorous studies?"

"Percy has been indisposed this week and left early today to visit the apothecary."

Priscilla offered him her linen handkerchief. "I see a dark smudge upon your cheek, Tom."

"Thank you, thank you!" With some awkwardness, he passed the handkerchief back to her after thoroughly scrubbing each cheek.

"Ink, most likely." Casting a long glance around the garden, his eyes widened. "Your father's pride is not misplaced. I can ill imagine the care he has taken to cultivate this place. Is it not like the first garden?"

"Very like." Priscilla sighed deeply, inhaling the fragrance of violets, and followed his gaze. "If only you could see it during the summer, when crimson roses cascade down yonder wall—or in spring, when golden tulips blanket the soil like jewels of the purest flame. Yes, *then* you would think so. You would say that such pleasures are too good for mankind!"

As she spoke, his grin melted and a demeanor of quiet reflection settled upon his face. "Poetic indeed! You never told me how well you can turn a phrase." He rubbed his jaw in seeming depths of thought. "I should like to see those sights, Priscilla."

A fresh wave of bittersweet sentiments guided Priscilla down different paths of contemplation. The memory of her father's warning assumed a pall of pettiness, even crudeness, against this verdant backdrop—as did her rash pledge. Determined to find expression for these sentiments, she punctuated her tone with emphasis as they began to walk down the lane. "This garden has always served as my refuge. Here, one forgets the trifling quarrels of this world. What must God think of us! We war with one another for the sake of lofty-sounding principles, which we betray with discord and violence." Scarlet ribbons encircling her hat, in addition to loose ringlets, fluttered lightly around Priscilla's neck with each shake of her head. "Do you not wish to forget, Tom? One might always know happiness then." She sighed as they approached the low brick wall on the far side of the garden. "Oh, how I envy the walls! They never change—and stand throughout the ages! They are immovable."

Pressing her palms upon the wall, she gazed at the various grooms as they leisurely led horses from the stable into the sunlight, brushing their already slick manes until they shone. In the opposite direction, she caught an angled glimpse of heavily laden carts as they rumbled over the cobblestones in the street and suddenly remembered that it was market day once again. Thomas's lingering silence arrested her attention, and she turned to notice a troubled glimmer in his eyes as well as tension in his jaw.

Whatever shape they took, these sensations appeared to fade as he meandered over to the gate nearest them and faced her again. "Shall we take a turn about the town? It is market day, after all. We shall not be missed."

Laughing, she skipped toward him with a childish air. "What vulgar enjoyments might we see *there*—when such peace and innocence can be found *here*? See, we are friends—as we once were."

Small lines creased his brow. "Any refuge may turn into a prison, and walls can enslave. We are no longer children, Priscilla. The world is changing quickly, and we must find our places within it—even the political conflicts at hand. I promised you before that we would speak of these things—"

She held up her hand in swift remonstration as she struggled to steady her voice. "Let us not speak of them today. Instead, let us bask in this glorious afternoon, for it will never come again."

Thomas's jaw muscles convulsed again, and, for a moment, he appeared as if he might make a distressed reply. Nevertheless, his features soon relaxed into a gentle smile, and he nodded slowly. As if to atone for any offense he might have given, he leaned over one of the neighboring topiaries, plucked a sprig of rosemary, and placed it in Priscilla's hand.

Threading the rosemary into her hair, Priscilla strove to maintain her composure amidst the doubts he had once more aroused—and their accompanying plateau of intellectual intrigue. Attempting to conceal her bewilderment, she assumed an amiable but nonchalant tone. "What shall you do this evening?"

"I hope to make an appearance at the Raleigh Tavern. Father and Will plan to attend a meeting of leading citizens in the Apollo Room—men who oppose the Crown's high-handedness. Rumor has it that Mr. Jefferson may be there. You know, Priscilla, I heard the great man speak once before—"

"*Thomas!*"

Priscilla gasped at the harshness of this voice, which sliced the air like a dagger and even stilled Frances's playing on a sour note. Priscilla glanced in the direction of its origin.

Mr. Eton's towering figure swathed her own father in shadow as the pair of men stood together at the garden gate nearest the Parr House.

Thomas winked at Priscilla as he advanced to rejoin his father with a long, quickened stride, leaving her to ponder his remarks for the remainder of the afternoon with some disquiet and much introspection.

Chapter 8

The Announcement

Whispers of great and mysterious changes hung in the air. Just as the spirits of Williamsburg's citizens had soared with the majesty of the changing leaves, breezes once glorious to the touch became frosty winds. It was as if anxiety began to swell the hearts of the masses. Priscilla vowed to forever remember this season of 1773 as one touched by the hand of fate.

October had not long dawned before such an alteration was wrought in the Parrs' hitherto peaceful lives. It emerged unexpectedly following a sumptuous family dinner.

Priscilla's brother wielded the mirth of his kindred to his own advantage. With little warning, he proudly rose and uttered a fateful announcement. "I intend to take a wife."

Never had Priscilla been so astounded, an emotion amplified by the abruptness of his declaration. Her lips parted, Priscilla stared blankly at him for some time. In her distress, she felt the blood drain from her face.

Ben scrutinized the dismayed expressions of his mother and sisters with evident satisfaction.

Priscilla's eyes darted in her father's direction.

He winked at Ben. "And who might this fortunate lady be?"

Mr. Parr's face exuded a glow of immense gratification. A conjecture arose in the midst of her tumultuous thoughts. Her father's enthusiasm suggested a prior knowledge of this development. His eyes glittered with pleasure, and zealous approval shone from every feature.

His broad shoulders squared, Ben straightened his spine. "I have sought Miss Eton's hand in marriage, and she has most graciously accepted my offer!" A triumphant grin unfurled across his lips.

At this proclamation, Priscilla was less bewildered. If Ben was to wed, she did not speculate concerning the lady's identity.

"Delightful!" Frances clapped her hands. "I wish you joy, Brother."

Priscilla winced at the assumptions that had inspired her sister's jubilation. The entire family followed Frances's congratulatory lead. Inwardly railing against the proposed match, Priscilla remained quiet. She risked no expression lest she provoke an unpleasant incident.

She was both burdened and restrained by certain invariable qualms. These grave misgivings, she now realized, had haunted her since she first espied her brother conversing with Miss Eton on the Palace Green. In the eyes of the world, Rachel's splendid lineage and appearance deemed her a prize for any man. But were such qualities sufficient to make her a pleasing wife, particularly given tales of her alleged madness?

Priscilla knew her brother's own fickle temper well. Could it coexist with Rachel's equally turbulent spirit? Her heart whispered the consequences of this marriage. Priscilla need not perform further examination to ascertain that her brother's passion for Miss Eton had sprung from blind infatuation alone. Such an inference was validated by the brevity of his pursuit. Surely the resemblance of their tumultuous natures ensured future conflicts!

The rest of the family did not share her angst. Seemingly oblivious to Priscilla's pensive silence, they sat laughing and chattering over bare plates for almost two hours. The merriment followed them into the sitting room. Ben loudly boasted of many ambitious and, in Priscilla's perspective, naïve designs for the future.

In the chaotic bustle of the evening, he drew Priscilla aside. "And what silences that tongue of yours, dear girl?"

"Doubts silence *me*."

"Doubts concerning what?" He grinned incredulously. "Pray, do not tell me that I have incited your displeasure for this venture."

"I have already declared my reservations, Ben!" she said, her courage mounting. "Do you not remember?"

Ben, his brow wrinkling in confusion, glared at her. She braced herself for a barrage of indignation.

Instead, his shock melted into a flippant laugh. "Ah, silly child that you are!" He chuckled again. "You must not fret so. Happiness never comes without hazard. Let us hear no more of your nonsense. Moreover, I thought we were in agreement upon that subject."

"My objections are sound!" Priscilla clenched her fists. "She has blinded you—as other men are so often blinded."

His tone hardened. "And you shall know that blindness once your own heart is penetrated—if it is not beyond the power of penetration. I will remind you then of your reproof."

Despite her penchant for debate, Priscilla spoke no more. She could not pierce a resolve so unassailable, so reckless, and yet so pitiable. In her mind, it appeared to bode little but evil for his prospects.

Nevertheless, a fresh fault with her brother's engagement surfaced in her mind.

"I confess myself astonished that you would consent to this marriage, particularly given Richard Eton's sympathy for the rebels' cause." Priscilla whispered to her father as the evening dwindled to its end. "Do you not remember the promise you extracted from me regarding my own associations?"

Mr. Parr drew back as if this objection had never before occurred to him. "Eton is my eldest and dearest friend. You do him injustice to rank him among the rabble-rousers."

"But you heard him, Father! He openly defended the seditionists at his own party."

Mr. Parr's eyebrows knit together in apparent irritation. "Eton heads one of the most successful law practices in the colony, as well as one of its oldest families. It is a fine match both financially and socially.

I want to hear nothing further about this matter—not even from *you*, Priscilla." In a lower voice, he added, "I have my reasons."

※

Days later, the engagement provided the primary topic of a lively *tête-à-tête* at one of the infamous teas. The tidings elevated the girls, who were hosted on this occasion in the parlor of the Adams House, to such rapture that Priscilla felt strangely out of place and frequently winced at their giddy exclamations.

Frances proved one of the most animated of all. "I can scarcely suppress my delight!"

Priscilla, in turn, could scarcely suppress a smile. "You must make an attempt, Frances."

"How am I to exercise patience before the ball at the Etons'?" Harriet wrung her hands dreamily.

"That cannot be helped, I suppose. I am also eager to see the pair side by side." Deep in thought, Priscilla drew the teacup to her lips.

"This marriage shall bring such joy in all corners, wouldn't you agree, Priscilla?" Frances lifted a tart from the silver serving tray and brushed crumbs from her lap.

Despite fondness for her younger sister, Priscilla was in no humor to indulge Frances's frenzy. "It shall bring more prestige than joy, I daresay!"

Margaret's eyes fixed upon her narrowly. "Priscilla, I forbid you to spoil our merriment."

"Margaret, hush!" Katherine rapped her younger sister on the arm.

"Their respective social stations make this an ideal match. No impediment may exist in light of such equality," Rosamund said.

"No doubt, no doubt, the affluence of their families is yet another advantage." Margaret twisted her linen handkerchief. "Yet, why must he choose her? Rosamund, are not you also a proper match in light of consequence? Are not Kate, Harriet, Jane, and myself suitable equals? Rachel is a shameless coquette."

"But a most successful one," Jane laughed. "You cannot deny that."

Margaret ignored the dissenting remark. "Mother has taken tea with her and considers her manners to be insolent. Rachel insulted her. You heard Mother, Kate. I cannot recall Miss Eton's language, but its arrogance is not to be doubted. Do you not hear the word from Richmond? They say that her moods turn black without warning; that she keeps to herself—and even hears voices."

These revelations merely heightened Priscilla's misgivings.

Chapter 9

The Outburst

Priscilla was at last afforded a glance of her brother and Miss Eton. During the Etons' ball, the two were thrown together for the examination of the world. All manner of probing eyes were cast in their direction, and no eyes delved more deeply than those of Priscilla. Resolving to know more, she advanced toward the pair early in the evening. She found them seated beside one another on the sofa. Rachel, her large fan unfurled, laughed wildly as Ben leaned over to share a confidence.

Ben's expression lost some of its mirth upon his sister's approach. *Surely he still resents my interference,* Priscilla silently surmised. When faced with his coldness, she suffered a pang of remorse for openly criticizing his engagement.

"I congratulate you, Brother." Priscilla managed a smile as Ben rose to greet her. "And you, of course, Miss Eton."

Ben's countenance instantly warmed. "I thank you, Priscilla." He gestured toward Rachel, who remained seated. "It is my wish that the two of you become friends."

Priscilla steadied her voice. "As always, I am resolved to show kindness toward those who truly seek your welfare and happiness."

Rachel's eyes flashed a challenge, and she turned again toward Ben. "*I* accept only those who leave your heart undivided. There you have it, my love! I am a jealous being and must have liberty to confess it."

"You shall have these liberties and more." Ben sank once more onto the seat next to her and gently caressed the dark curl that bounced upon Rachel's forehead. "I have secured your love, the only prize I desire. You have nothing to fear, Rachel. I shall be your lover, your friend—your sole protector."

Her presence seemingly forgotten by the couple, Priscilla began to contemplate the import of the brief conversation she had witnessed.

Spirited laughs, blushes, and whispers were freely exchanged between the lovers, and the interaction of their volatile tempers yielded every appearance of harmony. Priscilla had been amazed by their evident tenderness. She pronounced no judgment, however, since their characters remained cloaked beneath the often-deceptive guise of courtship.

"And so I gain a sister."

Priscilla's gaze followed the engaging voice that had interrupted her qualms.

Thomas Eton, erect as a statue, stood before her. His head, turned slightly to one side, was bent at a small angle toward her.

She broke into a smile to behold his endearing grin, and the concerns of previous moments shrank from her. "Yes, but I must caution you. I may now tease you at any hour or in any manner I wish! Before, I was restrained, saying, 'Old friends must not be taunted!' Now, I am freed from those chains of civility which bound me. We shall very soon be kindred by the law."

"But I fear your sharp wit. A giant intellect springs from its fiery embers!"

She arched her eyebrows. "And may singe a weaker understanding?"

"Aye, but there lies the enigma," said Thomas with a wink. "Such battles fail to stir a more fragile mind."

Their discourse abruptly halted, for the upsurge of biting tones was presently perceived. Only a few feet away stood a stern Phillip Parr, leaning one arm upon the fireplace mantle. Mr. Eton, Dr. Lee, and Mr. Adams were gathered in a compact circle around his form. William Eton lingered around the outskirts of the close-fitting ring.

The countenances of the men darkened ominously. The uneasy scene wanted no clarification.

Mr. Adams trembled with emotion from head to foot. "But the tidings from Boston wax more violent every hour! It must not lie far in the future."

"What must not lie far away?" Mr. Parr stiffened suddenly. "What fresh evil do you see, Adams? What vile event do you anticipate?"

"Rebellion! Rebellion! It is close at hand." Mr. Eton held his arm aloft in demonstration.

"Nonsense. A lie!" Mr. Parr's features twisted into a sinister frown. "Regardless of all their boasts, the threat of the British army hangs over their heads. They dare not forget it. The king shall soon tire of their treachery, and the leaders would be wise to heed the value of their lives. Perhaps they are witless enough to ignore the present consequences, but that is still the greatest obstacle to their desire. They are like children, whining to satisfy their whims. Certainly they possess more sense than to dash away all security!"

Dr. Lee shook his head. "Parr, I doubt that you fully comprehend this business. They have already transgressed the bounds of royal tolerance. Britain and her colonies cannot continue in this enmity. The bubble shall soon burst! You shall then behold the extent of the radicals' sedition. Very few days shall pass before the point of no return is attained at last. Britain and her colonies must clash!"

"They shall clash indeed—and God be praised for it!" A smirk contorted Mr. Eton's mouth. "We refuse to endure this degradation. The hour of our liberty draws near."

"Rubbish!" Mr. Parr's cheeks were aflame. "What result would issue from such a conflict? Who in all these colonies dare risk their fortunes and lives for the sake of a few taxes? Ha! Never in my life have I heard such a preposterous dispute as these rebels sustain—all for taxes. Now *there* stands a heroic cause!"

"We do not bristle at taxes, Parr. If Virginia were represented in Parliament, we would be the last to defy the Crown. No, this conflict shall be waged upon far more sacred grounds!" Mr. Adams's unbroken voice sent a chill through Priscilla's veins. "The glorious seed of freedom has been sown. Once the notion of liberty is planted within the mind of man, woe be unto all who attempt to retract it from his will once more. This novel concept, ostensibly doomed to failure, is nursed by Parliament's injustice!"

Large veins bulged in Mr. Parr's neck. "Parliament has a duty to crush sedition—just as traitors must be eliminated."

Priscilla shuddered as she noted the low, menacing resonance of her father's tone.

Mr. Adams was undeterred by the interruption. "Yet such oppression directs the march toward independence. The principle spreads like fire and threatens to reach beyond the present discord. The more rights are withheld, the more forcefully this purpose burgeons into bloom. God never intended mankind to choke upon the poison of endless tyranny. For many cruel ages, humanity's blood has been spilled, efforts thwarted, and lives manipulated by powerful oppressors. Oh, may the Creator's original purpose be achieved! May men at last be released from the shackles which have so long bound them! With this belief, nurtured by centuries of subjugation, smoldering within passionate hearts, what would the rebels deem as 'extreme means' to obtain their desire?"

"Treasonous dog!" Mr. Parr exploded with rage.

Priscilla's trepidation mounted. She had never witnessed such a fury. *What strange monster stood before her?*

He proceeded to issue threats that froze Priscilla's blood. She blushed wildly as heads turned, curious eyes darted, and everyone's attention rapidly converged upon the tall man near the fireplace. Lively murmurs arose and multiplied throughout the room. Mr. Adams, taken aback by the consternation his address had provoked, gazed in disbelief at his friend.

Frances suddenly crept up to Priscilla's side. Priscilla quickly discerned her sister's alarm. The young girl, unable to look upon her father, stared at the floor. Phillip Parr's tirade mounted in volume, and Mr. Adams's face continued to redden. The spectacle was fast in danger of becoming a brawl.

He must be stopped, Priscilla thought. *What a laughingstock Father shall be in the morning. He will be an object of derision in all the parlors of*

Williamsburg. What a prey for the gossips! His shame will know no end once he returns to his wits. He has scorned and alienated his longtime associates with a few thoughtless insults.

Fresh whispers amongst the room's occupants stirred her attention. The hum was born in the rear of the room and gradually rippled forward. Priscilla strained to behold the new object of the party's interest. Additional shock frayed her already-worn nerves to see Mrs. Parr, her august face pale, gliding toward the men. She approached her unruly husband and placed a slim hand upon his shoulder. He turned to her, and her gaze desperately entreated him to silence. Mr. Parr softened at her gentle advances. His eyes cooled as he drew his wife's hand to his lips. She then recoiled into oblivion.

"Pardon me, gentlemen, I pray." He retrieved a handkerchief and wiped perspiration from his brow. "These are dangerous times, and like other men, I can hardly distinguish friend from foe in the darkness."

Priscilla, although relieved, discovered that her heart could scarcely resume its former rhythm. Frances too seemed shaken and unlikely to return to her festive mood. Priscilla turned to Thomas and was amazed to note the same peculiar expression on his face as the one that had lingered there at the moment of their reunion almost two months ago. His intense gaze persisted, and, in his concentration, he scowled fiercely. She wondered at his absorption in the unpleasant incident.

The party's celebrations proceeded following the disruption, but Priscilla remained mystified by Mr. Adams's speech, her father's wrath, and by the ever-mysterious expression of her friend Thomas.

Chapter 10

The Prediction

"Thomas, I would like to pose a singular question. Surely you will humor me?" Priscilla peered at him carefully while she sketched his portrait.

The pair, eager to escape the chill of the day, sat leisurely in the parlor of her home. Priscilla had been delighted to receive a visit from her friend. Aside from the entertainment a call of this sort would occasion, she welcomed the opportunity for other reasons. She had been puzzled for days by Thomas's reaction to her father's outburst at the Eton home several evenings ago. Priscilla had largely overcome her bewilderment regarding his statements uttered within her father's garden—and was more intrigued than ever by his views. She yearned for a rational perspective to pierce the madness. This visit would provide a sterling opportunity to broach the divisive topic at the hour of her choosing.

Flushed with a quizzical smile, Thomas abandoned his pose. "What is it you wish to ask?"

"You were listening to a political debate the first night I spoke with you since your family's return. I shall never forget your unusual expression. Indeed, it has mystified me ever since! Following that dreadful uproar the other evening, I noticed it again. You must remember that the upheaval in Boston haunts my nights as well, even though it often pains me to speak of it. So many continue to dismiss the gravity of the turmoil – but *we* sense its magnitude.

You will forgive me...I was not prepared to discuss these matters in recent days. Fear and uncertainty overwhelmed me." Smitten with shame for her curtness during their last conversation regarding this topic, she bit her lip and glanced up from the sketch with every attempt at humility. "I implore you now—what is your true judgment?"

Even though Thomas smiled, the enigmatic look threatened to steal into his eyes yet again. He did not glance at her face but seemingly stared instead into the storm of his own thoughts. After a few moments of deep reflection, he whispered in a solemn tone, "Everything you have heard in the debates possesses a fragment of truth. The colonists of Boston verge upon revolt, and, in truth, I am of their persuasion. My view, however, was stated by Dr. Lee. Remember that he said, 'The bubble shall soon burst.' I recognize the precarious nature of the insurgence, and I shall not deceive you, Priscilla. Each day, I expect tidings of some extreme event that will place Britain and the colonies at one another's throats—"

"Tom, what do mean by 'extreme event'? I assume you predict an outbreak of hostilities."

"With the masses so near rebellion, can they simply forget their purpose? No! They *cannot* reverse their path. They will never be silenced until they unleash their frustrations with the yoke that has been placed upon them. And remember, Priscilla...they will not hesitate to employ violence in order to achieve their ends."

Stunned, she dropped her drawing pencils. "Are you certain that they intend to use violence? They may direct a peaceful protest."

"Never!" The sudden wildness of his expression almost frightened her. "Where lies my certainty? The rebels are in a vicious humor. Nothing save death shall hinder them now!"

"But surely their efforts will be thwarted by His Majesty's forces!" Priscilla, her thoughts in disarray, paused a moment to temper her words and tone. "Once 'the bubble bursts,' as Dr. Lee phrased it, the king will avenge this challenge to his rule. They must then be forced to return to their wits."

"His wrath will not stop them."

Priscilla laughed in order to disguise her confusion. "You entertain nonsense, my boy! Even the most careless among them must realize they haven't a hope against the motherland."

Thomas shrugged. "Perhaps you are right. But of this I warn you: men accomplish marvels if they fix their wills to an idea! This is probable—particularly with a principle as universal and intrinsic as human liberty," Thomas said, passion rising in his voice. Then, his tone deeper than ever before, he leaned so close to Priscilla's face that she espied bright golden flecks within his blue eyes—and even fancied that they flashed at her. "For my own part, I cannot blame them."

"*Cannot blame them?*" Gasping with disbelief, Priscilla rose from her seat. "Certainly *you* would not take part in this masquerade! You are far too sensible for that, Tom."

"It is the greater part of that sense which summons me to the very heart of this revolt."

Heart of this revolt? Surely he did not mean such words. Priscilla stared at her suddenly unsmiling companion. The gleam in his eye nearly proved infectious. She smothered her fascination. "Dying for taxes? I can scarcely believe it. Squandering your life's promise for some romantic vision that shall never penetrate realms beyond the dream? Shall perfect liberty ever exist in our colonies? Shall freedom ever flourish? No, for men are all the same. Their greed is eternal and overpowers all notions of good."

"Yes indeed! Their inherent evil shall never disappear." Thomas edged forward on the settee as Priscilla resumed her seat. "Nevertheless, the chance to forge a fresh, unsullied nation where liberty is law would be well worth the bloodstained toil."

Thomas's logic momentarily hushed Priscilla's tongue. A gradual comprehension grew within her heart. She not only recognized the beauty of his arguments but also their impracticality. Still, she trembled to hear him speak of these foreign concepts—especially with such passion.

"A lovely idea, but not feasible!" She lifted herself higher. "Its fulfillment shall prove particularly difficult in these parts. The Crown would never accept such a government."

She marveled that her old friend, possessor of a keen mind and lover of learned pursuits, should fall prey to the seditionists' propaganda. If the lowest rung of society, as opposed to its intellectual giants, fueled the rebellion like her father supposed, surely *they* could have no greater zeal for the revolt than the young man before her. Her heart wrestled with this realization.

Thomas nodded. "This is true; he would never tolerate it."

She held up a finger to emphasize her point. "There dies the prospect of liberty!"

"He shall be *forced* to grant our independence."

"How can that be?"

"I am ignorant of details. If courageous hearts have purposed its triumph, the world shall witness the dawn of a great wonder."

Priscilla laughed nervously as she retrieved her drawing pencils and continued sketching. "Your ardor nearly persuades me to support the seditionists!"

His countenance softened once more before resuming his pose. "Then I have done a great deed this day! The rebellion could have no braver champion. But think as you will, Priscilla. I highly regard any opinion of yours—and esteem intelligence wherever I find it."

Chapter 11

The Eccentrics

Happy, reckless acceptance governed the evening. The engagement ball of Benjamin Parr and Rachel Eton did not dissatisfy the expectations of mirth attached to it. Gaiety held sway, and the lavish festivities were clouded by no hint of the hostility so prominent at Richard Eton's infamous party. As humanity forever exults in youthful beauty and passions, the company rejoiced.

None were burdened by Priscilla's qualms, least of all the two individuals upon whom every eye was directed. She observed Ben and Rachel in the midst of the dance and cringed to behold the bond that united them. Such a fierce attachment, founded upon a brief courtship, appeared to her the height of folly. In Priscilla's mind, its rash nature signified an omen. She reasoned that infatuation had seized the now-affianced pair, for one cannot always behold the evil that lurks at the end of a sunny path.

Her trepidation, however, could not long be sustained at its present pitch. The celebratory nature of the gala momentarily allayed her most piercing fears. During a conversation with Katherine, Priscilla's walls of resistance were breached for an instant.

"These glorious events inevitably arouse certain sentiments," Katherine said slowly.

"Indeed." Laughing, Priscilla recalled secret misgivings. "All of our childish playmates disappear into that realm of no return. How I yearn for the old days! Defeat in our little contests formed my greatest anxiety!

The rebellion was a matter uttered only by our mothers and fathers, and our babyish intellects scarcely comprehended its importance."

"And, yet, our principles must never alter. Such values as have guided us thus far must continue to direct our respective courses. This path shall not fail any amongst our number!"

Priscilla could not resist a glance in Thomas's direction, whose recent conversation had kindled yet another firestorm of doubt within her. "I sense that we are approaching a time of great transition for all."

"Some changes, however, do not lie outside the common way." The corners of Katherine's mouth curled upward mischievously. "They are joyously expected!"

"You imply matrimony, I suppose."

"That was my meaning, yes."

"It is not an event I perceive in my near future. Therefore, I think little of it." With a twinkle in her eye, Priscilla further probed Katherine's meaning. "Pray, has some mysterious suitor prompted these musings?"

"No, indeed. Yet surely we must ready ourselves for that hour."

The conversation drew to a close as the guests shuffled into the immense dining room.

The banquet crowned the ball with lively exchanges and a succulent selection of rare dishes. Swept away by the merriment, many timid gentlemen were emboldened to spout long-treasured boasts. As the length of the table was served, numerous young ladies were also encouraged to bestow their smiles more freely. Phillip Parr's voice thundered throughout the room. His affability crested whenever he and his kindred found themselves the objects of universal approbation. Priscilla, despite her efforts, could scarcely restrain a smile, and Thomas's arrival at her side killed every attempt.

"I am overjoyed to see you, dear boy!" She extended both hands to him.

"Do not vex yourself upon that score." Giving her hands a firm squeeze, he chuckled. "I believe we are the least animated of all these revelers."

"Ah, yes." Priscilla smiled meaningfully. "We are a pair of eccentrics, are we not, Tom?"

He shook his head and released her hands. "Hardly eccentrics, Priscilla. The empty pursuits of youth never cease to dull the intellect and cool the heart's warmth. Virtues are not extinguished—only overpowered. I have witnessed such a piteous waste in one very dear to me. Indulgence cast a fatal frost upon the promise which once blossomed there."

Here he paused to glance at his sister, who giggled behind her fan a few seats away. Priscilla was stunned to glimpse untold sorrow clouding his keen expression. Lines she had never noticed before now bordered the outer corners of his eyes. The mournful trance, however, was brief. His attention was soon restored to Priscilla.

"So, you see, our peculiarities are not entirely destructive." He lifted the linen napkin and smoothed it over his breeches. "Why should I beg pardon for refusing to take part in the follies of my peers? Isolation and concentration, you know, are not enemies of the soul. Rather, they strengthen the human spirit."

"I have never heard it described thus." Priscilla stared at him in surprise.

It seems that I have always adhered to such beliefs, but he has made me recognize them, she thought.

Thomas nodded. "A life dictated by impulse and leisure can never aspire to greatness."

"Are you then a critic of youth and vitality?"

He gaped as if she had uttered heresy. "Never in a thousand years! The heart of youth also emanates the least corrupted principles known to man. Our spirits do not yet flag from the burdens of life, and our resolve is sustained by a fearless—perhaps naïve—zeal! What could mankind achieve by taming these vices and magnifying such merits?"

Thomas's address was broken off, for Mr. Parr rose from his seat and cleared his throat. The din of the vast room quickly hushed. Giggles, boasts, and jests were silenced by that gentleman's imposing presence, and all eyes were fixed upon him. Priscilla restlessly awaited his words.

"Less than a month ago, my son informed me of his intent to take a wife. That was a moment I had awaited with fear and anticipation since the hour of his birth. What sort of woman would best suit his prospects? I hoped he would marry into a distinguished family—in a manner which would most honor his kindred. This evening, it is my great pleasure to announce his success." Mr. Parr lifted his glass. "I propose a toast…to the happiness of my son and his handsome choice of wife!"

Rising also, Mr. Eton broadened the tribute. "To their fine posterity!"

"Here, here!" The room's occupants roared in deafening accord.

The sense of doom-laden inevitability returned to Priscilla as the cheers ascended. The tide had turned, and its progress could not be impeded now. Benjamin Parr had cast his fated lot, and Priscilla feared that his heart had been planted in barren soil.

Her soul screamed in anguish.

Oh, Ben! Why choose a madwoman to be the wife of your youth, mother of your children, guardian of your hopes, companion of your life?

Tears dimmed her eyes, and she glanced at her lap in order to conceal her distress.

She suddenly discerned a familiar giggle arise from the far end of the enormous table. Her eyes wandered to discover its source. Katherine Lee proved to be the origin of the exuberance, but plain Henry Adams appeared to be its inspiration. The two were seated beside one another, and the sight of their conversation seemed strangely suitable. Katherine's cool charm shimmered in his calm presence. His preference for her graceful smiles and soft grey eyes, which stared up at him from beneath long dark lashes, was evident.

Mr. Parr, making endless rounds about the table to receive everyone's individual congratulations, continued to beam. Priscilla often overheard his exclamations of approval concerning "the superior conquest" his son had made. Priscilla flinched at this boast, but she held her tongue and accepted the futility of speaking once more against the match. Despite this silence, she had never resented Rachel's aloof smiles and suspicion-doused taunts with greater fury than on the present occasion—when she held Ben's heart in her hands.

Chapter 12

The Marriage

"You held merry company last evening, Kate. A certain young man seemed to dominate your attention," whispered Priscilla mischievously.

The responsive twists of Katherine's features were illuminated by the sun's radiance shining through the parlor window. Her countenance was colored by no shame, but she smiled with amusement. No trace could be detected of her former animated state, which had so astonished Priscilla. Indeed, Katherine's tranquility had returned in such fullness that Priscilla began to doubt the significance of the recent scene.

"Mr. Adams is a young man of entertaining conversation, and his gentle manners are certainly capable of inspiring fondness." Katherine blushed to her hairline. "Indeed, a lady would be heartless to despise him."

"And so our little tea circle must lose another damsel to marriage!"

"Do not presume so much." Katherine giggled, roused from passivity. "Mr. Adams diverted me for the greater part of the ball with such respect, wit, and intelligence that I mourned to lose his company. Our discourse was agreeable to both parties, but *there* the matter ends."

"Oh, I cannot believe that!" Priscilla smiled incredulously. "I thought the son of old George Adams was a timid, whey-faced mouse until he carried on that spirited conversation with you the other evening. Admiration for you must have drawn out his livelier element.

I give my approval for the match; such a thoughtful young man as Henry Adams is worthy of you!"

"You tease me," Katherine began merrily, "but you yourself must also be open to romantic suspicion. I have noted one young gentleman in particular whose attentions you do not spurn."

"Who on earth?" Priscilla stared at her friend in shock.

"Young Thomas Eton has lingered at no side but your own. Your daring notions have clearly singled you out in his favor."

"*My* daring notions? The boy is a radical! This is the most absurd jest of all."

"Is it, though?" Katherine smiled softly.

"Yes indeed!" Priscilla dismissed her friend's suspicions with a toss of her head. "Thomas and I share curious views. Our minds work in parallel planes. Our tempers are so alike that no spark of love could ever arise between us. Can a flame ignite betwixt two stones, each set firmly in their own pillars of granite?"

"No, but two tributaries may unite to forge a river more powerful than themselves alone."

"Ah, I fear that we must differ, Kate." Priscilla sighed. "We should consent to a pact: our affections must follow their fated courses."

"I agree."

The members of the Parr family awoke the morning of the wedding with nervous anticipation. The groom's excitement never subsided. He wildly dashed about the Parr House like a small lad on the morning of his first hunting excursion. He teased his sisters mercilessly and continuously slapped his father on the back. Priscilla was struck by bittersweet gladness to behold both his boyish spirit and the ruddy glow of his cheeks. Mrs. Parr's eagerness rendered her absentminded, and even Ivy's sour temper was overcome by the bustle of the morning. Frances's childlike cries of joy could not be silenced by any force of nature, including a rebuke from her similarly distracted mother.

Phillip Parr bloomed into his full glory. He touted his son's great virtues, the beauty of his future daughter-in-law, the substantial fortune of the Eton family, and his likely future as the patriarch of a fruitful dynasty. The zenith of his ambitions seemed near indeed.

In the midst of such glee, what humor was left for Priscilla to exhibit? Her inner gloom briefly receded. What deed of hers could possibly amend such a dismal error on the part of a love-struck brother—if indeed it was an error? In this spirit, she resolved to smother her own fears and summon happiness for a beloved kinsman on this sacred day.

On the final day of October, therefore, Priscilla beheld the union of her brother with the person whom she had believed to be his doom. Desperation, impossible to appease, awakened. Despite struggles to the contrary, she was unable to quell this fear—a fear that culminated the moment Benjamin Parr and Rachel Eton become man and wife at the altar of Bruton Parish Church.

Chapter 13

The Guests

November disappeared with surprising haste, and the bleakness of winter stole into the town like an intruder. Following the advent of soberly scenic snows, the endless stream of Christmas parties, dinners, and balls began. The harsh weather, however, also conveyed certain nuisances. The austere conditions deprived Mrs. Parr, Ivy, Priscilla, and Frances of outdoor exercise. Consequently, the ladies were confined to the house with their new relation, Rachel.

The young woman possessed little adaptability, and the transition to her new home certainly worked no marvels upon her uncertain temper. Her daily routine mystified them all, for she sat in the parlor either reading, sewing, or making music for half the day but wandered restlessly from room to room during the other half.

Her new kinswomen, particularly Mrs. Parr, attempted conversation with her, but Rachel shunned their efforts. Making evident her wish for their absence, she never failed to issue an icy reply. Her upbringing as the only daughter in a prosperous family had worked its evil upon her disposition, and her removal to an unfamiliar home singing with the laughter of three daughters evidently unnerved her. The compassion subsequently directed at Rachel never penetrated her self-imposed loneliness. She remained bent upon isolation.

She quickly became attached to Mrs. Parr's harpsichord and sometimes played it for hours. During these periods, she only stared at the keys intently, flipped the pages of the music book, and never spoke. In one instance, Priscilla and Frances gossiped softly in the parlor while Rachel plied the instrument.

"Quiet!" Rachel's voice screeched with irritation. "You have ruined the score!"

Priscilla's temper rose. "Are we bound to silence for hours merely for the sake of *your* pleasures?"

Frances bit her lip. "Perhaps we were wrong to speak. The music is so lovely, after all."

An angry fever burned Priscilla's cheeks. "We were *not* wrong to speak, Frances. Let us continue our discourse!"

Rachel, however, resumed playing with such great volume as to drown any further conversation.

Similar scenes were not uncommon in the days immediately following Rachel's instatement as second mistress of the Parr House. Once Phillip Parr and his son returned home from an outing, however, her coldness melted like frost before the sun. She showered her husband with kisses. Following their embrace, the couple regularly burst into a torrent of conversation, which left the remainder of the family speechless and bewildered. They were puzzled by Ben's moody new bride, who now seemed to govern his thoughts, company, time, and attention. He fawned over Rachel and lavished upon her every possible gift, including trinkets, frills, and the pin-money to don the most expensive European fashions. Priscilla balked at his extravagance and reasoned that the judgment of her once-sensible brother had vanished the moment the beautiful Rachel had slipped his ring onto her dainty white finger.

The constant affection between them appeared sturdy. Rachel, although aloof to her husband's family, could ill bear his absence. She adored him to distraction and strove to please him. The two were inseparable at dinner each evening, and their relentless discourse resulted in a lack of exchange for the remainder of the Parr family. At the dreary close of most of those early December evenings, all but two of the family retired with a glum face.

One of Priscilla's greatest pleasures during this time arose from the Parr family's increased association with the Etons. The two households often enjoyed dinner together, and she usually chose a seat next to Thomas. He informed her of political tidings, or the lack thereof. Each time she spoke with him, she expected to be notified of a number of unthinkable disasters. For a time, she escaped such dreadful news.

Once more, she did not fail to observe Thomas's mournful manner regarding his sister. Priscilla once overheard a brief exchange between them.

Before dinner one evening, Thomas strode over to the harpsichord, where Rachel flaunted her musical proficiency. "My sister is in the bloom of health and happiness, I see!"

"Yes indeed." Smiling triumphantly, Rachel never lifted her eyes from the instrument. "My husband is a generous and protective man. I am adorned with greater jewels and gowns than ever I beheld in my life! Matrimony agrees with me."

"He spoils you, Rachel."

Rachel's fingers stumbled over the keys, and, having faltered, produced such a discordant noise that Priscilla winced. Her eyes blazing, Rachel wheeled around to assail her brother. "Who are you to make that judgment, impertinent young fry? What do you know of it?"

Though his lips twitched, Thomas's gaze never wavered. "I know more than you will admit. This has happened before. Remember when—"

"Hush now! You have always disliked me, Tom—confess it!" Brushing away a tear, Rachel returned to the instrument. "Leave me be! You interrupted my playing."

Priscilla pensively contemplated the scene. She seized an opportunity to broach the sensitive matter when she noticed Thomas's somber gaze directed toward his sister the same evening at dinner.

"Tom, why do you fix your eye upon Rachel thus?" Priscilla, eager to convey an air of mild nonchalance, sliced the mutton carefully as she spoke.

He did not break his brooding trance. Such preoccupied silence made Priscilla regret her query and wonder if she had offended him. Had the question reeked of an unseemly curiosity? She intended to introduce a more tolerable subject when Thomas finally parted his lips in speech.

His voice broke passionately. "I only imagine what could have been!"

"What do you mean?"

"Great gifts lie within Rachel, yet these resources are laid waste."

Priscilla waited as his features darkened with a sadness that nearly overwhelmed him.

"And I grieve for her, Priscilla!" His jaw trembled. "Such ardor and tenacity as hers could have been bent to a sterling purpose had they only been channeled into more appropriate paths! And that is not all, for something darker—something more powerful—enslaves her."

Priscilla was astounded to hear this speech. At such times, the simple boyish openness of Thomas's manner, as demonstrated during their rendezvous in her father's garden, seemed like a ghost—a bygone vision that breathed only within her memory. She often pondered that afternoon with something like remorse, as if an opportunity to drink more deeply from a rare friendship, a gift from heaven itself, had slipped from her grasp.

Nevertheless, following Thomas's confession, she beheld Rachel through very different eyes and strove to distinguish in her sister-in-law a hopelessly flawed heroine instead of a spiteful young shrew. Priscilla gradually became conscious of the source of Thomas's dejection. Rachel's self-seeking frivolity had erased all traces of purer metal beneath. Still, what darker force, as Thomas had termed it, worked in Rachel's mind? Priscilla pondered his statements for days. Indeed, they added credence to previous rumors.

Such gatherings of the two families yielded not only fascinating character studies but also indications of hidden motives. Ivy's self-possessed air, for instance, often acquired a softer edge whenever the Etons dined with her family. Her temper was rendered a great deal livelier by their company. Her eyes frequently roamed the table with agitation. Priscilla noted a strange eagerness in her sister's gaze. No tangible evidence justified Priscilla's theory—only small tokens. How could the continual elevation of Ivy's eyes at the mention of William

Eton's name be doubted? How could Ivy's searching stares of his frigid countenance be concluded as anything other than a budding interest?

The fancy, however, thrived only on the lady's side. The sullen William Eton never gave his admirer an unnecessary glance. One peculiar evening, however, he was forced to dance with her out of common civility. Priscilla, seated nearby, then overheard the most condemning evidence of all.

Ivy kindled the conversation. "William, I cannot comprehend why a man of your means has not taken a wife already. Perhaps your heart is a fortress that will not be conquered."

The shadow that fleeted across William's features did not escape Priscilla. He writhed in discomfort at his partner's flirtation. Priscilla leaned forward to hear his response.

"If I marry, my family will be the first to know of it."

"I am your sister now, William." Ivy's tone, though still ringing with warmth, sharpened. "Surely I may now be included in your confidence."

William made no answer. His annoyance was clear as he simmered quietly. A scowl further darkened his prominent brow, and the nervous energy of his steps indicated an eagerness to see the dance end. The bemused smile that curved his mouth, however, revealed some pleasure of vanity—and made Priscilla despise him. *He is both revolted and entertained by my sister's presumptions*, she thought.

Undeterred by his hostile silence, Ivy persisted. "I am no faithless keeper of secrets!" A strange light flashed across her steely eyes.

William's subsequent rebuke demonstrated more sneering insensitivity than Priscilla had yet witnessed in his character. "I share my private feelings with no one, Miss Parr, particularly a lady to whom I am bound by the most dubious threads of acquaintance. In the future, I shall thank you to leave off using my Christian name. These liberties hardly befit a woman of virtue."

The dance ended before Ivy could compose her wits to meet this direct insult. William hastened from her presence and strode over to Dr. Lee and Mr. Parr, with whom he spoke in hushed tones for half an hour. To Priscilla's astonishment, Mr. Parr, either ignorant or indifferent to the incivilities heaped upon his eldest daughter by that young gentleman, received him royally.

Priscilla calculated Ivy's aims. The chief of Ivy's interest in William sprang from his wealth and status. Beneath Ivy's bitterness seethed a single-mindedness that refused to rest until she acquired her desire—for good or ill. By failing to bless Ivy with wit and loveliness, nature had mocked her. These deficits, however, only inflamed Ivy's resolve. Her clever mind constantly devised the manner of her triumph. Her sole prospect for the deference she craved lay at the altar. She was determined to marry into greatness, and the various elements of her being labored for this one purpose. She had long ago vowed to pursue her objective to the last.

Despite the injustice of Ivy's abiding resentment toward her, Priscilla harbored some uneasiness for her sister. Ivy, she suspected, would sacrifice any principle for prestige in the world. Though Ivy read voraciously and might thus be expected to have imbibed discernment, Priscilla feared that she was blind to everything save her own advancement and, as demonstrated by her designs upon so aloof a man as William Eton, might someday become entangled in the web of her own ambition.

The month of December bred other surprises. Many visits by distant relatives were paid to the Williamsburg families. These visits often inspired parties in the guests' honor.

One such event was especially celebrated. Since the Adamses had issued their invitations, the insatiable murmur of the gossip circle had centered upon the guests of honor. This elite family had invited their illustrious cousins, John Seymour and his sister Anne, to pass the holiday in their Williamsburg home.

The pair arrived on a frosty Tuesday, and the party in their honor was scheduled for the following Friday evening at the Adams House.

Chapter 14

The Suitor

"The Adamses have endured much distress and stretched their resources to a ridiculous extent in order to accommodate the guests of honor this evening," observed Priscilla as she passed Thomas Eton at the beginning of the grandiose festivity.

"Indeed!" Thomas laughed, glancing at the gaudy decorations. "Absurd, I daresay."

"Why are people such shameless mercenaries, Tom?" Priscilla scoffed with disgust. "It is all a senseless business."

Bitterness suddenly scorched his tone. "Yet we see its footprint upon an even grander stage! Is not Britain the greatest mercenary of all?"

Priscilla, struck by his observation, turned to question him—only to find that he had vanished into the crowd.

She had no leisure to lament his disappearance, for tension soon flooded the Adams House in preparation for the descent of Mr. and Miss Seymour. The conjecture of past days reached a feverish climax as the guests abandoned all pretense of patience. Priscilla finally caught sight of Thomas, who had moved to his brother's side. Katherine, however, could not be spotted amidst the dense throng. The air inside the home grew thick and stifling as the entire assembly awaited the famed pair. Her eyes probing every countenance, Priscilla sat quietly in a dark corner of the room. Her concentration upon Thomas's wild-eyed remarks waxed so intense that she barely noticed the uproar that heralded the appearance of young Mr. Seymour and his sister.

"Priscilla, I should like to introduce Mr. John Seymour. Mr. Seymour, Miss Priscilla Parr," Jane Adams cordially said.

In the days preceding his arrival, the youth and riches of the much-anticipated Mr. Seymour gave rise to a great deal of lively discussion, but a later discovery had ignited rampant speculation. A report had surfaced that he was the sole owner of a vast plantation in the countryside after recently inheriting the estate in its entirety from his late father.

Another rumor had circulated that Seymour was heir to the massive fortune of his elderly uncle in Philadelphia. This uncle, the brother of John Seymour's father, had, as a younger son, been forced to make his own way in the world. He became a merchant and, in time, came to rule the commerce of Philadelphia. To his great profit, Phillip Parr himself had often invested in the trade ventures of George Seymour. Through his uncle George, John Seymour was closely associated with the premier shipping magnates of Boston. Tantalizing facts such as these kindled the hearts and ambitions of Williamsburg's genteel maidens.

John Seymour was, without a doubt, very well favored. He towered above almost every other man in the room, including the Etons. Like a Greek statue of old, his features exuded a chiseled splendor. He assessed Priscilla with sharp blue eyes beneath fair eyebrows, which he quickly lifted. His golden hair bordered his face in august style. His chin protruding, Mr. Seymour seemed to scrutinize Priscilla from head to toe. The subsequent admiring gaze heightened her uneasiness.

She attempted to puncture the silence. "How do you do, Mr. Seymour?"

"I do very well, Miss Parr," he responded, still seeming to take her likeness in his mind.

Shifting beneath his penetrating gaze, she smiled and sought an amenable topic. "And how does the capital suit you this season?"

"Admirably." He arched his eyebrows and returned her smile. "I had forgotten that Williamsburg bred such beauties—or else, I should have come more often before."

Heat doused her face, and she tucked her chin at his audacious esteem. His intense stare began to unnerve her, and the elevation of his jaw suggested an expectation of reciprocal flattery.

Leaning over to her ear so closely that his speech tickled her face, he whispered, "Dance the next round with me!"

Priscilla recoiled, searching his daring eyes. *What a liberty he had taken!* Still, to refuse him was unthinkable. The claims of civility forbade it. Swallowing hard, she accepted the hand he extended.

Mr. Seymour's flair for the dance amazed even Priscilla. She could only imagine the quality of instructors his father must have commissioned for him. His movements were both graceful and sure, and she inwardly acknowledged his skillful superiority to any partner she had ever encountered. His adroit maneuverings, however, were not confined to the dance. He struggled to spark a discourse with her.

"The hustle and bustle of this town excites me. Everyone dashing to and fro! The countryside, however, is more pleasing to the faculties—and easier upon the nerves. No rumble of carts and carriages disturbs my peace. Tell me, Miss Parr." His eyes narrowed to focus upon her face. "Have you ever sojourned in the country?"

"My Aunt and Uncle Wallace own a plantation there."

"How strange! They are indeed amongst my acquaintance."

"Truly? Why did we never meet?" Priscilla nearly bit her tongue upon unleashing the words. She did not think she would have *wished* to meet this pretentious man—even if she had known him to be amongst the inner circle of her aunt and uncle—and she did not want to give him a false impression of interest.

"Anne and I often dine with them nowadays, but we much prefer our own plantation to any other. Father, when he was alive, did not allow us many freedoms. We did not then often dine with friends, which would explain our never chancing to meet. At any rate, our plantation has indeed flourished during the past year. I respect the dead, but, in truth, Miss Parr, my father possessed none of that prudence which transforms a patch of mud into a thriving plantation."

"Yet, he left you sizeable holdings—such as many men would covet!"

He appeared surprised, but high-pitched insistence crept into his voice. "The plantation was in disarray until it passed to me. I have transformed it into a great enterprise."

"In six months?" Priscilla laughed, disbelief dripping from her words. What a pompous dandy, this young man who laid claim to his father's toil—all the while heaping adulation upon himself!

"The hand of inspired youth is swift."

Priscilla's tongue could no longer restrain its fire. "You should hide your face in shame for speaking of your late father with such contempt! You would not own the clothes on your back if not for him. If you did indeed carry out beneficial changes to the estate, you only improve upon the foundation he left to your keeping. You should value the precedents he instituted."

"You seem to be a rebellious spirit yourself, Miss Parr!"

"Yes, but I do esteem my father's noble life, even if our opinions may diverge on occasion."

"I am in no temper for a quarrel this evening." The livid spark lingering in his eye suggested that he was not accustomed to opposition and, having encountered it, was determined to conquer it. "You may strike a fair form, but are shockingly saucy. You may find it dangerous to cross me."

She met his gaze. "You will not find me easily cowed."

Mr. Seymour's features darkened with a malicious resolve that startled her. His face grew scarlet, and he fumed for the remainder of the dance. Shock at having received her impudence silenced him. His countenance twisted with pain at her reproof. The dance concluded none too soon for Priscilla. Barely had she fled his company before Katherine approached her and insisted upon hearing her impression of the prominent guest.

"If only you had danced with the popinjay!" Priscilla glared at Mr. Seymour, who brooded quietly in a far corner of the room.

Katherine's gloved hands flew to her cheeks. "Dear me!"

"He spoke so insolently of his late father, whom all recognize as an honorable man. Once I rebuked Seymour for his scorn, he said I would find it 'dangerous to cross him.' I will shun him, Kate."

"This is a wonder." Katherine did not bother to conceal her astonishment. "I have heard him described as 'charming.'"

Priscilla shook her head and scowled. "It was a false report then. It is impossible for an honest soul to grant his character mercy."

"Many of our friends will be disappointed in him, then."

"Some might, but the greedy adventurers shall not be deterred. It is hopeless. I will always be called a 'beacon of intolerance,' for I never can bear this ignorance."

Katherine's countenance suddenly brightened. "I have been introduced to Miss Seymour."

"Where is she now?" Priscilla's eyes searched the crowd.

Katherine cast a glance about the room and finally espied Miss Seymour's conspicuous form.

"There!" Katherine signaled.

"Where?"

"She dances yonder with Thomas Eton."

Sixteen-year-old Anne Seymour had aroused equal enthusiasm among the gossipmongers in recent days. Reports of this great beauty had preceded her, and she had consequently held the whole of Williamsburg's praise in the palm of her hand even before setting her elegant boot upon its snow-clad soil. These rumors, Priscilla presently perceived, were indeed true.

Miss Seymour danced as gracefully as her brother. Her rich golden locks were pinned in the most flattering arrangement Priscilla had ever seen. Priscilla could not distinguish the hue of Miss Seymour's eyes but assumed that they were glistening pools of blue like those of Mr. Seymour. Though diminutive, the girl's figure appeared well proportioned, and the tilt of her head suggested the same air of condescension manifested by her brother. Miss Seymour flashed a smile in her partner's direction, and Priscilla's heart ached.

Why did it ache so suddenly? The unexpected pain bewildered Priscilla. She recognized that the sight before her eyes had struck a raw place and levied all her logic in a struggle to slay the sentiment. All her might was focused upon its destruction as she strove to view the scene with indifference.

She could not suppress it. This realization proved even more devastating than the emotion's existence. Nevertheless, she knew that it must die quickly. As Thomas clutched Miss Seymour's gloved hand, the troublesome sting swelled into throbbing angst.

No! Priscilla vowed to smother the silly grief which had arisen with such ugly haste. The more vigorously she endeavored to stifle it, however, the more rapidly it pulsed. Which guise might these unsettling sensations assume? She hardly dared utter the one feeling that burst from her soul with the greatest volume and passion…

Envy!

Chapter 15

The Conspiracy

Priscilla suffered pangs of horror and disbelief in the days following the party hosted by the Adamses. No amount of rationalization could induce her to declare it a "success," the term of description employed and circulated throughout the neighborhood. Her distrust of Mr. Seymour escalated with the addition of a second burden. His company, an object for which she cared nothing, barred her from an honor infinitely more cherished.

If only to sever the chains that suddenly bound her! Suspended between dueling flames of confusion and expectation, she suffered a decline in artistic skill. Gloom and pleasure discovered a haven in the imaginative realm of her paintings, but chaos remained an intruder.

Her family's unrelenting praise of Mr. Seymour was heaped upon these woes. Their affections were won not only by his fortune but also the Grecian turn of his nose. Priscilla's aversion to the man was not swayed by their adoration, though her nerves were still agitated by the increasingly absurd tributes.

As the family gathered in the sitting room the afternoon following the Adamses' festivity, Mr. Parr first broached this subject. "Young Seymour is dignity itself! I think him as fine a fellow as ever was." Donning his spectacles, he unfolded the latest edition of the *Virginia Gazette* and eased into a chair near the window.

Priscilla's fingers defensively tightened around the spine of her book, and she sensed hot desperation boiling within her. "Are you certain that purse strings have no hand in it?"

"He certainly bears a pleasing countenance," Frances giggled.

Mr. Parr peered at Priscilla over the top edge of his newspaper. "And from a fine stock he is! His father, also John Seymour, was one of the wealthiest men in these parts. The young man stands to inherit yet another fortune…from Philadelphia."

This accolade summoned Priscilla from her silence. "I heard such a defamation of the dead from that rich gentleman's mouth as made my ears blush with shame. He boasted of his father's weakness—of his own might. He credited his own vigor and capacity as the joint creators of his prosperity. I delight in exposing a wicked claim. But for that wintry hand does he exist at all!"

"Tut, tut!" Mr. Parr, not without a line of alarm to crease his brow, quickly lifted his hand to subdue her. "Your tongue is merciless, Priscilla. Who would have guessed that I sired such a hawk? You know that I take much joy in your opinions, but, hear now! You may yet come to wish these things unsaid. It is time to dull those harsh interfaces—to broaden your circle of society. The hour has come to dwell upon certain truths—that principles should loosen and make room for order…for rational concerns."

A warm pulse throbbed in Priscilla's temples as her racing mind absorbed these insinuations. "To what end are these instructions directed?"

"He means that you are mistress of your own fate, Priscilla." Ivy's voice soared to a sharp pitch.

Stung by Ivy's interference and flushed with embarrassment, Priscilla glared at her as if to pose a challenge. "You speak in riddles."

"It is no riddle—on the contrary." Dipping her quill in ink, Mrs. Parr laughed calmly and began to compose a letter at her writing desk. "Surely you understand."

"Indeed, I find myself witless as a stone."

Frances's warm blue eyes remonstrated with Priscilla. "The wife of Mr. Seymour shall be a happy woman."

Priscilla flinched at her sister's childish enthusiasm. "I suspected an assumption of this sort. What ill fortune to be cast into company with a pompous crow, bedecked in vanity and swallowing up all other songs with one blast of his boast!"

Ivy flashed a bitter look. "Many would gladly endure such company."

Mrs. Parr suddenly laid aside her letter and turned to Priscilla. Something akin to dread lurked within her eyes. "Your saucy notions, my child, may do you harm."

Priscilla laughed. "But, Mother, why should I fear?"

"I often worry that your violent spirit can meet no peaceful end. A young woman cannot be too circumspect. Good sense, not sentimentality, is the best guide."

"Enough of nonsense now." Mr. Parr gestured with irritation. "What I intended to say is that flaws are inherent in the human race. Do not concentrate upon their abundance or lack thereof. Only think of Seymour's worth! He is a highly respectable gentleman—indeed, of the most respectable sort. Think of the advantages his wedded favor would bestow upon yourself and your kindred. You would take pleasure in a life of consequence and ease almost twice that into which you were born."

Priscilla's spirit rose like a wild creature in bondage. Resistance flayed her nerves. Why did they urge her so? Did the lure of worldly treasure blind their eyes to the heart's cry—indeed, to the demands of virtuous right? She suddenly yearned to paint, to soak the canvas with a thousand sorrows, fears, and desires. She thought it strange that a longing for liberty should overwhelm her at such a moment.

Even Frances, the sister upon whom she doted, conspired against her. Frances had always manifested a certain naïve obstinacy that troubled Priscilla. It suggested a stubbornness that invited all of life's chastisement to acquaint the soul with evil, pain, and grief. And yet, it seemed that the young girl wailed for such crushing knowledge—that such despair should arouse a deeper store of goodness yet untapped.

Priscilla was spared a response by the familiar, worn swing of the front door. The tread of lovers' feet was heard as the two sought refuge from the deepening shadows of dusk, and the forms of Ben and Rachel illuminated the sitting room doorway.

Chapter 16

The Interview

Days trickled into the obscurity of time following the Adamses' party. Hours waxed unbearable, and the hand of the clock rattled Priscilla with each gentle tick. While everyone around her slipped deeper and deeper into the airy glee of the season, Priscilla shrank from the merriment. Still worse, fate began to pour its fury upon her head.

The young gentleman she now scorned—but who seemed to have conceived an interest in her—appeared one Thursday morning. His smug grin suggested he had every expectation of a warm reception. Some measure of surprise and alarm from the lady's quarter must necessarily accompany the visit. Must he persevere after such impudence aimed to counter his own? Had the brute's injured pride suffered him to revisit his critic? Was her censure insufficient to frighten away all his hopes?

Priscilla had no leisure to decipher these mysteries. Following a brief exchange of civilities, Mr. and Mrs. Parr abandoned the gentleman to their daughter's company. After reluctantly offering him a seat, Priscilla settled upon a sofa across from him and promptly gave voice to her thoughts.

"You astonish me, sir." Her eyes fixed upon Mr. Seymour. "I rewarded the honor you bestowed upon me last Friday evening with taunts. I recall the nature of our quarrel."

"Why recall it?" He shifted in his seat.

Priscilla drew a sharp breath in an attempt to regain her self-possession before proceeding. "Because you demand it! By coming here thus, you revive the subject. I cannot engage in pleasurable conversation without resolving this matter."

Removing wrinkles all the while, he straightened his sleeves. "You misjudge me. I propose we begin afresh, deserting our former argument for more friendly discourse. I am willing to forget. My thoughts have returned to you often enough." He suddenly leaned forward. "Pray, is the hunter's glory redoubled in the capture of a mild robin? Nay, for his renown springs from the seizure of an untamed creature! The bird's resistance is proportional to the hunter's triumph. The ferocity of the prey is thus no stain but rather a brilliant badge for the predator."

She eyed him with all the suspicion of an encircled tigress. He removed his dark felt tricorne to reveal a golden mane, smartly tamed by a black ribbon. His lavish golden satin coat sloped away to reveal a white satin waistcoat, trimmed with gleaming golden buttons and crowned by a copious cravat fringing his throat. His ebony shoes shone like polished jade from the sunlight slanting through the window. His features were regular, his face pallid as if he had been outdoors only rarely in his lifetime, a rare trait for a young man reared on a plantation. A haughty spark peeked from beneath heavily lidded eyes, a paradox perhaps bespeaking certainty that others would do his bidding with minimal effort from himself.

A smooth ivory hand rested heedlessly upon the rich fabric of the furniture. His ease suggested a command of his surroundings as if he knew well the secret corners of the house. His person dominated the room as if he had sprawled across its plush fixtures for years past with every article of furniture impressed upon his consciousness. Never had he entered the door until that morning, and yet, in a moment, he became lord of the room. His detached authority could ill be contained, and even Priscilla was strangely drawn to its power.

She broke the silence. "Have you any tidings from Boston?"

Mr. Seymour's façade of civility splintered with her remark and was betrayed by the hot flush of displeasure that crept into his face. His eyebrows knit together in a tense weave.

"I have no reason to hear from Boston." His eyes swiftly narrowed. "You regularly speak of such things, Miss Parr?"

"I cannot help myself; my soul soars upon the wings of the momentous, the grand, the violent! Can you not restrain yourself when so many events of great import transpire within the space of hours? I pray for the conflict's resolution. While discord thrives, however, I will chase it—and know its significance. Are not all souls fascinated by dissension? Would you pause to behold a quarrel in the street—or rather a pleasant conversation?"

"These thoughts are beyond me. I never entertain them!" Bristling with annoyance, he withdrew his pocket watch and studied it. "You delight in this nonsense—this prattling with no logic? Not all members of your sex are drunk with their own wisdom. They chase neither the gales of politics nor the darkness of men's affairs. My dearest sister never touches these matters."

Mr. Seymour had struck a bitter chord within Priscilla that silenced the reproof that would have slid from her tongue in another moment. A thousand sharp sensations rushed back upon her.

Thomas! Thomas! Why should she heed it? Mr. Seymour had not perhaps known the force of his boast until he gazed upon her discomposed countenance.

Taking advantage of her silence, he proceeded to speak. "My most beloved hopes lie with Anne. She was born to make a brilliant marriage. Such virtues must in time win a coveted heart, and I only wish for the continued liberty of her own."

"Then you wish her to have a cold heart?"

"I shall never suffer Anne to cast herself into the wedded arms of an inferior. It would mean the death of all my aspirations."

"What does this signify—an 'inferior'? What can you possibly mean by this?" Fury choked her.

"I despise unthinking idealists."

"*Idealists!* You must then include in this category the Greek philosophers and the saints of old!"

"This is a different age, my pet." He tapped his knee impatiently. "The era of conquest and imperialism has dawned."

"Were the Romans not similar in their appetites? Were they not also brutes who lusted for the power to trample upon the rights of man?"

He shrugged. "The Romans brought stability. The rights of man are translated by fate. Some are strong; others are weak."

Rising from the sofa, she stared down at him in contempt. "Then can our Lord be blamed—when His blood was shed for all men to be free from these shackles of fate?"

"My dear Miss Parr, your sense is more closely aligned with that of the seditionists!" Mr. Seymour laughed unevenly. "I take my leave of you now. Where in that lovely head is this nonsense conceived? I wish to wrench it out by the roots! Perhaps someday I shall."

Chapter 17

The Ball

Fears of Mr. Seymour were amplified by the approach of the famed Governor's Ball.

Lavish gowns were retrieved from sheltered corners as the beauties of Williamsburg prepared for their most magnificent exhibition of the year. Affluent Loyalists and rabble-rousers alike were invited to the Palace, which was liberally ornamented with all the opulence of Britannia. The spirit of the season exploded in a night of majestic apparel, exotic dishes, and stately dancing.

The Parr household welcomed the ball with far less innocence. They remained fully aware of certain prospects that circumstances had offered them. The suggestive undertones of past days bubbled into a frenzy of expectation. All manner of exacting familial eyes focused upon Priscilla. They openly supposed that the ball proclaimed a prophecy of greatness for her destiny.

In the midst of scrutiny, she pondered Thomas's thoughts. She longed for the sight of him, for his face had not appeared to her for what seemed like weeks. Would he request to dance with her? Mr. Seymour's tyranny would surely consume the greater part of her evening. Why could not the Seymours be gone? Why had they intruded upon her dreamy little world?

Her fondness for Thomas had grown in the space of a few days—perhaps hours—into a sensation to which she dared not affix a name of any sort. His absence produced a void from which all hope and passion had fled. While Mr. Seymour loathed her ardor, Thomas had been its compass.

Priscilla still carried this fitful anxiety in her bosom as she ascended the steps of the Governor's Palace on a fateful night in December.

Indeed the grandeur of the ball failed to disappoint.

Upon entering the Palace, her cape was removed by a smartly dressed footman. Though she had passed through the front hall many times before, the scene never failed to overpower her.

She paused to admire the golden coat of arms—the great seal of the British Empire—which crowned the marble fireplace with imperial might. A circle of muskets, their bayonets converging upon a central point, adorned the high ceiling. An arsenal of other weapons, including polished pistols and swords, lined the walls. Though the cavernous space hummed with the gentle conversation of guests, an eerie peace was enforced by this display of martial might. Priscilla had often shuddered at the scene with a sense of dread and reverence, and the recent unrest in the colonies deepened the fear the room inspired in her.

Breathing deeply, she hastened into the adjoining passage.

Moments later, she entered the ballroom with as much ease as can be expected of a girl whose heart was engaged in a war of its own. She beheld the dancers, bejeweled in their nobility and struck by their own splendor. A triad of crystal chandeliers hung as diamond-kissed flames that threatened to illuminate the hearts and intents of the careless. The wooden floor had been polished to mirror the fanciful visions fleeting across its clear expanse. Portraits of George III and his queen—swathed in their finery—flanked either side of the entrance. Their eyes surveyed the scene with generous approval and embodied the looming presence, at once benevolent and imposing, of mother Britain. Even manifested in icy brushstrokes, the sovereign and his consort dared the brooding spirit of the rebels to tarnish the governor's glory.

Skirts whirled in the orchestral fanfare as the feet of Williamsburg's patricians pranced across the floors with genteel confidence. Indeed, the fury of youth was eclipsed by its exuberance. The dancers flew as birds unleashed from their cages, as if their spirits were emboldened by the mere hope of liberation. They created a world of their own passion, both wild and pure. In the midst of their merriment, however, reverberated tremors of frustration that threatened to fracture the foundations of an ancient land and to awaken the fury of an aching world.

Priscilla yearned to bring forth its power upon one of her fantastical canvases. The drama screamed to be captured. Her mind further strove to envision its essence. And yet she could not help but infuse into its truth elements of legend—fabled fairies that whispered into the ears of its darting subjects and bred the treacherous sentiments that abounded there. A momentary qualm seized her—something whispered to her own soul that no mythical creatures empowered Britannia's young lions.

Into Priscilla's reverie emerged the present, stark as a grim flame. Another image intruded onto her canvas. A young man had joined the dance of the elite. His familiar eyes betrayed a soul at once winsome and vulnerable. His unsoiled features evidenced a heart ruled by ideals but still a stranger to life's cruelties. Upon his arm flitted another, far more unsettling, vision. Anne Seymour donned a sumptuous gown of pale blue, which complemented her frosty eyes of the same tint. Her skirts cascaded about her dainty feet and rustled violently as she leapt to the music. Seeming to issue a flirtation, her décolletage slipped slightly short of indecency. Her golden curls were gingerly folded into a bun, although a few spilled down her shoulders. The enormous azure plume that crowned her head nodded softly throughout the dance. Her smooth features glowed in the secret knowledge of a small triumph, evinced by the deepening dimples of her smile. Priscilla's gaze returned to Thomas's uncharacteristically giddy face—

"And so, Miss Parr, wrapped in another world—as always."

Priscilla turned to identify the speaker and beheld the glittering figure of John Seymour. Surprise, mingled with an emotion she could not describe, enlivened his countenance.

She resisted the chill that shook her body and spirit. "Yes, and so shall the case ever stand while I am so ill satisfied with my own!"

A bemused smirk marred his features as he stretched his neck backwards to examine her face. "You are difficult, but even the most forbidding fortress can be overtaken."

"You assume much," Priscilla laughed.

"I must have your hand in the next dance. I *assume* you will not object."

"But I *do* object!"

His tone coarsened. "I think not."

Priscilla, in weakness and fear, could not suppress a slight trembling as he leaned into her ear and whispered, "You still do not know *who I am*. Else, you would not object."

Astonishment overwhelmed her senses as Mr. Seymour left her. She suddenly feared him. She feared his power to strip destiny from her. He had breached her walls of defense and exploited her weaknesses already. He had mocked the idyllic simplicity of her blameless girlhood, and, with a single stroke, he had barred her way to the wonders therein.

The Seymours' advent had signaled the loss of a friend never more precious, desired, and loved. Never before had Thomas seemed more lost to her, and yet her eyes looked upon him bitterly. He had slipped through her fingers in the passage of a moment. His gaze was now riveted from hers and locked in another. Lazy afternoons, careless words, and confidences of years and months past haunted her. They bore the lingering grief of legend, shrouded in the grave clothes of the past. Could she return to the innocence that once lived?

"Why, Priscilla!" Katherine's concerned voice disrupted her angst. "Are you well?"

Priscilla, resolving to conceal her sufferings from Katherine, smiled with hollow enthusiasm. "I am well, thank you."

"Why are you not dancing?"

"Never fear!" Inspecting her white gloves in order to avoid Katherine's gaze, Priscilla laughed resentfully. "Mr. Seymour has taken my hand for the upcoming dance."

"I see." Katherine nodded. "I am to dance with Henry Adams."

"Oh, that we might exchange partners!" Priscilla cried. "I so detest mine in every respect—all my better feelings rebel against him. You may think me unfair, Kate, or at the very least odd, when I say that he is a wicked man."

"You are severe! I accept that Mr. Seymour is an 'unpleasant' man or even a 'troublesome' creature—but 'wicked'? I cannot see this grave flaw in him."

Priscilla lowered her voice to an unsteady whisper. "I only know that, when he is near, he inspires fear in my heart."

"You must not fret." Katherine tapped her playfully with a closed fan. "You need only spurn him; or does some darker care burden you?"

Priscilla hesitated. How desperately she longed to share her uneasiness—to be consoled by a friend. She prepared to unleash her worries. Shame, however, drowned sensations of impending relief. She would be forced to acknowledge budding sentiments of warmth for the young man who was known to all the inhabitants of her world. Would Katherine think her indiscreet? Mr. Seymour's face towered in her mind above all her struggles and taunted her with fresh malevolence.

She was considering further concealment of her plight when another face encroached upon the dialogue.

"Good evening, Katherine...Priscilla," the young gentleman softly greeted the girls.

Katherine's eyelashes fluttered as he paused before them. "Mr. Adams."

Neatly, but not grandly, clothed, Henry Adams evoked little sense of either fear or awe. Still, Priscilla's gaze was drawn to his bright green eyes. Even in their warmth, the eyes waxed serene as a hushed sea, its surface deceptively still. Birth had blessed him with features of ordinary beauty, but they radiated strength and tenacity. His presence, although unlikely to intimidate, inspired respect.

After kissing Priscilla's hand, he turned to her friend. "Katherine, I still trust to receive the honor of your hand for the next dance?"

Katherine extended her hand for the same honor. "You have only to ask, Henry."

Eyeing her friend standing beside this simple fellow, Priscilla wondered at the awkward glances that flew between them. Surely this constituted proof of his designs upon Katherine! Amused, Priscilla cleared her throat. "I have yet to congratulate you, Mr. Adams, upon your graduation. Your father must be proud."

"I do believe he is, Miss Parr!" His round face convulsed with laughter. "It is my wish to honor him, for he has given me so much. I always endeavor to wield my resources for the cause of anything right and true."

"An attorney must always select his battles wisely, Mr. Adams!" Priscilla teased.

"Aye, indeed." Henry's eyes shone with the purity of youth and unsullied hopes.

"As I have frequently told him, Henry has been away from us so long that I can hardly absorb his presence!" Katherine giggled. "I have noticed that the law possesses a talent for sharpening one's sense of justice. That is to be expected, I suppose."

"More than you know, Kate." His demeanor grew solemn. "And yet, it is only a point of reference. It is only the scale of man's liberation and virtue. God alone remains its true Rock."

Katherine unfurled her fan. "Henry is of a seditionist persuasion, you see. Liberty has caught his fancy!"

"Ah, are we not all rebels of a sort?" Priscilla sighed.

"The rebellion has barely begun, Miss Parr." Henry chuckled again. "You may yet embrace the revolution."

"One may not always wield a sword, Henry, to defend radical sentiment." Katherine smiled. "Priscilla already proves herself a rebel."

"Oh, this will never do!" Priscilla waved in lighthearted protest. "Must conflict mar the happiness of this night? Let us be glad of reprieve. We may hear it often enough in the days to come."

"The music is fine, aye?" His foot tapping to the tune, Henry surveyed the dancers.

"Very lovely." Katherine stared at the back of his head. "Yet, I prefer the more delicate melodies."

Henry turned to meet her gaze again. "As do I, Kate." A flash of meaning shot through his voice. "They are often the bearers of greater passion and truth than all the animated reels in the world."

"Do excuse us, Priscilla." A telling gleam colored Katherine's expression. "The dance begins shortly!"

After the pair had departed from her, Priscilla's glance shifted over the breadth of the room. Her soul wailed for freedom. She toyed with the notion of forcefully refusing Mr. Seymour's directive. His dominion over her thus seemed to vanish for a moment. The resolution devoured all her qualms.

Scarcely had the determination hardened when an impediment emerged from the depths of her entrapment. How would such a feat, so worthy of public scorn, be received by Governor and Lady Dunmore? Would her rejection of a wealthy man and the subsequent debacle sink her into ignominy?

Thomas! Why did he not forsake his folly and return to her?

Priscilla, sickened by her own cowardice, extended her hand to the approaching Mr. Seymour.

"Despite what you may think, Miss Parr, I like your wit." Mr. Seymour led her to the dance. "Still, you are too brazen. I do not wholly despise female thought, but they should espouse ideas only in small company—and never to their husbands. It is the same with these colonies, you see. Like an ornament of empire, we are given liberty of a kind, but we pay tribute in taxes to London. We are bound to Britain like children—and must respect her."

Priscilla responded with a hard silence. She glanced around anxiously. When would the dance end? *Only then may I escape this loathsome diatribe*, she thought.

"What do you say to this, Miss Parr?"

Priscilla clenched her teeth. "It is an unjust comparison, and I reject it."

He feigned surprise. "I daresay your father thinks as I do."

For the remainder of the dance, he granted her the freedom of silence. She untangled herself from his grasp once the final note resounded. Demanding to be excused, she hastened to the opposite side of the room. Margaret Lee, idling nearby and looking peevish, suddenly snatched the hand of her elder sister Rosamund and approached Priscilla.

"Priscilla, do tell me if the gown is everything proper." Margaret whirled about as her cumbersome skirts threatened to swallow up her tiny form. "We were forced to tack up the hem, and I fear it looks appalling!"

"I do not wonder, Margaret!" Priscilla laughed. "It is quite an elaborate garment for one of your extreme youth."

Rosamund giggled as a raging blush, followed by a fierce pout, rose to her sister's plump cheeks. The brows of the latter merged in a ferocious little frown as her pale gray-blue eyes glared at her rival. For a moment, she turned to scrutinize the dancers.

Rosamund rolled her eyes. "It is her newest—from London."

Priscilla's glance followed that of Margaret as she noted the various partakers of the merriment. Mr. Seymour had finally taken a turn with forlorn Ivy. Priscilla's mind descended into cruel, albeit pleasing, thoughts. Such an occurrence would undoubtedly enrapture Ivy and give rise to a thousand swollen expectations. Priscilla's eye wandered to Mr. Adams and Katherine. Not only Mr. Seymour's advent but also the blossoming warmth between Katherine and her suitor signaled the vanishing of her childhood's simple haven.

"I believe Mr. Adams to be a great admirer of Kate's," Rosamund giggled.

Priscilla smiled once more. "As I suspected."

"But you entertain your own admirer, Priscilla." Rosamund pointed in Mr. Seymour's direction. "Dare I name him?"

Margaret fixated her flaming gaze upon Priscilla.

Priscilla's lips twitched in evidence of an already troubled disposition. "By all means, Rosamund, name him! Do not fear, for the gentleman to which you refer is *not* my admirer."

"Of course not." Margaret kept her cool eyes upon Priscilla. "If, in fact, his intentions are firm, her sharp tongue shall soon quench his devotion. Come, Rosamund."

The two girls left Priscilla as the dancers dispersed into a common throng. Isolation overcame her as quickly as the death of her naïveté. She seemed to rise above them and struggle free from some shackle, some chain, some burden she could not discern. And yet, a few restraints still remained, but never had they occasioned more suffering. Her heart throbbed, but her soul smarted with even greater force. Something whispered that an even darker day approached—that independence was borne on the back of sacrifice.

In the midst of her imaginings, Priscilla's consciousness was pierced by the weight of a hand upon her shoulder. Slowly, she turned and beheld the object of her ardor.

Never had her heart leapt so violently at the sight of him. His sapphire blue satin coat rivaled the unearthly beauty of his eyes and opened to expose a single-breasted waistcoat, embroidered with immaculate white lace. His lustrous locks were bound by a ribbon, which matched the shade of his coat.

Yet, his appearance stirred only minimal tenderness. Something else aroused all the love within a heart so keen. He stood smiling at her with the fondness of a friend. Priscilla, however, winced at his warmth, never more cold and forbidding to her than now. She felt that a barrier had been erected between them without her knowledge or consent.

Had she constructed it? How could she have prevented it? Why had she never beheld the empathy between them as the sign of a more mysterious and meaningful connection—perhaps set as an eternal seal upon their fates? Had she never sensed that, in the fleeting hours and days since their reunion last August, a force more far reaching than the sphere of their limited existences had sprung up and bound them together? Had she never realized that this same power had wreaked havoc upon the turbulent world which, even now, promised to ultimately separate them? Had the divinely sanctioned passion of the colonies shaped them so profoundly? Why had they thus tampered with destiny's decree? Perhaps she was mistaken. Perhaps she alone, with the aid of an unbridled imagination, was the author of such a fate.

"I must not lose sight of you, Priscilla." Thomas's laugh rang like music in her ears. "My dear little friend might be stolen away from me this night!"

"Stolen away?" Priscilla sensed a warm scarlet blush upon her cheeks. "Never! Are we not friends always?"

"As long as we both are willing."

Startled, Priscilla delved for any gleam of implication within those sapphire pools, which had captivated her. There, she beheld the same conflict that proved his perpetual struggle. Passion rang across the depths and vanished as a flame extinguished—only to appear once more.

"Thomas, are you well?"

The flame was snuffed out—the turmoil cooled at the utterance of his name.

He grinned with fresh nonchalance. "I suppose." Leaning closer to her face, his fierceness returned, and he whispered bitterly, "We mortals are so soon deceived, aren't we? This gathering strikes me strangely! Can you not sense that it is the last of its kind? It is like a final burst of vanity before the world is uprooted forever…and us with it. I feel akin to these colonies. Do not the same affinities course through your veins? Perhaps my tongue should not dare issue such fury. I find it impossible to—"

"There you are, my girl!" Mr. Seymour thus arrested the pair's conversation and terminated Thomas's disclosure. The latter's features clouded in an instant. Mr. Seymour seized Priscilla's quivering hand in both of his, and she was incapable of retracting it.

Mr. Seymour was followed by his sister, who glided to stand betwixt Thomas and Priscilla.

Miss Seymour's expression? A veiled vision, a cruel mystery. She smiled, exposing a line of gleaming white teeth. Her eyes twinkled like caverns of ice. The gaze, once fixed, seldom altered its object and thus bound her present captive in the form of Thomas Eton.

"You are certainly no stranger to me, Miss Parr!" Anne Seymour's ruby earrings swung like pendulums as her head bobbed. "Thomas, your accounts of her have some basis in fact! From all reports, Miss Parr, you are mistress of the canvas and partaker of the written word. Your lectures, I imagine, have thus changed the course of many an evening. I fancy the spirit of the dance may be sustained by tales of the usurper King of Scots—I forget his name—and a feast enlivened by recollections of that fatal fruit! Oh, yes, the scholar remains destined to spoil the masque, the artist to enrich it! A peculiar dichotomy indeed. To which are you most inclined?"

"Neither." Priscilla trembled to glimpse Miss Seymour's gloved hand resting upon Thomas's arm. "Festivity presents diversion for the scholar as well, for affairs of state are decided within salon and parlor, billiard room and ballroom alike. I see this always—I know it is true. Whenever men must meet, the cogs of fate inevitably turn. The artist merely provides the opportunity."

"Rubbish!" Mr. Seymour shook his head. "Do not encourage her, Anne. Remember, both Macbeth and Adam, whom you cited, fell by way of a woman dabbling in the affairs of men."

"But Eve, we must recall, was designated by God as the mother of all mankind." The wild gleam flickered again in Thomas's eye. "A woman was honored sufficiently to bear the Savior of the world."

"You see, John!" Anne gave Priscilla a condescending sisterly look and slipped her arm through that of Thomas. "Thomas defends the poor ladies against your attacks. Now, we shall dance."

"I tire of it easily, Miss Seymour! I must beg your pardon," Thomas airily chuckled, although Priscilla detected a strain of nervousness in his voice. "Moreover, my final dance belongs to Priscilla—she promised me months ago."

"Not that nonsense now, my pet." Anne, with eyes narrowing in spite of her smile, clutched his arm more possessively and led him away. "Whereas you will always have Miss Parr on hand, Miss Seymour's company is far scarcer. You shall not escape, naughty boy!"

"Neither shall you, pert little miss!" Mr. Seymour took hold of Priscilla's hand.

Priscilla's reticence ebbed with a view of her own fate. "Why engage in a mockery? I was never false…and shall not begin now."

"And shame yourself before all these people whom you have known?" Mr. Seymour smirked. "I think not. I must have your hand, Priscilla."

In that moment, hatred rose up in Priscilla's heart, for she knew herself to be within his power. "My heart cries otherwise."

"Heart?" Mr. Seymour laughed once more, this time cowing her with his eye. "Hearts have led men into great battles and hollow hopes. The soul's passion is no steady star by which to steer a troubled vessel through the sea of life. Only power—and security—may direct it into calmer waters."

"That shall never be my path."

"No? Have you any other?"

As hopelessness washed over her, Priscilla once again followed Mr. Seymour to the dance.

One further event provided an interlude to Priscilla's inner tempest. It transpired while she was seated across the table from her father and other spirited gentleman at Governor Dunmore's dinner. Wrapped in her own cares, Priscilla failed to heed their verbal jousts. The volume, even as it peaked and arrested less engaged minds, did not provoke her interest. Her attention, however, was finally riveted to the collision of intellects by the voice of one who had hitherto sustained a peculiar silence.

"Can we at all assist the rebels in their course…even now? Has anything—any plan, any design—been organized to aid them?"

The entrance of William Eton into the debate stunned even his father.

"Well?" William glared at the guests around him.

Henry Adams sputtered with surprise. "Why do you inquire thus? Forgive my ignorance, but I did not know you to be so ardent a supporter of colonial rights."

"I should be honored to convey any monetary gift—or gift of arms—to the Bostonians and therefore render service to this pledge of liberty!" William's fist pounded upon the walnut table, thus rattling the porcelain figurines that extended along its length.

"Watch your tongue, lad!" Mr. Parr barked. "Why indeed should we help the traitors?"

William sneered. "This is no revolt for an old man. Only youth can cast off these imperial chains."

Henry Adams beckoned to him. "I have the information you seek. We shall speak of this."

Priscilla heard no more since her gaze was fastened to the face of William Eton. In his eyes writhed ambition, lifeless without ideals. It reigned there as a tyrant to scorn principles and to mock his profession, the law. There stretched forth a desolate land, ravaged by avarice and echoing self alone.

As the dinner drew to a conclusion, Priscilla noticed William and Henry conferring in hushed tones near a corner of the supper room. She also observed that Henry often cast a nervous glance over his shoulder—as if to ensure secrecy. *What I would give to hear their discourse,* Priscilla mused silently. *What on earth could they be saying?*

The ball ended without further incident. As closing pleasantries were exchanged, Priscilla weaved through the mingling merrymakers as a lone wanderer, content to yearn for one and one alone, whose presence, as a direct imagining of a jealous and depressed mind, appeared torn from her. In this state, her eyes drifted among her peers and elders.

Then a shaft of time burst forth that, although scarcely observed at the moment, promised to emerge from a shrouded past and illuminate the future. William Eton, now unnoticed by the assembly, leaned over to whisper into the ear of Anne Seymour.

Part II

Chapter 18

The Defiance

It seemed inevitable that the fractious peace existing between Priscilla and Mr. Seymour should not be long sustained.

That fateful pinnacle was attained the Sunday following the ball while the parishioners mingled near the door of Bruton Parish after the service. Priscilla cast an occasional glance in Thomas's direction and secretly hoped for acknowledgment. His eye soon encountered her own. That agitation he had lately begun to evoke in Priscilla returned as he advanced toward her. She nearly trembled as he gazed at her silently. A fresh understanding, a knowledge mysterious and maddening, seemed to have arisen between them. All thoughts remained shrouded in unsettling secrecy, and yet uncertainty clouded his expression. His lips were pressed together as if he feared some dark secret might escape them.

Priscilla was eager to terminate the discomforting silence. "How do you fare with your studies, Tom?"

"Very well, I daresay, but it is a marvel." His voice steadied, and he removed his tricorne. "My mind has been otherwise engaged of late."

"You must not dally!" She started at the intensity of his tone. "An intellect such as yours? What a dreadful waste if you squander it."

Thomas grinned. "I will strive to achieve your standards of excellence, Priscilla."

"I am a hopeless hypocrite, you know, to upbraid you." Her eyes darted toward Mr. Seymour, who conversed with Phillip Parr and William Eton. "My own thoughts have wandered recently."

"What do you think of them—the Seymours?"

Her attention reverted to Thomas's features as he feigned disinterest. His eyes, however, betrayed him—his angst was unmasked. She paused for a few moments as she deliberated her response and weighed the effect of her words.

Never daring to trust her tongue for a guarded reply, she deflected his query. "Grant me this liberty: what is *your* opinion of them?"

Thomas bristled at her inquiry as doubt once again gripped his countenance. He evaded her stare while likewise appearing to struggle for a skillful answer.

At last, he burst into a laugh. "Miss Seymour desires to please me... my brother, at least, thinks well of her!"

Priscilla struggled to interpret his meaning, but she could not read him.

He returned the hat to his head, bowed to her, and departed.

Grappling with new feelings, she stood alone for some moments and watched Thomas as he boarded the Eton carriage with his family. As the carriage vanished down the street, she sensed a presence very near her.

"Your father permitted me to walk you home."

A large shadow fell over Priscilla. She turned and beheld Mr. Seymour behind her. She noted a particular smugness in the lazy shift of his eye. Still smarting from her conversation with Thomas, she dared not yet speak. Noting that the remainder of her family had already left in the carriage, she reluctantly accepted the arm he offered. She hoped to walk the entire distance in silence.

Nevertheless, they had barely crossed the churchyard when Mr. Seymour spoke again. "I have gleaned that your brother-in-law, the youngest Eton, harbors radical notions. I feel ill at ease concerning his affiliations with the seditionist movement. Since he admires my sister, I fear his activities for her sake. Tell me, does he actively collaborate or communicate with the rebels?"

Priscilla was so perplexed by the question that her step faltered. Cold fear gripped her mind. *I must tread carefully with my answer,* she thought.

"I know nothing of his deeds in that regard." She studied Mr. Seymour's profile with suspicion.

Mr. Seymour pressed her knowledge further. "Do you not hear him speak of his contacts among more powerful rebels? Or even those of his father?"

"I do not know. As I am of a Loyalist upbringing, it is unlikely that he would confide such details to me. Even if he had revealed them, I would never betray his confidence."

"Why not? You aid treason by refusing to divulge these matters."

She felt in that moment less confidence than in the remnant of the conversation. "I am not so idealistic as Thomas—or even yourself, John Seymour. I value friendship above all things."

"Shocking, Miss Parr." He drew himself up to his full height and stared down at her. "One cannot be impartial in matters so weighty."

"I was compelled to say it, sir."

"You are overbold." His crimson face turned a paler tint. "Notice that lovely girl of Dr. Lee's—Margaret is her name—and how meekly she behaves. Can you not learn from her way? You are capable of refinement, Miss Parr, and worthy of it. If you are as sensible as I believe, you will heed my counsel."

She was unable to bear this insult any longer in silence. "Mr. Seymour, I have no wish to reflect any demeanor save my own, certainly not that of so insolent a young woman as Margaret Lee. I have known her far longer and better than yourself, sir, and believe me—a scorpion lurks beneath the exterior. You have no call to slight me thus. I only speak my thoughts. Are wit and conversation great crimes? To be silent forever is to be a slave—a slave of society, of thoughts and feelings, which are all the more powerful when commanded to repression. I thank you for any remote kindness intended. Otherwise, I must advise you not to give me impudence."

Priscilla blushed with pride to have defied him, and she relished the sight of his shame. Such a man must be surprised by her strength of speech.

He blanched white with horror. "Miss Parr, you must reconsider."

"I shall never give it another thought after this moment."

His eyes landed upon Priscilla narrowly, but she neither melted nor fainted, despite suffering a storm of inner turmoil.

Mr. Seymour exploded with rage. "You had best give it another thought! I shall brook no impertinence from a wife!"

Wife? A flood of hot indignation shot through Priscilla's spine as she instantly understood the reason for his perpetual censure of her. He had intended *her* for his wife, but her character evidently did not suit him. He had therefore attempted to "refine" her. A thousand venomous words nearly tumbled off her tongue. With shrouded grit, she whispered, "You offer marriage to me?"

"After this exhibition, I will only marry you after I detect some positive alteration in your character."

Alter my character indeed! Priscilla straightened her shoulders and shot him a fiery glare. "Waste no more visits upon me. Find another young woman to flatter your fancy—and bend *her* will to yours."

"Another young woman?" Mr. Seymour laughed bitterly. "Impossible. Why should I?"

"I do not love you!"

"What is love but the song of poets? Marriages founded upon love are never prudent."

"Passion ebbs, but a marriage based upon mutual love and respect shall endure."

Another thought must have entered John Seymour's head, for a strange expression suddenly seized his fair features. "Surely you would not refuse me for a whimsical ideal."

"I do not understand you, sir. One moment, you insult me. The next, you express your intention to marry me. You clearly care nothing for me!"

"I have clearly explained my wishes, Miss Parr. Why else would I make the offer?"

Priscilla summoned all her courage. "If this be your mind, I charge you—take your intentions elsewhere! If you loved me, you would not mutilate my feelings. I neither love nor like you nor even respect you! Furthermore, if I were a man, I would not spare you a sound thrashing for your roguish conceit. This subject is forever closed. Be gone, blackguard, and trouble me no more. I am leaving you now, Mr. Seymour."

"My dear Miss Parr, you are too hasty!" He restrained her forcibly as she turned to go. "You will regret this scene once your fit of passion cools."

At this statement, Priscilla tossed her head in his direction. She was powerless to subdue this long-suppressed flame of temper. Her left eyebrow arched as she wrenched free of him. "Mr. Seymour, I am not, nor shall ever be, *your* Miss Parr. Good day, sir."

With another toss of her curls, she disappeared, leaving her unwelcome suitor scarlet faced and incredulous upon the street corner.

Mr. Seymour ceased bestowing his attentions upon Priscilla. She concluded that his smitten pride would not allow him to cast a side glance at her again. Following the quarrel that had arisen between them, he ignored her.

As Priscilla had expected, the subject was revived during a tea hosted at the Parr House shortly after their confrontation.

"It is strange that Seymour should desert you, Priscilla." Rosamund's large brown eyes softened with sympathy.

"He once confided to Henry that he wished to marry you." Jane sipped her tea. "Shocking indeed."

"I have more to add." Margaret's eyes glittered with triumph. "I heard him tell Father that, though he liked you at first, your manners soon repulsed him."

"Only a woman unwilling or unable to contradict John Seymour would *not* repulse him." Priscilla smiled with secret knowledge. "I rejoice that he no longer foists his smirks upon me."

Even freedom from his attentions, however, bore a price. Priscilla's family, excepting Frances, burned with rage toward her.

Her father spoke coldly to her for a week afterward. *To have his daughter alienate a perceived matrimonial prize is almost more than he can bear,* she pondered. She could but poorly brave her father's displeasure for even that brief interval. His disapproval delivered the keenest blow.

Chapter 19

The Incident

Christmastide was the most delightful time of year in Priscilla's eyes. She was fond of the balls, the delicacies, and the mirth it occasioned. She disliked, however, the day-long foxhunts that her father, her brother, and the other gentlemen loved so well. During the days of hunting, Priscilla brightened once she heard the familiar sound of tired footsteps plodding down the hall while shaking the snow off their boots in the evening. During those days, Rachel waxed more cross than usual. Her mood did not become bearable until those heavy footsteps were heard and she rushed into the strong arms of her returning husband.

Priscilla still hoped to penetrate her sister-in-law's reserve. She attempted to begin a conversation, but it was all in vain. On Christmas Eve morn, she presented such an attempt while sitting in Rachel's company. From time to time, Priscilla would introduce a topic, but each was subsequently killed by Rachel's frosty silence.

Finally, Priscilla, frustrated, cried out, "Pray, tell me, once and for all—why do you refuse to love us as your family? May I ever be a true sister to you?"

The icy beauty of Rachel's countenance grew colder still as she smiled, though Priscilla noticed that her lower lip quivered. "You waste both your time and mine in striving to secure my good graces, Priscilla. Do not wear that angelic expression for me. I detest it! I know your character. I have been told of your incivility toward Mr. Seymour. Everyone whispers of it."

"On the contrary!" Priscilla was quick to correct the rumor. "It was the reverse. Mr. Seymour is a conceited man, lacking in all forms of gallantry. Furthermore, *he* is not the author of your enmity toward me. You nursed it long before he came to Williamsburg."

Rachel ignored the reference to herself. "I do not believe you. I judged Mr. Seymour to be an excellent gentleman. At the Christmas Ball in particular, your manners toward him were atrocious. He once considered you for matrimony, and, with your rudeness, you shunned a wise match. Did you think that this affects only yourself and has no implications toward your kindred? Still, all is as it should be. You did not deserve such good fortune."

Despite the tension thus occasioned by Priscilla's refusal of Mr. Seymour, Christmas Day at the Parr House did not disappoint. Mr. Parr's aunt, Mary Laurence, celebrated the holiday with the family. Mrs. Laurence, a well-preserved and venerated lady, was famed for her sharp wits at such a great age. She lived down the street from the Parrs and was never in want of visitors. Many of the town's most prominent families called upon her, for she always wielded tasteful humor.

Despite Rachel's insolence, Priscilla cherished her evenings with the Etons, which became more frequent during the holiday. In the years to come, she would recall one such evening in particular.

During the evening before dinner, she sat with her sisters upon the drawing room sofa. Rachel idled fretfully in an obliging chair while William Eton and his brother stood lazily near the elaborate fireplace. The rest of the company meanwhile lingered in the parlor of the Parr House.

Priscilla and both her sisters were close enough to overhear a softly uttered conversation between the two brothers, although neither young man ever seemed to become aware that they were heard.

"I must tell you, Will…I have unearthed a rare jewel…a lady of peerless wit," Thomas murmured in a low voice. "Though I am young, I am quite certain I shall never find her equal."

Cadence to Glory

Priscilla's breathing faltered. *He speaks of Anne Seymour!* Her forlorn spirit sank further.

Drawing his thick black eyebrows together in mocking disbelief, William laughed. "You? In love? You do not even know what it is to love."

Deep in thought, Thomas stared at the floor. "She is the better part of me, although I am not certain she yet knows it herself."

William shook his head in a vulgar fashion, or so Priscilla thought. "You have not been enough in the company of women, Tom. I wager you'll forget her tomorrow, when another wench passes by!"

The brief conversation died there, but its damage had been inflicted upon the hearer. Priscilla's anxieties, however, were soon occupied by another matter in the following days. Less than a week had elapsed after Christmas Day before she received important news. These tidings, which shook her frame exceedingly, were delivered by the very one she now longed to see at all times.

Thomas called quite unexpectedly at the Parr House. After he was announced, Priscilla rose and presented her most flattering smile. Her spirits in a flutter, she prepared to offer him a seat. The smile faded as Thomas, his face scarlet and flustered, rushed into the room.

"You could never fathom what has taken place!" He gasped for breath.

"What has happened?"

"The bubble has burst, Priscilla." His voice ascended in ecstasy. "It has burst at last!"

Such an uproar followed news of the Boston incident throughout Williamsburg and the rest of the colonies that even Priscilla feared the ramifications of the deed.

After Thomas delivered the news to her, she hurried to her father's study and pronounced the tidings that still rang fresh to her ears. Mr. Parr's eyes clouded over ominously, and he bounded from his seat. His hands contracting and relaxing in spasms, he paced to and fro in front of his bookcase. The man was visibly enraged, and any other young woman would have recoiled from the room.

"Traitors! They should be locked up, every one! Who ever expected such a radical act? Have the hotheads any sense? Any sense at all? Ha! Lunatics! To have cast tea into the harbor! These Sons of Liberty should be hung from the tallest tree in the land, their bodies a repast for the vultures!"

Priscilla was shocked by his savagery. "Calm yourself, Father! I fear for your health a great deal more than this development in Boston."

The man seemed to remember himself at her concern. He ceased pacing and turned to her. "Priscilla, what have you to say about it?"

"Only this: I believe they were impassioned at the hour of this irrational act. They shall regret it when they feel the heat of His Majesty's—and Parliament's—wrath. Who can tell what drastic measures he will take?"

"How right you are!" His countenance glowed at the punishment the rebels were sure to receive. "Whatever the consequence, they have invited it."

At that moment, Priscilla recalled her own questions upon first receiving the tidings from Thomas.

In accordance to one inquiry, his brow had heaved in confusion. "I have learned that the act was done quietly. Sam Adams, they say, was at the center of it. The company came disguised as Mohawks. Take none of this for fact, mind you. I have only just left the Raleigh, where I received this information. Even there, rumors are so rife that I cannot separate truth from propaganda!"

"This will surely arouse a commotion in Parliament. It was a statement of supreme rebellion, which cannot be erased with mere apologies."

"No doubt!" Thomas had rubbed his chin thoughtfully. "It was extreme, but, at least we have arrested British attention at last."

Priscilla, still reeling from shock at the time, had clutched the arm of a chair for support. "What grievances must have tortured them to do this thing?"

He shook his head sadly. "I wish it could have been resolved by negotiation. But the British are a stubborn people. One cannot reason with them."

"But *we* are British, Tom."

"Are we indeed?"

The news sparked even more heated debates within the House of Burgesses. Mr. Parr invited powerful men to dinner, then debated the matter with them following the meal. The tone of these "debates" rose to its usual hostile pitch. Her father retired to bed many an evening with a dark face and overcast eyes. Priscilla feared for his health and continued to discourage these fiery discussions. However, whenever she ventured to do so, her father only scoffed. "Nonsense! I am robust as ever. How else shall I participate in these struggles?"

Most supporters of the radical cause, including Thomas, loudly proclaimed that the hour of reconciliation had passed and that further action must be taken to halt this oppression by Britain. Tories such as Priscilla's father believed, however, that a single administration of punishment by King George and Parliament would end the revolt once and for all.

Priscilla was no extremist at heart, but she decided the colonists had crossed a line. Britain's penalty must be severe, or else the rebellion would continue to infect naïve minds like heresy. However, she also realized that a harsh punishment might fuel the already rampant flames of sedition.

Chapter 20

The Illness

Priscilla had been so consumed by the growing political turmoil that she had failed to notice a significant change in the life of her friend Katherine. One icy Sunday morning in January of 1774, Priscilla encountered her friend in the churchyard of Bruton Parish after services concluded. Newly eighteen, the eldest Miss Lee appeared a more blissful young woman than in the fall. A new vivacity quickened her step.

Priscilla removed a hand from her muff and waved merrily. "I am overjoyed to see you, Kate—and you as well, Rosamund, Margaret!"

Katherine returned the salutation. "It has been many days since we have seen you informally."

"And much has happened. Priscilla, did you know that our Kate is to marry Henry Adams?" Rosamund giggled fitfully.

Priscilla cast a quizzical look at her friend, who colored wildly.

Katherine turned to Rosamund and Margaret. "Run along, dears. I shall come to the carriage shortly."

After her sisters had skipped away amidst a chorus of girlish laughter, Katherine whispered, "Surely you saw this coming, Priscilla."

"I considered it, but, of course, you assured me that my suspicions were hasty and false. Tell me this, and I shall be content with silence. Do you love him, Kate?"

"Very much." Katherine's tranquil eyes were brimming with stars. "He may not be the most handsome man in Williamsburg, or the most fashionable perhaps, but I do love him. He returns my sentiments in equal measure. You know, if I should die this moment, I will never be happier than I am today. You may think me a silly child for saying this, but I shall never love another as much as plain Henry."

"I am not so ignorant of these matters as you believe. These tidings please me so well." Priscilla squeezed her friend's hand. "I wish you joy."

"I pray you may soon experience the same happiness. I particularly think of Mr. Seymour's conduct toward you. Do not think me ignorant of the injustice."

"Kate, Kate!" Priscilla laughed, careful not to mention Margaret's connection to the matter. "Do not mourn for me. He was no loss at all. He was intoxicated with his own greatness. I despised every moment of his company. I told you as much myself. He left my heart intact—in truth, relieved and enlightened! I tell you a secret, Kate, if you tell no one."

"I shall not tell."

"He asked for my hand."

"And you refused him!"

"Of course. To do otherwise would have been the error of my life and a betrayal of every conviction. Are you cross with me now?"

"Quite the opposite. I have heard Henry, Jane, and Harriet speak of his arrogance. They are well acquainted with his pride since the Seymours have spent the past few weeks beneath Mr. Adams's roof. I do not believe he would have suited you."

"Neither do I!"

It should be no surprise that one of the happiest moments of Priscilla's life arrived the hour that Mr. Seymour and his sister departed from Williamsburg. She was elated to know them miles away—particularly Anne. Thomas had not behaved like an infatuated boy, but Priscilla recalled his remarks that evening in her father's drawing room. He appeared like his old self with her, but something was lacking.

Thomas frequently became troubled and appeared burdened with cares too weighty for his youthful mind. He, like Mr. Parr, was much graver than usual during the cold and contentious weeks.

One afternoon, Priscilla questioned him. "Thomas, are you well? What troubles you?"

He resumed an uneven smile, though he peered at her with softened eyes. "Nothing of significance distresses me. I am indeed well."

Priscilla secretly wondered if his despondency stemmed from Miss Seymour's absence.

"I was surprised that the Seymours left so suddenly," she said.

Thomas's jaw tightened. His eyes flew to her face with a fierceness she had never before seen in them. His gaze then shifted to the window. "Indeed."

Though she briefly pondered further exploring this subject with him, deeper objections quickly overcame the urge. Indeed, she fancied a fearful glimmer in his eyes—a glimmer bespeaking wariness of that topic and a fear that it might be drawn into the light of scrutiny. Priscilla thus decided to forego the discussion entirely. Indeed, Thomas seemed to share the sentiment, for mention of either Mr. or Miss Seymour never crossed his lips. Priscilla viewed his reticence as additional evidence of the mysterious wall that seemed to have arisen between them since the Seymours' advent.

The following afternoon, however, as Priscilla sketched his profile yet again, he astonished her with a small outburst. "I can conceal some matters from you no longer, I suppose."

Suspended between hope and fear for the words he would speak, Priscilla held her breath as her heart pounded.

Thomas completed his thought after a lengthy pause, during which he rubbed his temples and closed his eyes. "If the colonies respond even more violently to the king's punishment, it could herald war. War signifies death, bloodshed, and nearly every security torn from us. If a war should erupt for the cause of liberty, I must support it with all my heart—and join the great struggle."

"Hush, do not talk so!" Priscilla struggled to suppress angry tears. "I pray that the trouble never reaches that inevitable point."

Her heart cringed at the cause in which he so desperately believed. She was revolted by the colonial rebellion, even though it had haunted most of her life. To turn upon the mother country!

Only a miracle from God could secure victory over the king's forces. Then, afterward, what of government? If it existed, what form would it assume? Chaos! A certain failure from the very morning of its birth.

The cause of tax-weary colonies, however, did not seem quite so disgusting when pronounced from Thomas's lips with such passionate devotion. The two young friends did share a common thread. Both seemed to fear the violence expected by many. Still, his heart lay in the perilously obscure future…with these colonies. Hers lay with the established but increasingly threatened past…with Britain.

Katherine married following a brief engagement.

The ceremony was conducted on the frigid morning of January 15, 1774. Thick cascades of dark curly locks were bound up to frame Katherine's face. Priscilla noticed that her friend's cheeks were singed by the blush that is so common to virgin brides. During Katherine's wedding, Priscilla recalled their childhood. Katherine had grown into a stylish and well-developed, though not beautiful, young woman. And here she was, being joined forever to good and cheerful but plain Henry Adams!

Priscilla's eyes met those of Thomas during the ceremony. Her heart rose to her throat as he responded with a wink, a flash of that winsomeness she loved so well. She was struck by an unsettling sensation. At that moment, she knew that an era of her life was drawing to an end, fading into the dusky mists of memory.

During late January, a spirit of gaiety pervaded the Parr household, for Rachel was expecting a baby in the fall. Priscilla's brother had never been so happy since his wedding day. Even Rachel paused to make herself pleasant. Where suspicion had once brooded, tranquility took residence. Rachel even withdrew from the harpsichord for a time and ventured forth to mingle with humanity.

While Priscilla, Ben, and Rachel were sitting together one afternoon, Priscilla posed a playful query. "Do you foresee a son or a daughter? Pray, what is your prediction?"

Ben lovingly caressed his wife's rosy cheek. "A son!"

"Oh, now, now." Rachel's dark blue eyes smiled into his. "We cannot know until my time is fulfilled. Should you be angry with me if it is a daughter?"

"Never, my darling!" Ben seemed amazed that his wife would consider discord between them possible. "But I believe it shall be a son."

Priscilla observed that Ben's passion for his wife had endured thus far. She began to question the validity of old forebodings, supplanted now by cautious optimism.

The chill winds of February seemed to usher in an abundance of sickness. This year's victims within the Parr family included Mrs. Parr and Priscilla. Priscilla was not initially apprehensive for her own state. Each year, she suffered a cold, but it usually persisted for a week at the most. After her mother's indisposition had spent, however, Priscilla's seemed to worsen.

Dr. Lee's expertise was required, but the remedies he prescribed worked little effect upon her case. Instead, she weakened. Whenever Katherine or Thomas came for dinner, they were struck by Priscilla's ghastly aspect and harrowing cough—and declared it openly. During her decline, Thomas called upon her more than usual.

One especially frosty morning, she was forced to take to her bed, and Dr. Lee was summoned again. She had taken ill with a fever, and rest was essential to her survival. She was not long so miserably subjected before Thomas Eton hastened to the Parr House and requested to see her.

As he entered, Thomas rushed to her side and enclosed her feverish hand within his. "Oh, Priscilla! How do you fare now?"

"Not well, I fear." She was too drained of spirit to feel great pleasure—even in his company. "I am surprised that you have come."

"Why should I not come? How could I abandon my dearest friend to this malady?"

"Unthinking child! Do you not dread infection?" She stifled a hoarse cough. "You risk your life thus."

"I would be a worthless friend if I allowed you to lie in such misery and never darkened the doorway to console you." Leaning over the small table beside the bed, he poured cool water from the pitcher into a silver basin. Dampening a freshly pressed cloth that had been laid out by the maidservant, he gently pressed it to Priscilla's brow.

The tenderness and strength of his touch sent a strange shiver through Priscilla's frame—a chill she could scarcely attribute to her illness. "So you have come to cheer me?"

"I have come to make a valiant attempt." He drew up a chair to the bedside and retrieved a book from his coat. "I shall read to you."

"I have no sunbursts of wit to share today, no anecdotes to amuse you."

"I have not come for amusement." His blue eyes pierced the labyrinth through which her soul was wandering. "Only rest—I am content with that."

Priscilla would later cherish recollection of the days of her recovery as some of the most pivotal of her life. Thomas, his father forbidding him to come for more than an hour each day, returned to her sickbed every afternoon at the same time. He read to her from the Bible, from Milton, from Shakespeare, and from other classic volumes. His words were punctuated by a passion for life and all its enigmas. A thousand startling realizations rushed upon her. She understood how closely his interests and feelings were allied with her own. Fresh, more puzzling sensations also struck in the most unexpected moments. Her cheeks warmed at the pressure of his hand upon hers. His winsome smile often compelled her to look away. As he delivered bittersweet passages, she absorbed his pronunciations, expressions, and emotions with rapt attention.

These encounters aided her in a swift convalescence. Before the absolute conclusion of her illness, however, Priscilla was emboldened to act upon a notion that had been germinating in her mind.

She summoned his attention for the revelation of a secret. "It lies within the second drawer of that bureau." She directed his focus in the proper direction.

Thus invited, he moved to the ornate article of furniture. His search was brief; a thick stack of ruffled papers lay united by a single string. He painstakingly lifted the papers from their position into the open air. After wavering a moment between either perusing the pile or handing it to the rightful owner, he proceeded to place the stack in her hands.

She refused the papers. "I would be honored if you would review these—my own creations—and state your frank evaluation of them."

He eagerly examined each work. She observed his brow, which was faintly lined by the violence of his concentration. Fierce activity darted across his eyes. Her impatience to learn the nature of these sensations grew. She anxiously studied his face until, at length, he glanced upward form the paintings.

Astonishment convulsed his every feature. "You amaze me, Priscilla!"

Priscilla's heart sank. "You disapprove of them?"

"I have only finished looking upon the shadow of genius!"

"They amuse you then?"

"I would never make light of these works!" He held the papers aloft. "Such uncorrupted artistic expression is rare. Your talent possesses great promise."

"No one prefers these art forms, Thomas. Shall I face contempt always?"

"The world is an unsoiled canvas before you, Priscilla." His eyes blazed with purity undimmed by the skepticism born of experience. "Although you must trek across a wasteland of hostility, you must dare to dream. Unless you follow your vision to the furthest reaches of belief, the fires of artistic power and expression will surely be extinguished. All hope shall perish with it, and hope, my dear girl, is the light of the soul. You must chase these lofty aims, for the future presents an enigma—exciting in its mystery but rife with hidden snares. Yet, oh, for that virgin opportunity to escape the corruption of the past!"

Trembling, she beheld a faint glimpse of something not altogether mortal—something not altogether of Thomas. As his gaze held her fast, his ruddy glow cast its own gleam across her soul. She suddenly realized that he spoke not only of her creative struggles but also of the tumult that embroiled the young and troubled land of her birth. Emotions, both fresh and alarming, flooded her vulnerable breast.

A desire for freedom and destiny was awakened from a dormant slumber.

A love long budding in her soul burst into violent bloom.

Chapter 21

The Excursion

Priscilla rose from her bed in late February on strict orders from the physician to stir out of doors as little as possible. Mrs. Parr, Ivy, Rachel, and Frances fitted the sitting room facing the street for Priscilla's comfort. The four ladies, with varying degrees of patience, strove to care for her needs. Her heart warmed with appreciation of their efforts, but even Frances's lively chatter annoyed her. Only silence permitted Priscilla to consider the changes that had occurred during her illness.

By now, she understood that she had fallen in love with Thomas Eton. But that she now entertained such feelings for an old friend disturbed her. His very presence suggested that of a brother and protector. The question of revealing the altered state of her heart proved a source of indecision. He behaved with tender sentiments but uttered no romantic intentions.

I should keep these thoughts silent for fear of losing the precious friendship I now share with the young gentleman, Priscilla thought. *What shame I shall suffer if he spurns my affections! I would face him in Williamsburg forever! Our friendship, which I prize, would be lost. No, it is wise to remain silent. Perhaps such feelings shall dwindle with time.*

But, no! How vain were her inward assurances. With each visit, they weakened, and he seemed not so far from her grasp. Her spirits lifted with every good-natured word she received from him, with every laugh they shared, and with every smile they exchanged. Why would he call so often if he did not share her feelings? She fancied herself knowledgeable of his character. He would not call so often unless... she held some charms for him. Every similar inference threatened to elevate her to the sweetest hope she could imagine. Her good sense failed to chain it.

Love, it seemed, paid no heed to her puny struggles. During these days, she would raptly gaze into his countenance and wonder if the same affections trembled within his own soul. She wondered—not without fear—if he could penetrate her expression and detect the adoration she harbored within her breast.

The notion of confessing her emotions to him returned again and again; however, she finally spurned it and rebuked herself. *What a savage idea!* No matter how often his kindness evoked admiration, or his gentleness a leap to her heart, or his grin a blush to her cheeks, she would never tell him. At any other time, she would have spoken her opinion concerning a matter. Love, however, had silenced bold lips—a feat that neither gossip nor censure could achieve.

Following her recuperation, many surprises and pleasures appeared, particularly in the arrival of her Aunt and Uncle Wallace.

Mrs. Wallace was Elizabeth Parr's sister, and the couple's advent provided sorely needed diversion for the Parr family. Mr. Wallace cut a tall, distinguished figure and displayed every ideal of a Virginian gentleman, schooled in every courtly gesture. Although not vain, his attire was always impeccable. His chuckle proved infectious, but, having previously served in the House of Burgesses, he also boasted a sharp eye for politics and government.

His wife exhibited no less of a commanding presence. Although less of a beauty than her sister, Mrs. Wallace voiced controversial perspectives with greater frequency, spirit, and intelligence. She and her husband, although country dwellers, regularly entertained illustrious guests from Williamsburg, Richmond, Philadelphia, and, as was their rare delight, Boston. With seven daughters married and dispersed throughout the colonies, the Wallaces found the liberty to do as they liked. Such freedom and idleness of mind allowed them to cast their considerable intellects and energies into political dealings. Although a former civil servant, Mr. Wallace still played a central role in the intrigues of the fiery House of Burgesses.

The Parrs invited the couple and received them well, but none welcomed them more gladly than Priscilla. Such company stimulated her eager mind. Many evenings were passed in lively exchange, during which Priscilla mingled Thomas's opinions with her own. Therefore, she was not much surprised when her aunt and uncle expressed a desire to form his acquaintance.

When told of Thomas's family, Mrs. Wallace beamed with a realization. "We know his Aunt and Uncle Eton very well, for you are aware that their plantation lies near our own. They dine with us often. Mr. Eton has spoken of a nephew named Thomas. He has not come to visit them since he was a small child. Is your friend a sensible young man?"

Priscilla smiled proudly, although an arrow pierced her heart while extolling his graces. "Oh yes, he is very fine, blessed with virtue as well as wit."

Mr. Wallace rubbed his protruding chin. "He sounds like a lad of excellent character."

Mrs. Wallace leaned forward with curiosity. "What are his future plans, Priscilla?"

"He is being tutored extensively at home, and he hopes to attend the College of William and Mary a year from this autumn. Following graduation, he will study the law."

Mr. Wallace chuckled. "His designs are well formed. Is he a wise fellow?"

"Very wise. You shall meet him tonight. He and his family are dining with us."

※

Priscilla introduced her Aunt and Uncle Wallace to Thomas accordingly.

As always, Thomas proved attentive and cordial. His tasteful wit and boyish smile did not fail to win the visitors' admiration and respect.

"My husband and I particularly value golden sense in youth." Mrs. Wallace bestowed an approving look upon Thomas while sampling the venison placed before her. "Most young people in our acquaintance are inclined toward shallow concerns—such as the gleam on their buttons."

"Everyone frets over these things from time to time." Thomas laughed a little self-consciously. "Still, I cannot understand why so many are oblivious to the British hubris."

Priscilla smiled. "Do not say that in Father's hearing. Else, you will never be welcome in the house again!"

Mr. Wallace addressed Thomas. "You study history, I suppose."

"Yes, sir."

"What does history reveal to us in the present age?" Mr. Wallace reclined from the mahogany table.

"We are free people—like the Athenians, who, with numerical odds stacked against them, drove back the mighty Persians."

Though her heart fluttered when he spoke, Priscilla laughed incredulously. "You equate King George with a Persian despot?"

Thomas never flinched. "Indeed I do, and despots are toppled when lovers of liberty stand firm."

"An uncompromising stance." Mrs. Wallace smiled with amusement. "I like that."

Priscilla only gazed at him. Something new awakened, and, though she resisted it, she was almost ashamed of her own pragmatism. His principles seared her conscience, and all that she had previously believed briefly fell open to doubt. His heart was like the wild eagle, imprisoned to no one—lest his purpose falter.

Mr. Wallace's voice sliced through her reverie. "When next you call upon your aunt and uncle in the country, you are welcome to dinner."

Thomas grinned. "I should like that most of all, sir."

For the remainder of the evening, Priscilla mulled his words. Through the havoc-laden fog of her thoughts, he represented clarity. His moral certitude shone into her mind like a lamp, exposing hidden crevices. She yearned to touch that which she most believed to lurk behind his brow—*greatness*.

These silent reflections were disrupted by an incident that transpired later in the evening after the Etons had departed and most of the household had retired.

Unable to drift into slumber, Priscilla remembered a treasured volume she had left on a side table in the parlor. In hopes that reading might entice her to sleep, she resolved to fetch the book. As she descended the stairs, however, a hushed conversation emanating from the central hall arrested her step.

She first recognized her mother's voice, which sounded harsher than usual. "She thinks herself mistress of this house over me. I will not stand for it, Benjamin."

Ben's pleading tones next arose. "Rachel means well in all things, I assure you. It is harmless, Mother."

"Harmless?" Mrs. Parr laughed bitterly. "She tried to dismiss one of the maidservants today—on the mere pretense that the girl displeased her. Rachel is easily displeased, I have learned! And what can explain her odd murmurings when she fancies herself alone? Have you not witnessed those? It almost frightens me." Priscilla started violently. *Perhaps Rachel is mad after all!* A fresh anxiety pulsed through her bosom as she sank down onto the stair step and leaned forward to listen.

"I beg you will not speak of my wife thus." Ben's voice grew indignant. "She is wearied by her condition, and I cannot—"

"Heed your mother." Mr. Parr's rebuke suddenly boomed throughout the hall. "I have reason to believe that your wife has been in my study—sorting through my papers. And that is not all! You cannot afford to shower her with trinkets and gowns as you have done. In these turbulent times, our resources may be compromised."

After a few moments of troubled silence, Ben replied with wearied resignation. "Very well. I will speak with her."

Priscilla subsequently heard the shuffling of footsteps. Fearful of being discovered, she hastened up the stairs again and returned to her bedchamber.

The arrival of unwelcome tidings followed that of Mr. and Mrs. Wallace.

The news ventured forth that Parliament had passed the Boston Port Act. This controversial legislation closed the port of Boston to trade, beginning with the first of June. It would be enforced until the tea that had been dumped into Boston Harbor was paid for by that city's fiery citizens. The sum was to be paid entirely—not a shilling less! British soldiers under the command of General Thomas Gage were sailing to Boston to impose the despised act.

This news rocked the foundations of Williamsburg. Views remain mixed, but, whether defending or protesting the act, emotions flared. On one side, this decree meted out just discipline for a terrific scandal and deplorable treachery. On the other side, the act was a grossly unfair wrong inflicted upon all because of a few renegades. What had once been a gracious town had, like Boston, degenerated into a hotbed of tension, quarrels, conspiracy, and hostility. The undercurrents in Williamsburg waxed ominous.

Britain and her colonies had bickered for years. The situation, however, mounting in both gravity and proportion, exploded daily. Every hour, gunpowder was added to the rising flame. Priscilla approved of Parliament's judgment, but she also dreaded its consequences. The deafening town of Williamsburg bustled even more ferociously than before. Insecurity reigned supreme not only in the House of Burgesses but also in Priscilla's heart and in the heart of every other law-abiding citizen amongst her acquaintance.

Priscilla's father and brother were almost gleeful upon receiving these tidings. "How proud we shall be of a sovereign and a government that break insurgence with a pitiless hand! Perhaps those liberty-mad seditionists shall repent of their radicalism." At each meal, she carefully listened to her father and brother boast of the royal power and ridicule the rebels. She frequently thought their language verged upon the fanatical, a tone she despised.

Yet, despite her father's show of approval, Priscilla noticed a heaviness about him in the days and months following the arrival of this news. He withdrew to his study after dinner far more often than usual and received a greater volume of correspondence from the port cities.

She pondered the effect the Boston port's closure would wreak upon her father's investments—and guessed this consideration to be the source of his concern.

Amidst these conditions, the Wallaces sojourned with the Parrs for a month. The former enjoyed their leisurely stay and dreaded the impending separation. Priscilla and Frances especially entreated them to remain for an additional fortnight. This proposition, however, was impossible. Mrs. Parr, never famous for longsuffering hospitality, quickly made it clear that she did not care to entertain visitors—even her sister—in the house for another hour.

Mrs. Wallace, however, advised a different plan to Priscilla and Frances. "You should both spend the summer with us in the country. Devon Hills is the most agreeable place during this season. Does this please you, girls?"

"Marvelous, Aunt!" Frances clapped with delight.

Priscilla's spirits climbed. *"Of course* it pleases us!"

Mr. and Mrs. Parr were applied to for their consent, and it was eventually given. Both were initially hesitant to approve the venture. Mrs. Parr, perhaps given her own tainted past, did not believe it proper for young ladies to be frolicking in the country, particularly at the vulnerable ages of fifteen and eighteen. In contrast, Mr. Parr opposed the scheme since he knew very well that Mr. and Mrs. Wallace were adamant supporters of the rebels. He did not wish for his daughters to remain alone beneath the same roof with a couple whose sympathies were so firmly aligned with the Boston radicals. Since both Mr. and Mrs. Parr appeared unwilling and stated the reasons behind their opposition, it seemed that the girls' dreams of a lovely summer were to be forgotten.

Priscilla, however, refused to relinquish these hopes, and she held a lengthy audience with her father. His resolve gradually loosened. The prospect of having two less in the Parr House over the summer outweighed his philosophical objections, and he was persuaded in favor of the proposition. Since her husband had agreed, Mrs. Parr reluctantly complied as well.

Everything was then settled.

Chapter 22

The Plantation

On a cloudless May morning, Priscilla and Frances set off with their aunt and uncle. Priscilla had obtained a promise from both Thomas and Katherine to write her each week. Both had heartily pledged to do so. She knew without a doubt that their letters would furnish the happy zenith of every week.

The party arrived at their destination in late afternoon. Mr. and Mrs. Wallace were exhausted, but the change of scenery seemed to infuse Priscilla and Frances with new life. The two girls embarked upon a leisurely walk through their uncle's orchards after leaving the carriage. Priscilla enjoyed the ramble thoroughly. How the sunshine bathed her face with warmth! After a winter and spring of little exercise and few excursions, this balm to her health was welcome.

"Frances, is this not beautiful?" Priscilla clutched the brim of her ribbon-laced hat as a sudden breeze threatened to sweep it away. "Was it not kind of our aunt to suggest this? She must have seen how we ached to be out and taste such pleasures as these."

Inhaling the scent of apple blossoms, Priscilla's eyes searched the horizon. She espied a glimmer of the York River in the distance, which bordered her uncle's plantation to the north and facilitated the transportation of his goods. She even caught sight of a small ship lingering near the banks, no doubt loaded with produce and destined for some distant port. Priscilla gazed with longing at the shore, thinking that if only she could board that ship and travel the seas, separated forever from civilization in all its decadence and strife, she could find her own soul.

Frances, her eyes glittering in the sunshine and her feet skipping along the stony path, interrupted her thoughts. "It was indeed kind of Aunt Wallace. I know that you were restless at home."

"And you?"

"I was also restless. What a lovely summer awaits us!"

True to Frances's expectation, their first week at Devon Hills was marred by nothing. Priscilla was relieved by the absence from home—to be away from her father's political rants, Ivy's silent schemes for snaring William Eton, Ben's temper, Rachel's moods, and all the monotony that home represented in general. These things taxed even Priscilla's iron nerves. Prior to their departure, Frances, Priscilla noticed, had also been miserable. She had grown taciturn and had lately acquired a rather melancholy air. A year ago, Mr. Parr had been a firm but sensible father, Mrs. Parr had been a calm mother, and Ben had played the role of a loving, although strong-willed, brother. Even Ivy had not been half so disagreeable. Priscilla had then possessed the great comfort of Katherine, whose life now revolved around the needs and desires of her husband.

Immediately following the addition of Rachel to the family, however, Ben had become consumed with pleasing her and had paid little heed to anyone or anything else. Rachel's fickle nature had proven, in the past months, a considerable influence upon Ben. Following the discovery of Rachel's condition, Ben's anxiety for her had coarsened his naturally stubborn temper. The Boston tea incident and news of the Coercive Acts had deeply troubled Mr. Parr. The depressed spirits of her husband and son, compounded with the swinging moods of her daughter-in-law, had ruffled even Mrs. Parr's peace of mind. In addition to all this, Katherine had become a wife. This circumstance had limited her presence at the Parr House. These recent losses of so many of Priscilla's pleasures had struck a blow. Her escape had finally arrived, and she intended to make the most of it.

On the Wednesday morning following their arrival in the country, she resolved to compose her promised letters to Thomas and Katherine. She first wrote to Thomas.

Dearest Tom,

I apologize for my tardiness in writing. I can only excuse it by relating my utter happiness with my aunt and uncle. The hours disappear so swiftly here—like clouds fleeting before the tempest. Dearest Aunt and Uncle Wallace remain so generous to Frances and me. I ride horseback each day except the Sabbath. The weather always cooperates with my every whim. The country refreshes my soul. I have taken countless walks upon the grounds of Devon Hills, and they never exhaust me. My aunt urges me to play her harpsichord. What is more, I believe that my aunt and uncle take the keenest pleasure in my performance.

I repeat: I have strengthened. It is the host of fresh life, an energy altogether new to me. My bout of illness is but a memory now. It is happiness to see dear Frances's cheeks, which waxed ashen a mere week ago, now illuminated by a curious rosy glow. I retain great hopes that she will become a beauty at last! The day of our departure from this place will be mournful indeed. It is folly to dread an occasion so relatively distant. I intend to glean all the joy offered by this adventure. I have also chanced upon a magnificent discovery. Life is intended for enjoyment—not in wild pursuits but in the pure pleasures of God's provision.

You must tell me, Thomas Eton, my dearest friend. How fares my family? Are they well? Is your sister Rachel well? What does or does not occur in Williamsburg now that I am gone? Please write to me soon. Your faithful friend—Priscilla.

After sealing the above letter, she scrawled a missive to Katherine. When it was also finished and sealed, she placed the letters upon the mahogany desk in the corner of her bedchamber. She was interrupted by Frances, who expressed a sudden desire for a walk. Priscilla dispatched her letters following the stroll and remained content to await two lengthy replies.

"It must be quite a marvel to have this entire plantation to yourselves." Priscilla silently admired her aunt's ceramic flatware at breakfast one morning.

"Indeed!" Mrs. Wallace acknowledged the compliment with characteristic zest. "Our daughters, well, we miss them, of course. However, although you will think me wicked to confess it, I prefer having our home filled with guests of intellect who bring the world and all its conflicts to our secluded nook of civilization."

Priscilla turned to Mr. Wallace. "Uncle, I wonder if you have heard any news from Boston?"

His expression waxing grim, Mr. Wallace cleared his throat and spoke in a deep voice. "General Gage arrived two weeks ago. I know you fret as we do, Priscilla."

"I do not know what is to become of these colonies," Priscilla said. "From all I hear, their paths meet upon a sure road to destruction."

Mrs. Wallace lifted a finger in genial protest. "Or upon the road to uncharted liberty."

Priscilla shifted slightly. "I wonder how the citizens will tolerate soldiers upon every street corner, monitoring each transaction."

"Not very well, I believe. I am plagued by great anxieties for our movement. The pressure of Parliament and the redcoats may strangle it in the end." Mr. Wallace shook his head in disgust.

"Thomas would dispute that," Priscilla smiled. "He insists that oppression will only inflame the cause."

Mrs. Wallace glowed with agreement. "That is precisely my view! Your Thomas has a fine head upon his shoulders. We colonists have been left to ourselves for so long that we have no tolerance for British domination of our affairs."

Feigning fascination, Frances sat listening dutifully but, after many moments, broke her respectful silence. "I did not believe the situation to be this serious."

Giving Frances a grave look as if alarmed by her naivety, Mrs. Wallace nodded. "It is quite serious, child."

As if to relieve the awkward silence that followed, Mr. Wallace changed the subject. "My dear, let us extend the invitation to our nieces."

Mrs. Wallace fastened her gaze upon Priscilla and Frances. "We are entertaining other guests for dinner this evening. We have invited our neighbors, Mr. and Mrs. Eton. Their plantation, you might recall, is a mere five miles away."

"We have also invited John Seymour and his sister of Cawdor Plantation." Mr. Wallace beamed as if he believed himself to be the bringer of happiness. "They are young, you see, and may be pleasant company for both of you."

If Priscilla had not been such a steady girl, she would have dropped her fork at the news—and what devastating news it was! To have escaped Mr. Seymour and his sister once had been a blessing in her eyes. But to be forced into their presence once again! Nevertheless, Priscilla maintained her countenance.

Mrs. Wallace seemed disappointed by her niece's lukewarm reaction. "This news is not pleasing to you, Priscilla?"

Frances squealed with joy. "We are already acquainted with Mr. Seymour and his sister. Are we not, Priscilla?"

"Indeed we are." Priscilla noticed that her voice was barely louder than a whisper.

Mrs. Wallace's large eyes broadened with curiosity. "How did this transpire?"

Priscilla drew a deep breath to banish her distress. "Mr. and Miss Seymour visited their cousins, the Adamses, this past Christmas."

Mr. Wallace's countenance glowed with remembrance. "Ah, yes. I had already forgotten that John and Anne passed the holiday in the capital."

Priscilla remained silent, for she did not trust herself to speak again.

"Well, then, I am sure that this is a pleasant notion to both of you." Mrs. Wallace dabbed her lips with the linen napkin and rose from the table. "Miss Seymour is about your ages—although closer to yours, Priscilla. And I believe you shall like Mr. and Mrs. Eton. They are the finest company for any occasion. Priscilla, this must be of particular interest to you since they are close relations to your friend Thomas."

Chapter 23

The Letters

Priscilla found Mrs. Eton to be one of those rare, serene individuals who seem untouched by the imperfection infecting the remainder of humanity. Her mild nature contrasted sharply with that of the assertive, opinionated Mrs. Wallace. Of politics, she spoke not a word and avoided with peculiar stubbornness. Priscilla once broached the tender subject, but Mrs. Eton merely laughed politely.

When Priscilla informed Mrs. Eton that her nephew Thomas was a dear friend, nothing could subdue the woman's benevolence. Warm blue eyes twinkled in the midst of that stout, rosy face. "Was my nephew well when last you saw him?"

"Oh yes, he was quite well, Mrs. Eton."

"You see, Miss Parr, our nephews and niece claim the greater half of our hearts and are all the world to us, particularly since my husband and I have no children of our own. We have seen nothing of Rachel since her marriage. Will remains occupied with business. Thomas…" here the lady paused in sweet remembrance, "…he has not come into the country for many years. He is tutored excessively, you know, for he plans to enter the college soon."

Priscilla sighed woefully to contemplate the separation that such a day would occasion. He had only returned to her life for nearly a year. How dull—how meaningless—every moment must have been before his return to Williamsburg! How would she ever do without his encouragement? *Perhaps I truly loved him at his father's party last*

Cadence to Glory

August—the first time I spoke to him since childhood, she realized with a pang.

She understood that he knew her only as a close friend and nothing more. Priscilla recalled that evening in her father's parlor when he had just as much as assured William that his heart belonged to Anne Seymour. Still, Priscilla harbored the hope that Thomas was too young to marry and that Miss Seymour would soon accept one of her other suitors.

Priscilla was now convinced that no other man would be more suitable to her character, interests, and aspirations than Thomas Eton. Indeed, she clung to the belief that he represented her surest chance of happiness. Their minds were accustomed to tread the same well-worn paths. His notions of liberty maddened her—and enthralled her. The more she resisted his ideals, the more she was drawn to *him*.

These sentiments dogged Priscilla throughout the dinner, although they steadied her to encounter those whom she most distrusted.

His sister upon his arm, John Seymour strode into the parlor before dinner. All rose to greet him. In preparation for his advent, which had occasioned Priscilla much anxiety in the preceding hours, she had imagined his smile in its most cruel form, his eyes frozen, his voice more nasal than usual. Nevertheless, when his gaze finally settled upon her face, she found her consternation to be far less than imagined. His piercing stare aroused more fear in her memory than in the flesh. She was surprised to detect a new haggardness to his features, which even inspired her pity.

"Miss Parr." Mr. Seymour failed to meet her eye as he bent over to plant the mandatory kiss upon her hand. Priscilla shuddered to feel the familiar chill of his lips upon her skin. He then turned away sharply to converse with his host, Mr. Wallace, as well as Mr. Eton.

As he hastened away, however, Priscilla found herself face to face with Anne Seymour, whose golden eyebrow arched although she smiled.

"Well, Miss Parr, it is an honor to see you and your sister again! How well you both look." Miss Seymour voiced her crystal laugh—a laugh which, although still lyrical, pierced the air like a well-aimed arrow released with quiet but deadly accuracy—as she extended her slim, gloved hand to both Priscilla and Frances. "I declare that I have never been so delighted as during our visit to Williamsburg. I daresay my brother and I discovered the most agreeable, stimulating, and *fiery* company we have ever encountered. We are thinking of a second visit in the autumn, having been accorded such a *rousing* welcome at Christmas! Would you like that, Miss Parr?"

During the course of the evening, Mr. Seymour did not pursue Priscilla in the least. Though genial to the Wallaces and the Etons, he had no kind looks for the Parr girls. The man's resentment toward her still smoldered. During dinner, Mrs. Wallace whispered to Priscilla. "Mr. Seymour has been less than courteous to you and Frances. Indeed, his conduct is monstrous! I am determined to confront him."

"I beg that you will not, Aunt." Priscilla laughed, amused by the frenzy into which Mrs. Wallace had risen. "I cannot speak for Frances, but I am not at all offended—rather, the opposite."

Mrs. Wallace, her bosom heaving with anger, appeared unconvinced. "And how can that be?"

Priscilla rolled her eyes with a smile. "If only you knew!"

Despite the early preservation of peace, the evening would not pass without disruptive announcements.

As the company rested in the drawing room following dinner, Mr. Seymour rose to address them all. "I do not know if you have heard the tidings from Williamsburg."

Mr. Wallace's leisurely expression melted. "What has happened?"

"The House of Burgesses has lately adopted a most intriguing resolution."

Mr. Eton, his attention similarly arrested, leaned forward with interest. "What did this resolution proclaim?"

"They proclaimed June 1st as a day of prayer and fasting in Virginia."

Mrs. Wallace's bejeweled hand flew to her breast in astonishment. "The very day that the Boston port is to be closed."

"Well, this is somewhat better news!" Mrs. Eton sang with joy, rocking from side to side.

Priscilla raised her head in defiance. "These are much more welcome tidings than we have received hitherto."

Mr. Seymour glared at her for the first time since their mutual cold acknowledgement earlier in the evening. His back stiffened with a jolt. He was most likely, Priscilla surmised, regarding the lack of alteration in her pert manner since they had parted. This time, he held his tongue.

"I believe it to be a very rational proposal." Mr. Wallace's features relaxed once again.

Mr. Eton hummed in concurrence. "And I."

Mr. Seymour's lips twitched with a nervous, violent energy—a gesture that marred his manly beauty. "Nothing need be argued." Seeing that none contradicted him, he continued with renewed confidence, stabbing the air with his forefinger. "Traitors cannot quarrel from the end of a rope!"

The ladies gasped in revulsion. Mrs. Eton in particular was reduced to hysterics while Priscilla and Frances rushed to console her. The other gentlemen did not attempt to conceal their shock at Mr. Seymour's remark.

Mr. Wallace immediately leapt from his chair and scowled at the younger man. "We shall have none of that language before the ladies, John!"

Mr. Seymour colored vivid crimson. His pride was evidently mortified, and he said no more. He sulked throughout the remainder of the evening. His shame paralleled Priscilla's gratification upon his public reprimand, and, at that moment, she thought her uncle the finest man in Virginia.

Two days later, Priscilla received her desired letters from Williamsburg.

She read Katherine's epistle first. Although unfailingly cordial, it did not communicate the details Priscilla desired to know concerning matters in the capital. She continued with Thomas's letter.

Mary Beth Dearmon, MD

Dearest Priscilla,

I rejoice to know that you are well in body and spirit! Your days in the country shall, by all accounts, never be forgotten. As you well know, my Aunt and Uncle Eton also live in the countryside. My aunt will certainly be fond of you.

Forgive me for abruptness on this next subject. Much has transpired in the capital since your departure. The port of Boston is to be closed, and that city will soon be swarming with redcoats. You understand what this means to all of us. You are most likely already aware that the House of Burgesses has declared June 1 as a day of prayer and fasting. On that day, the port of Boston closes.

What I communicate next shall disturb you considerably. Governor Dunmore has adamantly opposed the resolution. Today, to the angst of this city, he dissolved the General Assembly! I can imagine the shock you feel upon reading these words—they cannot have surpassed my own upon hearing them. You understand the violence of my sentiments only an hour ago when Father and Will returned from the office earlier than expected with the dreadful news. Father was cast into a frenzy of anger. His rage, however, is not to be compared with that of my brother.

I never dreamed that Dunmore would disregard our rights and deny our most basic liberties. My pen can ill convey the horrors. Dunmore will stop at nothing. Freedom, though intoxicating in all its impossible glory, is a dearly bought vision! We must be prepared for the deluge. Nevertheless, the first of June, we shall seek divine guidance, which is the greatest aid this colony can receive.

I dined last evening with your family. I wonder if the affection between your brother and my sister has not cooled.

It is unavoidable! My thoughts return to the present catastrophe. Forgive me, but I envy your refuge in the country. I am furnished with a view of the street while I pen this missive, and these very streets, I am certain, have never been more rocked by confusion, deception, anger, unrest, and suspicion as they are at this moment.

I must now return to my tutor's lesson. He must not suspect that I write this letter. Yours affectionately—Tom.

Upon reading his letter, Priscilla, her mind spinning, collapsed upon the nearest sofa.

Dunmore had dissolved the General Assembly!

She would not have been more astounded to hear that King George himself had graced the streets of Williamsburg in her absence. Dunmore, she inwardly admitted, had trespassed an invisible boundary. What a monumental abuse of power! How fateful a step!

The situation echoed not only from distant Boston, but rumblings of war resounded at home—in *Williamsburg*. Priscilla shared Thomas's urgency and dread. Virginia, she was convinced, had been stripped of the self-determination it had hitherto possessed. It would be a colony devoid of freedoms—suppressed beneath the thumb of this autocratic governor.

As she reread the letter, she noted his mention of Ben and Rachel Parr. Priscilla was startled by the reference but, remembering the conversation she had recently overheard concerning Rachel, surmised that perhaps her initial misgivings had been justified. She was frustrated that he offered no more details concerning the matter. Taking up a pen, she composed the following reply:

Dear Tom,

I received your letter in possession of the knowledge you conveyed—save that of the dissolution of the House of Burgesses. I had heard nothing of it. My own astonishment can hardly be expressed. I know for certain, however, though I have received no communication from them, that my family opposes you in principle. I favor impartiality while you champion the rights of the colonies. I shall never allow this matter to sever our friendship. It is essential to my life.

I mourn to hear of difficulties betwixt Ben and Rachel. Allow me to disclose my true feelings to you at another time when we may talk without interference. It is such that cannot be written.

I have seen your aunt and uncle and find them genteel indeed. They have dined with us twice. Mr. Seymour and his sister have also seen fit to delight us with their company.

Here Priscilla ceased writing. She suddenly sensed a strong urge to reveal the ugly particulars of her experiences with Mr. Seymour. She lifted her pen with trembling excitement. Before she could make another mark upon the page, however, she decided against it. Her heart was too full to write a coherent account. She concluded with the following:

Please write again soon. Give my love to all whom I left behind. Your sincere friend—Priscilla.

Chapter 24

The Visitors

June 1, 1774 heralded a day of heavy hearts, searching souls, earnest fasting, and much supplication by the people of Virginia. The Wallaces traveled with their two nieces to church, and the entire morning was spent in reverent humility before God. Priscilla prayed most fervently for guidance and courage since her heart ached with the rebellion and all its swiftly approaching consequences. Her aunt and uncle prayed that Britain would reconsider current policies. Priscilla, however, petitioned God with different motives. She prayed that the rebels might be subdued without bloodshed and that peace would reign once more in Williamsburg. She prayed even more ardently that, if God willed war, He would spare Thomas's life.

Shortly thereafter, Mr. Wallace's long-standing correspondence with several of his former colleagues in the House of Burgesses brought news of fresh developments in Williamsburg to Devon Hills. The dissolved body, it seemed, had convened in the Raleigh Tavern and was proposing to boycott all items imported by the East India Company with few exceptions. The members pledged to resume their assembly, holding a sort of "annual congress." Priscilla despised these tidings, but still she condemned the governor for provoking the House of Burgesses and thus inflaming hostilities.

"Dunmore can hardly expect the Burgesses to accept his insult without protest," Priscilla declared after her uncle delivered the tidings.

Surprised by the thrill of pride that reverberated down her spine, Priscilla added, "It was a mistake. He has awakened a pack of lions!"

The General Assembly and most of the general public were infuriated. Each time Britain slapped a restriction in the colonists' faces, their retaliation was both swift and fierce. As the month of June slipped away, Priscilla was tormented by these events. *Until Parliament employs tact for dealing with certain demands,* she thought, *there will be no peace for the colonies!*

To Priscilla's great astonishment, Mr. Seymour and his sister called upon her one afternoon in late June. Priscilla had never been so dismayed. Mrs. Wallace sat with her to receive them, and, considering the callers and the history of their association with Priscilla, she welcomed her aunt's strong and orderly presence. In addition, Priscilla did not wish to be alone with the Seymours. She and her aunt received them, however, with all courtesy and grace.

Miss Seymour hailed them with a smile. "We trust to find you both well?"

"We are indeed well." Priscilla rose to greet them.

"Please sit down." Mrs. Wallace waved the visitors toward two blue damask chairs near the harpsichord.

The guests found seats easily enough. Mr. Seymour began to clear his throat while Anne maintained her customary smile, which often gave the impression that, though outwardly bent upon courtesy, she was inwardly laughing at the object of her attention. Priscilla seemed at a loss concerning the best approach for continuing the conversation.

Mrs. Wallace came to her rescue. "I believe you saw my nephew and nieces in Williamsburg recently."

Though he addressed Mrs. Wallace, Mr. Seymour's eyes alighted upon Priscilla's face. "It has been five months at least. Hardly recently, madam."

Hearing him speak so smoothly as he scrutinized Priscilla evoked sour memories in her breast. Those piercing blue eyes possessed a peculiar talent for discomfiting the usually composed Priscilla. Thomas, she thought fondly, exercised quite the opposite effect upon her. She wished with all her heart and soul that he was there, sitting next to her, to distract her from the probing stares of the Seymour siblings. Nevertheless, he was miles away, and, thought Priscilla with a pang of sorrow, perhaps not thinking of her. Perhaps his thoughts lingered upon the self-possessed, manipulative girl whom she faced at that moment...

Mrs. Wallace's unruffled voice broke Priscilla's contemplation. "Pray, did you like the capital?"

"Of course. That city, you know, is famed for biting wit! Most enjoyable it is—if one owns a temperament which delights in quarrels." Anne Seymour's small white fingers slid down the harpsichord admiringly as she spoke. "We *did* relish the festivities, if that is your meaning."

Mr. Seymour gazed at his sister proudly. "Anne won quite a few admirers during that brief tenure."

"I cared not a whit for any of them." Anne wrinkled her nose and giggled. "Funny little creatures they were—their heads swimming with odd notions. Yet, they worshipped me!"

She ridicules Tom! Fury seized Priscilla, and she glared at Anne.

"My sister's modesty is unparalleled, is it not?" Mr. Seymour grinned. "Anne, you cannot deny that you preferred one in particular."

Priscilla guessed the identity of the young man to whom Mr. Seymour referred. Old, unpleasant feelings revived. She struggled to still the nervous tremor that suddenly afflicted her hands.

"Well..." Anne's voice trailed off as a triumphant smirk twisted her lovely red lips. "...I sought and discovered an equal in wealth, temperament, and even in allegiance."

Priscilla balked. This description did not resemble Thomas. Perhaps Anne referred to someone else after all—someone whom none, not even her brother, had suspected. Priscilla's fears turned upon a new path, and, for the first time, she wondered if Anne Seymour had used Thomas for devious ends.

Cadence to Glory

Still, Priscilla could not stifle a laugh. *What foxes these Seymours were!* What a comical pleasure to observe how deftly they could fixate the entire conversation upon themselves!

Mr. Seymour snapped to attention, and his cold eyes swung upon Priscilla. "Miss Parr, why did you laugh?"

"No reason."

"Come now, Miss Parr, tell us." Miss Seymour's tone adopted a pleasant but insistent resonance as her eyes narrowed.

"Why did you laugh?" Mr. Seymour stamped his foot as a purple flush darkened his cheeks.

Priscilla's frame shook with indignation—the culmination of much insolence directed toward her.

Nevertheless, she fortified her gaze. "I liked the sound of it, sir!"

The gentleman then smiled at her in a complacent, searching manner. She frowned at the intensity of his grin, which reflected his demeanor during his sojourn in Williamsburg. She glanced toward her aunt for assistance.

"Mr. Seymour, would you and your sister remain for tea? Shall I call the maidservant after all?" Mrs. Wallace hastened to ring the bell.

"Take no trouble, madam." The strange grin disappeared from his features. "We shall be leaving now—I thank you."

Miss Seymour, her lips drawn into a pout as if displeased by the conversation's curtailment, gathered her heavy skirts to leave. "Good afternoon to you both."

"I shall see you to your carriage." Mrs. Wallace ushered them toward the door.

Mr. Seymour vanished from the room with his sister and Mrs. Wallace.

When her aunt returned a few moments later, Priscilla proceeded to probe her opinions. "What do you think of them?"

"I have known them since their birth, and I knew their parents long before that. Their mother, God rest her soul, was an angel, and their father was a principled gentleman. His son is clever but lacking something of common courtesy. If only he could find a virtuous wife! She would, I believe, exercise a lasting goodness upon his character."

"There I must disagree with you, Aunt. There will be no altering men like that, unless by God's doing. Even if a true gentlewoman crossed his path, he would abuse her kindness and ill-use her efforts to mold him."

"I might not go so far as that." Mrs. Wallace laughed. "Miss Seymour is not so churlish."

"They are a strange sort of people. Their arrogance is second to none."

"I have always thought their father's indulgence responsible—for young John's pride, at least. Their mother, humble as she was, did not oppose him in anything."

"I despise them, aunt."

Mrs. Wallace's voice sank into a whisper, and a mischievous smile shaved years from her face. "Would his character at all improve in your eyes if I declare my belief that he admires you? He confided to your uncle that you received his attentions with enthusiasm in Williamsburg."

Priscilla was indeed surprised. Where was Mr. Seymour's mortification? Her fury mounted. What right had John Seymour the Pompous to spread lies concerning her? Perhaps he could not bear that she had rejected his proposal and thus sought to soothe his humiliation.

Priscilla had not intended to reveal her charges against him to her aunt, but, given this new fragment of information, she could not now restrain herself. "He did call upon me, yes, but I made it clear during his final visit that I did not wish to see him again. He had posed questions of a most inappropriate nature to me, and it was on this account that I declared my disinterest. Why does he circulate such falsehoods? I never admired him. He is a knave!"

"Come, come. I believe you, child." Mrs. Wallace placed an assuring hand upon her shoulder. "He was unkind to you?"

"Yes, Aunt. You will not mention this to my uncle?"

"I will say nothing—if you so wish."

Chapter 25

The Rendezvous

Priscilla faced the burdensome chore of meeting the Seymours again a week later. Nevertheless, their appearance inspired annoyance, rather than trepidation, within her breast. Her old nature, content to dare the disapproval of such a man as John Seymour, was returning in great force. Priscilla pondered these things as she gently applied the final touches to Frances's hair in preparation for the guests.

"It shall be only a month more until our return to Williamsburg! It will be ever so melancholy to leave our dear aunt and uncle." Frances sighed as she scrutinized herself in the looking glass.

"And I." Priscilla strung pearls across Frances's neck. "Do not forget Mr. and Mrs. Eton—they have also been kind to us."

"Oh no, I cannot forget *them*!" Frances stared up at Priscilla apologetically.

On this particular evening in mid-July, Priscilla wore an elaborate cream-colored silk gown, a diamond necklace draped lightly across her throat. The gown, along with the accompanying jewelry, had been borrowed from Mrs. Wallace, who insisted, against all protest, upon Priscilla's wearing it. Frances, in contrast, donned a dark green frock, which complimented her reddish-brown tresses.

Before another word could pass between the sisters, Mrs. Wallace opened the door of Priscilla's chamber. "Girls, come down as soon as possible. Our guests will arrive any moment."

Priscilla and Frances, careful not to trip on the hems of their gowns, hastened to follow their aunt down the stairs and into the central hallway. They immediately heard the cumbersome halt of Mr. and Miss Seymour's carriage. A few moments later, the Seymours, faultlessly attired as ever, entered the house with a great deal of ceremony.

"How do you do, Miss Parr?" Mr. Seymour paused to kiss Priscilla's hand.

"Very well, I thank you." Much to her dismay, Priscilla began to fret again. *Why did he behave so politely toward her now?*

The Wallaces had scarcely finished greeting Mr. Seymour and his sister when the Etons' carriage pulled to a stop upon the lawn. Priscilla turned away to regain her wits after Mr. Seymour's perplexing conduct. When she turned around again, she observed the Etons through the open door as they disembarked from their coach. But, then...

"Wait a moment!" Priscilla gasped suddenly as her pulse accelerated. "Who is that with them?"

She strained for a clearer view. Her face flushed scarlet with shock as Thomas Eton strode through the doorway.

The sight of him whom she had cherished in such warm remembrances during her absence from Williamsburg sent a burning blush to her cheeks. He filled the doorway like a lost hope. Even his shadow awakened forsaken dreams. Once he entered the room, his gaze settled upon her face.

Mr. Wallace slapped Thomas upon the back. "How goes the capital? We hear a great many things!"

"Most of them true, sir!" Thomas laughed.

"Thomas, I think you have given poor Priscilla the shock." Mrs. Wallace drew back with a bemused smile.

"Did you know about this?" Priscilla, burning with shame at the transparency of her feelings, addressed her aunt and uncle. "I mean his coming, of course."

"Indeed we did!" The Wallaces sang in unison.

"We hoped to surprise you, Miss Parr, with a visit from a friend," Mr. Eton smiled.

"Thomas also entreated us to say nothing of his arrival." Dimples pitted Mrs. Eton's plump face as she giggled like a woman half her age.

Thomas grinned. "I hope to find you well, Priscilla?"

"You find me very well, I assure you." Priscilla struggled to compose herself again.

Then, as the other guests moved toward the parlor for conversation before dinner, Thomas approached her in a low tone as concern clouded his eyes, which were particularly sharp. "We *did* startle you, Priscilla. Your face is like to catch fire. Are you well?"

"Yes indeed." She blushed at the weakness that still rattled her voice and strove to meet his gaze, which struck Priscilla as particularly penetrating on this occasion, in her usual playful manner. "Dearest Tom, do not fear for me! The sight of you gladdens me beyond expression."

True to his custom, Thomas sat beside Priscilla during dinner. They had much to discuss.

She ate very little, preferring instead to savor his presence. "Was Rachel well when you left Williamsburg? I think of her often."

"She was well." A moment later, after some reflection, he leaned over so closely to Priscilla that her face smoldered with modest sensations. "I must know your thoughts concerning those events which have occurred in your absence."

"What on earth can I think? I have been so astonished. It has all taken a perverse turn. I do not believe that the rebels will stop now. As far as Dunmore is concerned, I cannot pardon him."

"Since I wrote to you, additional happenings are afoot. At the beginning of the month, some sort of 'convention' is meeting in Williamsburg to discuss these events."

"London will not tolerate these and other insults—*this* you know."

"These were my very thoughts! I can see nothing but war looming on the horizon. It is something of which I must partake."

"Why, Tom?" Unable to repress her passion in light of losing him, she abandoned cautious reserve. "Why must you do this? Why cast your life away for some silly notion of liberty? Are your days so unhappy that you will discard them without a thought, without a single attempt at reason? Britain holds supreme authority over our lives and deaths. It will *never* change. You are falling into that age-old snare, Tom—that trap which is the graveyard of great men and all the youthful hopes they carried!"

She had not intended to react violently and immediately regretted having done so.

Thomas, however, merely smiled and stared at her in fascination. "I was wrong to discuss these matters this evening…when we have not seen one another for many weeks."

Priscilla, eager to banish the memory of her outburst, assumed an expression that she hoped would convey mischievous curiosity. "Tell me—how *did* you simultaneously write your letter to me and receive Mr. Percy's lecture?"

"Percy paces while he lectures. I kept my writing paper beneath my book. Whenever he turned his back, I quickly lifted up the volume and scrawled a few words."

"Naughty Tom!" She giggled incredulously. "It must have taken a long time."

"An hour!" He threw his head backward and laughed.

"How did you persuade your father to allow you to visit your uncle and aunt when you should be preparing for college?"

"I could not convince Father alone. Mother intervened on my behalf. She argued that even the best scholars must have occasional reprieve from mental exercise. The next moment, Father conceded. It was Mother's doing, you see."

"I am very glad she was successful." Vastly encouraged by his merriment, Priscilla paused to gather her thoughts. "In your letter, you intimated that a domestic crisis has arisen within my family since last I saw them…particularly concerning Ben and Rachel. Enlighten me!"

Thomas glanced downward with discomfort at the subject. "Very well."

Her pulse throbbing, Priscilla leaned forward to hear his narrative.

His eyes overcast, Thomas laid down his knife and began his account of the event.

"The conflict erupted during a dinner hosted by your father. The ladies were all speaking of the new fashions from London—as ladies will do. Your mother and mine were urging our fathers for money to indulge these trends. It was all in jest! They merely laughed and assured our mothers that their beauty lacked nothing. It then began. Rachel turned to Ben and commented with a coolness of manner that she had significant need of the fashions since he had reduced his spending upon gowns for her. Your brother seemed put out by this, and he countered that they had discussed this before and would not flaunt it before guests.

"A few moments later, my sister revived the subject with vehemence. She asked why he had limited her purse funds. He replied that, with the port of Boston to close—it was not yet closed at that time, mind you—he could not manage the additional expense of procuring the luxuries of London by unconventional means. I shall never forget his words: 'You would do well to shrink from a spectacle here. The woman who bears my name, my ring, and my child shall know me as master of my own home.'

"Rachel rose from her seat abruptly and confronted him in a rage. She said, 'I am no slave—and shall *not* be commanded. You once protested your devotion. Am I a trinket…to be trotted out before the world as your plundered prize? I despise that which I loved! You only coveted the prestige of my father's house in marrying me. Shall I not even receive the trappings of my position as compensation?'

"Your brother colored so deeply and shook so violently that I feared he would suffer a fit. He said, '*Your* father's house? Your father is a mere attorney. Mine is a gentleman. Who is the true mercenary, I ask you? Answer me! Yes, you have learned well from your seditionist set. Avarice does not favor you.'

"My sister broke into a scream. 'You dare accuse *my* family of treachery! *I know things which are hidden from your eyes,* and you would be wise to humor me!' Strange words, are they not, Priscilla? Both of them were oblivious to the guests by now, and everyone seated at the table squirmed upon witnessing the quarrel. Will finally interrupted the scene, stating, 'Your conduct shames us all, sister.'

"This only inflamed Rachel and emboldened Ben, who shouted, 'I find myself in the universal predicament of men throughout the ages who married a scheming shrew!' This remark, coupled with William's rebuke, stripped my sister of all composure. She unleashed another scream and flew at her husband. When the guests moved to restrain her, she collapsed and fell into convulsions. Delirium took hold. In truth, it alarmed me sorely. All the guests were dismissed except Dr. Lee, and he proceeded to examine her. It was feared for some hours that the child within her womb would be lost. When the danger had passed, the physician advised rest and repose."

"I can scarcely believe it!" Priscilla gasped when he had concluded the dismal tale. "Have they reconciled? Is she now recovered of the fit?"

Deep anxiety marred Thomas's visage as he spoke. "Your brother was at once remorseful for his part in the provocation. He apologized to her profusely when she regained her senses. They established a truce of sorts—more on his side than hers. She has been obliged to sit near the window of your father's home since the incident, but the slightest noise agitates her and sends her into incoherent mumblings. She even speaks of voices inside her head—and often stares in an unworldly way. The day before I left, she suffered a relapse."

"How did it happen?" Priscilla asked.

"She accused Ben of humiliating her before all the citizenry of Williamsburg. She called him her 'tyrant and murderer.' When he departed the house in a rage, she cried out for him to return and then succumbed to the fit again. It was milder than the first, however, and she recovered sufficiently to weep that afternoon when, grief stricken and repentant, he returned to her. I fear, Priscilla, that..." Thomas struggled to complete his statement as his countenance fell again.

Priscilla was amazed to behold the shadow of pain fleet across his eyes, distorting his beautiful features. "What do you fear?"

"I fear for her mind." He seemed to peer through the haunting corridors of memory. "It has always been a fickle thing, even in the best of times."

"What did she reference...some secret knowledge which might prove ruinous to my family?"

"I cannot say. That was curious, was it not? Perhaps her distress at the moment shook her judgment so that she imagined—"

At that moment, Mr. Wallace's booming voice ascended above the clamor of his guests and curtailed the discourse between Thomas and Priscilla. "John, tonight, the toast is yours."

Mr. Seymour held his glass aloft and flashed a peculiar smile. "This evening, I must toast to..."

Silence reigned.

"...the lovely Priscilla Parr."

Every glass was raised in her honor, and a celebratory chorus ensued. *"Here, here!"*

Priscilla could never have been more bewildered and embarrassed. How could Mr. Seymour bring himself to toast to her? Had she not been rid of him?

She smiled nevertheless. Glancing swiftly at Thomas, she noted that mysterious expression she had observed on his face at his father's party in August—when she wondered who he was and what he was thinking. *How she longed to peer into his mind at that very moment!*

Following dinner, the company retired to the drawing room. When everyone had settled themselves, Mr. Seymour burst into a hard-edged laugh. "Why shall we not have some dancing?"

"Splendid, John." Miss Seymour nodded her approval.

Frances seconded the notion with applause. "How lovely!"

The senior members of the party, being somewhat fatigued by the day's deeds, voiced cheerful opposition.

"How easy for you to suggest it, John! You are young and strong. But we old ones suffer rheumatism and various aches. In short, we shall be content with our boredom." Mr. Wallace, whose good nature had evidently forgiven Mr. Seymour for his recent breach of civility, chuckled loudly and slapped his thighs.

Stroking her chin absently, Mrs. Eton hesitated. "I am quite exhausted—and not up to dancing. You will forgive me, of course?"

"We need a stir, ladies and gentleman." Mr. Seymour planted a fist in his other palm. "Come now, I shall not take 'nay' for an answer."

"I might play the harpsichord," Mrs. Wallace said.

Because of the hostess's willingness, the entire party reluctantly complied with the proposition.

Almost immediately, Thomas turned to Priscilla with a laugh that enthralled her. "Dance with me, Priscilla! You owe me that pleasure, as I recall."

Locked in his earnest gaze, her reply sank into a husky whisper. "You know I can never refuse *you*, Tom."

Even as she spoke, Priscilla glimpsed Mr. Seymour's form approaching. A large grin exposed his snow-white teeth.

A frightening gleam, half concealed by his gallant air, darted across his eyes. "Miss Parr, I must claim the first dance."

Priscilla glared at him resolutely. "Thank you for the honor of it, sir. However, I am already—"

"I have already claimed the young lady's hand for the first two rounds." Thomas completed her sentence.

Priscilla's eyes flew to his face in astonishment. His jaw tightened with furious excitement.

She addressed Mr. Seymour with renewed energy. "As Tom has informed you, I have already engaged myself, sir."

Mr. Seymour drew one deep, incensed breath and strode away without a word. Priscilla and Thomas continued to observe Mr. Seymour as he approached Anne. Mr. Seymour whispered something to her. Miss Seymour's eyes widened with amazement as she flashed an angry look in Priscilla's direction.

The remainder of the evening, Miss Seymour barely acknowledged Priscilla's presence, and Thomas never asked her to dance. Priscilla thought it odd that he should pay so little heed to the young woman who had seemingly been, only a few months before, the object of his attentions. It was almost as if Thomas no longer admired Anne even though his inclination for basic courtesies remained. He maintained his disturbed gaze for the duration of the evening, and his expression continued to agonize Priscilla. She wondered if more violence raged beneath that placid brow than even she suspected.

As the hosts bid good evening to their guests, Thomas proceeded to kiss Priscilla's hand. After he entered the carriage, however, she discovered that he had deposited a small scrap of paper into her hand. Curiously, she unfolded it and read the following words:

Tomorrow
Half past three
Mr. Wallace's field that claims the tremendous oak
Come alone

Chapter 26

The Confession

Priscilla awoke the next morning with her mind still meditating upon the vague message that Thomas had given her the previous evening. Some dilemma required prompt attention—perhaps something fresh concerning either the rebellion or her family. It was a matter that he, for some reason, could not reveal to her the day before for fear of being heard. A fever of wild speculation had prevented her from sleeping that night.

The day passed indolently. She drove herself mad with curiosity throughout its entirety. Each hour seemed longer than the one before, particularly as the clock chimed two in the afternoon. She resolved to meet her appointment early. She explained to her aunt and uncle that she would be riding alone for a brief while and should return in an hour. Fortunately, her hosts agreed, and Priscilla assured them of her obedience.

She rode out of the stables at a faster pace than usual. Her interest intensified. Prodded onward, her steed began to gallop at an alarming speed. The breeze ripped her painstakingly arranged hair, and her tresses soon tumbled down her shoulders. The wind slashed through her thick locks as she leaned forward upon her horse.

For these moments, she experienced the greatest exhilaration of her life.

She tasted liberty! What a marvelous, innocent sensation! She felt so unfettered and free from all her worries concerning the colonial

Cadence to Glory

rebellion! The sun shone full upon her face as the wind swept through the grass. She suddenly fancied herself a creature passing into an imaginary tale—such as she had never before envisioned.

She came upon the field where the large oak tree stood in all its regal glory, like a great and wise king of the ancient ages. From a distance, she discerned Tom pacing beneath the oak while his horse idled nearby. As she rode toward him, he looked up—and stood quite still.

"Hello, Tom!" she called to him.

"Priscilla!" He answered with a wave.

As Priscilla approached him, she slowed her horse. He assisted her to dismount and, she noticed with some surprise, trembled as he did so.

Her heart raced. "What it is you wish to discuss with me? Can it be news of the rebellion?"

"No."

"Further news of my family?"

"Not at all."

"One of our acquaintances?"

"Far from it."

"Then, you puzzle me, Tom. What is it?"

He paused for a moment and then, facing her suddenly, spoke in deep, strong tones:

"We have been intimate friends for many months now. I have shared thoughts with you which I have never voiced to another, and I know you have guarded them faithfully. Your friendship is of utmost value to me. Speaking as I now must is no simple task, but I am driven toward it, Priscilla."

Alarm rose to her throat and choked every syllable. "Please tell me!"

Tom turned his face from hers. He leaned against his arm, supported by the trunk of that indomitable oak. His eyes glided across the vast fields as if his heart sought some well-concealed treasure within the verdant folds. She longed to view his face and discern the sentiments stirring within his soul, so staggering in its depth and mystery. His silence proved of such considerable length that she wondered if he had forgotten her presence. After many moments, he parted his lips in speech.

"A great change approaches, Priscilla." His voice came forth resolute with purpose but tremulous with passion. "It beckons to my soul as an invitation whispered upon a divine wind, haunting and yet alluring to the deepest expanses of my being. Two paths loom ahead, and I must soon set out upon a course. One path boasts security while the other warns of peril. This uncertain course conveys a great risk—to lose all in the quest of a tantalizing, glorious, but impossible dream."

Priscilla was drawn inexplicably into his inner turmoil. His words failed to puzzle her as an understanding was suddenly born within her soul. She stood in rapt amazement. Thomas was laying bare his soul, the treasure that was so precious to her. She could not remove her eyes from his face, as witnesses to great marvels and disasters alike cannot look away from the spectacle before them.

Thomas turned to focus his attention upon her with an intensity that frightened her. "What motivates a man, Priscilla, to cast aside all reason in pursuit of an unattainable glory? When the vision remains so far from his grasp as to drain all hope from his weary soul, what drives him onward? What compels him to brave so many dangers and trials, to struggle along a lonely road, taxing even unto the grave, with no surety of victory at the journey's end? Why does he press forward from the wealth and corruption of Egypt to pursue a destructive trek through the heart of the wilderness…with only the distant luster of a pristine land to light the dark way?"

She was transfixed by his ardor and her own wonder. "Which land is that?"

"*This land!*" He outstretched his arms and gestured toward the rippling sea of green surrounding them on every side. "These colonies! This is my land, Priscilla. My true land! Only consider—a blank canvas, a virgin soul, uncorrupted by the filth of tyranny, by the dark shadow that has plagued the world since the fall of man, by the sorrow which has haunted human government since the dawn of the ages!"

Absorbing his words, Priscilla stood rigid as a stone. Her heart believed and trusted him as a child never dares doubt its protector. A love for this land of his heart grew within her.

"My path lies before me, stretching through a vast and barren desert. Yet, the path is mine." His eyes shone with purpose. Without warning, he captured her hands. "I can offer only my devoted love and loyalty. Will you brave the journey by my side?"

Priscilla's thoughts froze, and all power of speech abandoned her. Shock reverberated throughout her frame. The heat of his penetrating gaze struck her violently. Her eyes, however, did not waver from his. A silent communication passed between them.

"How can I beg you to accompany me through such woes?" He seemed to search her own soul with a longing that seared her innermost dreams. "Because I love you with all the depth and ardor by which I love these shores! If God will judge us fit to reach that haven of opportunity, if this land becomes a nation, I desire nothing save your beloved presence. Whenever I envisage that horizon of hope, your form alone strikes a silhouette across its expanse. Can I ever deserve your hand—that you may stand beside me forever through all the tempests of this cadence to glory?"

Hot tears streamed down her cheeks. "I know not what terrors lie across my path, Thomas Eton, but I vow this day to brave them with you. No device that cruel fate may invent shall part us. From this moment, my life, my fortune, and my destiny are bound with yours!"

With a sudden sharp cry, Thomas caught Priscilla in his arms. Burying her face within his heaving shoulder, she sobbed all the more violently to sense the warmth of his own tears upon her neck. In a moment, the joyful weeping of lovers gave way to mirth—the laughter of liberation—as Thomas, maintaining an almost jealous grip upon his sweetheart, lifted Priscilla into the air, her skirts swelling in the breeze and her eyes locked into his own.

An understanding of sentiments long concealed lay between them like an imperishable thread, sealing their bond. When at last they did part that fateful afternoon, each withdrew with spirits prepared to surmount the fiercest barrier. The oak, a silent witness to their pledge, may very well stand today, tall and majestic in its royal might. If so, it is unlikely that any token remains to mark for posterity what passed beneath its boughs one decisive day long ago, the forging and fusing of two destinies. It may well be imagined, however, that, as the wind ripples its haunting melody through the leaves in ages yet to come, some hint of great mysteries long forgotten may stir.

Chapter 27

The Return

The days to come would never be equaled in exultation during Priscilla's lifetime. Her heart slowly began to adjust to the great changes that had occurred. It seemed that she had never experienced life—the sort of life that gives breath to the soul—prior to Thomas's confession. The era of her childhood seemed but a bleak haze, illumined only by frustrated, misguided passions. She had unconsciously been searching for some purpose in which she could invest her fierce hopes and energies. In the expanse of one afternoon, a great discovery had been made.

Thomas's presence became a regular fixture within the Wallace home in the ensuing days. His visits became more frequent than the summer breeze. The Wallaces' general lack of acquaintance with him was remedied as his lively laugh and somber political insights became standard additions to the dinner table. Curiously, Mr. Seymour's visits dwindled as those of Thomas increased. Since Priscilla and Thomas often strolled arm-in-arm through the Wallace's lush groves, lingering several paces behind their hosts and Frances, more intriguing revelations were made. She probed him for details, such as the moment his love for her was born.

He warmly covered her hand, which rested upon his arm. "I always admired your intelligence and courage, and I was never insensitive to your beauty—regardless of what you may have thought at the time! Our daily familiarity, however, blinded me to deeper sentiments. At

Christmas, though it shames me now to confess it, I was taken with Miss Seymour. Her beauty and wit beguiled me. Humans are the most easily deceived of all God's creatures, aren't they? The Christmas Ball was the hour of her unveiling. I shall not elaborate here—do not ask me to do so, Priscilla. Only suffice it to say that she is no selfless maid but rather a calculating coquette, a deceiver of men. It was also in the Palace when my heart first leapt at your sight, as I watched you dance with Seymour. Soon, rumors began to reach me—rumors of your engagement to that—that braggart!" He grimaced as if the very words were distasteful to him.

"I curtailed my visits for fear that I would fall at your feet and beg you not to marry him. Every instance of explosive news concerning the rebellion produced fresh grief. I could see only you beside me in the midst of advancing terrors. My dread increased as your second letter from the country communicated an upcoming encounter with Seymour. This was torture enough! Immediately afterwards, however, my uncle's letter arrived. A startling line recounted Seymour's declaration of his admiration and intent to court your favor once more. It was enough to alarm me. I pleaded with Father for leave to come here. Seymour's attentions toward you once I arrived seemed more than enough to justify that fear. I became desperate—and resolved to make my feelings known."

Priscilla giggled like a giddy child, her present gladness enabling her to jest at past miseries. Her heart was light with the freedom to reveal previously concealed sentiments that had hung between them. "Miss Seymour drove me mad with jealousy. No other explanation remains to be offered. You cannot comprehend my shock. I should never have believed you loved me."

"I thought it obvious." A wicked twinkle illuminated his eye.

"Do you remember, Tom, that December evening in my father's parlor when you told William that you had conceived a passion?"

"You heard that, aye?"

"When you were describing Miss Seymour." For the first time since his confession of love, she peered at him uncertainly, and past hurts rushed back to mar her joy. "My heart was broken—you know not how completely."

"Brilliant irony," he laughed uproariously. "I was speaking of *you!*"

Priscilla's cheeks burned as a mystery was solved with ease and satisfaction. A mountain of distressing events was explained by these recent developments. *Could such excellent fortune truly exist?* she wondered. *Was it only some cruel vision?*

His step slowed, and he faced her anxiously. "I beg you not to speak of her again, my love. I know my heart's own trickery. Let us begin anew without record of Anne Seymour. To do otherwise flaunts my shame."

"One matter, however, still remains for discussion."

"What is that, darling?"

"You know not the nature of Mr. Seymour's pursuit of me. You are aware of his arrogance, but his heart is consumed by darker forces than you know. What I say now, you must never reveal to another soul."

"You have my solemn word."

She proceeded to narrate the entire account of Mr. Seymour's connection with her. No details were spared. Frequently interrupting to pose questions, Thomas focused upon her story with rapt attention. At length, she completed the narrative.

"He is a truer blackguard than I thought. I will confront him." Thomas's fists clenched tightly.

In his anger, Priscilla thought fondly, *he has forgotten that he is only eighteen years old while John Seymour is a grown man.*

"Pray, do not!" She laughed at his misdirected chivalrous instincts and pressed his arm lovingly. "I have that which I desire. All wrongs have been righted—now that we understand one another. Distance, in this case, empowers forgiveness. Come, let us be of good cheer this blessed day and leave him to the caprices of fate."

Despite the happiness that Priscilla and Thomas now realized, it proves no uncommon occurrence for interruption to awaken mortals from the otherworldly delights of a dream. It speaks harshly, slicing through ecstasy and calling souls back to the bleakness of the practical world. Such a call reached Priscilla on the eighteenth of July in the form of the following brief message from her father:

Dearest Priscilla,

Praying that you are well, my child, I pen this note to require your prompt return home. You and your sister are to leave the country on the twenty-fifth of July. I wish both of you to be present upon the birth of your brother's heir, whose advent is considered imminent.

Hoping that your journey may be a pleasant one, I remain your loving father—Phillip Parr.

Priscilla had not expected her father's summons until the early part of August. The twenty-fifth of July loomed a week away! It seemed only yesterday that she had arrived, ignorant of the destiny awaiting her. These had been the most joyous days of her life. Her health and spirits had recovered from her illness in the spring. If she had not come, Thomas's love might never have been so ardently aroused.

Her hosts, particularly her aunt, were past consolation.

"We did not expect you to abandon us so soon." Mrs. Wallace brandished her cup for emphasis over tea that afternoon. "We thought to have you another fortnight at least."

"I wish we could remain," Priscilla sighed feelingly. "Frances and I have loved this place so well."

Frances teetered on the brink of tears. "Oh, Priscilla, could we not entreat Father to delay our journey for at least a week?"

"I am afraid not, dear. I should like to linger as much as you do, but Father's note was urgent. I fear his wrath if we were to disobey him."

Frances's lip quivered in resignation, and she stared at her lap. "I suppose you are right."

Arrangements for their departure were made immediately after Priscilla received her father's notice. Four days before their return was scheduled to occur, Priscilla had the pleasure of receiving Thomas.

"It is such a lovely day, and the gardens beckon to me." Mrs. Wallace waved toward the drawing room window, which overlooked the terrace.

"How about it, lad?" Mr. Wallace reached for his hat. "Join us for a jaunt."

Smiling, Thomas winked at Priscilla. "I should like that very much."

Thus resolved, the five of them quitted the house and passed through the garden gate. As at other times, Thomas and Priscilla tarried behind the rest.

A tender silence hung between the pair until Thomas spoke at last. "Though I did not tell Mr. and Mrs. Wallace, I received a letter this morning from my father. He requires that I return the day after tomorrow. I fear I must bid goodbye now."

"Goodbye? We shall not be apart for long."

Thomas clasped her hands and pierced her gaze with his eyes. "You must know that we will be forced to delay our marriage until I have completed my time at the college."

Though this observation pained her deeply, the same fierce emotions which had flooded her soul that afternoon beneath the regal oak rushed back upon her now. "What are a few years to a lifetime? They are nothing to me—if only you love me still at the end of them."

Glancing around to ascertain that the rest of the company had ambled into the distance, he slipped his arm around her waist and drew her hand to his lips. "Have I leave to seek your father's consent upon our return?"

"It is yours."

They meandered through the hedges together in silence, basking in the ethereal grace of the afternoon and in the burning light of their love. A violent sorrow threatened to bewilder Priscilla's soul as she watched the sweetest and truest chapter of her life close forever, never to be opened again.

Priscilla's dread for her return intensified a few days later as she finally boarded the carriage that would convey her home. She waved to her aunt and uncle until their familiar forms were no longer visible. As the countryside rolled past her window, slipping through her fingers, she could no longer suppress tears. Frances wailed with concern for her sister's distress. Priscilla, who attributed her tears to grief at their departure and joy with promises of the future, could not reply.

On to Williamsburg!

Chapter 28

The Engagement

Priscilla breathed nothing but excitement by the time the carriage rolled through the familiar bustling streets of Williamsburg. As she passed the Eton house, she espied the back of Thomas's head through the window. He did not see her, however, since he was in the midst of lessons from Mr. Percy. Priscilla smiled. Thomas would soon know of her presence in town, and then, she reasoned, their plans would be formally approved.

The carriage swayed to a halt before the Parr house. Her father and brother, who were standing upon the lawn, awaited the returning travelers. The two men quickly strode to the carriage and helped the girls to disembark.

Mr. Parr welcomed them with open arms. "Priscilla! Frances! I rejoice to see your pretty faces again."

Ben managed a smile. "The house has suffered from your absence."

Priscilla immediately noticed an alteration in her brother's mien and manner. Agitation wrinkled his brow, strained his voice, and excited the dark flame in his eye. His unsettled gaze darted wildly.

Nevertheless, she returned the compliments with a giggle. "And we have missed you both dreadfully."

Mr. Parr, suddenly struck by some peculiarity, drew back to study Priscilla. "You have changed."

"Truly, Father?" She was a little perplexed by her father's vitality. "In what manner?"

"The great improvement in your health and spirits quickens even these old bones! You are even more of a beauty than when you left us. And your cheeks—what bonny roses I see there! Ah, you resemble your mother more every day. The sojourn has even added to your magnificence. And you as well, Frances! My daughters both look well. Come, dears, let us go inside before we melt beneath the blaze of this sun."

The four of them entered the house and, subsequently, the parlor, where Mrs. Parr, Rachel, and Ivy awaited them. Priscilla found herself swept away by such a joyful temper that she hastened to each of them.

"My Priscilla!" Mrs. Parr warmly embraced her daughter.

Turning next to Ivy and Rachel, Priscilla saluted them. "My heart rejoices to look upon your dear faces once again."

With a lofty tilt of her head, Ivy unleashed a hard-edged laugh. "You have trespassed long upon our good uncle's hospitality—and must have grown fond of his swine or some such, I daresay."

Priscilla's exalted state of mind allowed her to overlook every offense. She even embraced her sister-in-law, whom she found to be very large indeed. "Rachel! How lovely you are looking."

"Quite," Rachel replied, her pale lip trembling and her eyes red rimmed. "I see that you still possess that irritating talent of throwing unpleasant truths into one's face."

Even this insult did not succeed in ruffling Priscilla.

In the succeeding days, Priscilla pondered the changes to come. She awaited Thomas's announcement with a full measure of both bliss and apprehension. Her father's insistence that she spurn young revolutionaries gave her some cause for alarm. However, if he believed Richard Eton to hold only partial devotion to the rebellion and therefore insufficient justification to block the match between Ben and Rachel, perhaps he did not likewise grasp the scope of Thomas's radicalism—and would raise no objection to her own engagement.

Mr. Eton's reaction to the arrangement also troubled her. He had, after all, disapproved of William's association with the Richmond Tories. Nevertheless, he had also consented to his daughter's marriage to Ben—a firm Loyalist—presumably due to his long friendship with Phillip Parr.

Priscilla was not long suspended in this state of uncertainty.

Four days following her return, Thomas and his father called upon the Parr family. Priscilla saw the Etons' carriage pull up in front of the house that afternoon. For the past few days, she had remained seated at the parlor window, awaiting their advent. Her restlessness had mounted hourly as she twitched without ceasing and proved unable to endure any one employment for more than a few moments.

On this particular day, Mr. Eton and his youngest son were announced promptly and shown into the parlor. The family had been accustomed to Thomas's friendly calls upon Priscilla. Now that Mr. Eton called along with his son, as he had seldom done before unless invited to dine, the entire family hastened to assemble.

"Richard! What a pleasant surprise." Mr. Parr welcomed his friend. "And Thomas, dear lad. Do be seated—both of you. Now, what prompts you to honor our home with your presence today?"

Mr. Eton appeared sterner than usual. "It is not I but my son who wishes to speak with you."

Mr. Parr glanced with astonishment from Mr. Eton to Thomas and back again. "Your son has business with me? What purpose?"

"You shall see, my friend." Mr. Eton poorly suppressed a grin.

Thomas stepped forward and, glancing briefly toward Priscilla, met Mr. Parr's stare without blinking. "Yes, sir. I must speak to you—alone."

After a moment of what resembled indecision, Mr. Parr squinted suspiciously. "Very well, then. We shall confer in my study. This way, my boy."

Phillip Parr and Thomas Eton made their way to the study. When they returned to the parlor an hour later, few could have guessed what had passed between them. Thomas's eyes glistened with that ethereal flame that burns so brilliantly within the hearts of idealistic youth, unscarred by the severity and suddenness of life's trials.

While he stood before his family, Mr. Parr's trembling jaw evinced that he still doubted the agreement that had been reached. "I have a singular announcement."

Priscilla was ignorant of neither the subject nor the result of the interview by gazing into Thomas's confident eyes.

Mr. Parr placed his large hand upon Thomas's shoulder. "This young man has just given me one of my life's most remarkable surprises. He has just applied for my consent."

"Consent for what?" Mrs. Parr stammered with poorly concealed wonder.

"My consent to a union between himself and Priscilla...upon the completion of his education." Mr. Parr, who appeared increasingly satisfied with the proposition, burst into a grin.

The entire room was struck dumb.

Mrs. Parr was the first to speak. "But, Priscilla, I was under the impression that you were only childhood companions."

"We were, Mother. Yet, we are no longer children. Childhood and its attendant feelings are long past."

Mrs. Parr could not check a smile. "I confess that your manner is altered since you returned. I had suspicions—but never in connection with *him*."

Ben manifested the first excitement that he had displayed in days. He immediately rose and shook Thomas's hand with a touch of his old zest. "Well, Thomas, it seems we shall be made brothers twice. I congratulate you."

"Thank you, sir. This good fortune overwhelms me." Thomas's eyes furtively found his sweetheart.

To be the object of those clear and forceful eyes sent a thrill through Priscilla's frame once more. She hastened to his side so that she might entertain a closer view of his ardor. He clasped her hand, drew it to his lips, and lingered as if he savored the deed. The touch of his lips upon her hand aroused a curious sensation, and, for the first time, Priscilla's cheeks burned with a womanly fire.

Unaware of the self-conscious looks passing between the now-affianced couple, Ben chuckled. "She is a fine specimen. You are right to boast of her acceptance. Believe me, Thomas, I know her peculiarities like a book. My sister would never give her hand unless the fellow proved his virtues. I feared spinsterhood for that one!"

Priscilla feigned offense with a mischievous toss of her head. "I heard that, Benjamin Parr!"

Her bosom heaved with intense relief as she shed the weight of four days' burden of anxiety. It seemed that her engagement would be warmly received after all.

Frances tapped Priscilla on the shoulder as the room erupted in the chaotic din of joy and surprise. "Priscilla, I never suspected it. I wish you all the happiness in the world!"

"Neither did I guess that our visit to the country would hold such implications for destiny." Priscilla, wheeling around to face her sister, giggled. "Surely you must have thought something amiss when we lingered behind you all during our rambles across the grounds."

"I have little seen such things." Frances's cheeks were aflame with girlish modesty. "I remain ignorant in the ways of the world. Perhaps I shall learn someday."

The entire Eton family was invited to dinner the following evening. A night of unparalleled happiness ensued. While Ivy could scarcely avert her eyes from William Eton, Thomas seemed incapable of extracting his own from Priscilla's face. Even the fact that Ben and Rachel Parr, brooding in their own miseries, barely acknowledged one another failed to mar the occasion. Rachel's mind, although clearly disturbed, maintained a silent storm. Ben and his wife thus avoided a shameful scene, and, for this mercy, Priscilla was inwardly grateful.

Following dinner, Priscilla was implored to play the harpsichord for the entire company. As her dainty white fingers swept over the delicate ivory keys, she glanced upward to see Thomas gazing at her with the greatest admiration in his powerful blue eyes. The world and all its confusion were suspended by the adoration of her great love, Thomas Eton. The dubious yet inviting future loomed like a perilous path of glory before them. As long as her hand was enclosed within his own, she believed, her courage would remain intact, her purpose unaltered, and her determination unshaken.

Chapter 29

The Birth

News concerning the engagement of Thomas Eton and Priscilla Parr, including the distant wedding day, spread amongst the gentry of Williamsburg in the space of an afternoon. It was met with open amazement by those who remarked on the prospect of a second Eton-Parr alliance. Indeed, some whispered that perhaps such a degree of affinity between the two families was not a thing to be borne. Most, however, greeted the news with enthusiasm. Katherine Lee Adams and her husband called upon Priscilla bearing congratulations as soon as the tidings reached them.

Flushed with joy, Priscilla quickly offered them seats upon the settee. "And does this please you, Kate?"

"How could it not please me?" Katherine grasped her friend's hand in both of hers. "I had suspicions at the very first—which soon faded. The two of you deceived me for so long. Did you suspect it, Henry?"

"Of course, darling. I knew it from the beginning!"

Katherine, delighted to her fingertips, giggled with a backward tilt of her head. Then she commented to Priscilla in a lowered voice, "You know he would receive all the praise for his powers of perception, but only when everything is said and done!"

Priscilla noted her friend's bloom of spirits. Katherine's cheeks flamed with the rosy health of wedlock. Priscilla smiled to ponder such a fate.

It was during this period, when Priscilla's bliss rendered her incapable of thinking about anything that did not directly pertain to her own destiny, that Rachel Parr began her confinement. Rachel had been lately indisposed due to the friction that had arisen within her marriage and the turmoil that had afflicted her mind. Mr. Parr had been particularly concerned that such discord would injure the child. The flurry of excitement occasioned by Thomas and Priscilla's engagement was thus swallowed up by another sort of agitation in scarcely less than a week. Everyone happily awaited the birth.

Still, developments occurred in the first week of August that did much to endanger Priscilla's contentment. The much-talked-of convention assembled in Williamsburg. This convention proceeded to adopt resolutions against goods from Britain and against the importation of slaves following the first of November. In addition, they adopted resolutions against the exportation of goods to Britain following August 10, 1775. Seven men were chosen to represent the Virginia Colony in a Continental Congress, which was scheduled to convene in Philadelphia a month later. These delegates would include Edmund Pendleton, Peyton Randolph, George Washington, Richard Henry Lee, Benjamin Harrison, Richard Bland, and Patrick Henry, several of whom Mr. Parr had known for years.

Even these events could not touch Priscilla's happiness. Though the inns of Williamsburg teemed with those who had assembled to decide the fate of Virginia, she blinded herself to these things. Let the storms rage—she defied them! Let them ring in every ear! Let them topple every wall! None of it, she reasoned, would affect her. She rested in a happy fortune.

That resolve was soon tested when, in the first week of September, Rachel began to experience birth pains. The midwife was summoned with all due haste. It was clear by noon of that day that Rachel was in great suffering. Screams and shrieks haunted the Parr house, those same walls against which laughter had bounced but a few days earlier. None could sleep for the clamor of Rachel's agony. Ben's resentment toward his wife melted into wild remorse. He wrung his hands to see her, but his father only warned him, "Leave her be. Men do not belong in such places. It is not done—and would only distress her."

Rachel's misery awakened Priscilla from her daydreams. She feared for Rachel and the child. Ben edged closer and closer to the precipice of insanity as the screams reverberated throughout the house that night. Everyone most likely would have been forced to remove themselves from the premises for presence of mind if, in the early hours of the next morning, a daughter had not been born.

The sex of the child disappointed Phillip Parr, but the young father, who had prepared for the worst, was only relieved that the mother's life had been spared. The child, named Sarah, was well formed and healthy, and the entire household quickly conceived an affection for her. Ben visited his wife the day following her deliverance, and they reconciled for the present.

Amidst the celebration, little attention was paid to the health of the woman who had borne the child. Her complaints of pain were dismissed by those around her as customary for a woman in her condition. Two days following the birth, however, Rachel contracted a fierce shivering fit, and Dr. Lee's services were required.

Upon his arrival, the physician's brow wrinkled with alarm. "I suspect childbed fever."

Ben wrung his hands desperately as a sickly pallor swept over him. "But will she live?" He sank into a nearby chair and shook his head violently as if to banish the nightmare. "Oh, what did I care if she were mad? Why did I not dare the world to scream about my ears? I shunned her when she needed me most. What I would buy for her this day—all my inheritance to clothe her precious form! Yet, what does it matter now? What have I done?"

Priscilla, who gathered with the family to learn Rachel's prospects for recovery, mourned for a brother so wretched—and so wracked by a doomed passion.

Dr. Lee, placing his hand upon Ben's shoulder, gazed down at him with grave sympathy. "I have witnessed a few patients recover from this fever, but most have not."

This prognosis was sufficient to plunge the entire household into a state of consternation. Celebration was rapidly swept away by despair. The Etons were summoned. Ben could not be coaxed away from the bedside of his ailing wife. For two long weeks, he sustained this vigil with the self-sacrifice of a monk. During this time, Rachel's condition swung from stable to critical. At the end of this bleak period, she asked for Priscilla.

Priscilla hastened when called, and she sat down beside the bed. The death-scented sheets clung to Rachel's thin frame, which shuddered in swift gasps for breath. Priscilla, remembering how she herself had lain is such a dire state only months ago, disliked the scene. She gently clasped Rachel's trembling hand. "What is it that you must say to me, Rachel?"

Priscilla's pulse quickened, for she wondered if her sister-in-law intended to reveal the secret knowledge referenced during the quarrel Thomas had recounted.

Rachel's grip tightened with a jerk. "I am dying, am I not?"

"Dr. Lee himself said that some have recovered from such a fever as yours. Your constitution is hardy enough to withstand sickness. You shall be one of the few, I am certain."

"A fortunate few." Rachel sighed softly as tears gushed down her cheeks. "Do not lie to me—I detest that. I shall not survive the week, and everyone knows it!"

This feverish outburst evoked profound sadness in the hearer. Priscilla studied those tired, pale blue eyes that had once been vivacious diamonds, shining for suitors—and then shining for Ben alone. Rachel's once glowing skin had faded into a sickly, flushed hue. Her once graceful hand now faltered. Her gleaming dark locks now lay piteously strewn across the pillow behind her gaunt face.

Rachel's bosom heaved as she struggled for breath. "I have asked you to come because…because I should like to receive your pardon. I have been unkind to you. Let me cast this burden from my soul and die in peace with the forgiveness of those whom…those whom I have treated ill."

These words brought violent pangs of remorse to Priscilla's heart.

Surely she had misjudged Rachel?

Rachel lifted her head slightly. "Well, you cannot forgive me?"

"You have any forgiveness I might offer. You know that. Only recover your strength, and all shall be well again."

Priscilla expected Rachel to send her away, but she did not do so. What Rachel next uttered mystified even Priscilla.

"Life!" Rachel gasped a bitter laugh as she closed her eyes and writhed in pain. "A useless game! I have fallen. It is almost humorous. All the efforts lead to...to so little gain. And here I am...dying for my own blindness! The blackness of the grave...it draws near. I can sense the chill of the earth in my heart. It kills me...little by little. *Oh, do not leave me alone!* What have I to do but relent? My child...to live without a mother! Her road will prove harsher still. These voices inside my head...how they torture me...how they *slay* me! Can you not hear them as I do?"

The speech so utterly stupefied Priscilla that she wondered if the fever had ravaged her sister-in-law's brain. These ramblings belonged with the ravings of madmen.

An otherworldly agitation suddenly seized Rachel. Her eyes began to dart wildly, and her jaw contracted fitfully. "Death is coming...it comes for *me*! Go, or you too may be taken!"

Ben burst back into the room as Rachel plunged into delirium. A cold sweat bathed his brow as he turned upon Priscilla with a mixture of fear and rage. "What have you done to her?"

"Nothing—I have done nothing." Priscilla, overcome with grief and shame, fled the room.

The minister arrived before sunset.

※

The room where Rachel lay remained cloaked in deathly silence. Soon after the minister arrived, Mr. Parr delegated his two youngest children to the sitting room downstairs.

Twisting her hands together, Frances now sat quietly by the fireplace. She slowly turned her frightened, childlike eyes toward a portrait, painted not long ago, that was displayed on the opposite wall. Priscilla followed her gaze and found Rachel's visage staring coolly back at her. Considering the present turn of events, the painting's subject cast a chilling pall over the room. The sight of Rachel's familiar face unleashed the flood that had threatened to break loose in Frances for many days. The child collapsed in the chair and sobbed violently into her handkerchief, which was not designed to accommodate such an outpouring of feeling.

Priscilla hastened to console her, but Frances refused to receive comfort in her distress. Priscilla then attempted to hush her—all to no avail. For a time, Frances could say nothing. Sorrow choked every word.

After several moments, however, she was able to whisper her sorrow. "Will Rachel die? She cannot, I say! We must imagine ourselves months ago, when we were all merry and Rachel free from care. Why can we not go back? Now, we shall never be glad again."

The girl rocked back and forth, bursting into a fresh wave of tears.

Such paroxysms of woe further burdened Priscilla. "Frances, you are weary. I shall take you to bed."

Frances offered no resistance to her sister's initiative. They slowly entered and passed through the hall. As they ascended the stairs, the dimness of the upper hall became apparent. They finally reached the second floor. The two walked quietly, hardly daring to step lest the floorboards should creak. Priscilla's chest constricted with heartache for there, at the far end of the hall, was the room where Rachel lay dying, surrounded by the minister, the physician, and her two families. No sound of any kind escaped from its confines. Only a few cold rays of candlelight issued from underneath the door.

Frances burst into a second wave of weeping at the mournful sight. Priscilla swiftly ushered her into her bedchamber.

Frances clutched Priscilla's arm. "Do not leave me!"

"I would never leave you. Wipe your tears, Frances, and say your prayers. Ask God to spare our sister-in-law if it be His will." Priscilla clothed her inconsolable sister in a nightgown and tucked her beneath the canopied bed's heavy covers.

Priscilla's suggestion sparked an onslaught of fervent prayers from Frances's quivering lips. Priscilla repeated the prayers even after Frances had drifted into a fitful slumber.

The hours crept by. An eerie mist of silence cloaked the halls of the house. A strange loneliness stole into Priscilla's soul. Memories and images preyed upon her mind. She remembered Rachel at the engagement ball. Only weeks before, Rachel had been a vibrant soul among them. Had it all come to this? Her life now stood upon the brink of mortality. It ebbed away a few rooms down the hall—death weaving its poisonous web like a patient but unyielding predator.

Priscilla suddenly thought of Thomas, who remained with his family in Rachel's sick chamber. *What pain must torment his soul*, she wondered. Priscilla longed to go to him, but she was bound to Frances's bedside.

Priscilla was sick at heart, and she began to ponder the great change that would beset her home after such a calamitous night. Without realizing it, she fell asleep. Her slumber was disturbed by nightmares that haunted her and by visions of the past, which wrought an even greater anguish.

She awoke after what seemed like years of agony. Her attention, however, was immediately arrested, and she was gripped by fear. No sound engaged her focus, but she recognized a nightmarish silence more terrifying than the one to which she had fallen asleep. It was an intuitive knowledge more powerful than she had ever sensed before. At that moment, Benjamin Parr's hopeless, maddening cry suddenly rose out of the dark stillness.

Priscilla covered her face and wept.

Rachel was dead.

The house plunged into mourning following the death of Rachel. The needs of the newborn child were attended, but all thought lay with the grieving father. Benjamin Parr, pale and oblivious to the world, sank into a miserable state as death carved its path of ruin across his soul. He would speak to no one, refusing even to see his daughter.

Priscilla's heart ached for him—and for Thomas. She had never seen either of them so forlorn as the day when Rachel was laid to rest in Bruton Parish cemetery. Frances sobbed without ceasing. Mrs. Eton wept softly but otherwise seemed to bear the sorrow with greater fortitude than was expected of a woman who had lost her only daughter.

Rachel had perished in her twenty-third year. This was the young woman with and without whom Benjamin Parr could not live. She was the sister of Thomas Eton, and Priscilla grieved to witness her burial. Her tale was a tragedy that would later revisit Priscilla's mind in the strangest of times. In the years to come, she was often haunted by the youthful, haughty face of Rachel Eton Parr.

Chapter 30

The Widower

As if all the world disregarded the gloom that now shrouded the Parr household, explosive tidings reached Williamsburg during the autumn months.

On the first of September, General Gage had confiscated the stock of gunpowder at Charlestown, Massachusetts. During the months of September and October, the new Continental Congress had convened in Philadelphia, and, excepting minor details, its resolutions matched those of Virginia. These pronouncements thus signified that the colonies intended to defy England with every sinew. Priscilla, however, did not discuss these happenings with Thomas, whom she knew to be enveloped by grief for his late sister.

These proved bleak times for the Parr and Eton families. Black was strictly donned every day with no exceptions. Ben's fearless temperament faded into the tragic mists of the past. His eyes at first seemed drained of all life, their lack of expression disguising the storm within. Once the initial shock had subsided, however, his grief began to manifest itself in irrational fits of fury and violent swings of remorse. He bemoaned every harsh word he had ever uttered to his "dearest darling." He attended each meal, but, before retiring, often vented indignation upon one of his relations.

One day, he selected Frances as the target of his ire. "Methinks I see scarlet satin beneath your frock."

Frances gasped, her eyes broad with shock. She dropped her fork in confusion. "Of course not."

"We are in mourning!" Ben roared.

"Please do not accuse me wrongly. I am not—"

"Go to your chamber at once and take off that vile color. Do you think to make yourself a harlot?"

Frances covered her face and unleashed a petulant cry. "I wear only black!"

"Does no one harbor a shred of respect for the dead—"

Here Ben paused with a painful gleam in his eyes.

"—*for my wife!*"

In that instant, Priscilla wished that he had never set eyes upon Rachel Eton, for she loathed to behold the crumbling ruins to which union with that ill-fated woman had reduced his soul. Yet, how she loved him! If only he did not suffer so. He was now a man, but to Priscilla, he would always be that boy who lovingly fussed over her, teased her, and tended to her small needs. Such a childish fit directed against innocent Frances boded ill for him.

Ben not only attacked his parents and sisters but also avoided his child as much as possible. He finally agreed to see her—but only for a moment. Whenever he glimpsed the infant, he seemed to envision only the dying eyes of Rachel, staring back at him with a haunting reproach. He left her to the supervision of the servants, particularly a wet nurse whose services Mrs. Parr had recently sought and secured. Consequently, the Parr women often found themselves caring for the child, and Priscilla soon developed a great attachment to her.

Nevertheless, as the first sting of sorrow passed, Priscilla's thoughts returned to the political turmoil at hand.

She then judged it safe to hazard a question to Thomas, who had begun to recover his wits from the shock of Rachel's death. "What are your thoughts concerning this parade of conventions, Tom?"

"It confirms the seriousness of the rebellion, a thing we have long suspected, you and I."

"Are they serious enough for war?"

"Yes."

"Parliament will react with vengeance."

"We can deduce that from General Gage's deeds in Massachusetts."

Priscilla cringed at talk of war. She was aware that Thomas would join this army since he was a member of the militia. He longed for nothing more than the opportunity to bring lofty ideals to fruition, though he was consigned to a tiny portion absorbed by the greater whole. In action, not theory, he discovered his passion, and Priscilla found her true rival for his devotion. This war, she reasoned with a shudder, might even interrupt their plans. She struggled to assign these fears to a neglected corner of her consciousness.

It was out of necessity—not affection—that Benjamin Parr married again.

Even in despair, he was not insensible of the need for a mother to his infant daughter. In addition, he had sired no son. A male offspring formed one of the primary two results he hoped a second marriage might afford him. His sole alternative was to remarry.

He sought a kind woman who would accept the child as her own. For his own sake, he desired a compassionate soul who would tolerate his grief, which still loomed over him like a shadow. As a mourning man, he needed a benevolent touch. Ben also preferred a woman who would be Rachel's opposite in every way. He wanted nothing to remind him of her. To Priscilla's astonishment, he acknowledged these requirements to his family.

He soon discovered a young lady who suited his unusual criteria in Rosamund Lee, the sister of Priscilla's closest friend. Rosamund was a homely girl of fifteen with mousy brown tresses and unremarkable brown eyes. Despite these defects, she and her temperament were well known to the Parr family, and she was generally regarded by them to be gentle and dutiful. These characteristics spoke so strongly in her favor that Ben promptly proposed marriage.

Rosamund's own feelings were confided to her dearest friend Frances, who, with a little persuasion, repeated them to Priscilla. From

Frances's account and from all the knowledge springing from past acquaintance, Priscilla deduced that Rosamund's ideals concerning matrimony were more pragmatic than romantic. His was her first offer. Furthermore, Rosamund viewed the match as desirable on an objective level. He stood to inherit a great deal of wealth, and an alliance with the House of Parr was more than respectable. She also believed the match to be satisfactory on a personal level. She viewed him as a sensible gentleman, and, as a young girl, she was far from blind to his good looks. In addition, she observed the grieving widower in him. She therefore understood that, if they married, she would be forced to deal with him, for the first few years at least, in a tender manner. In Rosamund's own mind, her mild nature rendered this no immense challenge. Her parents also strongly favored the match.

Therefore, at the youthful age of fifteen, she accepted him. They were married very soon after the proposal and two months after Rachel's untimely demise. Priscilla observed that Ben was no longer the lighthearted youth she remembered with so much fondness. He rarely smiled and never laughed. She did not even recognize the bitter man he had become. Priscilla, however, rejoiced in hopes that Rosamund could exert a calming influence upon her brother. *With Rosamund at least,* Priscilla thought, *the family will never be subjected to an encore of poor Rachel's lunacy.*

The wedding day itself was not a blissful occasion for Ben. Despondency weighed upon his brow throughout the entire ceremony, and the heavy pall cast by Rachel's memory hung over the proceedings.

The latter half of October brought far different tidings, for it heralded the return of Mr. Seymour and his sister to Williamsburg. The formal explanation was circulated that Mr. Seymour came to settle some unpaid debts incurred during his visit the previous Christmas. The Seymours were again staying with their cousins, the Adamses. Priscilla was no longer agitated by their advent. In fact, now that Thomas's affections were secure, she viewed their return with indifference.

Part III

Chapter 31

The Warning

In late October, George Adams hosted a party at his home. This gathering proved remarkable both because of the events that preceded it and the discourse to which these occurrences gave rise.

The house hummed with conversation. Most of the older gentlemen, along with William Eton, congregated in their own corner of the room. The speeches, as usual, were fiery and aroused.

Mr. Parr's voice ascended above the commotion. "I marvel at this Continental Congress. I never expected matters to take such a brazen turn. I thought that King and Parliament had ended this entire affair by sending Gage across the ocean."

Mr. Eton shrugged. "Perhaps London will now see its folly. We cannot allow Parliament to trample upon us any longer."

William nodded in agreement. Priscilla examined his countenance carefully. She had heard him say little since his outburst at the Christmas Ball. Instead, he had relapsed into his old reserve, seeming always to watch and wait in the shadows. He thus appeared to read the thoughts of those around him without ever revealing his own.

Dr. Lee suddenly arrested Priscilla's attention as he arched his eyebrows. "That is a strong statement, which, frankly, borders upon treason. Even though I realize the serious nature of this situation, I remember where my loyalties lie. *You* also must not forget."

Cheeks aflame, Mr. Parr stamped his foot in frustration and stretched his arm across the fireplace mantle for support. "My question is how far the rebellion will go."

Dr. Lee paused thoughtfully before replying. "Quite far, I fear. The rebels are emboldened at present."

"You believe the revolutionaries are set upon war, do you, Lee?" Mr. Parr's frame convulsed in a shudder. "The thought is despicable."

Grinding his teeth, Mr. Eton answered for the physician. "I am certain of it."

Such was the concern and extremity of the chatter on one side of the room. On the other, the innocent youths remained oblivious to the calamity.

Priscilla, eager to ignore further rumblings of debate, sought and found her friend Katherine.

"Tell me how progresses your marriage!" Priscilla, flush with delight to see her dear friend, clasped Katherine's gloved hands within her own. "I have not spoken with you since my return. 'Tis far too long an absence!"

"Yes, though it seems that I have not been sorely missed, for you had other company in the country, I believe." Katherine smiled, glancing over her shoulder at Thomas, whose tall frame presently stooped beneath the doorway.

Priscilla's bosom heaved as she espied him. "He is far too good a man for me, Kate, and yet I cannot refuse the blessing offered me in his love. Would I not be the greatest simpleton who ever lived to reject it?"

Katherine feigned offense in good-natured protest. "Hush, now! He is *not* too good for one such as you, Priscilla. Pray, do not say such things! Do you not both possess independent minds—and free tongues, at that? It is a splendid match."

At that moment, Henry Adams's approach spirited Katherine away. Pressing her friend's arm with utmost affection as she withdrew, Priscilla turned toward Thomas, who, catching sight of her, was advancing toward her when he was engaged by the warm conversation of an elderly gentleman.

"How handsome your Thomas looks this evening."

Priscilla turned to Frances, who, peering across the room at Thomas, now crept to her sister's side.

"I cannot agree with you more." Priscilla sensed a blush flood her cheeks.

"I am delighted for you both." Frances abruptly switched the subject as she glimpsed Ben, who, lounging upon a chair nestled in the corner of the room, gloomily immersed himself in a tattered copy of *Oedipus the King*. "Our brother is a slave to his melancholy. It smites my heart."

"And he breaks mine ten times over!" Priscilla shook her head. "He is an altered creature. There is nothing left of his old swagger."

"Your knowledge of human nature surpasses my own so completely. You could clarify this mystery."

"What mystery is this?"

"Our brother certainly admired Rachel at one time. After he married her, he seemed to love her a while longer. Then his affection waned, and he regretted the marriage. As she lay dying, however, his love revived with great violence. But now, he has wed Rosamund. Has he forgotten his first wife? How can one's ardor wax so fickle?"

Priscilla had pondered the question often enough in the months following Rachel's passing. Ben's actions both before and after her death were almost too puzzling to contemplate. She had stirred the waters of his soul in indefinable ways, and love had marred him. Yet how could Frances grasp these complexities?

Priscilla thought deeply before hazarding an answer. "His feelings for Rachel were unchanged. Was it love, passion, or even lust? That is not for me to say. God rest her soul, I cannot speak ill of her."

She had barely concluded her statement when Thomas approached them.

He performed a bow for comical effect. "I was just informing yonder gentleman how lovely you both look. I must be careful with you now, Priscilla. I am like the rich man who, though worshipful of his wealth, fears that a thief may come and steal his plunder."

"Plunder! Is *that* what I am? Take care, my love!" Priscilla, intensely relieved that he had not overheard her discussion of his sister, wound her arm through his. "You are mine, Tom, and I am yours. Did we not seal our bond by the most solemn of promises beneath my uncle's tree, with heaven itself as our witness?"

As Priscilla uttered these words, Mr. Seymour, in all his pompous glory, strode up to their party.

Thomas, his eyes still luminous from the assurances of his sweetheart, snapped to attention and cast wary eyes upon his former rival, as if suspicious that he meant to renew his addresses toward her. She could not help but laugh at this flash of jealousy in one she loved so dearly, whose arm she pressed.

Nevertheless, Mr. Seymour grinned in a chilling manner that sent shivers up Priscilla's spine. She sensed a lingering dread of his intentions. To her surprise, however, he acknowledged neither Priscilla nor Thomas. Turning his back to them, he stretched his height to its full dimensions. To Priscilla's horror, he grasped the small hands of Frances. "When the dancing commences, Miss Frances, I should like to claim your hand for the first three. Will you do me this honor?"

The first three! Priscilla trembled. She glanced at Thomas anxiously, who returned her clouded gaze. Could Mr. Seymour harbor an interest in Frances? Priscilla cringed to note the manner in which he studied her sister. She recognized that glare. Mr. Seymour had flashed the same expression last Christmas—and the previous summer.

Frances, hiding behind her fan and gazing from underneath long eyelashes at Mr. Seymour, whispered an answer. "I am delighted, sir."

After the dancing had begun, Priscilla expressed her concern to Thomas. "Could it be possible that Mr. Seymour has taken a fancy to my sister? Or am I only swept away by agitated imaginings?"

"It is no act of imagination—only observation. It certainly looks as if Seymour means to pursue her."

"John Seymour boasts a smooth tongue but also the cleverness of a weasel and the cunning of a serpent. He will not entrap my sister. I will not allow it!" Priscilla vowed in a sharp whisper. "Do you think she reciprocates? Can you tell, Tom?"

Thomas glanced sideways at the pair with a stony gaze. "I do not know. Only time will reveal the truth. I do not like to fancy your sister—or any young woman with a grain of innocence and decency—within his clutches."

Priscilla espied her sister dancing and struggled to deduce the girl's thoughts from the candor of expression. The maiden's soft cheeks glowed crimson, but, in Priscilla's mind, this signified little. Such a modest girl as Frances, she reasoned, was destined to suffer discomfort upon her first encounter with male attention. Frances's eyes glistened with their usual serenity, but her small mouth curved into a coy smile, revealing deep dimples at each corner.

Priscilla wrestled with an impulse to forewarn Frances of Mr. Seymour's duplicity. After all, was she to remain silent as he embedded his hooks within her sister's soul? Still, a revelation of his villainy would necessarily entail a narrative that would require knowledge of the human heart's darker crevices—a knowledge that Frances utterly lacked. *She can scarcely comprehend that mankind is capable of folly, much less deceit,* thought Priscilla. Priscilla realized that such a lesson can only be learned by the loss of innocence, a loss as irrevocable as our first parents' expulsion from paradise.

Given these considerations, which haunted her for the remainder of the evening, Priscilla ultimately resolved to hold her tongue until fate either removed the threat posed by John Seymour or forced her into a painful discourse with Frances.

November swept into Williamsburg like an intruder. None desired the passage of time, for it inevitably brought distressing tidings. Priscilla, however, welcomed it. At such an hour, she was in need of an opportunity to watch her sister's dealings with Mr. Seymour. Did the girl manifest symptoms of love?

Priscilla had not long to ponder these riddles. Mr. Seymour called at the Parr House on several occasions following the party hosted by George Adams. At all three times, Frances was allowed—and encouraged—to receive him alone. The family guessed his intentions before the first visit was over.

Mr. Parr danced with delight as the family, having abandoned Frances to Mr. Seymour's company, assembled in the sitting room. "What a trophy our Frances has won!"

Mrs. Parr, embroidering a cap for baby Sarah, immediately frowned. "But she is so young."

"I must say—having John Seymour court two of my daughters is a great honor." Mr. Parr suddenly flashed a smug grin and rubbed his large hands together. "You know, Priscilla, you should not have driven him away. But for that saucy tongue, such good fortune might have been yours. You were outdone by your younger sister—ha!"

Priscilla swiftly glanced upward from a book which, in her agitation regarding Frances, she only pretended to peruse. "I am more than content with my present situation, Father."

Ben, who buried his head in the *Virginia Gazette*, managed a quiet rejoinder. "I hope Frances knows what she is about."

Mr. Parr sniffed in contempt. "It is high time she learns."

Priscilla noticed in the ensuing days that Frances seemed much more lighthearted than usual. A curious glow often tinged her soft cheek, particularly after she had been in the company of Mr. Seymour. Her eyes often glimmered like stars, particularly when they fixed themselves upon his face. She even spoke of him fondly. Priscilla was pained to notice that her sister melted beneath his gaze.

Priscilla, always cognizant of her changed relationship in regard to Thomas, confided in him with less reserve than ever before.

She opened her heart regarding her sister as she walked across the Palace Green on his arm one afternoon. "I cannot decide what to do. I cannot remain idle while she is taken in by his trickery. What does he want from her, Tom? We both know her to be a naïve and self-effacing girl. She has never even held a lengthy conversation with a man other than Ben and Father. Suddenly, John Seymour—rich, forceful, and, when he contrives to be so, charming—seeks her regard. Compounded with all these pressures, the family badgers her daily to accept his advances. This leads to an enormous amount of sentimental vulnerability. Seymour knows this. I believe she has already been deceived by the worthless dissembler. She encourages him!"

"Have you warned her of the danger she is in?" Thomas asked.

Priscilla sighed. "I would like to do so but am uncertain that she is prepared to hear of my own experience with Mr. Seymour."

"Perhaps you could tell her that you entertain grave doubts as to his character?"

As was her custom, Priscilla thought his counsel sensible and shrewd. Recognizing that her initial reticence had been an error, she proceeded to act upon his advice. Later that very afternoon, as the Parr family lingered lazily in the sitting room before dinner was announced, she purposely sat next to Frances in an isolated corner. Priscilla had already spent a few moments planning a tactful approach when Frances unexpectedly simplified the dilemma.

"I find Mr. Seymour to be the most excellent of men." Frances absently toyed with the ruffles on her sleeve. "He is courteous, handsome, witty, and unfailingly kind to me."

Priscilla shook her head uneasily. She could guess the likely direction of the coming dialogue and braced for the difficult task before her. "What are your feelings toward Mr. Seymour, Frances?"

Frances smiled as if harboring a precious secret. "I like him very much. In fact, I think I *love* him!"

Priscilla winced. The prospect of Frances devoting the love of her untested heart to this particular man revolted her. Mr. Seymour performed a flowery act, complete with all the devices of theatrical craft, and Frances's senses, so inexperienced with deception, were fully beguiled. Priscilla was compelled to caution Frances at once.

A quizzical stare displaced Frances's elation. "You are displeased?"

"It is my duty to warn you."

Frances leaned backward in surprise. "Warn me?"

"As you know, Mr. Seymour once paid court to me."

Frances nodded. "I remember."

"I know him well even from that brief period, which proved of sufficient duration to convince me entirely that he is not the man he seems."

"What do you mean, 'not the man he seems'?"

"He is consumed by arrogant cruelty, and he is not above manipulation."

"You must be mistaken. Not Mr. Seymour! I have heard no cross word from him since I have known him. He is a dear creature."

Priscilla measured her words and spoke slowly. "He may act the hero's part, but he is a dark man, such as you have never met with before."

"That cannot be so!" Frances's hand trembled upon her throat.

"I refuse to lie, Frances. It is indeed true. He is a selfish, proud being."

Frances averted her gaze in agitation. "This is not like you to speak so harshly of others. How can you be so certain of Mr. Seymour?"

Priscilla was floored by her sister's defiance. "It is no mistake! I know this man thoroughly."

When Frances glanced at Priscilla again, her eyes shone with tears. "How can you say such a thing?"

Priscilla, overcome by desperation, placed a warm hand over that of her sister. "You must believe me!"

"I beg your pardon." Frances wrenched free her hand. "I cannot think ill of him. I misjudged him once and shall not repeat the offense."

At that crucial moment, the servant entered and announced the completion of dinner preparations. Following this declaration, Mr. Parr and his family, save his two youngest daughters, left the sitting room in pursuit of the dining room. Frances rose with firm grace and fixed her glare upon Priscilla before sailing out of the room. "John Seymour is the finest man I have ever known."

This episode proved difficult for Priscilla to digest. The obstinacy evidenced by Frances, who had always proven so docile, was a new marvel. Priscilla, who had often wished to see more liveliness in her sister's manner, now longed for the days when Frances, thinking herself far too humble to voice an opinion, had submitted to her own advice in everything. These anxieties, as well as uncertainty concerning her present course, drove her back to Thomas's counsel.

She reopened the subject with him a few days later. "Frances would not heed my warnings."

"She wouldn't?" He froze with amazement.

Priscilla groaned. "She demonstrated no impartial mind when I confronted her. I have never seen stubbornness in Frances before. John Seymour has utterly duped her."

"My brother talked with Seymour only yesterday." Thomas's voice quavered with concern. "Apparently, Seymour confided that he means to propose before the month is out."

"Oh no!" Priscilla wailed in despair. "I feel I must tell her, with no ugly detail spared, of what I know regarding Seymour."

"That would be wise."

"I may break her dear little heart forever—and bruise her innocent mind."

"She will thank you for your forthrightness, I warrant. It is better that you expose Mr. Seymour's faults now than to have her discover them herself within the bonds of matrimony!"

Chapter 32

The Confrontation

In the second week of November, the expected evil news reached Williamsburg. The Boston Tea Party had been repeated—only closer to home. Two half-chests of tea imported by John Prentis & Company, a Williamsburg enterprise, had been cast into the York River near Yorktown, Virginia. Priscilla's father and the other older gentlemen snatched this fresh piece of news about which to quarrel. Thomas's anxiety escalated as the rebellion drew nearer. These tidings, it seemed to Priscilla, merely strengthened his staunch belief that the revolt would inevitably degenerate into war. She dreaded war worse than the last gasp of air she would draw upon the earth, for war would snatch him from her. The conflict battered her heart's hope. The storm gathered and would soon break loose. Its force threatened to shatter her sheltered world forever.

Amidst these worries, and perhaps because of them, Frances's peril weighed upon Priscilla's mind. Marshaling her courage, Priscilla considered the manner in which to best approach her sister. After much contemplation, she resolved upon a direct confrontation, though with lingering doubts regarding the suitability of that method.

One evening, she opened Frances's chamber door before the young girl slipped into slumber. She found Frances propped up by two particularly thick pillows, the remainder of her small frame nestled beneath the covers. Her long auburn hair woven into a thick braid, Frances had already changed into her silk nightgown.

Upon Priscilla's entrance, Frances was staring at the ceiling with a peculiar luster in her blue eyes. "Priscilla!"

"Dearest sister." Priscilla sat down upon the edge of the bed.

Frances answered Priscilla with her characteristic smiling, wide-eyed stare. "What troubles you tonight?"

"It was not my original intent to tell you this before, but circumstances have compelled me thus," Priscilla began with an equally solemn countenance. "It may be the only path to your heart. You are my sister and friend. Silence would violate my duty."

"What do you wish to tell me?" Frances brought her knees up to her chin.

"I wish to disclose my particular experience with Mr. Seymour."

Frances's childlike eagerness vanished in an instant, and she turned her face away from Priscilla. "No. We have discussed this once before."

"Please, Frances—you must hear me!"

"No. I do not wish to hear such things."

"I implore you, Frances! If not for your own sake, listen for mine."

Frances deliberated the choice carefully. Then, facing Priscilla once more, she gestured in permission. "Very well. I will listen."

Priscilla drew a deep breath and began her account. Endeavoring to recall and relate every particular, she spoke as placidly as possible. She searched for expression in Frances's face but found it blank. When Priscilla concluded her narrative, she awaited Frances's response.

At long last, Frances sat up quite rigidly. "Whatever his past, he must have changed. I know that he is now the dearest gentleman in the world. This has been *my* experience."

Priscilla strove to suppress her rising exasperation with Frances's implacability, and, though sensing the anger in her own voice, she did not shrink from a scene. "Men like Seymour do not change. He performs an act in order to ensnare your affections. He is cruel, clever, and very, very cunning. So he was, and so he is. So he will ever be!"

Frances's eyes searched those of her sister. "Why do you advise me so expressly against the dictates of my heart?"

"Our hearts must submit to the rule of our heads in some cases. We must heed the advice of those whom we respect. I view Mr. Seymour objectively, whereas your blind fancy will never allow an honest assessment of his character."

"You were led by your heart when you accepted Thomas Eton," Frances said coolly.

Priscilla reeled from her sister's sudden change of manner. *I can scarcely believe it—she means to defy me,* Priscilla thought. Was it possible that Seymour's hauteur had influenced her? Priscilla struggled to maintain her composure lest any symptom of weakness on her own part emboldened Frances. "Yes, but I was also led by my head. All those whom I respect approved of him. I can truthfully claim that we were first the best of friends. Can you say as much?"

"I know nothing – only that I will love John Seymour forever."

"Poor, naïve Frances!" Priscilla laughed in order to conceal her mounting angst. "You do not know not what love means."

"I know that John Seymour loves me."

Priscilla was overcome by a sudden terror. "You would not marry him, would you?"

Frances stared down at her small hands, which were trembling as they fingered the loose ends of her braid. "If ever he requests my hand, I shall accept him."

Priscilla's knuckles paled as she clutched the oaken bed post for support. "You cannot understand the magnitude of your own words! You propose to take a great burden upon yourself and purchase your own misery. Suppose you marry him! Once you are wed, *you belong to him.* Do you understand that, Frances? He will be your master! His true nature is certain to emerge. When your fancy for him ebbs, as it certainly will, you will see him as he truly is—a black-hearted villain who has deceived you. You will be left with only the shell of empty hopes for comfort. Small solace indeed—when you mourn your marriage and despise him more with each passing hour for the rest of your life! These woes will strangle the last breath from your tender soul. Do you realize that you choose servitude—and death?"

"Stop!" Frances covered her face. "A rift has never arisen between us, Priscilla. Why do you construct one now?"

"Do you think I would take such pains to rescue you from a good man—or even a decent one? Never!" Priscilla leapt to her feet in desperation. "You have been more like a child to me than a sister. All these years, I have advised you, guided you, and offered a shoulder upon which to pour all your grief. Are you resolved to disregard my counsel now—when your entire life hangs in the balance?"

Frances's eyes were swimming. "Only leave me to myself!"

With this final request, Frances collapsed, sobbing violently into her pillows. Priscilla wished to console her sister but decided that Frances was in no humor to be persuaded. After drawing the gauze bed curtains, Priscilla returned to her own chamber, which was situated next to that of Frances. For an hour that night, Priscilla heard the desperate sobs turn to muffled murmurs—then cease. Each sob assailed her fiercely maternal heart.

Priscilla could not suppress tears the following Sunday after church services as she related to Thomas her disastrous encounter with Frances. "The more I attempted to dissuade her, the more her resolution hardened."

"You have exhausted all alternatives, Priscilla. It is a tragedy to see Frances waste herself upon that cur!" Thomas drew her aside gently. "Nevertheless, every being must decide his or her fate—for good or ill."

"I beg your pardon!" Priscilla's mouth fell open in disbelief. "Would you have her marry that despicable tyrant?"

Thomas's color rose, but his voice remained unshaken. "You know very well that I would not. Still, you have warned her. She must choose her own path."

In her heart, Priscilla recognized the merit of his assertions. It seemed he always won her agreement, perhaps since he appealed to her upon grounds they both revered. Self-determination was, in her eyes, one of the premier virtues—the very antithesis of tyranny. She could not deny these values, and, by challenging her in so many forms, Thomas cultivated a burgeoning realization that the rebel—or in this case, the free individual—often bears the truest banner of both loyalty and conscience.

Chapter 33

The Unmasking

A few days following Priscilla's conversation with her sister, Mr. Seymour called upon the Parrs and requested a private audience with Frances once again.

The fears inspired in Priscilla by his arrival can well be imagined. Despite the sudden trepidation she suffered, she was not unprepared for this development. She had been expecting such a call for some time. Priscilla and the rest of her family removed themselves from the parlor, the former with great heaviness of heart. Leaving Frances to Mr. Seymour, they relocated to the sitting room, as was their custom.

Mr. Parr attempted to compose a business letter, but, after a few moments, he pounded his fist against the writing desk. "What on earth is that young man doing in there?"

"He is most likely asking her to marry him." Rosamund clasped her hands. "What a great lady she will be."

"Do not be so certain," Ivy said. "Mr. Seymour has called upon her before, and he has not yet proposed."

Priscilla suspected that Ivy resented the fact that Mr. Seymour had slighted her for two younger sisters.

"But that does not signify he will not do as much this time." Mr. Parr peered down the hall anxiously before returning to his chair at the desk. "What a glorious alliance! It seems our family shall receive a golden second opportunity after all."

Turning to Priscilla, Ivy smiled half-teasingly. "How shall you like it to live with the knowledge that you lost such a prize to a younger sister?"

"Quite easily." Priscilla was amazed by the fury that possessed her own voice. "Thomas Eton is a thousand times the man John Seymour will ever be."

"That is rather harsh." Ivy laughed in mock disbelief.

"I wonder how Frances likes Seymour." Mr. Parr strode to where Priscilla was sitting and towered over her. "You should know, Priscilla. She confides in you alone."

Her heart fell to reveal the truth. "I believe she is favorably disposed toward him."

Ivy tapped her foot. "What does that matter?"

"Ivy speaks truly." Ben rose and strolled to the window, where he observed the street's activity with a stony expression. "Love is a dangerous emotion—and one to be avoided like the plague. It ends in useless heartache."

Rosamund flinched a little at her husband's opinions. Priscilla, however, thought only of the peril at hand. She knew that Frances sat in the parlor, pledging her hand to Mr. Seymour at that very moment. Even though Priscilla suffered pangs of sorrow, she did not endure the aches of a burdened conscience. She had fulfilled her duty. Frances chose her fate without ignorance.

"I do not entirely favor this match." Mrs. Parr's voice suddenly wavered as if she held something back. "Girls do not even know themselves at fifteen. She is still a child in many ways."

At such a dark moment, Priscilla was somewhat surprised—and consoled—by her mother's reluctance to endorse the marriage. *Perhaps hope remained after all!*

Mr. Parr appeared vexed by his wife's qualms. "It is an opportunity, Bess. Surely you would not have her spurn it."

The voice of Frances suddenly shattered the subsequent silence.

"Father!"

Her relations bolted from the sitting room at the shout. They saw only Mr. Seymour, dashing out of the parlor, seizing his coat and hat, and slamming the front door as he exited the home. The dismayed party then proceeded to the parlor, where they beheld Frances, her eyes scarlet with weeping and her cheeks deathly pale.

Mr. Parr glared at his daughter. "What happened, child? Explain this spectacle at once."

"He proposed to me, and I refused him."

"Why did you shout?"

Frances's eyes fixed upon the floor. "He would not tolerate my refusal."

Mr. Parr's face reddened with rage. "Why did you reject his offer, Frances?"

"Please do not be angry with me." Frances suddenly fell at his feet as tears flowed freely. "I cannot bear it, Father. If only you had witnessed his conduct to me just now, you would have no daughter of yours accept him—*even for all the king's gold!*"

Priscilla could only smile through tears of relief. She raised her eyes toward heaven and silently expressed her boundless gratitude.

✦

Priscilla was destined to know more concerning this remarkable set of events. She received a surprise visit from Frances before she went to bed that evening. Frances entered the chamber, her dainty feet treading the floorboards with the airy lightness of a sprite. Her sister's entrance curtailed Priscilla's perusal of a book.

"Oh, Priscilla." Frances perched upon the foot of her sister's bed. "I am terribly sorry for flouting your advice regarding Mr. Seymour. Convinced that he loved me, I blinded myself to the truth. I see that now. Can you pardon me?"

Priscilla offered her sister a benevolent smile. "Of course."

"It will cause me great distress, but I must tell you of his churlishness this morning." Frances sighed, biting her lip. "The matter is far too weighty for concealment."

Priscilla swiftly closed her book. "I hoped you would bestow your confidence upon me."

"The family had hardly withdrawn from the room when Mr. Seymour began to exchange pleasantries. We entered into petty conversation for a few moments. Unexpectedly, he sank to his knee and said, 'Your beauty overwhelms me to senselessness. Your charms eclipse my every thought. Marry me! Take pity upon a poor man who suffers a great deal because you are not his wife.' As you may imagine, I could scarcely breathe! He is my first suitor—and far more passionate than I ever imagined men to be. He flattered my vanity, meager though it was.

"I was on the point of stating my compliance when a strange uneasiness afflicted me. I was struck by a mysterious awareness that this marriage would prove to be my undoing. Only God could have whispered this knowledge and inspired such terror in my heart. Your qualms weighed heavily upon me. With Mr. Seymour on his knees before me, however, I resisted the urge to reject him outright. Stating that such decisions as these deserve further time for consideration, I asked him to return at the same hour tomorrow. The lover's ardor faded. He seemed irritated and snarled, 'What is your intent, Frances? What is there to ponder? Have you not encouraged me with every word and look?' Yes, Priscilla, he used my Christian name—and in no affectionate tone! I replied that my sole desire was to be certain of my choice.

"He then became a transformed creature altogether. His gentle eyes burst into dark flames, and his soft expression warped into a glare. I was dismayed! He whispered, 'You will marry me, Frances! I will have no other way. I have besmirched my dignity in order to please you. You may never receive another offer!' My entire frame trembled, and his true character lay unmasked before me. The proper course, however, was then clear. I said, 'You have just revealed a facet of your character which cannot be overlooked. I cannot wed a man who speaks to me in this manner. Indeed, I am sorry.'

"When I had finished my speech, in which I was surprised by my own courage, he arrested my hands in his fearsome grip. His eyes pierced mine. I shall never forget that dreadful expression upon his face! His tirade still rings in my ears: 'You will not play games with me, Frances Parr. This family shall not deal falsely with me a second time. I am not a man to be trifled with. I bore the insult with your sister. I shall not be slighted again!' The strain proved too much for me. I wailed for him to stop. This plea did not subdue him in the least. He mocked me and shouted, 'How dare you refuse my fortune—all I have to offer! How dare *you* refuse *me*—John Seymour! You *will* be my wife, little wretch.'

"He severely hurt my hands. I was so frightened, Priscilla. I believed he would truly injure me lest I screamed for Father. This I did, and Mr. Seymour immediately leapt to his feet. 'Not a word of this to anyone! Do you hear?' He thus warned me. He hurried from the room, and the next thing I heard was the front door closing. I then saw the faces of my family, demanding to know every particular."

Priscilla could only stare in shock at the conclusion of Frances's account. "He tormented you and insulted our family! I knew he was a devious man, but not quite that fiendish."

"He is the very knave of which you cautioned me—and much worse." Frances hung her head. "I am only relieved to have escaped his clutches."

"Why did you not relate these details to Father?"

"I feared Father's reaction."

Priscilla smiled. "You may be right, for there is no telling what he would do to Seymour with that fiery temper. He might really murder the cad!"

"That is true."

Priscilla studied her sister compassionately. "Poor little dear. Is your heart broken?"

"I am ashamed to have been so misguided." Tears welled in Frances's eyes.

"Do not be so glum. Only rejoice that his faults were unmasked *before* you married him."

Frances sighed sorrowfully. "Yet how wrong I was to doubt you."

"Your courage was extraordinary. Nurture it! We must always heed those who advise us, particularly those whom we respect."

"I understand. Thank you for everything."

"Enough of this gloom! Time for sleep now."

"Good night, Priscilla."

"Good night, Frances. Rest well."

Frances left as quietly as she had come.

And Priscilla slept soundly that night.

Frances was out of danger.

Chapter 34

The Holiday

It did not seem to Priscilla that December should so soon recur, for much had taken place in the colonies and in the Parr household since the last winter had passed.

For Priscilla, it was the happiest epoch of her life.

Thomas Eton was the light of every hour, her dearest friend, and the love that burned more brilliantly every day within her heart. Despite the cool judgment of which she had always boasted, her mind dwelled upon him every moment. Scarcely had she sought and found a new purpose to which she might divert her thoughts did memories of his boyish grin, his deep voice, his gentle manner, and those striking eyes pierce her heart with redoubled force. She knew full well that he would attend the College of William and Mary the following autumn. Still, the delay did not yet torment her. If she only contemplated their future happiness, Priscilla reasoned, the years would pass more swiftly.

Priscilla had also established a pleasant rapport with her new sister-in-law. Rosamund had always been Frances's dear friend, but now they grew even closer. The three girls—Priscilla, Rosamund, and Frances—shared many common bonds. They were regarded as sensible young women and were very near to one another in age. Priscilla was not long in developing a high respect for Rosamund, whose easy temper she had always admired. Rosamund's perceptive nature, however, was masked by a childish manner. She skipped about the house playfully, singing with innocent openness.

It did not seem to pain Rosamund that her new husband, now nearing twenty-seven years of age, did not adore her. She occupied herself by showering her infant stepdaughter, whom she treated as a costly porcelain doll, with love and attention. She cared for the child as her own. By showering the infant Sarah with affection, by clinging to practicality, and by keeping company with her two youngest sisters-in-law, Rosamund was able to tolerate her husband's coldness. Priscilla always hoped that Rosamund would win Ben's love and respect in time. She also believed that Rosamund, whose own heart was far from insensitive, would soon come to smart at his neglect.

Christmas 1774 thus proved to be a very different sort of holiday.

Tension was on the rise in Williamsburg. Men were quicker to assign sinister motives to one another, even in cases where none existed. The Tories struck openly against the rebels. Among Mr. Parr's closest friends, ever deepening divisions appeared. Phillip Parr and John Lee were Tories. They were inflexible men who remained loyal to the Crown and looked with horror upon the sedition surrounding them. Fiery men touting utopian ideals of freedom for all, Richard Eton and George Adams sympathized with the rebels. Even these old friends, now keeping their own counsel, glanced over their shoulders at one another with a degree of suspicion.

The Christmas Ball offered Priscilla ample opportunity to observe the rifts that had been driven between friends—both old and new. Perennial friendships were withering. Jane and Harriet Adams were kept away from the Parr girls by the formerly genial but now prejudiced George Adams, who feared that his daughters' associations might taint his own revolutionary pedigree. Even long-term fancies perished. Ivy and Margaret, two young ladies who would once have attempted any number of ridiculous feats in order to lure William Eton, avoided him as much as possible. The Seymours, however, endured little transition in this regard. It was no change at all for them to simply avoid those whom they did not care to acknowledge. Priscilla was inwardly grateful that Mr. Eton had not resorted to a similar level of irrationality. Without Thomas, she knew not how to bear these vicissitudes. Drawing upon his strength had become a natural inclination.

The ball also stirred old reflections that had been intolerable in past months but were not unpleasant in that pleasant hour.

"This time last year, I believed I had lost you...and how my heart pined for you!" Priscilla whispered to Thomas during the reel.

This confession drew a warm hue to his cheeks. "And this dance is far belated. I almost struck the smirk off Seymour's face when he steered you away from me! In this room, I first understood that I loved you."

Priscilla, intoxicated with joy, could not look upon the ballroom—the site of her humiliation the previous year—without a sensation of triumph. Nevertheless, as in each hour of great happiness, when a man struggles to verify that no ploy of fate may blight his present ecstasy, so did Priscilla, protective of her bliss, ponder the prophesies of doom that had long agitated the Williamsburg citizenry. "I could never lose you now."

"You know, my love, there may come a time when..."

"Please do not speak of it, Tom!" Priscilla's eyes suddenly moistened. "I cannot bear it. Do not mar this lovely evening with such talk."

For a moment, silence lingered between them as the dance progressed. As in all times when he descended into troubled thoughts, the musculature of Thomas's jaw convulsed. Priscilla, immediately cognizant of his distress, regretted her outburst, if only for the pain it had occasioned him—and for the disappearance of the grin that had grown so precious to her.

She resurrected their conversation with a quick glance about the room. "What a tragedy to behold these breaches of friendship! It seems that our fathers are not as intimate as they once were."

"I notice it all too painfully." He gave her a troubled look. "What a disheartening sight—to see people who have been friends for many a difficult year become as enemies! That is an inevitable misfortune of life. When principles are at stake, friendship is always sacrificed."

"Cannot people agree to differ peacefully?"

"*That* is a rare accomplishment." Thomas suddenly grinned. "This is a reversal indeed! Now *you* have become the idealist and I the pragmatist."

Priscilla noticed that Mr. Seymour ignored Frances as well as the entire Parr family, save her father. What would once have enraged Priscilla merely conferred relief. Frances had barely escaped that scheming creature, and Priscilla wished him as far away from her sister as possible. Indeed, she wished her entire family to be eternally safe from his menacing clutches.

Priscilla also rejoiced that Frances seemed to take the disappointment in good part. Some vital part of Frances, however, had altered. The youthful ignorance had vanished, perhaps forever. Rivers of innocent flattery no longer poured from her lips. She was now more mindful of her words and manner, and Priscilla celebrated this transformation.

With these characteristics, however, Frances had acquired a touch of general distrust. Although her natural gentleness of heart remained, a shade of doubt had darkened her bright blue eyes. Priscilla bemoaned the fact that this doubt had destroyed Frances's purity of mind. An air of gravity now hung over the girl like a veil. This increased degree of judgment, however, did result in a benefit. Priscilla had previously hidden some matters from Frances for fear that she had not the maturity to comprehend their import. Priscilla could now reveal much to Frances without fearing an unwise interpretation.

At the ball, Ben danced twice with his child-bride. His motives, however, were purely objective. In the past month or so, Dr. Lee had hotly expressed his conviction, in the hearing of many friends, that his daughter was neglected by her husband, Benjamin Parr. Ugly gossip was beginning to circulate. These rumors reached the ear of Phillip Parr, who feared the condemnation of all his acquaintances. In Priscilla's hearing, he ordered his son to pay more heed to Rosamund at public gatherings. Ben submitted to his father's demands but failed to remedy his indifference to Rosamund in private. Priscilla, however, never forgot that Rosamund was a girl of only fifteen years and quite young to be burdened by such apathy in her marriage. Rosamund, however, seemed to understand her high-strung and bitter husband, and, at the first, she braved his frostiness in exceptionally good spirits.

In contrast to the ball, Christmas was a tame occasion in the Parr household this year. Phillip Parr's aunt, Mary Laurence, visited for several days as usual. Priscilla, it seemed, was thrown together with her aunt quite frequently during the course of the holiday.

The elderly woman, each of her knotted knuckles adorned by jewels of a different tone, opened a welcome subject one morning as Priscilla prepared to paint her likeness. "I was delighted to learn of your engagement to that excellent young man."

"I thank you, Aunt Laurence." Priscilla smiled as she measured out the oils. "I think myself blessed indeed."

Mrs. Laurence's large round cheeks, strangely bereft of lines for a woman of her age, bounced as she laughed. "You have my approval for that enterprise."

"I am glad of that."

"His mother visits me often. Augusta's a dear lady. And her husband as well—in his own way, of course. You know he is only four years younger than me, do you not? Richard Eton resided here when I left my pedestal atop English society in order to journey to these colonies. My brother came also with his wife and son—your dear father. But, of course, you know that story well enough already." The jewels, catching sunlight streaming in from the window, glinted as she waved her hand. "Richard was only eighteen at the time. He was touching upon thirty years when he married Augusta. She was nineteen then, if I recall, and such a pretty little thing. Rachel was the very image of her mother but thirty years before. It pains me that Rachel was taken at so youthful and promising an age. Her memory, it seems, hangs like a shadow over Benjamin."

The matriarch became quiet, compelling Priscilla to glance up from her work. She sat staring at the floor with a grave expression, so much so that Priscilla thought tears might fall from her eyes in another moment. The older woman's bosom heaved before, drawing out a handkerchief, she dabbed her eyes.

Priscilla, overcome with tenderness and vulnerable to tears herself, abandoned her canvas and rushed to condole with Mrs. Laurence. "You are very much in the right, dear Aunt. I wish it were not so. I hope to remonstrate with him soon."

Mrs. Laurence shook her head and grimaced. "Tread gently, child. He has been dealt a great blow." Her voice broke as she enclosed Priscilla's smooth hand within her crooked one. "In my sixty-five years, I have learned that one cannot wield too much caution when dealing with the whims of human sentiment."

Chapter 35

The Remonstration

Before Priscilla realized it, Christmas had passed. January also quickly vanished. Mary Laurence returned to her house down the street, where, despite her advancing age, she always insisted to live alone.

The situation in the colonies could scarcely be worse. Some boasted that Britain could not refuse colonial demands, particularly noting the conventions assembled the previous year. Others, like Mr. Parr, insisted that no matter how ferociously the colonies protested, the king and his Parliament would never yield since the rights they upheld were ancient, married to precedent, with history as their basis—and thus were far more sacred than the grumbling of subjects who loathe to pay taxes to their lord.

In such times as these, the pleasures and dilemmas of domestic life, no matter how mundane, provide a welcome distraction. In this way, the Parr family was briefly diverted by an intriguing morsel of news delivered by Henry and Katherine Adams during this hour of rising political tension. As the guests were announced one icy morning, Priscilla smiled to see her friend once more. She had not often been in company with Katherine lately, for the latter proved to be an attentive wife. Katherine's visits had thus fallen few and far between. Priscilla reasoned that the couple must possess a great deal of tidings to call in such austere weather.

As Katherine entered behind her husband, Priscilla rushed to greet her. "How lovely it is to see you again! We have been far too long absent from one another."

Katherine's cheeks glowed with pleasure. "I have missed you also, Priscilla."

"It does not seem that you should be married, Kate." Priscilla sighed. "Why, I remember when you, Thomas, and I scampered upon the Palace Green—free from care!"

"So can I." Katherine's eye seemed to wander back to those days. "Time has certainly elapsed."

"Hasn't it, though?"

"Yes. That was a wonderful era."

"Those days are lost forever, you know."

The emotions shared between the two girls waxed fiercely poignant. Each well understood that her beloved might be slain in the catastrophe that approached in the burgeoning flames of colonial rebellion. Priscilla recalled those dreamy days of their childhood with bittersweet pangs. Their lives had changed tremendously since that faraway period of innocence. In the course of a single year, lighthearted joys had suddenly given way to the heartrending anxieties of adulthood.

Katherine then excused herself and turned to greet her sister Rosamund with a kiss to each cheek.

Henry suddenly addressed his wife. "Now, Kate, shall we deliver our news?"

Katherine broke into a fanfare of giggles. "I could not rob you of the pleasure even if I wished."

Awaiting this revelation with impatient curiosity, the entire Parr family leaned forward.

Henry grinned at his wife and stood before the small audience. "Father just received word this morning that Seymour's uncle in Philadelphia has died. His fortune, as you may be aware, is large."

Numerous gasps fluttered about the room. Gripping the arm of his chair for support, Mr. Parr appeared particularly stunned.

Katherine's manner suggested that she herself had still not recovered from amazement. "The even greater astonishment is that this morning, after he was informed of his uncle's death, Seymour rushed to my father's house and proposed marriage to my sister Margaret. They are to wed next week. Their plans are to depart for Philadelphia immediately afterwards. After Mr. Seymour claims his fortune, they shall return to his plantation."

Priscilla could hardly believe this turn of events.

Mr. Parr glowered with unconcealed anger upon Priscilla and Frances. His mouth twitched violently, as if restraining his rage in front of the guests was intolerable. To think that Mrs. Seymour might have come from among them. To think that they had received two opportunities for such an honor. To think that Priscilla and Frances had both scorned this golden prospect! These, Priscilla deduced, were his thoughts toward her.

Her face changing color rapidly, Ivy stamped her foot. "If he can be happy with that spoiled child, then let him be gone!" Covering her face with her hands, she then flew from the room in a great temper and bitter tears.

Priscilla did not even flinch at the redoubled attack of furious stares. She maintained her countenance. Frances lowered her eyes, and Priscilla could not discern her sentiments. Henry and Katherine appeared to sense the emotions smoldering within the room, for they soon glanced uncomfortably at one another. Katherine's eyes suggested to her husband that they should perhaps leave. Henry nodded his assent.

In the week following the visit afforded by the young Adamses, Phillip—and even Ben—Parr waxed cold and uncommunicative toward Priscilla and Frances. Ivy's bitterness, however, reached a particularly painful zenith. She was even heard to moan, with indignant tears in her eyes, "If only he had paid his addresses to me! I would *never* have refused his offer."

Despite lingering resentments, the wedding date for John Seymour and Margaret Lee arrived with haste. The Parr family attended the ceremony, but only for the sake of appearances. Priscilla remained content throughout the event. She remembered that Mr. Seymour had admired the vain Margaret once before. He had even once suggested her as a model for Priscilla's own character!

This proved an instance of human folly for Priscilla to consider in the days to come. In her view, these two individuals performed their act to perfection, but both were villainous frauds. Each had schemed to secure the other. Priscilla had no doubt that, once wed, their natural selfish inclinations would collide. *After all,* she whimsically thought, *one cannot mingle fire with gunpowder and expect anything less than an explosion!*

Following the departure of Mr. Seymour, his child-bride, and his sister from Williamsburg, Priscilla was left with a trouble that distressed her exceedingly.

To Priscilla's surprise, Rosamund had shown no disdain toward her sisters-in-law for refusing Mr. Seymour.

"I might have once condemned you both, but not at this moment." Rosamund had swept back a wayward strand of hair from her face before lowering her stepdaughter into the cradle one morning. "I have learned that wealth and prominence do not ensure a worthy husband."

Priscilla, who had accompanied her sister-in-law to the nursery in order to see the child, had first attempted to hold her tongue. This sad confession, however, had moved her. Sudden anger at her brother's conduct had arisen upon glimpsing the deep well of pain in Rosamund's eyes. This fury had conquered discretion, and Priscilla had said, "I will speak to Ben. 'Tis shameful that he is so cruel!"

"I beg you will not, Priscilla," Rosamund had replied while learning over to rock the cradle. "I must maintain my wits. That is all."

Remembrance of the scene plagued Priscilla as she now strolled in the garden behind the Parr house one chilly February afternoon. She knew that she risked contracting a cold by emerging in such temperatures, but her need for solitude eclipsed all other qualms.

She despaired that Ben's heart was broken, but she also mourned the fact that he did not even respect his new wife. Despite Rosamund's plea to the contrary, Priscilla was planning the proper opportunity to speak with him when suddenly, she sensed a hand resting upon her shoulder.

She turned to see her brother.

His eyes startled her with their desolate gleam. "You should not go forth in this weather."

"I know." Priscilla considered how best to proceed.

Ben extended his arm to support her. "Very well, then, I shall stroll with you."

They walked on for a few moments without a word exchanged. Priscilla sensed that his indignation toward her concerning the Seymour affair had run its course. She glanced observantly at him. His eyes appeared to glimpse some faraway, intangible scene, rocked by the tempests of his heart's anguish.

His voice, ravaged by this desperate malady of soul, quavered. "I remember when I used to traverse this divine haven on many an afternoon…with Rachel."

"You cherished that, did you not?"

"Indeed." Ben's voice faded into a strained whisper. "I count those days among the happiest of my life."

"Your new wife also loves this garden. I have often seen her here." Priscilla turned to face him slowly. "She would be most honored, I am certain, to walk with you here as well."

Ben's features suddenly hardened. His jaw twitched violently, and the melancholy in his eyes was consumed by a dark energy. "No."

"Can you not reserve a small place in your heart for her?"

"That is not possible."

"She holds the right of a wife to be loved."

"She fulfills her purpose, Priscilla. Her kindness to my child pleases me. I expect that, in time, she will furnish me with a son. I am satisfied with our present arrangement. Furthermore, I believe it suits her."

Priscilla could not suppress the sarcasm that crept into her tone. "How could coldness and neglect suit any woman?"

"What?" Ben's gait jerked to a halt. "You cannot stand before me, Priscilla, and declare that Rosamund Lee loves me. *Her* heart is untouched. She wished to marry the same affluence into which she was born. She is like every other ambitious girl—a cold, scheming mercenary!"

"Perhaps she entered into the union on those grounds." Priscilla steadied her gaze. "I doubt, however, that she expected such incivility from *you*."

"Incivility? What would she have me do? Kiss her feet? She does not understand the agony I suffer every hour."

"She desires respect. Is that an unreasonable hope?"

"I do respect her. She is a pleasant girl, and, under different circumstances, I might well learn to like her. I certainly wish her no harm."

"Your behavior to her is guided by the basest cruelty and selfishness! It is sheer insolence."

He flashed an accusatory glare, and, for a moment, Priscilla feared that he might strike her. "You do me injustice, Priscilla. It would not be the first time. You never liked Rachel—and once warned me against her!" A wave of pain suddenly contorted his features. "I *do* respect Rosamund in my own peculiar manner, but she will never be my beloved. My love lies beneath the earth of Bruton Parish cemetery!"

Though stung by his reproach, Priscilla continued with even greater forcefulness than before. "Rachel's body may there rest, but her soul is at peace. Four months ago, you chose a girl—a mere child—with whom to spend the remainder of your days. Your choice was freely made—by your own will. Rosamund did not seek your favor. You offered it! If you cannot adore her, at least honor her as your wife—for her sake and for your own."

Ben's eyes glistened for the misery within, and his voice choked with feeling. "I *cannot* care for her! It is hopeless! Every hour, day and night, I see Rachel. I see her eyes—so beautiful in life—tormenting me in death! At night, I pretend she is there, but the bleak truth returns. She haunts my every deed, my every word, even my every thought! I cannot forget her. I never *shall* forget her. Even as I lay dying, I shall see her—smiling so mysteriously at me. Don't torture a man so near to madness that it breathes upon him!"

With a fierce look, Ben turned upon his heel and stormed down the path toward the house, slamming the garden gate shut as he went.

Priscilla pulled her wrap tightly around her shoulders as the merciless wind blew about her face—and her soul.

Chapter 36

The Riot

February and March proved uneventful. Little news escaped the maelstrom brewing in Boston. Priscilla's heart lightened, for lack of tidings, she reasoned, could only portend good.

Thomas was not so sanguine. "The crisis may subside for the moment. A storm, however, may only be increasing in strength, preparing for eruption any day."

Perhaps not even Thomas, however, could have foreseen the magnitude of that storm.

A distinct clamor outside the window stirred Priscilla from her sleep in the early morning of April 21, 1775. Even the sun had not risen. Still dazed by her sudden awakening, she was struck by a piercing thump that seemed strangely near. The sound of drums! This realization brought her upwards in the bed as fear seized her. Pitching back the covers, she sprang to the window of her chamber and threw it open.

The scene below nearly stifled her breath. Utter chaos greeted Priscilla. Still dressed in their nightgowns, countless citizens of Williamsburg poured out of their homes. Men gripped their rifles as the restless glow of torches illuminated the dark street below. Out the people rushed as their feverish cries escalated in both volume and frequency. Brandishing their weapons and torches, the masses had been stirred. Nearly all the windows lining the street were pushed open. Young women like herself leaned over the window frames, surveying the riot with horror. Most observed the scene for only a moment before disappearing—presumably to join the madness.

The shouts were deafening.

"Filthy redcoats!"

"We can't let him get away with it!"

"Dunmore! He'll suffer for this!"

"We must stop them!"

"Come on, men!"

As Priscilla overlooked the street, she went unnoticed. She was a mere spectator to this anarchy. Thoughts soared through her mind like formerly caged birds, nearly as ferocious and dizzying as the uproar in the street below.

She could not hope to determine the cause of this tumult from her present position. The drums signified some momentous incident that had ignited the hearts and wills of the townspeople in the dead of night. The air had been drenched by such a plethora of rumors in the past year or so that she would be surprised at nothing.

Oh—for the din! She could barely think.

She then heard a general rustling in the hallway. The roar, she realized, had also roused her family from slumber. She deserted the window for the hallway, where she found her father, mother, sisters, brother, and sister-in-law assembled. Their faces were blank with terror.

Mr. Parr rubbed his eyes drowsily. "What is going on down there? What is that frightful noise?"

Mrs. Parr's eyes were wide with dread. "I cannot fathom it."

Ben's stance shifted, as if in eager anticipation. "Let us see, Father."

The entire family descended the stairs, rushed down the central hall, and scurried out the front door.

When they all reached the front lawn, Mr. Parr turned and lifted his palm before the ladies. "Remain here."

He and his son ventured closer to the street. Mr. Parr stopped one of the throng by grasping the lad's coat. He turned the young man around. A spark of dumbfounded recognition ignited both their countenances.

It was Thomas Eton!

Ben held his head in disbelief. "Thomas!"

"What is this, lad?" Mr. Parr seized Thomas by the collar. "Speak without delay!"

Priscilla, standing several paces behind them, was forced to strain her ears in order to overhear his explanation, so thunderous were the shouts surrounding them.

Thomas heaved for breath in excitement. "The redcoats are attempting to steal gunpowder from the Magazine!"

Ben squinted in the torchlight. "Who gave them access?"

"Dunmore—*the tyrant!* This is all his doing." Thomas freed himself from Mr. Parr's stranglehold.

Mr. Parr's eyes narrowed with interest. "Why do *you* join this mob?"

"We must stop them, sir! They *mock* our liberties!" Thomas, not at all cowed by the older man's disapproval, drew himself up to his full height.

A livid glance of meaning passed between them before Phillip Parr, turning on his heel, returned to the house without another word, leaving both Ben and Thomas upon the street staring after him.

Priscilla would never forget the gaze Thomas next flashed toward her—a torn look of longing, mingled with pain and fury, such as she had not seen from him before. It afflicted her powerfully, and, as a valiant emotion awoke in her breast, she yearned to run toward him.

Despite these sudden feelings, her own fears were drowned in the turmoil—and the calls for vengeance. The sinister glow from the torches blinding her dazed eyes, Priscilla was convinced that she would never behold a more unsettling night.

***

The days following the infamous riot were likewise troubled and disorderly. The militiamen, who had drilled perpetually of late, were mustered. As men between the ages of sixteen and sixty, Phillip Parr and Ben were required to serve in the militia. Both were horrified when the group was ordered to assemble.

"If they assume I shall defy Dunmore, who acted as any loyal servant of the Crown should, they are mistaken!" Mr. Parr's eyes blazed over the breakfast table.

"But *you* must, Ben." Rosamund gazed at her husband pleadingly. "Else, you will be fined."

Ben retorted with a scornful smirk. "We shall pay the fine!"

"What is the commotion? I cannot understand what has so enraged the seditionists." Mr. Parr dusted his mouth with his napkin in an angry flourish. "Dunmore was removing the gunpowder from their reckless hands. They are like disobedient children, assailing those who would shield them from peril."

"Have you heard, Father, that Mr. Henry has mustered volunteers from Hanover County?" Ben's voice ascended with emotion.

"Patrick Henry. Bah!" Mr. Parr sneered at the name. "The ever-busy troublemaker! They say that he delivered the most impudent speech in Richmond at the second convention—a mere month ago."

At this final sentiment, the family grew silent. The second convention for Virginia had been organized since Britain still refused to submit to the demands of the colonies. The most vocal colonists, it seemed, were in no temper for intimidation.

Priscilla broke the uncomfortable silence. "When is this to cease, Father?"

"I do not know." Mr. Parr, his shoulders slumped, looked like a broken man.

As fate would decree, Patrick Henry led Hanover County volunteers toward the capital. Payment or the return of the gunpowder was harshly demanded. With all other alternatives lost to him, the governor finally agreed to pay for the gunpowder. The true disturbance, however, would appear a few days afterward when the Lees invited the Parrs, the Etons, and the Adamses to dinner in early May. All gathered for a delightful evening of gossip, laughter, amusement, and lively discourse.

Upon her arrival, Katherine Adams seemed troubled by her sister Rosamund's appearance, marked as it was by a pallid aspect and unsmiling lips. The girl's naturally lively spirits were subdued. Rosamund was unhappy and, in Priscilla's opinion, had come to regard her marriage as a grievous error. After Katherine finished conversing with Priscilla before dinner, the former spent a great many moments speaking quietly with Rosamund.

Thomas had lately been occupied with training for the militia. The rigors of the drill had noticeably fortified his resolve and heightened his courage. The contours of his face were hardened by the discipline and emboldened by the challenge. He retreated further and further into his books—and his ideals. An enigmatic, distant stare now haunted his eyes to the point where Priscilla often despaired of penetrating his moral seclusion. Such thoughts visited her frequently, particularly when she encountered him during this memorable festivity.

When she glimpsed his tall form advancing toward her, she abandoned the harpsichord she had been playing and rose to greet him. "I have missed you of late!"

"And I, you. Tell me that some gallant has not stolen your heart from me!" A mischievous spark leapt in his eye as he kissed her hand. Leading Priscilla toward the nearest sofa, he sat down next to her.

"You know that is impossible." Priscilla blushed with gratitude for this hint of his former gaiety. Then, adjusting the lace on her petticoat with trembling fingers, she asked, "How do matters stand with the rebellion? I know you have been reading the papers."

"They are worse than ever. They are more than worse—war is upon us." He lowered his voice to a grim whisper. "There will be no peaceful compromise, Priscilla."

Hopelessness washed over her. "Why not?"

"This rift has passed beyond all hope of reconciliation."

"You cannot join this madness, Thomas!"

His countenance became firm—and deeply troubled. "I thought you understood what I must do. I am destined—nay, *determined*—to fight, Priscilla, and have always said so. How can you not have known this?"

Although he reached for her hand, Priscilla, turning away from him, fought back tears at his reproachful words, which seemed all the more reproachful in their gentle delivery. "I cannot understand your reasons!"

So flowed the discourse on this occasion—candid and heartfelt—as Priscilla remained unaware of the momentous jolt that awaited them all. A courier arrived at the Lee house, and a letter was handed to Dr. Lee at dinner. This arrival was regarded with little interest at first, for much conversation prevailed. The dismal expression that colored Dr. Lee's countenance, however, finally silenced the room.

George Adams spoke first. "What is the matter?"

His brow shaded by concern and his lips quivering, Dr. Lee folded the letter with much uneasiness. "I have just received news of great import."

The entire room seemed to freeze with anxiety. Priscilla scarcely dared breathe. A sense of dread took hold. Only death, she thought, could have inspired this degree of solemnity.

Visibly shaken, Dr. Lee resumed his speech in a grave tone. "Battles have erupted in Massachusetts. I do not know particulars, but it seems a confrontation occurred between His Majesty's soldiers and the local militia in Massachusetts—at the towns of Concord and Lexington. Casualties were suffered. As to number, I cannot say."

A heavily silence shrouded the dining room. Priscilla's heart felt as if it would burst with anguish. Thomas's face was overcast with a knowing sorrow. From the first, she realized, he had known that this day would come. He had sensed its advent as one detects the tremors foretelling an earthquake. At that moment, she could view the future stretched before her to the horizon. She would be forced to part with him soon. He would join this conflict. Of that, she was certain. Her heart pounded with the stark realization…

War had begun!

Chapter 37

The Decision

The very foundations of Williamsburg were rocked by the news that hostilities between Britain and her colonies had begun in earnest. Shouts of zealous enthusiasm rang from one quarter while cries of angry distress resounded from another. The Parr and Lee families, in particular, uttered the latter exclamation. Staunch Tories, the patriarchs of both households were shocked, enraged, and shattered. Denial had become a mockery now that the rebels were on an unalterable and deadly rampage. They would stop at nothing. With heavy hearts, these two men acknowledged the grievous truth.

Their old friends, George Adams and Richard Eton, supported the cause of the rebels, which was fast becoming a war bound to something greater—liberty and respect for the rights of man. A great breach had been wrought between these four men, who held equally implacable convictions. None of them wished to recognize the chasm, but it remained inevitable. The Etons and the Parrs, however, still maintained a degree of closeness embodied by Sarah Parr, their mutual progeny. Nonetheless, the intimacy that had previously flourished between the two families had cooled. All seemed to forget the engagement of Thomas and Priscilla.

Priscilla had been stunned by news of the battles. Numerous anxieties beset her mind. Would the two families still honor the betrothal? Would Thomas be slain in this approaching conflict? All her distress was multiplied a thousand times by the staggering announcement her father made the following day at dinner.

Mr. Parr rose rather unexpectedly from his chair, his meal only half-consumed. "I have something of utmost significance to say."

The tone of his voice induced everyone at the dinner table to lay down their forks. They listened with all possible attention, their eyes keen with interest.

Mr. Parr gripped the back of his chair for strength. "For the past year, I have conducted a correspondence with our cousin, Sir Henry Blount. I have lately begun to fear that blood would be shed in this present crisis—and that an armed revolt would result. Months ago, I sought and procured Sir Henry's consent that we might claim his hospitality should any conflict erupt. Contrary to what we had all hoped, or even believed, the day of decision is upon us. Neutrality is now futile. I fear that war has indeed begun."

Ben lifted his hand in dissent. "It is unlikely that these skirmishes will continue. After all, how long would this rabble persist with redcoats upon their heels?"

Mr. Parr would only shake his head. His large eyes shining, he seemed to wrestle with his own emotions. His hand, resting upon the chair, trembled ever so slightly. Priscilla knew that her father at last realized the dark truth.

"No. There will be war, and our presence here might imperil our lives. We are well-known supporters of the Crown. As such, we would be the first to taste a rope about our necks. My mind upon this matter is fixed. I shall not be dissuaded." Mr. Parr breathed deeply, presumably in order to maintain his composure. "We leave this house and sail for Britain at the end of the month."

Faces turned ashen in one accord as a series of gasps escaped the room's occupants.

Mr. Parr took advantage of the heavy silence that followed. "Upon our arrival, we journey to Kent to meet Sir Henry and Lady Blount. We shall reside there until we can find a suitable house, either in London or in the country."

Priscilla's attention was drawn by a small clamor to her right as Frances slumped forward in her chair. Though revived by the attentions of Mrs. Parr as well as sips of water from Priscilla's own cup, Frances awoke from her swoon in a state of nervous energy, as manifested by her wild eyes and tearful sulks.

The entire family vacillated between fear and amazement for nearly a fortnight. They whispered little amongst themselves, for their pondering was weighty. All remained too astounded to maintain their usual airs. Upon each Parr countenance instead roamed a gaze of listless confusion—like that of lost, wandering lambs.

No one's inner tumult, however, could have exceeded that of Priscilla. Anxiety, sharpened by shock, pounded upon her heart like a hammer, never relenting for an instant. Never in the history of her life had she been hurled into such consternation. Following her father's announcement, even as Frances had recovered, Priscilla had sat trembling, feeling her lips grow white as a December frost. All life and color had drained from her soul, and she was unable to eat for days. This development shed an entirely different perspective upon the direction of her life, for, if she departed for England as her father desired, she could never marry Thomas.

In the fog that had descended upon her mind, Priscilla resolved to reason with her father. She could not leave Thomas! Her love for him never burned so clearly as that hour, when she realized that she would lose him forever. She wished to meet him—to whisper her love into his ear once more.

She saw him less frequently now. With the estrangement between his family and hers deepening every day and with the now continual practice of the militia, their encounters had become rare and precious. *She could not leave him!* She would have enjoyed more time to deliberate this great question had the departure date been set in the more distant future. As matters stood, she was given less than a month to chart the course of her future life.

Mr. Parr was bending over paperwork when Priscilla, her cheeks raw from weeping, entered his study.

"Father."

With this tender address, he glanced upward. His eyes seemed to pierce her with particular intensity.

"I must speak with you, Father." She struggled to maintain the evenness of her voice.

"You need not tell me." He removed his spectacles in rehearsed fashion. "I have known this interview would come."

"Father, I cannot leave."

An expression of pain twisted his features. "It is rare to find a lad less given to vain pursuits than Thomas Eton. I have always thought so—else, I would never have consented for him to wed my dearest child. Still, I underestimated his treasonous fervor—and that of his father. In truth, he is the very sort of youth against whom I once warned you!"

The mention of that interview, in which she vowed to shun those who dared lift up their sword in rebellion, stung Priscilla. She was struck by the imprudence of such a promise, extracted from her before she had tasted the bitterness and ecstasy of love, as well as the reversal to which she was now driven.

After examining her expression for some moments, Mr. Parr resumed his address in a firmer tone than before. "War is thrust upon us, calling us away from our truer lives. Fidelities deeper than fancy steer our paths, and sacrifice will test us. This is no age for doubt—all shall stand on one side or the other. Will you stand with *me*?"

"I shall not choose between principles, Father!" Priscilla threw up her hands in desperation. "Rather, would you have me leave my soul behind?"

"The soul is not so easily abandoned." Mr. Parr scoffed. "After all, England is not bereft of handsome faces."

She labored hard to dismiss the pain delivered by his flippant observation. "How can I ever consider another when he has no equal? I would rather cast my fortunes with these colonies, suffering the travails to independence, than forget that which I have adored with so pure a love."

"You speak like a child—a mere woman! It is beneath you." He seized her by the shoulders. "Is affection for a father nothing? I have held you in greater esteem than all my children—even above my heir! His temper—so hotly and darkly it burns—scorches even me. You are superior in virtue, wit, and judgment. Your allegiance to me is not so cheaply discarded. You have only to measure your contemplated actions against his own disastrous entanglements to know my meaning!"

Noting her sufferings, Mr. Parr's features softened and his jaw relaxed. Pacing before his desk, he stared intently at the floor and slipped into deep reflection. He held his head in his hands and mumbled violently, as if a sharp agony of soul had captured him. "Surely she will not! Oh, no, she will not."

So great was his mental affliction that Priscilla wondered if all the miseries of his life bent their havoc upon him in a single moment. He clenched his teeth and shook his head forcefully. Suddenly, he hung his head in silence. Little by little, his dignity returned, and his back straightened.

After some moments, he met her gaze again. "What I shall next propose I would not have considered for all the Crown's wealth if you had not already promised your hand to young Eton—and if I had not given my consent. Your fate lies before you. Choose wisely!"

Priscilla awaited his proposition with much eagerness.

"Henceforth, you may live with my Aunt Laurence—and thus remain in Williamsburg. In this way, you can marry the lad for whom you profess such devotion…but you will never see any of us again."

Priscilla nearly fainted with shock. She was astounded from head to foot. All her strength was required to prevent her collapse upon the floor from the force of this blow.

"How can I make such a wrenching choice?" She wrung her hands. "Do not cast this burden upon me! Can we not all remain in Williamsburg?"

His expression froze in an instant. "That is impossible."

Her temples pounding, Priscilla wondered if her father thus intended to shame her into submission. Still, the gleam in his eye suggested sincerity. His countenance seemed fixed in this matter. A distaste for indecision was reflected in the hardness his features assumed as Priscilla pleaded that he reconsider the offer.

Indeed, the sharp edge of his voice startled her when he next spoke. "Do not address me again lest you have an answer. You dishonor me with equivocation. I hope not to have reared a child with so little certainty of her own convictions."

Finally convinced that her father had no intention of yielding to her entreaties, Priscilla released all pretensions to hope. Whatever sufferings she had previously endured did not compare to the ensuing misery. Any shred of tranquility unraveled. In an instant, she was forced to decide her entire existence. How could her father be so cruel? A horrible anguish descended upon her as she contemplated her two choices.

In her distress, she considered those whose loss to her now hung in the balance. Priscilla was never more inclined to overlook their faults than in the present calamity, and her feelings turned to frenzied reflection. She thought of the man who stood before her—the proud, doting father. Elizabeth Parr had been a strong yet devoted mother. Ben had once proven a protective brother. His first marriage and the death of Rachel, however, had transformed the high-spirited boy into a tormented, preoccupied man. Ivy had never loved Priscilla and was ruled instead by spiteful ambition. And Frances—oh, the dear sister who now trusted Priscilla implicitly following Mr. Seymour's courtship and whose innocence had been marred by that man as well! And then, there remained Thomas, who returned the only devotion that had ever deemed itself worthy to enter the well-fortified gates of her heart. How she adored him!

At the present moment, trembling in her grief and urgency, she felt her connection to him perhaps more powerfully than ever before. His idealism and convictions, so unstained by the corruption that a broader acquaintance with the world might introduce, drew her at all times. He looked always forward, and it never escaped her notice that the landscape of her mind had undergone a radical alteration since the renewal of their friendship. She now understood that her character had long been ripe for the change. It seemed to her now as if she had been born to meet him—and to walk with him through the trials that would beset them both. A life without him would plod forward as but a series of meaningless events, inflicting her with memories of a grand love painfully yearned for across the unfeeling distance between them and the cruel sands of time.

She attempted to consider affection for her kindred. All in vain! She loved them dearly, but her life with them already seemed like a treasured artifact. A new path stretched before her, and passion for Thomas steadily eclipsed all other sentiments. She had already embarked upon another course by promising her hand to him beneath a cloudless sky that summer. The wind of that day still rippled through her heart like a gale—and held her fast. She suddenly realized that her journey, once begun, was not of a kind to permit retreat.

Priscilla Parr whispered the fateful determination.

"I must remain in Williamsburg."

Her father's stoic silence became maddening. Only his lips, tightly compressed, betrayed the violence of his emotions.

"I have promised myself to Thomas in marriage. I cannot revoke that pledge."

He ground his teeth. "You have made a costly choice."

Priscilla was stunned to silence as she watched her father's ire seize control of his faculties. He shook with indignation, her shocked silence only serving to inflame his boiling rage. "I have loved you all these years. *This* is how you repay my affection—by deserting us forever." His voice boiled with pain and vehemence. "I shall never forget your blatant ingratitude. Such treachery as this is unpardonable. I gave you a choice, and you have abused my liberality. Never did I suspect this choice from you—*you*—who I believed but a few moments ago to be the brightest and most promising of all my children. You have disgraced us. Leave my study this instant—ere my wrath kills me!"

With this directive, his strong finger pointed unsteadily toward the door.

The Parr family was stunned to silence.

Priscilla stood before them still as a statue, her father having forced her to enlighten the remainder of the family as to the resolution that had been made. He sat in the shadows, unwilling to defend her during the expected onslaught.

She had long surmised his thoughts toward her. He was too wounded by a sense of supreme betrayal to allow more natural inclinations to hold sway. A child who would abandon her kindred for the sake of romantic notions of her own was the basest of all creatures. To shirk duties to the hands which gave life proved the rebellious youth an ingrate of the most despicable sort. Likewise, to pursue a tantalizing hope while neglecting all sense of inherent gratitude validated the hopelessness of the idealistic traitor. The love of country governed all other loves, and, in scorning it, an individual negated all faith in redemption and all claims to honor.

Britain remained the beloved motherland, where, for centuries spent laboring beneath the hands of brutal tyrant and chivalrous king alike, families had carved out positions of prosperity and reverence. In Phillip Parr's perspective, the rugged coasts of the colonial wilderness boasted certain comforts, but the riches and security of England surpassed all pleasant outposts. Why continue in a land struggling to free itself from the maternal bond, from which all blessings and prestige stemmed and without whose lordship it was doomed to wither at the very hour of its birth? *Yes*, Priscilla thought bitterly, *I have heard him extol these notions long enough to know the shape of his disdain for me!*

Ben suddenly leapt to his feet in indignation. "You would disown us, Priscilla?"

She steadied her nerves and mirrored his glare. "It is *you* who disown *me*—and our home."

A small fanfare of weeping erupted, and she turned to see Frances sobbing into her handkerchief. In contrast, Rosamund sat open mouthed, her chin quivering at the news. She glanced toward her husband, but he held Priscilla in a furious gaze.

Ivy sat motionless, a faint bemused smile playing about her lips. "Let her go, Brother. Let her taste sedition in its fullness! I am sick of cruel comparisons. Having one less sister with whom to contend for the affections of great men is a welcome prospect."

"Hold your tongue!" The fury churning beneath Mrs. Parr's voice startled Priscilla.

"I am not surprised by these sentiments." Priscilla, though pained to the core of her being, fixed a fearless eye upon her elder sister. "At least my motives are sincere. *Your* ambition overrides faint stirrings of sisterly affection. Effecting the breach will be an effortless task, for envy knows no brother—and claims no friend."

Frances stood in a sudden frenzy, her cheeks stained with sorrow. "How am I to endure this most miserable separation of my life? You are my sole confidante, Priscilla, and necessary to my peace. You even saved me from the eternal despair of an unworthy husband." She turned to her father and tugged his sleeve in desperation. "We cannot abandon her upon these war-torn shores!"

Mr. Parr waved Frances away. "Priscilla has chosen exile. I am happy to oblige, don't you see?"

Rosamund stared at her lap. "I am sorry to lose such a dear friend."

Rosamund's innocence had been dispatched by an uncaring husband, but her impulsive goodwill remained. Nevertheless, Priscilla understood the source of her reluctance to say more. Rosamund could ill afford to openly defy her father-in-law for fear of losing the few strands of tolerance that bound Benjamin Parr to her side. She was most likely compelled to maintain her silence—and would thus be a secret, though ineffectual, ally.

All eyes, however, were soon arrested by Mrs. Parr, who was seized by such agitation that she hurled aside her needlework with great violence.

In a mere moment, she bolted from the sofa and struck Priscilla. "Miserable ingrate!"

Priscilla reeled from the blow. Unable to stand any longer, she collapsed onto the settee and caressed the brutalized cheek.

Mrs. Parr, her eyes flashing with wild rage, towered over her like a mountain. "I know the wastelands into which young girls wander—*I know them well!* You seek love like a golden land, Priscilla, but it will destroy you."

Tears blurring her vision, Priscilla rushed to her own defense. "I have done nothing against my virtue, Mother—nor would I ever do so!"

"We shall see!" Bitterness twisted the corners of Mrs. Parr's mouth. "Is not one disgrace the prelude to another? I too once rebelled against those who gave me life. It brought infamy to my family—and shame upon my own head. A girl who would forsake her father's house is capable of anything. Yes, you have cast your lot, but I will have no part in it from this day forward. *Get out of my sight, you wretched child!*"

Arrangements were concluded for the sale of the Parr House.

It was sold to a prosperous lawyer, a Mr. Edward Guildford, whose small family included a wife and one adult son. The facts remained scarce. Mr. Guildford briefly traveled to view the house and was prepared, after an hour of observation, to sign the deed. The transaction was achieved without further delay.

Mr. Parr made a prolonged visit to his venerable aunt, Mary Laurence. He concealed the particulars of the interview from Priscilla, only communicating with aloof equivocation, "My Aunt Laurence has been so kind as to take you in." Priscilla wondered regarding her aunt's true sentiments. She knew the woman to be warm and witty. Would she consider Priscilla an intruder? These, however, were but trivial anxieties.

Mr. Parr also planned a farewell dinner for the twenty-fifth of May, only five days prior to their consequential departure. All their close acquaintances were invited, including the Etons and the Adamses. Revelation of the imminent schism within the Parr family had not yet been accomplished. Mr. Parr would soon be forced to disclose the truth to the world. Priscilla initially feared the exposure, but her logic hindered her from drowning in apprehension. She was burdened with enough heartache without lamenting the condemnation of society. Thomas did not yet know of the sacrifice that she readied to make for the sake of his love. He would discover its existence soon enough.

The hour of this farewell gathering arrived at last. Priscilla feared it with a terror that seemed to conquer her sense and fortitude, regardless of her resolve. Once the guests began to appear, her pulse accelerated. She donned her customary expression, but a sea of turmoil churned violently beneath it.

Her heart particularly suffered when Katherine, with tears gathering in her eyes, approached. "I am so grieved, Priscilla. When Henry passed the news to me, I could barely eat or sleep. We must always correspond once you have reached England."

Moved by Katherine's heartfelt sorrow, Priscilla only smiled sadly at her friend's ignorance of how matters stood.

Priscilla's attention, however, was soon riveted to the somber discourse of the older men.

Mr. Parr raised his glass in nostalgic homage. "Well, my friends, this is 'farewell,' I suppose."

"It is not 'farewell' to my family, Parr. We leave for London in three weeks," Dr. Lee said.

Priscilla glanced toward Katherine, who was situated within hearing distance of the dialogue. As soon as her father uttered those words, Katherine's eyes began to swim with grief. Priscilla noted a single shining tear slide down her friend's waxen cheek.

Priscilla's concentration was recalled by the sharp mention of her own name by Mr. Eton. "What of Miss Priscilla's engagement to my son?"

Mr. Parr colored violently, and his jaw stiffened. "My daughter will not be persuaded otherwise. She is determined to fulfill it as previously planned."

Mr. Eton bristled with irritation. "How can such a union be achieved, Parr?"

"Priscilla shall remain in Williamsburg with my Aunt Laurence."

"I beg your pardon?" Mr. Adams's snow-white eyebrows converged in amazement. "She departs not with the rest of you, then?"

"That is true." Mr. Parr slapped his thighs. "Let us not sink beneath our troubles this evening, gentlemen. After all, we shall seldom meet again after this night."

Priscilla, immersed in her turbulent thoughts, suddenly sensed a warm hand resting upon her arm. Thomas stood before her in grave dignity, and her heart stirred to his presence.

A strange expression had overtaken his features, and she knew at once that he had heard. "Come. We must speak alone."

Her heart pounding within her chest, Priscilla rose. The two slipped from the crowded room so as not to attract curious stares. They made their way to the garden.

Thomas turned to face her. "I know what you intend to do, Priscilla."

"Yes?"

"I am a selfish creature—and would chase you to the wilderness end in order to have you for my own." He suddenly caught her in his arms. "Your fire is my strength, and once it has singed me, I cannot live without its power. Yet, a deadly conflict awaits me, and my fate is doubtful. When you suffer agonies on my behalf, are you certain you will not despise me for it in the end?"

"Is it that your love has so soon wilted?" Priscilla cried. "Beneath my uncle's oak tree, you beseeched me to suffer gale and tempest by your side. I knew no particulars, but I did not doubt the violence of the journey. Can you cast me aside this effortlessly when I have forsaken everything? Oh, Tom, you and your fickle dreams! My father placed the choice before me. I have resolved upon a path, and I shall remain here. I see the road before me—and nothing else."

His eyes searched hers deeply, and she could feel the wisps of his breath upon her face. "How strange I felt when my heart first loved you. Seymour was leading you to the dance. As long as I live, I shall never forget. My feelings frightened me then. Their violence seemed improper, even worthy of shame. But now! How I could ever have looked upon you without passion? Only when I believed your smiles would be bestowed upon another did I run mad with envy and pursue you. How could I ever have been blind to you, Priscilla Parr—to a tongue that shatters falsehood—to a spirit that cannot be broken?"

He held her closely for some moments in silence. Indeed, Priscilla realized that he had become a refuge and a lantern of hope in the storm that had enveloped her. A great passion wracked her soul as she clung to him. "Shall we go in again?"

"Of course." Thomas, slowly releasing her, extended his arm.

Only when he turned did she notice the tears standing in his eyes.

They slipped back into the tapestry of mirth just as quietly as they had disappeared from it. They had not been missed.

Chapter 38

The Departure

The morning following the farewell dinner, Mr. Parr instructed the maidservants to begin gathering Priscilla's belongings. It proved a dismal task for Priscilla to witness, and, despite her efforts, she frequently broke down into weeping. Frances and Rosamund both remained with her for purposes of consolation. Within two days, the said possessions were collected and transported down the street to Mrs. Laurence's home. Simultaneously, Mrs. Parr, Ivy, Frances, and Rosamund labored to draw together the remainder of the family's belongings, which, once collected, were sent ahead to England. Such tasks were accomplished with a lack of fuss, but a spirit of gloom pervaded the proceedings. Mr. Parr conveyed only one item of his to Mrs. Laurence's home for Priscilla's charge. The object was an old, dust-encrusted chest that was, according to Mr. Parr, "full to capacity of useless, silly, sentimental old things that would be of use to no one."

The final evening spent with her family taxed Priscilla's nerves and resolve to the limit. Mr. Parr reported travel arrangements, the schedule, and the ship that would bear them across the ocean. Despondency cloaked the evening. No embers of merriment threatened to slice the desolation of the night.

The next morning arrived.

Priscilla awoke to feel the sun from her chamber window bathing her face. For a single fleeting moment, she did not recall the import of the day, only a vague sensation that a season of misery lay before her. Then, her memory returned.

She rose from her bed unwillingly. Desperation and fury threatened to equal her sorrow. She beheld her beloved bureau, emptied of its cherished contents, for the last time. Her heart absorbed every article of furniture in the room. Priscilla forced herself away as a fresh wave of anguish swept over her.

She sat with her family for their final repast together. No words were spoken, no insults were exchanged, and no regrets were voiced. The only perceptible sound was the faint splash of Frances's tears against her napkin. Nearly all other faces were hardened by resentment and dignity, their fierce sentiments successfully contained. They rose with their usual formality from the table, never to dine there together once more.

With an astonishing lack of disorder, they silently filed into the hall. One by one, each passed through the door. Priscilla lingered behind the others. She glimpsed back one final instance as an inhabitant of the home. Her senses played cruel deceptions, for there, in the spacious hall, she perceived the forms of five spirited children, skipping through each room and leaping up the stairs with no effort. She could almost hear their rousing cries beckon to her from the mists of the past. With feverish bitterness, she closed the door upon their ghosts.

The Parr family boarded their two carriages, and they rumbled down the street to Mrs. Laurence's house. In the foremost carriage, Priscilla, Mrs. Parr, Frances, and Rosamund were seated. The infant Sarah was nestled within her stepmother's arms. In the second carriage, Mr. Parr, Ben, and Ivy were situated comfortably.

The mood within the first carriage proved tense. Frances did not attempt to restrain her sorrow. Her lips pressed together, Mrs. Parr stared out the window. Rosamund avoided Priscilla's gaze by focusing her attention upon the child she held.

The carriages halted with a lurch. The entire family, with few words exchanged, disembarked their conveyances and entered the Laurence House. They were ushered by the maidservants into the parlor, where Mary Laurence sat to receive them with a disarming smile.

She rose and outstretched her arms to Mr. and Mrs. Parr. "Welcome, Phillip, Elizabeth!"

Courtesies were traded with all due ceremony.

"Will you sit down?"

"No, thank you." Mr. Parr smiled faintly. "We must be on our way, I fear."

"So soon, Phillip?"

"Yes, Aunt."

"Shall I see any of you again?" Tears flooded her fading blue eyes.

"Most likely not, I am afraid."

"Farewell, then!" Mrs. Laurence quivered as she beheld the son of her dead brother for the last time.

Mr. Parr's countenance relaxed somewhat at the sight of her grief. "Do not despair, madam. Bess's sister and brother-in-law, the Wallaces, still dwell in the country. You will also have my daughter's company to console you."

Mr. Parr did not linger to witness his aunt's lamentations. Upon his instruction, the Parr family returned to the carriages outside. Priscilla followed behind them with rapid steps. Mr. Parr, Mrs. Parr, Ben, and Ivy stepped into the carriages with haste. Only Rosamund, clutching Sarah, and Frances did not hasten to depart.

Rosamund stepped forward first. "Goodbye, Priscilla. I shall never forget your kindness to me. God keep you and bless you all your life."

Priscilla smiled. "Thank you, Rosamund. I have also been glad of your friendship."

She then gazed into the brilliant blue eyes above the dimpled cheeks of Sarah Parr. "Farewell, little one." She tenderly stroked the baby's flaming auburn wisps of hair. "May you be as beautiful as your mother and as strong as your father. Long life, my dear, and much God-given prosperity!"

Rosamund quickly returned to the carriage with the child.

"Come, Frances!" Mr. Parr rapped his gold-topped cane against the side of the carriage.

"I—I must bid my sister goodbye." Her bosom heaving, Frances threw her arms around Priscilla and gave full vent to her misery. Many moments passed before either of them spoke. "It is unbearable, Priscilla, to be parted from my truest friend in the world! I shall be lost without you."

"No! You must bear up against the caprices of circumstance. Ruthless as they are, they must not triumph. Though you defied me once, I saw an indomitable spirit that would not suffer defeat."

"I promise to write to you faithfully."

"Goodbye, dearest sister."

"Goodbye, Priscilla!"

Mr. Parr flinched at this display of emotion. "Let us go, Frances—*now*!"

Priscilla released her weeping sister. Frances retreated to the carriage and settled upon the empty seat next to Rosamund.

Priscilla stared with longing at her remaining family members. "Will you not kiss me this final farewell?"

"No." Mr. Parr averted his stern glare from her face.

"Mother?" Priscilla pleaded.

At this entreaty, Mrs. Parr arched her eyebrows and stared at her lap.

"You refuse to perform even this small, formal courtesy to one of your own—one whom you will most likely never see again?" Her voice trembled as she surveyed the unyielding countenances.

Mr. Parr's look of contempt burned its wrath into her soul. "That particular 'one of our own' has abandoned her kindred and deserves none of our sympathies now."

Before Priscilla could utter another syllable, Mr. Parr signaled the drivers to direct the conveyances forward. As the two carriages rolled down the street, hot tears of pain and betrayal cascaded down her cheeks. Her heavy heart only brightened somewhat when she saw Frances lean out from the window and wave to her. Priscilla returned the gesture and shouted, "Goodbye!"

Cadence to Glory

The carriages suddenly slowed as they proceeded past Bruton Parish, the cemetery that housed the graves of her grandparents, her dead brother Charles, and Rachel Eton Parr. Her pulse quickened at the thought that, even at that moment, her father might suffer a change of heart.

It was not to be.

After some moments, the carriages hastened onward, and her gaze followed them as they vanished down the street.

Chapter 39

The Remembrance

Priscilla spent the first day apart from her family in nearly absolute silence. Her hours passed at the window, her listless gaze concealing a heart wracked with grief. Despite Priscilla's attempts to discourage conversation, Mrs. Laurence was not offended. She seemed to genuinely pity her young niece's predicament and proved to be all that was obliging. She posed few inquiries to Priscilla, even when the young woman did not dine with her and retired prematurely.

That night, Priscilla lay awake, seeking tranquility in the darkness. The tumult of her mind prevented slumber. She had grown weary and could not feel easy. The serenity of the night was eerily overwhelming. Little was heard except the gentle clicking of the clock in the hall and her own fitful intake of breath. She turned over restlessly.

It was too quiet! Too placid! Altogether too peaceful! She despised it. The Parr house had never possessed such odd silence. She recalled how as a child Frances would slip down the hall when nightmares haunted her. Priscilla would console her, take her hand, and lead her back to her chamber. There, she would tuck the covers over Frances once more. Priscilla's mind wandered to years past. She would herself, as a little girl, seek solace from her father, mother, or brother when she suffered horrifying dreams. One of the three had always alleviated all her puerile dread.

Stop! She was looking backward! Priscilla cautioned herself. Such recollections, she reasoned, were perilous. She wiped away the cold beads of perspiration that had coalesced upon her forehead. As much as she strove to check it, her mind continued to roam the obscure, distant fields of the past.

Her mother—her dear mother. How she loved her. How she yearned for her comfort already. Despair at Mrs. Parr's betrayal returned. An image of Phillip Parr also appeared in Priscilla's mind. How gently he once hoisted her into his lap. He was always strict, but he adored her. The thought of disappointing him, as she had surely done, pierced her to the heart.

Do not betray your family, your friends, every love you have ever known. Most of all, dear girl, never betray England! Always remember that you are British. Remain true to the empire, and you shall forever stand proud!

His words from nearly a year and a half ago echoed through her head with terrible penetration. Like an icy whisper, they haunted her. She tossed over, as if changing position would banish the terrors that now descended upon her mind. The burden of neglected responsibility to her father fell upon Priscilla. In his eyes, she represented a lost hope. Had she failed him miserably? She was suddenly shocked that she could look back upon her resolution.

She endured woe unlike any other her soul had ever experienced. Within the west organdy bedroom in her aunt's home on that quiet summer night of 1775, loneliness engulfed her like waves of the sea. Frances had always believed her fearless, capable, and strong. Priscilla realized that, in truth, she was but a frightened, heartbroken child. She was so alone in the world—*so utterly forsaken!*

She would most likely never see her family again, never pass an evening with them again beneath the roof of the dear old Parr house, never dine with them to imbibe her father's political grievances, never share the same pew with them in Bruton Parish Church, and never celebrate Christmastide with them once more. The joys and miseries of childhood had become inseparable in her mind.

She did not regret her decision. Thoughts of Thomas forbade it. Nevertheless, the injustice of it all imposed upon her thoughts again and again.

She could no longer resist the power of her grief. The anger and resentment she had suppressed for hours fell away like a poorly fastened cloak. The tears that had long gathered in her eyes spilled over her cheeks. Before Priscilla realized it, she was sobbing into her pillow, softly at first, then overwhelmed by a ceaseless flow of fear, shame, and heartache.

<hr />

In the ensuing days, Priscilla floundered at a low ebb. Misery rendered daily tasks intolerable. Every thought revolved about her family, and her mind ran rampant with oppressive memories. Her sufferings were compounded by the visitation of splitting headaches, which seized her suddenly—most often at night.

The darkness of the night thus posed her worst battles. As the moon stretched its lonely, mysterious gleam across the floorboards of her new bedroom and she stared at the walls, her fears—those delirious remembrances—seemed to exploit the lack of diversion, sound, and color to attack her with vehemence.

She gleaned numerous revelations from her sorrow since it provided ample opportunity for frank self-examination. She had often prided herself on her strength of spirit. As the walls of her life collapsed around her and she hourly surveyed the piteous rubble, however, her famed courage unraveled.

In all her trials, however, she was not friendless. Mrs. Laurence proved to be a compassionate listener, an understanding guardian, and a valuable counselor. The venerable lady quickly conceived a deeper affection for her niece and soon inspired a reciprocation of devotion from Priscilla. As the final kinswoman of the elderly woman, Priscilla became a cherished soul once more. She would often notice some spark of tender recollection stir within her great aunt's deep blue eyes, which became pools of untold grief. Priscilla never inquired.

Fresh company somewhat enlivened Priscilla's bleak days. The Guildfords arrived to inhabit the Parr house soon after its evacuation. Priscilla closely observed the family at church. Edward Guildford was a small, lean man in his early sixties. Always eager to please, he exhibited affability in dealing with his new acquaintances. His wife appeared to be a quiet, composed little woman who carried herself with dignity but who was not nearly as sociable as her husband.

The couple's sole progeny was a young physician who brimmed with all the vitality of youth. Like his father, he was capable of evoking friendship and fidelity, but his humor occasionally took a bitter, sarcastic turn. He seemed aware of his charismatic powers, in which he basked, and often wielded them to his purposes. He was an attractive young man with dark brown hair and raven-colored eyes. Priscilla noticed that Harriet and Jane Adams frequently glanced his way during services. In a flash of her old wit, she laughed at the sight.

Thomas called upon Priscilla a few days following her family's departure. Mrs. Laurence made polite conversation with him for some moments. For a time, Priscilla feared that her talkative aunt would not grant them solitude. When Thomas asked if he and Priscilla might stroll in the garden, however, Mrs. Laurence was quite amenable to the plan.

She pleasantly replied, "I hope you will excuse my abstaining from the ramble. An old woman's infirmities prevent her from taking exercise as she would wish!"

Thomas then led Priscilla to the garden where he immediately addressed her. "I cannot bear to see you in such morose spirits."

"I am indeed quite downcast."

With quiet incisiveness, he examined her. "You regret your decision?"

"Never!"

"When I gaze ahead to all the years we shall be forced apart, I cannot but groan in my soul." Thomas squeezed her hand.

Even after two years, the admiration in his eyes possessed the power to make her cheeks flame. "Let us not speak of that separation, Tom. Indeed, hostilities may continue for months, not years."

Thomas's brow furrowed.

She searched his expression for some token of affirmation. "Perhaps the conflict will soon end."

A dark cloud overspread his features. "I doubt it. The redcoats form a fighting force vastly superior to our own. Lest some other European power be induced by enmity for Britain to join the war on our side, we have only the militias! No, I am convinced that our struggles will be bloody, our battles numerous, our principles tested. Our best hope lies in the strength of our cause. We speak of dreams, but how can we know if our plans will be affected?"

Her anger rose swiftly. "Can we not speak of our plans for a single moment without arousing the very subject that you know is so distressing to me? I hear of it perpetually! Do you not know that my heart nearly fails me with terror each time I think of the future? Why must we talk of it?"

Thomas held her against his heart, so closely that she could hear its quickened cadence. She understood that his predictions seemed probable enough. If only he had known the nights of sleeplessness that she had so miserably suffered. If only he had known of the piteous prayers offered to God at all hours of day and night. The suffocating grip of uncertainty closed about her struggling soul.

Her fears escaped in a desperate sob. "What shall become of us after all?"

He cradled her cheek in his hand and gazed into her eyes. "Only God can know for certain. Still, Priscilla, believe me when I say this: We shall triumph in the end, regardless of all. Some divine assurance whispers to me. A haven of opportunity lies at our path's end—yet unseen by mortal eyes!"

Governor Dunmore and his family fled Williamsburg during the early morning hours of June eight. Did such a maneuver suggest an imminent invasion of the capital by British soldiers? Were Dunmore and his family escaping prior to the designated onslaught? Speculation was enough to plunge all Williamsburg into an uproar.

Neither the Parr family nor that of the governor was the only Loyalist household to depart Williamsburg. Katherine Lee was divided not only from her parents, who sailed for England the second week of June, but also from her two sisters since the Adamses had no intention of returning to the mother country. Jane and Harriet even shared a letter with Priscilla. Its author was none other than their cousin, John Seymour. He wrote that he did not even intend to return to his plantation before journeying to England. Mr. Seymour planned to conduct arrangements for the property's sale by correspondence. According to the letter, he had suspected explosive developments in the conflict and would thus take with him only his most prized possessions, including his sister and his child-bride.

In contrast, it soon became well known that Priscilla Parr had been abandoned by her family. Although she had determined her own fate, others around her did not accept the truest version of events. The rumor circulated, and, to her surprise, much pity was expressed for her sake. The only pleasure of being awarded such compassion was the company it produced. She received numerous visits from the three "tea" friends who remained in Williamsburg, namely Jane, Harriet, and Katherine Adams. Jane and Harriet, though sympathetic, stared at Priscilla in great wonder when the latter explained the cause of her present status.

"Your father offered you a choice?" Jane stared wide eyed at Priscilla.

"I cannot believe that." Harriet shook her head as Mrs. Laurence offered her tea.

Priscilla nodded. "Indeed he did."

"Had we been thrust into a similar situation, Father would never had allowed us choice—would he, Jane?"

"Never." Jane straightened the wrinkles on her frock. "Why did you stay for Thomas's sake, Priscilla?"

"I could never go back upon my word, and I love him."

"Oh, that is a pity, is it not, Jane? I would love to meet great lords and mingle with the cream of London society." Harriet giggled. "It would put dear old Thomas to shame—though I confess I did rather like him at one time!"

Priscilla received more heartfelt consolation from Katherine, who projected a peculiar empathy upon calling at the Laurence house one afternoon. "You behaved honorably in adhering to the engagement."

"Yet, I was half-guided by selfish motives!" Priscilla cried. "A life without Thomas? Kate, surely you know how much I love him. You understand that I could not bear it!"

"Of course. I know how wrenching this ordeal has been for you." Katherine bit her lip in thought. "I lost my family as well, and my husband's life will soon be thrown into a precarious state."

"And I fear for Tom! The deluge has already drawn him in, Kate. I am hourly tortured by this indefinable dread. I know that you feel it for Henry."

For an instant, Katherine's countenance convulsed with pain. Nevertheless, she continued with a strained note of cheer. "Yet, the day is not lost...though our fortunes are still adrift. I have my beloved Henry, and your friendship furnishes me with much comfort, Priscilla."

Priscilla smiled with gratitude. "And yours offers an untold amount in return."

"Moreover, I have good news to tell." Katherine's fingers rested upon her slightly distended girth as happy tears rolled down her face. "There is new life!"

Priscilla squealed with delight.

Katherine was with child.

<hr />

Priscilla occupied her days with painting—or rather, using the poor materials available to attempt do so. Trade betwixt Britain and her colonies was presently jeopardized, and the sort of artistic resources to which she was accustomed was scarce. She frequently sat at the window while recalling the happy days she had spent in the country the previous summer. That distant era seemed to have vanished forever. Various sentiments, each contradictory and equally forceful, beset her. Although Mrs. Laurence strove by various methods to entertain her, Priscilla's heartache refused to accept diversion in any form. Her thirsty, burning soul wandered in a desert of pain, yearning for something she could not determine. She thought of her family always.

Such visions of extreme woe she painted! One image portrayed a weeping young woman. The subject's fierce beauty was marred by tears for her beloved, who was leaving to fight a great battle. Tears streamed down the girl's fair cheeks. Her handkerchief, clutched only by her waving fingers, danced in the wind. The young man looked grave, as if he viewed her fresh face for the last time.

Mrs. Laurence often observed Priscilla as she painted. The elderly woman risked no comment for a time but instead sat attentive. She finally said, "Priscilla, you are a true artist! Can you not, however, render pleasing scenes—scenes which celebrate the nobler aspects of the human spirit?"

Priscilla looked upward from her employment. "Such as what?"

"Such as…" Mrs. Laurence's voice trailed off as she immersed herself in thought. "Such as a loving family by the blaze of a roaring fire, the wedding of two long-divided individuals, a grand ball, the splendor of a walk in the countryside, or the victory of right?"

"Those prospects arouse no fire within me, Aunt. I am passionate, you understand."

"I thought these things appealed to every heart. Why must you prefer mournfulness to joy? Why would the public gaze upon a work of art which fills them with melancholy? Would they not prefer a view which inspires them to enlarge their lives? It would be passionate, as you say. Truly, I cannot understand how you can paint such scenes without falling victim to sadness beyond compare. It is gloom without purpose!"

"In this period of my life, that is the only sentiment which strikes any chord of familiarity within me." Priscilla could barely stifle her resentment at her aunt's interference. Returning to her work with renewed determination, she peevishly wondered how the old woman, secure in all her comforts, could presume to lecture her.

Breed's Hill.

It had been one of the first of many battles, and fortune smiled upon the august British.

News of the redcoats' victory had not been unwelcome news to Priscilla. If the colonists were shaken to their senses by this episode, she reasoned, perhaps they would perceive the utter futility of their campaign against the British. Rumors percolated so wildly that it was difficult to distinguish truth from myth. Yet, details did not touch her. She hoped for good to result from this Boston combat—a complete reconciliation with Britain and a swift cessation of hostilities.

A few days earlier, Williamsburg had learned that George Washington, a Virginian plantation owner and old acquaintance of Priscilla's Aunt and Uncle Wallace, was charged with commanding the colonists' military force—the Continental Army. Priscilla recalled meeting him once during one of her childhood visits to Devon Hills. She remembered only a towering gentleman with powdered brown locks tied in a queue, a veteran of the last war, whose dignity and reserve rendered those around him all the more attentive whenever he deigned to voice his opinion. The size of his hands had particularly amazed her. Even to a child, such as Priscilla had been at the time, he had inspired respect by his dignified carriage, measured speech, and resolute gaze. Nevertheless, behind reverence for the man, fear had smoldered, as though the sleeping lion might be roused at any moment.

Indeed, mused Priscilla upon hearing the news of Mr. Washington's appointment, *he is a man most worthy—and far more suited than any other—of leading a revolution against the greatest nation on earth.*

Chapter 40

The Confiscation

The sun poured its wrath upon Thomas's head as he rode his horse beside the company of men marching in file down Duke of Gloucester Street.

Revolution was in his heart on this day of days, when he cast off the restraints of youth to strike a blow at tyranny.

This opportunity had surfaced unexpectedly that morning when his father, returning home early, burst into the library, begged Mr. Percy's pardon for interrupting the lesson, and turned to his son in anticipation. "George Adams stopped by the office a few moments ago. It seems that Henry is leading a deputation at noon to confiscate arms from the Palace. They are meeting first at the Magazine. I assume you would have a part in it?"

Thomas had risen immediately, throwing aside his text—*The Annals of Tacitus*—as he did so. Thoughts from the previous moments had dwindled into minutiae. After all, how could merely reading about the Germans' struggles against the Roman Empire compare to tasting a similar revolt for freedom in one's own day? Without another word to either Percy or his father, Thomas had fled the library, retrieved his horse from the stables, and galloped toward the Magazine.

Now, as the solemn party made their way toward the Palace, his mind was more fully engaged by the repercussions of this adventure. The Magazine arsenal must be replenished by arms from the thief's own supply. This was a logical conclusion and a reasonable plan. Still, it constituted an irrevocable statement of disloyalty, for Dunmore was the Crown's representative under the law. Likewise, the Palace was the seat of royal power in the Virginia Colony. In legal terms, they marched to steal weapons—and thus raw power—from the king himself. With a single stroke, this deed would brand them all traitors forever.

Thomas had long coveted the distinction, and his courage grew as the group finally advanced upon the Palace Green. With Dunmore gone from Williamsburg at last, resistance was improbable. Still, a sense of danger shrouded the proceedings. Frustrations that Thomas had suppressed for years threatened to erupt as he neared the Palace, and he clutched the reins with a fierce grip.

The band of men suddenly drew to a halt.

"Try the door first!" Henry Adams's voice rang clearly across the Green in the humid air.

Thomas, swiftly dismounting, tied up his horse to a post.

A path cleared amongst the men, some of whom carried smaller blocks of firewood. A large log, however, was hoisted in their midst as a group in the center aimed it toward the door. In one accord, they rammed the entrance. Several other attempts followed with the same result. The door, it seemed, was locked tightly on the inside.

"Thomas—come hither!" Henry beckoned his friend toward the front window.

Seizing a stick of firewood, Thomas rushed to the window and broke it open with a single heave upon the glass. Followed by Henry and a knot of other men, Thomas climbed over the shards of shattered pane into the spacious entrance hall.

Henry suddenly turned to the group that had passed through the smashed window. "We need Ogilvy—the blacksmith."

The name was shouted to those who waited outside, and within moments, a tanned, burly man entered through the window and proceeded to ply the lock. Thomas heard a soft click. At Henry's directive, he wielded his club to bludgeon the now-weakened chains. The door fell open as the men came pouring into the hall with a great shout and made for the weapons that lined the walls.

Thomas himself leapt upon one of the red damask chairs. Flushed with the peril of the moment, he began tearing carbines, sabers, and muskets from their exhibition upon the wooden panels, and his companions did likewise with systematic efficiency. A massive pile rose in the center of the room on the black and white marble floor as the gentlemen dismantled the display of arms.

As he went about the daring business at hand, Thomas beamed with pride. *This tale shall be recounted to my descendants for generations—if I am not hung first,* he thought. Still, he reasoned that this hour of glory would render his life worth its misery if he and his compatriots dangled from a rope in the morning.

And then, with a sharp pain to his heart, he thought of Priscilla.

In this very Palace, he had conceived a passion for her. He still recalled her appearance that fateful evening at the Christmas Ball. A luxuriant golden plume, matching her silken gown, crowned a bounty of light brown curls, which, though partly pinned behind her head, tumbled down the nape of her pale neck. Her sea-green eyes, though keen with some agitation, were unblinking. The mesmeric smile that lined her lips belied the fierce courage and intellectual fervor she had always manifested. He could imagine her in that instant—exactly as she had been that night.

His reverie was disrupted by the sudden exit of the men, who, gathering muskets and swords from the small mountain of arms, reassembled upon the Green.

As Thomas reached for an armful of weapons, Henry tapped him on the shoulder and thrust a single pistol into his hands. "You will be on horseback, I presume. If anyone should try to hinder us from reaching the Magazine, you will restrain him. You must do the same when we return for the remainder of these arms."

Thomas nodded gravely and strode toward the door. Glancing backward, he almost gasped to behold the nearly naked walls—half-stripped of their warlike majesty. Stooping as he passed through the door, he returned to his horse outside. Mounting hastily, he rode near the flanks of the company as they marched slowly down the Green and turned onto the central thoroughfare.

Clusters of townspeople gathered in curiosity, gaping at the men as they passed. Some cheered loudly; others merely watched the small parade in silence.

The sight of these onlookers sapped his boyish glee as the implications of his charge settled upon him. What if someone accosted them? Even worse, what if the mouth of his pistol failed to wreak its intimidation upon the assailant? Shuddering at the prospect, he assumed a fearsome expression in hopes of discouraging any interference.

Suddenly, a white form emerged in the corner of his eye. His fingers tensed upon the pistol as he turned to see a young woman, her skirts billowing behind her, rushing toward him.

Priscilla!

His heart pounded violently. Ever conscious of the danger surrounding the present situation, he galloped to meet her.

Her face, though wan with horror, remained hard as granite. "What are you doing?"

"We are transferring Dunmore's weapons to the Magazine. Priscilla, you must stand aside." He leaned down urgently toward her and said in a lower voice, "It is a perilous act that we do. Under no circumstances must you involve yourself in this business."

"Why have you done it in the light of day? Anyone can recognize your face—and testify against you!"

"We are not ashamed. At least we have more honor than Dunmore, who stole our gunpowder in the dark of night—when decent folk are in their beds."

Her lips twitched vehemently. "They will hang you for this. I know it. Why have you done it?"

He stiffened, suddenly realizing that she awakened in him greater emotion—both love and anger—than any other being. "I would rather hang than accept the dictates of a despot."

"What about my fate, Thomas—when you are gone?" Tears gushed down her cheeks. "You are everything to me now."

The sight of her pleading eyes almost drove him to desperation. Balancing the pistol on his lap, he reached down for her small hand. "I love you."

Cadence to Glory

She said nothing, only captured his hand in both of hers.

He nodded toward her and returned to his place beside the unruly cavalcade. As the company marched toward the Magazine, attracting spectators in its wake, he glanced back over his shoulder.

She was still standing on the street corner—a solitary figure swathed in pearly white, gazing at him as he went.

Chapter 41

The Repudiation

July marked an escalation of the strife that had recently erupted in Williamsburg.

A resolution was demanded by the Continental Congress, declaring the necessity to take up arms against Britain. The Virginia Convention met in Williamsburg, and a Committee of Safety was established. In addition to the already-existing minutemen and militia, two regiments were organized.

In addition, the blood of Williamsburg seditionists continued to boil against Dunmore—and their sovereign. In a sign of rising confidence, the rebels took occupation of many notable buildings. The soldiers steadily multiplied in number and might about the city. Their haunting presence served as an inescapable reminder to all citizens of the nightmare to come.

On a cloudy August morning, Thomas pondered the events of recent days over the breakfast table. The raid on the Palace, particularly the incident involving Priscilla, brooded heavily on his mind. The crippling expression of hopelessness she had worn as he rode away haunted him. It was so unlike her fiery nature.

Grasping his fork, he listlessly fiddled with the cold ham upon his plate.

Mr. Eton's flat voice pierced his troubled reflections. "You are not to see the Parr girl again. Do you understand?"

Thomas glanced upward with a jolt.

The evenness of his father's tone suggested a joke at best, a mockery at worst. Still, the harsh glare of his eyes could hardly be mistaken for levity.

Knowing from experience that his father would capitalize upon any token of weakness, Thomas tensed his jaw. "What is the reason for this injustice?"

Mr. Eton scowled at his son. "I am your father. That is sufficient cause. Do you expect me to honor any promise I made to Phillip Parr, who betrayed the glory of Virginia, fled these shores without even an acknowledgement of our long friendship in parting, and tore my only grandchild from your mother and I forever? I was his friend and benefactor when he was nothing in the eyes of the world. My vengeance merely falls upon his seed. Why do you still fancy the Tory wench—when she has been cast off by her own household? Perhaps she seeks to draw our family into her disgrace."

Mr. Eton resumed dining as if he had been speaking of the weather or other such commonplace matters. Thomas's fury toward him mounted along with his confusion. He clenched his teeth, and, for the first time, felt as though he might strike his father.

Mrs. Eton quickly placed a hand upon her husband's sleeve. "Richard, this is too harsh an edict."

William, leaning back in his chair, surveyed the spectacle with amusement, as evidenced by the smirk that twisted his mouth.

Thomas sprang from his chair in great anger. "She has no part in the sins of her father. Our engagement was an agreement that you undertook in good faith, and it *must* be honored."

His black eyebrows merging, Mr. Eton laid down his napkin and stood calmly. "I will not be defied."

Thomas's angst multiplied, although he endeavored to conceal his struggles. "She was not cast off, Father. On the contrary, Mr. Parr held his daughter in such high regard that he presented her with a choice."

"Then she made a foolish decision."

"I cannot—*I will not*—abandon her! If I am to marry, it is her hand alone I will accept."

Mr. Eton's eyes flashed livid, and he advanced toward his son sternly. "You will do as I demand, or you may be likewise disowned. You have yet to receive an education toward your livelihood, and the purse strings are *my* prerogative. Should you like it if I turn you into the streets to beg your living? That is the place for ungrateful progeny."

Thomas became numb with grief and rage. The threat carried much weight, and he believed his father fully capable of acting upon it. He would be reduced to a pauper, and even if he took Priscilla as his wife, he would not be able to provide for her.

He knew that he could never relinquish her. He recalled her image as she rode toward him across Mr. Wallace's fields, her hair flowing down her shoulders and glistening beneath the sun's luster. He closed his eyes with anguish at the memory.

His mind raced, grasping wildly for a solution to this dire impasse. "I must see her."

Mr. Eton nodded but held firm his gaze. "Yes, you shall see her—one final time—to make clear my wishes."

Thomas called upon Priscilla quite unexpectedly. From the moment he entered the parlor, Priscilla suspected that something was amiss. He appeared fitful and, as civilly as possible, entreated Mrs. Laurence to grant him a private audience with her niece. Mrs. Laurence, on this occasion, was happy to oblige. Her withdrawal proved expedient.

Once they were left together, Priscilla immediately interrogated him. "What is the matter, Tom?"

Thomas fell forward on the chair, his head collapsing into his hands desperately. "I know not how to live, Priscilla!"

"Pray, is there some trouble?" Panic froze her heart to see him thus—as she had never seen him heretofore.

"How shall I tell her, God?" he prayed aloud, shaking his head in confusion. "How shall I tell her?"

She grabbed his wrists and forced him to look into her eyes. "Thomas Eton! Tell me the evil this instant. You know that I will survive it."

"This morning, Father ordered me to renounce our engagement." Pain tore his features and staggered his voice. "He demanded that I pay this visit for that very purpose."

Priscilla released his wrists and limply dropped onto the chair out of which she had leapt. Her head was embroiled in a whirl of sensations—chaos, anger, agony, and despair. She was lost in a daze, feeling that she might faint. Priscilla, however, was of no fainting stock, and she recovered her wits sufficiently to ask him, albeit in broken tones, "Why?"

"He said that you are but a disgraced child cast out by her family. He bears much ill will toward your father. I confronted him, and he broke into a rage. He threatened me, vowing that, if I married you, he would not finance my education—and would turn me into the streets."

Priscilla was sobbing violently now, her head clutched between her hands. All was lost.

To the heavens, she cried, "Please, God, help me! Do not allow him to commit this base cruelty!"

As she wailed, Thomas took her into his arms and locked her in his embrace, allowing her pitiful tears to fall upon his shoulder. In her presence, he seemed to have composed his battered wits somewhat.

He whispered into her hair. "I shall write to you. We can meet in secret until I complete my education. At that time, we can marry—and make our union public." His chest heaved sharply. "But, no! With the conflict at hand, my entrance to the college is uncertain. Yet I vow to you, as I vowed once before, that our fates are *one*. Nothing is lost, you see, as long as our will remains unshaken. We shall yet surmount this trial—and someday look back upon this dark season with that joy which only springs from long-withheld triumph."

Priscilla gleaned hope from his words, which mirrored her own thoughts as they slowly took shape.

When forced to choose between Thomas and her family, she had believed herself a veteran of the greatest miseries known to mortals. She had been proven incorrect in her conceited assumption. Now, she endured this fresh agony.

She had always fancied herself indomitable as a mountain, but the past few months had exposed her own deficiencies.

Chapter 42

The March

Considering the recent turn of events, Priscilla was given the most pleasant shock of her life when Thomas called upon her a few days afterward.

"How I have longed to see your face!" She threw her arms about his neck. Then, with a start, she drew back with concern. "Your father will know that you have come."

"His esteem is of little consequence now."

The solemn cloud in his eyes, which avoided her, did not escape Priscilla's scrutiny. "What else is wrong, Tom?"

His voice waxed frigid though pain softened his features. "I am to leave this afternoon. I march with the Virginia Regiment."

The dreaded hour had arrived at last. Its blow was sharp and incisive. Nothing could have prepared her for the force of that moment.

She searched his countenance for any contour of either untruth or jest in its solid outline—and discovered none. "No! You cannot!"

"I must! Do you not covet liberty and justice for these colonies? Do you spurn the cause I am prepared to champion?"

Panic at his impending departure freed Priscilla's tongue to express long-suppressed sentiments. "If you lose your life in its defense, I shall never believe in it!"

"This is a mystery to me." At last, Thomas fixed his piercing eyes upon her face. "Did you not pledge your faithfulness and steadfastness beneath that mighty oak?"

Priscilla held her head, which throbbed. "What did I promise? My memory, beset by so many miseries, grows weak!"

Thomas searched her gaze. "You do not mean that, do you, Priscilla?"

"Yes, I do! This cause and I shall forever be enemies! What do I care for liberty if we must be parted? I have given you my heart. Do you no longer love me, Thomas? Have you deceived me for nearly a year? Have you not seen the horror I have suffered at the very mention of losing you to this rebellion? Can you not see? Can you not see that I would willingly lay down my life for you? I feel as though I have done as much! Can you not see that, without you, my life would be devoid of hope? My poor, cruel boy! How can you stand there so calmly when you see that my heart is breaking? Thomas, where is *my* liberty?" With this desperate appeal, Priscilla sobbed into her hands.

Thomas had striven to remain placid, but this new agony seemed to tax his already-fraught nerves to the limit. He clasped her face between his hands so tightly that she expected to be crushed. "How can you say that I do not love you? I draw no breath without thinking of you—and loving you. Do you think that my own life would be worth living if ever I lost you? Do not cry, my love. I cannot bear it! Your broken heart is breaking mine."

"I scorn ideals! They cannot shield me from the dark times—or smile upon me through sorrow's mists. What do they mean to me if I cannot have you?"

He regarded her sternly. "Neutrality is out of place in this age, Priscilla. Even *you* must choose your side."

"You speak like Father—and John Seymour!"

"If they speak thus, then they speak the truth." His tone pulsed with emotion. "I fight not only for the independence of the colonies but also of humanity from tyranny—that one dictator shall not enslave the world, that mankind should not be subject to his machinations of terror and whims of cruelty, that his caprice shall never rule our sons and daughters, that no drop of our life's blood shall be spilled by his treacherous will! History is littered with such oppressors. Who should have guessed, love, that these small outposts upon the shores of a wild, untamed land should sound that sacred cry of liberty to all the nations? We shall witness this marvel, Priscilla!"

She was overcome by despair. This passionate idealism, his heart's fire, only intensified her desire for him. It had first drawn her spirit to his. Why strive against it? Why wrestle with a soul so compelled by a divine purpose? The ardent gleam in his eyes seemed to melt her stubbornness to nothing.

She loved him more than ever before at that moment, and she carved his image into her memory for the future months of absence. Fate had betrayed her obstinacy, and the inevitable had taken her hostage. "Will partings forever remain bitter? Must I always be torn from those I love and adore?"

Thomas took her hands gently, but his grip gradually became possessive. In his countenance glowed not only zeal for his intentions but also grief for the breach at hand. "Remember what I say now, and never forget! Burn these words into your memory! As God is my witness, I shall return. My heart is consumed by a multitude of fervent cries, but *you* are my greatest dream!" He abruptly released her hands and, with shining eyes, uttered his final plea: *"Wait for me!"*

Without another word, he turned upon his heel and hastened from the room. A stark realization accompanied the closing thud of the front door. He had scarcely withdrawn from her presence when she fled to the window for one last glimpse of him.

She ached with desolate longing. She was helpless now against the tide of fate, for it had mocked her most valiant efforts. As she watched the young man stride across the lawn and turn at the street corner, his head bent beneath the fog's obscurity, she fell onto the settee in violent weeping.

She understood that she might very well have looked upon him for the last time.

Part IV

Chapter 43

The Scholar

Priscilla was obliged to inform Mrs. Laurence of Thomas's departure. Indeed, the old woman's sympathy was more than sufficient to make Priscilla regret her recent resentment.

Priscilla wistfully watched the departure of the regiments but was unable to locate Thomas amongst the mob. Nevertheless, she noted the familiar forms of William Eton and Henry Adams as they passed. Roger Guildford was the only young man of the gentry not joining the regiments; his profession furnished him with a convenient excuse to remain in town.

Gazing out over the sea of men, Priscilla discerned that most were lads, donning rifle frocks in lieu of official uniforms. Almost as one entity, they marched with a swagger, the blood rushing to their faces, as if embarking upon a grand adventure. Strutting in step with the fifes and drums that went before them, some even grinned. With great bitterness, Priscilla thought, *Will they still dare the redcoats to strike, taunting lofty ideals with each step, once they enter the fog of war, the stench of blood polluting the air, the flight of bullets past their ears, the chorus of faceless screams sending terror through their hearts, and look upon the broken bodies of their compatriots, mutilated by bayonets and cannon fire?* Thoughts such as these drew fresh tears to her eyes, and she wondered how many of these young men, their tongues ringing with the praises of war and liberty, would return.

With the departure of the regiments, Priscilla was left with only ashes to endure the storm of her life. Fear became a persecutor that drained all hope from her exhausted spirit. This war would endanger Thomas's life. She might bear the separation more easily if she was certain of his safety for its duration. Yet she claimed no such assurance, and his final parting admonition—to wait for him even in the absence of communication—afforded little consolation.

She first turned to the God who bends human events to His will. Priscilla presented supplications for her love's protection and guidance for her weary steps. Second, she turned to painting. Aunt Laurence never uttered another syllable questioning Priscilla's artistic decisions. She would only glance occasionally at her niece's paintings over the rim of her spectacles before returning to her book. The painting of the lovers parted by war had assumed fresh import for Priscilla.

Further comfort arrived.

Priscilla had not so soon anticipated a letter from Frances. Although Frances had promised to write, the events of the past few months had so consumed Priscilla that any recollection of such a pledge had been blocked. In one respect, she was elated to receive word from her sister. In another, however, it presented a poignant reminder of those whom she had lost forever.

My dearest sister Priscilla,

I sincerely hope that your health is good. I am dreadfully remorseful for my tardiness in writing, and I pray that you will pardon me.

Even though we are all well at present, the voyage was harsh. My abhorrence for the turbulence of the sea overpowered any romantic notions. Sickness came upon me almost at once. Rosamund, however, suffered most. She remained indisposed for the greater part of our journey. A most sensible physician, however, sailed with us. He prepared a mixture from such materials as he carried with him on the vessel. His medicine brought a measure of relief to her during our trek's final week.

We landed at Portsmouth and suffered another lengthy journey to Kent. Sir Henry and Lady Blount were expecting us and were well prepared for our arrival. The house is a vision. My own apartments quite bewilder me. Such sights are rare in Williamsburg, and my eyes are unaccustomed to this opulence.

One can often remain ignorant of all wonders and injustices beyond his or her realm of influence. I feel I shall never be the same again. An empty heart further exposed to excess can only sink deeper into chaos.

Father has begun to seek a house, either in the country or in London. I shall be content with his determination. Father carries himself in his usual manner. He is delighted with Sir Henry's library, which is full five times as large as the one he left in our old home—and not nearly as forbidding. I have requested and received permission from Sir Henry to partake of his books. I confess that your absence is the partial cause of my literary enlightenment, for I find that memories of you are most vivid when I take up employments of which you would approve.

Mother is well, of course, although the rigors of the voyage stirred a touch of rheumatism. Since her recovery, however, she has sewn the most charming little frock for the baby. I wish you could see it. The child speaks now! Each day, we await some new feat from her. At least she is robust and not often ill. I wonder why our brother does not love her well. One can only suppose that he blames the dear little thing for her mother's untimely end. It is a pity! She favors him most.

Ben is not often about. His fondness for fox hunting is indulged by our genial hosts since he is allowed use of their park for the sport. Even so, he is perhaps much more idle than before, and—forgive me—I think it unfortunate. He has taken to strong drink of late, something which you know he never before touched. He still slights poor Rosamund. If her heart was cold upon entering the marriage, it is no longer so. She loves him—I am certain of it. I sometimes pass her quarters, and, if the door is ajar, her sobs may often be heard. Ivy, I fear, does not fancy our accommodations. She frets that country life does not permit the number of social engagements to which we have been accustomed and hopes that Father can acquire a house in London soon.

As you may have deduced, I dearly love our hosts. They remain most understanding of our present situation. Sir Henry and Lady Blount are the parents of six children. The eldest son is a student at Cambridge. He is currently at home on holiday. A friend and fellow student is visiting him—a certain Richard Carey—who will obtain his degree ere long. This Richard is a singular fellow! His manners are open and gregarious, but I never suspected that deeper metal lay beneath until yesterday.

Mary Beth Dearmon, MD

I stumbled upon him in the library, where he was leaning over a thick volume.

Before I could retreat, he engaged me in conversation regarding the book. "Mathematics—have you much experience with it?"

When I replied in the negative, he pointed toward the complicated figures in the book. He burst into lavish praise for the subject's merits, and, in spite of myself, his description intrigued me. "It is absolute, you know. Only a single answer exists. Like good and evil, all is clarity. No gray areas to cloud the mind! Not even history and politics can equal it."

"After this account, I almost wish to learn myself," I said.

"I shall teach you, if you wish, in this library—at a certain hour—until my holiday is over."

We agreed upon a regular time, and I retreated to the corner of the room in order to conclude my own reading. Later in the afternoon, I set out upon my daily walk. As I sat alone in one of the many arbors in Sir Henry's gardens, mournful thoughts of you returned. A soft rustle interrupted my reverie, and to my astonishment, young Carey stood only a few paces away. He did not share my discomfort upon meeting alone twice in the same day.

I rose in distress, but he gestured for me to remain seated. "I did not intend to curtail your leisure! Please sit."

I assumed my former posture and expected him to leave. He did not. Instead, he stood admiring the glow which the afternoon sun cast upon the topiaries.

He suddenly smiled. "Kent forms quite a vision this time of year."

"Yes, indeed, but I must confess, sir, that my heart is far away. I pine for my little home in Virginia—and the sister I have lost."

My complaint seemed to strike some tone of empathy within him, for his eyes turned upon me with great gentleness. His cheer melted into riper sentiments. I had not yet seen him thus and was taken aback.

"You dearly loved your sister?" he asked me softly, for Sir Henry's son, lately enlightened by our own father, had mentioned the reason for your remaining behind in Williamsburg.

"Very much indeed." I lowered my eyes to conceal the tears. "She was not only my closest friend but also my most trusted counselor. I have not the soul of a lion. Her guidance was, of all things, most essential to me."

He mused intently for a moment, most likely deliberating whether or not to speak. A struggle seemed to rage beneath his brow, and one side eventually triumphed. "I am also no stranger to loss," he finally said.

My interest was aroused, and I leaned forward for more.

"The first seven years of my life were spent in London, under the cautious eyes of my adoring parents. I was their sole progeny, a blessing from God after a decade of barrenness. They instilled in me a pride, not entirely evil, for my talents. Even at such an age, I dreamed to be a great statesman—to play a vital role in the workings of history. My hope and confidence swelled. My father was a modest gentleman, my mother a sensitive woman in all her ways. Life's promise dimmed when my father was struck by a sudden illness and died within months. My mother, ravaged by grief, perished a year later. I found myself alone in the world. One of my father's elderly brothers, a man of means, agreed to take me in. I was profoundly grateful to him. Tragedy is a cruel teacher, but an efficacious one nonetheless. Only the flaming aspirations which had long compelled me sustained my hope by refusing to be stifled. The harshness of the path often threatened to drown all my efforts, but ambition drove me to the culmination of my aims. I shall soon receive my degree, a step toward my greatest desire. You may wonder why I reveal such things to you—a stranger. The human heart seeks its own destiny, Miss Frances, and only the individual holds the power to seize it! Such blows are difficult to survive. They forge an even darker fate, however, if they are allowed to obliterate the dreams of the soul." He smiled again. "It is straightforward—like mathematics!"

Although awed, I was also perplexed. Can a person ever truly recover from such calamities as you and I have lately suffered? Is it possible? I shall ponder his words...they are still mysteries to me. Your loving sister—Frances.

Priscilla certainly noticed a new intellectual vitality in Frances's language and perception. Her own troubles, however, prevented her from dwelling long upon her younger sister's expanded interests. She set about the unpleasant task of enlightening Frances as to the sad events that had arisen in her circumstances since the family sailed for England. Priscilla penned her missive with much love for a sister whom she hourly missed. She signed the letter, which was mailed the following day.

Despite the pleasure afforded by Frances's letter, more tangible comforts were scarce. Christmas, Priscilla realized, would be lonely. Indeed, the presence of more than two hundred independent militiamen stationed in and around the city, separate and distinct from those regiments which had marched, forbade forgetfulness. She would be plagued by painful memories, but she resolved to weather them. Few parties were to be found this holiday season, but Mary Laurence and her niece were invited to a small festivity hosted by the Guildfords. Priscilla was mortified by the prospect.

Still, Mrs. Laurence insisted. "Come now, dear! It will do you good. You have been too long shut up in this house. Your pretty face must be shown to the world more often, not left to waste away in this hermit's lodge!"

Priscilla smiled and knew herself defeated.

The party was a nice little affair, but no grandiose gala. Priscilla was grateful for the simplicity since she had neither heart nor stomach for extravagance. She noted that her old home, under its new owners, had assumed an entirely different character. Laughter, rather than disputes, now rang within its walls. Airy white calico curtains now fluttered in place of her mother's heavy crimson silk panels. Expansive Turkey carpets blanketed the floorboards instead of the lavish Scotch coverings she knew well. The cumulative effect of these alterations made the rooms appear far more spacious than Priscilla otherwise remembered.

Mrs. Guildford proved to be a gracious hostess, but she did not shrink from delicate topics. She was particularly attentive to Priscilla. "This will be an unpleasant holiday for you, no doubt, as you are not surrounded by the solace of family this year."

Priscilla nodded with some discomfort. "Yes, I am afraid so."

"I pray that our little gathering furnishes a measure of delight."

Gesturing toward the curtains, Priscilla hoped to distract the well-meaning hostess from this raw subject. "I was admiring the new window treatments, Mrs. Guildford. Where was your home before coming to Williamsburg? I forget."

"Richmond." The hostess smiled as she fingered the crystal rim of her glass. "My husband and I loved Richmond, but we wished to live at the center of social and political life in Virginia. Where else were we to go but Williamsburg?"

"Indeed!"

Her smile revealing poor dentition, Mrs. Guildford whispered to Priscilla behind her fan. "Yet, I believe we received more action than that for which we bargained, if you comprehend my meaning."

"It has proven a great deal too much for me as well." Already suspecting Mrs. Guildford to be a woman of shallow intellect and character, Priscilla allowed herself to smirk. "Your son, however, was permitted to remain here. Fortune has smiled upon you in that regard."

Mrs. Guildford nodded. "What you say is true, and my husband has seen too many years. I suppose that is one great advantage in Mr. Guildford's being twenty years my senior. For the safety of the unlucky ones, though, I beseech God daily. Many, like poor Mrs. Henry Adams, have watched their husbands join this debacle."

Priscilla's voice thickened. "Some will not return."

Mrs. Guildford clapped her hands. "We must not brood upon unhappy things tonight. After all, how can our anxieties ever benefit them, protect them, or end their woes?"

Priscilla could scarcely suppress the tide of bitterness that washed over her as she heard a woman, never intimately connected with the horror of the age, glibly dismiss the present terror. Priscilla's initial impression of her hostess further soured, and she was not sorry to lose the latter's conversation and company.

Priscilla was sitting alone when she observed young Dr. Guildford approaching Jane and Harriet Adams. He advanced upon them gallantly. Within moments, the sisters were whispering to themselves, giggling at his witticisms, and blushing at his grins. Priscilla watched with disgust. His gaze suddenly swung around toward her, but she averted her eyes.

She was both puzzled and irritated when he strode across the room to her chair. "You are Priscilla Parr, are you not?"

She eyed him with suspicion. "Of course I am."

"I am Roger—Dr. Roger Guildford." A naughty twinkle illuminated his black eyes. "It is always my pleasure to meet a beautiful woman."

"And I see you make an art of pleasing them!"

Bending forward, Roger Guildford roared with laughter.

Priscilla blinked with confusion. "What have I said, sir, to effect such merriment?"

"I like your spirit, Priscilla!" He tilted his head toward her. "You read me well."

"That is *Miss Parr* to you!"

He continued to laugh until his face colored scarlet and he was forced to sit down. His guffaws soon drew the attention of the entire room. Priscilla resented the humiliation his absurdity had occasioned, and, gathering her skirts, she hastened away from him.

Katherine's child was a boy.

The labor was difficult, and not long after the midwife was dismissed, Katherine fell gravely ill. The expertise of Dr. Guildford was consulted, however, and his care was credited with her subsequent recovery. Any lingering doubts regarding his fitness to service the citizenry of Williamsburg were forgotten.

The entrance of David Adams into the world on the second of January was heralded in all corners with joy, but the child was not greeted by his father. The infant was also of a fragile constitution, and fears for his welfare quickly consumed Katherine. The birth also conveyed another measure of grief to Priscilla. She had encountered Katherine only sporadically since the latter's marriage. With a sickly child to rear and a husband at the battlefront, Katherine would see Priscilla with even less frequency. It seemed as though both girls had lost another friend. They had, of late, lost so many.

Chapter 44

The Physician

Even though war raged, the spring of 1776 was rather uneventful on a domestic level as far as Priscilla was concerned. While her days were never happy, her activities settled into regularity, which provided a degree of stability. She was finished with tears, which she had discovered to be futile. Her hours were consumed by painting and books, and they became her sole pleasures. She did, however, receive another letter from Frances in April.

My dearest sister,

I cannot express the profound joy with which I received your letter. Your penmanship is still strong and fluent. Your words never fail to inspire me. My life has been dismal without you, but I now realize that I must make my own happiness.

Your recent misfortunes are grievous indeed. I mourn with you regarding the double losses of Mr. Eton's consent and of Thomas to the war. Still, I am confident that God shall bring about a union between you in time. This expectation is the greatest solace I can offer you, dearest sister. Inexperienced as I am, I shall hazard nothing further.

Father has procured a house on Dover Street in London, and we are now settled. The house is much finer than even we have experienced. Since our family took possession of the place, we have attended an endless stream of balls. Ivy, I daresay, is delighted. I am of the opposite sentiment. I have always been timid and ill suited to the dazzle and clamor of these gatherings. Yet, I must go in order to please our dear parents.

Mary Beth Dearmon, MD

My friend and sometime-instructor Richard Carey has returned to Cambridge. He did not labor in vain. I still study mathematics every day, only now in the library of our new home, and I now aspire to proficiency. Perhaps astronomy shall be my next pursuit. The confines of my own world seem narrow and stifling in comparison. Perhaps you will be proud, Priscilla, that I have learned ambition at last!

Our Sarah is utterly precocious. She has long been walking, and her quick ways remind me of you. She is a comfort and delight to Rosamund.

I despair for our brother. Since our move to London, he has fallen in with a very dissolute set of young men, for whom drunken brawls and gaming are commonplace. These things have been shielded from me, but I accidentally overheard Father berating Ben for his newly acquired vices. Ben ignores Rosamund as much as ever, and it pains me so. Sarah is nothing to him. He never speaks of Rachel, but she fills his heart. He keeps a lock of her hair pressed between small fragments of paper within his breast pocket at all times. I know this to be true since, when he is unaware of my eyes, I have often seen him withdraw the token and kiss it. I sometimes wonder if he is wracked by guilt for their quarrels prior to her death.

Praying that this note finds you in health, I must conclude this letter. I am your devoted sister—Frances.

Once Priscilla had finished reading the letter, she simmered.

How could Ben commit such an injustice? How could he abuse and humiliate his loyal, longsuffering wife by his obsession with a woman who—God rest her soul—had lain in the grave for over a year? Rosamund was barely beyond girlhood! How could he shame his innocent child so?

Priscilla seized her pen and with tremendous energy began the following note:

My dearest sister Frances,

I have just read your epistle and must confess that the tidings shared therein have incensed me. My thoughts shall be expressed plainly and unreservedly. I have never been so overcome by indignation as when I read of our brother's selfish deeds and shameful conduct. You share these sentiments. I never thought him capable of these evils. Please convey my sincere empathy to Rosamund. I am certain that Sarah is as brilliant as you report. I long to see my young niece. You are such a dear to care for her so. Without the heed which you and Rosamund pay her, from which quarter would she receive the love and affection due her?

Few noteworthy events have transpired since my last letter, other than Katherine's being blessed with a son. The family that now occupies our old home is a decent one. Old Mr. Guildford is a model of courtesy, and his lady seems pleasant enough. My goodwill, however, does not warm to their son. Even though he is a capable physician, his unruly manners sicken me.

It is perhaps well that you are gone. Some militiamen still remain about the city, and distrust is rife. Many suspected of mixed loyalties have been brought in for questioning, and I must guard my own tongue, sharing unorthodox opinions only in private company, though it goes against my nature.

I have no further news to impart.

Dispatching my most heartfelt wishes for your health and happiness, I am your loving sister—Priscilla.

"What do you think, Aunt Laurence?" Priscilla asked.

"Concerning what, dear?" Mrs. Laurence peered over her book.

"The war!"

Mrs. Laurence laid aside her volume and examined Priscilla with a benevolent, thoughtful gaze. "Of what consequence is an old woman's opinion? I am flattered indeed."

Priscilla was struck by astonishment.

"Why…it matters much!"

"On which side do you believe me to be?"

"I suspect that you support the rebels. Else, you would not dwell here still."

"I still reside here, but not for that cause. My years are waning, and this frame of mine would never survive a lengthy voyage to England."

"Sometimes I wish that I were in England."

"Do you indeed?"

"I sometimes wish that I were miles away from this war which has doomed my prospects. I yearn to be with my family once more. But then, I remember…"

"What do you remember, Priscilla?"

"Tom." Priscilla lowered her eyes to her lap. "I fear for him so."

Mrs. Laurence gestured with her spectacles. "You must have faith! God will shield him from both bullet and bayonet. You will see."

There was no more talk, for one of the servants entered the sitting room. "A caller, Madam."

"Who is it?" Priscilla brightened at the prospect of a visit from Katherine.

"The name is 'Guildford.'"

Mrs. Laurence hummed in recognition. "He is the attorney whose family occupies your old home! We attended his Christmas party. I believe he took William's place in Richard Eton's law firm."

"Yes." Priscilla's spirits flagged in disappointment.

Mrs. Laurence turned to the servant with a gracious nod. "Please tell the good man that we shall receive him in the parlor presently."

Mrs. Laurence and Priscilla migrated to the parlor soon after the servant had hastened from the room. To their keen amazement, however, old Mr. Guildford was not their visitor.

It was Dr. Guildford, his son!

He paraded into the room. "Good morning, ladies!"

Priscilla could not suppress a scowl.

Even Mrs. Laurence's hands, slightly deformed by rheumatism, trembled with bewilderment. "Good morning, young man. You will forgive me for the misunderstanding. I was prepared to receive your father."

"I am sorry to disappoint! Perhaps I may stand proxy for him and entertain you all in his stead?"

Mrs. Laurence's mouth wrinkled with amusement. "Pray, be seated, Dr. Guildford."

Once the three of them had attained a measure of ease, Mrs. Laurence said, "As you must remember, Dr. Guildford, my name is Mary Laurence. This young woman is my niece, Miss Priscilla Parr."

Priscilla's old pride resurfaced with a smirk. "Unfortunately, we have already met."

"Yes, most memorably." Dr. Guildford smiled mischievously.

Mrs. Laurence, rising with the vigor of a woman half her age, walked to the window and parted the curtains. "The weather is very fine, is it not?"

"Yes, very fine." Dr. Guildford winked at Priscilla.

Following an awkward period of silence, Priscilla smote him with a fierce look. "Dr. Guildford, I would like to know—have you come to trade pleasantries, inform us of the latest news, or waste an afternoon? Pray, state your business at once."

"I have come to call upon *you*, Miss Parr."

"Me? Surely you jest!"

"I am perfectly serious!" He laughed.

Priscilla could hardly believe her ears. "You are lying to me!"

"I would never do such a thing."

"If this be the case, you are disgraceful." Priscilla turned away from him. "I am sorry for your having undertaken a trip for nothing, but—"

He leaned forward with a grin. "Miss Parr, Roger Guildford is not so effortlessly rejected."

"Not only a shameless flirt, but impertinent, too!"

Dr. Guildford sprang to his feet with a glimmer in his eye. "You may be the victor this time, but I shall return. Good day, Miss Parr… Mrs. Laurence."

After his exit, Mrs. Laurence stared at her niece in surprise. "That is an odd one. He does not behave like others of his grave profession."

"Not at all!" Priscilla still smarted from his flippancy at her expense.

"It is my advice to leave him be."

"I have no intention of encouraging him." Priscilla nodded firmly. "His actions at his father's party did not escape my notice. Surely you remember him there?"

"Indeed, I do remember him." Mrs. Laurence tapped her fingers upon the arm of her easy chair.

"He trifled openly with Jane and Harriet Adams. I have no patience for scoundrels. How shall I be rid of him?"

"Ignore his attentions. He will leave you to yourself in time. Yet, one can never be certain!" Mrs. Laurence added upon second thought, "Coldness from you might further inflame his fancy."

Priscilla suddenly battled nausea at her recollection of John Seymour. "How do I manage to attract the most unwelcome—yet most determined—suitors?"

"I recall one courtship which was most welcome to you."

"Yes." The mention of Thomas cast Priscilla into fits of anxiety for his safety and wellbeing.

Roger Guildford's resolve, however, proved more tenacious than even Priscilla had anticipated. He called upon her frequently. Strive as she may, she was sorely taxed to shake off his attentions. Still, he was not nearly so unpleasant as Mr. Seymour. Despite all her efforts, she enjoyed his company, and he possessed a keen talent for inspiring gaiety, a sentiment of which she was in need.

Priscilla retreated to her aunt's harpsichord when he called one afternoon. "You might as well cease all attempts, Dr. Guildford."

"Why?"

"I do not love you—nor ever shall."

"I have just begun my chase!" He chuckled.

"Wicked man!" Priscilla giggled in spite of herself. "I may be as a friend, Roger, but never a sweetheart. If you persist in calling yourself my suitor, I shall be forced to become dreadful."

He turned the pages of the music book as she played. "We would not want that, would we?"

"I mean it thus." Priscilla clinched the smile that threatened to surface. "I shall not allow any man to court my favor, particularly when my beloved is at war."

"Who implied that I court you?" Looking offended, his spine quickly straightened.

"*You* implied it but a moment ago!"

"That was a moment ago. It is not the present. A moment ago, I was your suitor, but we are now as friends."

"Have I your word?"

"My word of honor."

"You are impossible!"

"I thank you kindly for the compliment."

"And absurd!"

"If I do say so myself."

"And highly vexing!"

"Why, of course, mademoiselle."

She wheeled around to face him. "Oh, *do* be quiet!"

"Now the lady has presumed to give me orders!" He gasped in feigned astonishment.

"Someone had better." With a smile, she returned to her music.

Given his assurances that he now harbored no improper motives, Priscilla experienced liberty—liberty to laugh at him. She now remained free from the fear of betraying Thomas by her wit. Yet, she sometimes wondered if Roger Guildford was sincere. She occasionally noted him staring at her in such a striking manner that she doubted his honor. She gradually became confident, however, that his intentions toward her were such as he proclaimed them to be—nonexistent. He had, after all, pledged his word of honor.

In any case, Priscilla's dreary existence did not permit discrimination as to her sources of amusement. Dr. Guildford's humor filled a great void in her lonely days, and it soon became clear to her that comparisons with Seymour were unfair. She resolved not to spurn him. In the spirit of their mutual understanding, the pair soon established friendly relations.

"You do not behave like a physician." She studied him squarely.

"How so?" Intrigued, he sat forward on Mrs. Laurence's drawing room sofa.

"You are not dignified to the degree that befits a man of your somber calling."

"No?" His brow creased with mock astonishment.

"Not in the least."

"I always thought that a grave face frightened the patients and put them ill at ease! For instance, who would have their blood let by a physician who does nothing but brood throughout the procedure? Would it not do their hearts more harm than good and work upon their humors not a little evil?"

"I can envision that exactly as you describe it!"

"No, I am resolved to be as amusing as possible in my patients' company. Perhaps if more physicians exercised the full measure of their wits, their patients would improve more swiftly. Moreover, I abhor bloodletting. No patient of mine has ever been subjected to the leeches. It is an archaic and barbaric practice—ill suited for this enlightened age of science."

"That is a revolutionary concept, Dr. Guildford. Quite a heretical theory in the medical world, I daresay!"

"Roger, if you please."

"What?"

"Use my Christian name."

"I prefer *Dr. Guildford.*"

"Well, I am sorry for it. It must be *Roger*. I will not answer to 'Dr. Guildford.' Tell me, Priscilla, a lovely little girl like you would probably have many admirers. Where are they?"

"The only admirer I wish to entertain is a member of the Continental Army. Do you not remember? I told you as much before."

Dr. Guildford expressed surprise. "Only one?"

"Yes."

"Do you love him?"

"With all my heart," Priscilla answered without hesitation.

"Who is he?"

"Thomas Eton. We grew up together—as 'childhood chums,' you might say. His family moved to Richmond when we were both quite young. Then, two years ago, the Etons returned to Williamsburg."

"The son of Richard Eton, with whom my father practices the law?"

"His youngest son."

"We knew his family when we lived in Richmond," Dr. Guildford said. "We often met them at assemblies but never formed an intimate friendship with them. How did you learn to love him?"

"It is a lengthy narrative…and lovely, though it has been beset by many turns and obstacles." Priscilla sighed. "We were the dearest of friends for quite a long time, it seems. Then, he began to court the favor of another. I knew then that I loved him. We both traveled to the country last summer. The beautiful irony was that, while I supposed that he had fallen in love, he feared that I had succumbed to the same fate! He declared his devotion ere we returned to Williamsburg.

We agreed that the marriage should occur after the completion of his education."

"Quite a tale!" Dr. Guildford slapped his thighs. "What happened afterward?"

"The war erupted, and Father forced upon me a stark choice: my family or Tom. I had given Tom my solemn word, and my love for him was as strong as ever. Before Tom departed for the war, however, Mr. Eton refused his consent to our union."

"What shall you do now?"

"What *can* I do?" Priscilla shrugged as the old flood of hopelessness threatened to drown her. "I can await his return. Perhaps some blessed turn of fate may mend the dilemma completely."

His fingers intertwined upon his knee, and a daring grin flashed across his features. "You will think me a great knave to declare it, Miss Parr, but I never trouble myself for this conflict. It is of no consequence to myself, and its final result shall neither gladden nor distress me. I owe loyalty to no man, allegiance to no nation."

Priscilla gasped in horror, perhaps more violently since her own heart had once entertained such sentiments. "Have you no honor, sir?"

"You are wrong, Miss Parr." Evidently pleased by the effect which his heretical opinion had produced upon his hearer, Dr. Guildford beamed with pride. "My honor is intact. I am Roger Guildford, a most respectable physician—whether Englishman or independent American!"

"It is difficult to hear you speak so flippantly." Priscilla winced at his words. "I once thought as you do."

"No more? What altered your philosophy?"

"I do not know." Priscilla faltered as she probed her own thoughts, like some dark and unexplored territory. "Repeatedly, I have been forced to take a side. A war of ideas, you know, often leaves no heart untouched. I thought myself exempt from the struggle, but I was mistaken."

"Do not be ashamed." Dr. Guildford shrugged. "I have a proposition and would like to talk of something else."

"What is it?"

"Your hours, I expect, are idly spent?"

"I paint. I read. That is all."

"Your intellect is keen. I need an assistant—merely to aid me during procedures."

"I know nothing of medical science!"

"You can make yourself familiar with my instruments and fetch them as needed. Surely you can accomplish minor tasks such as these. I can compensate you but little for your labors, but a small fee is possible."

The thought of an occupation startled Priscilla, and she was hesitant. Yet, at the same moment, she could not deny that some secret delight took hold. Whether it was a result of the prospect of usefulness, an eagerness to expand her mind, or a longing for friendship, she could not tell. Neither could she check the smile that rose to her lips.

The idleness of her days, she realized, had perhaps exacerbated her melancholy. She was naturally curious, and such an employment might excite her intellect. After all, her father had kept a book of physiology, which he had often lent her, within his library.

Following several moments of reflection, she lifted her chin. "I accept the offer."

A pattern was hereafter established. Dr. Guildford lent her his own scientific books, which she quickly devoured. He sent her a note of summons—sometimes in the middle of the night—when an emergency arose, and she rushed to the house of sickness. Her dedication and sincerity were soon praised by Dr. Guildford's patients, and his dependence upon her assistance steadily increased. In return, since adversity had taught her humility, she persuaded him to expand his practice to include less affluent families.

Dr. Guildford, along with Priscilla, was frequently called upon to treat the various fevers and colds that afflicted young David Adams.

Katherine was comforted in her distress by the sight of her dearest friend at the physician's side. Still, Priscilla could not help but notice the lines that concern for the child had drawn across Katherine's brow.

Chapter 45

The Inheritance

Priscilla received a very unexpected letter from Frances in late May. *Some momentous event must have occurred for her to have written so soon after her last note,* Priscilla reasoned while opening the missive. Then, her heart trembled at a sudden thought. *I hope no one has perished!* She devoured the following words with much haste.

Dear Priscilla,

 The most extraordinary thing has occurred. Your mind shall never give it credence! Never in my most untamed dreams did I imagine such a turn of events which has come to pass. I scarcely know where to begin.

 You are aware, of course, that we have wealthy kindred in this land—most notably Samuel Parr, our father's cousin. This relative has been ailing. Only a month ago, he passed from this life. No one was surprised, for his illness had heralded approaching death. Yet, our family could not have been more stunned than when the tidings arrived—but a week following our good cousin's demise—that his only son, a high-ranking officer, had been among the few British casualties sustained during the Continental Army's assault on Quebec this past December. Although my familial grief could not have been greater, I was astounded when Father explained the ramifications of these two deaths. As it stands, Father is now the nearest living male relative to our late cousin Samuel. In short, my dearest sister—and here is the shocking truth—Father has inherited the whole of our cousin's fortune and estate, Kennet Hall!

 Priscilla dropped the letter. A thousand sensations flooded her nerves at once, making her incapable of speech and movement. Her mind sputtered with amazement. Her father had inherited a grand fortune. Not just any fortune, but the lordly fortune of his cousin Samuel! She sank into the nearest chair and sat still a few moments waiting for her heart to slow its desperate flight. She still could not overcome the wonder and incredulity of the entire matter. Her family had been affluent before, but now they were rich beyond all imagination!

When she had composed her wits to a minimal degree, she took up the letter once more and commenced to study its remaining contents:

Father resolved to retain our London residence for future seasons in town. We have settled in Kennet Hall in Buckinghamshire, and oh, I must tell you of its perfections and our glorious advent!

As we were conveyed across the gently sloping hills, my eyes first beheld the majestic cupola piercing the fair morning sky. Atop its regal head fluttered our banner, seemingly inviting us to seek refuge within the towering walls. The house's breathless height was crowned by tall balustrades and its breadth marked by a proud line of Venetian windows, each adorned with a balconet. The Greek portico was supported by four imposing Corinthian columns, which stood as graceful pillars of stone. My heart leapt at the sight of them. A pair of staircases rose to the central entrance of the house. Before the estate bubbled a lavish fountain, upon which a multitude of angels descended to earth in a heavenly retinue. I was moved by the cherubic beauty of their gilded faces. As long as I draw breath, I shall never forget that day which transcended a thousand yearnings, delights, and miseries of my life.

Imagine entire rooms lined with red damask—long galleries flanked by portraits of our noble ancestors—libraries with books too numerous to count—a park populated by scores of deer for hunting—vast halls ennobled by soaring Baroque plasterwork. These are the glories of our new home.

We have visited court and knelt before our great sovereign and his consort. He is a man of gentility and conviction. I beheld Her Majesty's beauty and elegance with wonder. Her queenly grace of legend is no myth. Rather, it is a truth for all to witness.

Father has purchased for me attire reflecting our new status. I wear such sumptuous raiment with gratitude. I remember my origin and shall not fall prey to vanity. If God has blessed me thus, I refuse to betray His favor with arrogance.

Your absence in the midst of these marvels strikes me as particularly strange. I cannot but guess that you would have surpassed us all, your tastes and demeanor remarkably suited for such grandeur. Your wit, upon reflection, seems to have been intended for the adoration of the elite, the jewels of a patrician lady, and the glow of royal favor.

Here I must stop. I tread upon perilous ground, for it is not my place to rebuke or demean the chosen fate of one so dear to me. I am your affectionate sister—Frances.

By the time Priscilla finished reading the epistle, its revelations stung her with even greater ferocity. An emotion akin to remorse drowned all familiar voices of conviction. She envisioned the rewards of destiny—the noblewoman's existence, the stately affluence, and the marked deference. By her own free will, she had renounced them.

The darkness of uncertainty crept into her consciousness. Frances's letter had delivered one of the most staggering misfortunes yet! The lure of riches seized her soul and wrestled with deep-seated loves. Doubt, however, was succeeded by fury and animosity for her father. She had been abandoned by her kindred, the young man she loved, and all tangible hope. Bitterness leaked its poison into her spirit. She recalled, with rising ire, how her father had extracted from her an agonizing choice, such as no daughter should have been given. She blamed him with a malice unequalled by any that had ever sprung from her stormy breast. Her resentment grew roots of iron.

At that pivotal moment, she resolved never to forgive her father—to bear against him an eternal ill will that would terminate only with her death.

Chapter 46

The Prisoner

Given the tempest that the arrival of Frances's letter had aroused in Priscilla's mind, it was perhaps fortunate that she was called to accompany Dr. Guildford on a peculiar errand the following afternoon. She received the following note from him shortly past noon:

Priscilla,

> Our services are required. I will come for you at half past two. Yours, etc. —Roger

The summons puzzled her in one respect. On previous occasions, when Dr. Guildford's skills had been consulted, his note had bidden her to meet him at their destination, wherever the patient might be located. Then, her perplexity gave way to suspicion, and Priscilla sensed a reemergence of her old doubts regarding Dr. Guildford's intentions. Yet, the memory of his willingness to train her in his profession smote her conscience.

His chaise halted in front of Mrs. Laurence's house at half past two, a moment neither early nor late. The contraption jolted as he leapt from the driver's seat. With a few light strides, he met her as she advanced toward the vehicle. Though his expression had assumed the solemn air so peculiar to his vocation, his features yet struggled with agitation of some sort, as suggested by the curl of his lip.

"Good afternoon, Priscilla," said Dr. Guildford, handing her into the chaise.

"Good afternoon." She dared not hazard further reply, for she was bewildered by his manner.

Climbing into the vehicle, which he himself sometimes drove to the homes of his patients, Dr. Guildford took hold of the reins, and they began to rumble down Francis Street.

"You are likely curious as to why I came for you. Do you think it will be a terrific scandal?" Dr. Guildford, pausing at this point, glanced sideways at Priscilla with laughing eyes, most likely to observe the effect these remarks had evoked in her.

"The threat of scandal has lost its hold over me. What could be more scandalous than a young woman living apart from her parents? Nevertheless, your insistence upon conveying me this afternoon, which you have never before done, piques my curiosity." Then, turning in her seat to confront him, she asked, "Tell me…what are you about, Dr. Guildford?"

Dr. Guildford, looking straight ahead, grinned and gave a swift nod. "Wait a while, and then all will be clear."

Though still dismayed, Priscilla was somewhat comforted by this mysterious reassurance. Her mind began to rest again, and she was thus at greater leisure to observe the fresh sights—tokens of a new age—which greeted them both. On either side of her, she began to glimpse the independent militiamen who had remained behind. The men drove wagons piled high with weapons and supplies to the storehouse.

Drills were carried out on every street corner by men who, having missed the first march, were desirous to fight. She even espied a few young men who could not have been older than fourteen, and thus could not have satisfied the age requirement, riding atop the wagons and cleaning their muskets with scarlet cheeks and shining eyes. *Such was Thomas, content to chase his liberty to the ends of the earth, blind to the cost,* thought Priscilla as tears clouded her vision and she was forced to avert her gaze.

She was not long beset by these bitter sentiments, for something else soon arrested her attention.

As they drove past the capitol, their progress was impeded by thick crowds that clogged the street as men entered and quitted the building in unceasing flow while some, loitering before the arcade, murmured amongst themselves in animated tones and waved freshly printed broadsheets in the air.

"What is happening at the capitol?" Priscilla asked her companion.

"Word is that the Convention voted last week to recommend independence at the Philadelphia Congress." Dr. Guildford wrinkled his nose as if the words were distasteful to his palate.

Priscilla gasped. "That is not possible!"

"We shall see. It is of trifling concern to me." Dr. Guildford set his jaw and narrowed his eyes. "I care only that I was spared from this madness. If other men value their blood so little, then let them spill it. *Not I!*"

Priscilla was struck by the scorn that inflamed his voice, a sour note which painted the physician in an unfavorable light. Why his diatribe rendered her uneasy, she could not determine. His thoughts, uttered with such candor and fury, mirrored those which she had entertained for so many years. Nonetheless, she cringed to hear them voiced by him—self-interest laid bare, cowardice exposed, naked disloyalty. Against his rant, Thomas's self-sacrifice and courage appeared all the more radiant in her eyes. Yet, to whom was Dr. Guildford disloyal? Surely she did not mean disloyalty to these colonies?

"You are quiet today, Priscilla," said Dr. Guildford in a much calmer voice. "Are you well?"

"I feel better than ever." Priscilla shivered, as if to shake off the oppressive questions that dogged her mind. Nevertheless, she lapsed into silence again, still unable to forget the spectacle she had just encountered.

She soon espied the Public Gaol in the distance, which grew larger and larger as the chaise approached it. The Gaol, bordered by a white picket fence in the front, was a small brick edifice crowned by several towering chimneys and flanked by a lengthy courtyard. Priscilla was acquainted with the jailer, Peter Pelham, as were most of her circle since he also served as organist at Bruton Parish Church. Priscilla laughed to herself upon recollecting that two Sabbaths past, he had brought one of his prisoners to the service for the purpose of pumping the organ.

She turned to Dr. Guildford with a smile. "Do you not remember that a few weeks ago, Mr. Pelham brought…"

Her voice faded as the chaise lurched to a halt in front of the Gaol.

"What is the meaning of this?" She faced him again, this time with round eyes. "Why have you brought me here?"

Dr. Guildford flashed a knowing smile. "Our patient is here."

Her thoughts began to race. "Surely Mr. Pelham…or his wife…or perhaps the children are—"

He cut her short. "No, Priscilla. Our patient is a prisoner."

Apprehension gripped Priscilla in swift fashion, despite her struggles to limit its mastery. And yet, quite another emotion, still without distinct form, emerged. An opportunity, swathed in both darkness and light, to explore further a world of human suffering that she had only first begun to taste tempted her. It was the same sort of urge a man feels when he is drawn to peer into an abyss; it lured her with promises of a wisdom she yearned to grasp.

Priscilla attempted to even her pitch. "What is his—or her—crime?"

"Desertion."

The word, even murmured with peculiar nonchalance by the physician, struck a discordant note in her ears. She cringed. "How was he injured?"

"That, I do not know. We shall see, I suppose. Mr. Pelham sent me a note an hour ago. It seems that I was the only physician in town willing to treat a deserter." Dr. Guildford beamed at this latter statement. "And why not? This poor wretch is a human being, like you or me." He sighed. "Well, let us go in and see him."

Reaching for his bag, Dr. Guildford hopped down from the chaise then assisted her in dismounting. Together, they passed through the white picket fence and followed the crooked path to the door, which Dr. Guildford rapped thrice. As they waited, a single crow circled overhead, an occurrence that did not escape Priscilla's notice and did little to lessen her trepidation.

Within a few moments, the door was opened by a rotund man of medium height, deep in middle age, his saucer-like brown eyes shaded by an overhanging brow, the slightest odor of liquor clinging to his person, a set of keys jingling from his belt.

Priscilla smiled and nodded toward the jailer. "Good afternoon, Mr. Pelham."

Upon seeing Priscilla, he touched the corner of his hat and flashed a quizzical look toward Dr. Guildford.

"Miss Parr is now employed as my assistant," the physician replied.

Priscilla glanced sideways at Dr. Guildford. In the brief time she had worked with him already, she had observed a curious phenomenon. Upon entering a patient's dwelling-place, his jovial irreverence disappeared and methodical efficiency usurped its place. Indeed, he became as grave as any monk in Christendom.

"I see." Mr. Pelham chuckled. "Thank you for coming." He gestured inside the door. "After you, Miss Parr."

"Thank you, sir." Priscilla stepped across the threshold in the direction of his hand.

Dr. Guildford followed fast behind her and, after the door had creaked to a close, accosted the jailer with inquiries. "Tell me about this man. From whence does he come? How was he injured?"

"He is a Williamsburg man." Mr. Pelham, fumbling for his keys, motioned for them to follow him. "Marched with the first group! It seems he had not the heart for battle after all. One cannot help but pity the poor lad. 'Tis a hard thing to look upon death at his age."

"But how was he injured?" Dr. Guildford persisted.

"It was no easy task to arrest the boy. He fought us blow by blow, and his shoulder was wounded in the scuffle. He will make a fine soldier yet!"

"What will happen to him, Mr. Pelham?" Priscilla asked.

The jailer shrugged. "It is difficult to say. His hearing is tomorrow. But if I were a betting man, I would place my money on a good flogging."

"Only a flogging?" Priscilla cried. "I expected it to go far worse for him!"

Mr. Pelham shook his head, grinning with that morbid humor so customary to those well acquainted with the pain of others. "Three hundred lashes is still a harsh sentence, Miss Parr."

The jailer, then opening a second door, ushered them from his own lodgings into the spacious courtyard, which was enclosed by high brick walls. Into the side of a wall was cut several doors, each secured by a rust-encrusted bolt. He turned his key in the lock of one of these doors, and it swung open with little effort.

Upon entering the room, Priscilla stepped onto a floor blanketed with straw. Her eyes scanned the cell. She glimpsed a small window, sunlight streaming through the iron bars, on the far side of the room. A scuttle, presumably through which a prisoner's fare might be thrust, penetrated the wall. Soft moans punctuated by the clanking of shackles drew her attention to a shadowy corner in which a young man lay writhing, his leg irons clashing against one another.

Dr. Guildford and Priscilla, moving slowly so as not to startle him, advanced toward the prisoner.

Priscilla was astounded to realize his extreme youth. His long curly raven hair twisted in an unruly mass behind his head, the boy's face turned toward them. His forehead damp with perspiration, the warm color of pain flushed his cheeks, which were plump like a child's. Keen black eyes shifted from Priscilla to Dr. Guildford, finally resting upon the former. He began to tremble, and a tear trickled down to his chin.

"Do not fear *us*!" Priscilla, overcome with pity, knelt beside the young man and placed her hand upon his brow. "We have come to help you."

"For a moment, when first I saw you, I thought my sister had come to visit me." The boy's lower lip trembled as he addressed Priscilla.

"What is your age, young man?" asked Dr. Guildford.

"I am but a month past fifteen, sir."

A fresh pang throbbed within Priscilla's breast for this boy. The childlike softness of his face, thought not his tears, recalled Thomas so strongly to her mind that for a moment she envisioned him there, manacled and lying upon the straw in this young soldier's stead. Perhaps he was indeed injured and suffering in some tent, far removed from her devotion.

Dr. Guildford knelt on the soldier's opposite side. "Where is your pain located?"

Groaning, the boy reached toward his right shoulder with his other hand. Dr. Guildford, first stabilizing the boy's right arm, palpated the shoulder in question. "Feel his shoulder, Priscilla."

Priscilla touched the joint but applied little pressure for fear of exacerbating the injury.

Dr. Guildford fixed his eyes upon her in a probing manner. "What do you observe?"

Priscilla, disquieted by his stare, shook her head. "I…I cannot say."

"That is because you do not *feel*!" Dr. Guildford sneered. "You think it improper to touch the patient? I have no need for weak-willed assistants hindered by propriety!"

"It is not propriety which holds me back!" Priscilla, her temper rising, returned his glare in equal measure. "I might harm him—or inflict pain!"

Dr. Guildford lowered his voice. "Perhaps I was too severe just now. Only you must understand, Priscilla, that I never help a patient but that I may likewise harm him. It is the nature of healing—and medicine. Do try again."

Her indignation somewhat soothed by his softened tone, Priscilla pressed her hand against the affected joint. The boy grimaced. Priscilla paused, endeavoring to shape her tactile sensations into words. "This is no smooth surface—like that of other shoulders. It is…it is like a box!"

"Yes!" Dr. Guildford's eyes glittered, and he clasped his hands. "The shoulder is dislocated from its socket. The square surface is the chief clue. Have you a piece of cloth which you might spare?"

Without further thought, Priscilla, her spirits soaring, tore a fragment of cloth from the hem of her skirts and placed it within Dr. Guildford's hand.

He turned again to the young man. "You will suffer even greater pains than before as I restore this joint, but you will soon have relief enough to compensate for your troubles. Open your mouth, if you please." Nodding, the young man obeyed him without question, and the strips of cloth were soon packed within his cheeks. "Hold his arm, Priscilla."

Priscilla, eager to regain his confidence, did as she was commanded.

Dr. Guildford, bending the same arm at the elbow, rotated the limb first across the boy's abdomen and then to his side. Ignoring the young soldier's muffled screams, he continued this motion until the limb swiveled in the joint like the gears of a well-oiled timepiece. The boy's shrieks diminished as he fell to soft panting. Dr. Guildford extracted the padding from his mouth.

"The pain is less," the boy murmured, his eyes closed. "I thank you, good sir—and lady."

Priscilla's bosom heaved with joy. Though her part was small—indeed, miniscule—she could not cease smiling. Her hands had transmitted healing! The great power of this realization filled her with ecstasy and gravity all at once. She gazed at her tiny fingers with newfound wonder, as if participation in this one deed were enough to consecrate them forever.

Reaching inside his bag, Dr. Guildford withdrew a sling, in which he placed the boy's right arm.

"He brought some money in his satchel," said Mr. Pelham, who, lingering at the door, had witnessed the event. "Perhaps he can recompense you from—"

A small smile escaping him, Dr. Guildford shook his head as he rose to leave. "There is no charge. I will not take money from this child, for such is he."

As for Priscilla, she sat gazing with tender eyes upon the recipient of their services. "What is your name?"

"Charlie, ma'am. Charlie Dixon," he answered, smiling at her.

Tears sprang to her eyes, and her voice splintered. "I once had a brother with that name! Had he lived, he would have been about your age now."

"Do I favor him?" asked Charlie, leaning upon his left arm to sit upward.

"No, for he had a red mane, not a handsome curly black one like yours." Priscilla laughed, dabbing tears from her eyes. Then, as a sudden notion seized her, she spoke to Charlie in a whisper. "Tell me,

Charlie, do you remember Thomas Eton? Perhaps you marched alongside him when you first left Williamsburg?"

Charlie, a healthy glow returning to his countenance, bit his lower lip. "I do not remember anyone by that name, but perhaps I did meet him at some point. You see, we were already beginning to run out of supplies, and equipment was scarce. I had not even ink and paper to write Mother!"

Placing her hand over her heart, Priscilla suddenly understood why Tom had not yet written her. Doubts that had tormented her for months dissipated. Somewhere, Thomas surely longed for her with a passion that could be satiated by none but her. Her heart brimmed to overflowing.

"God bless and keep you, dear Charlie!" Standing to her feet, Priscilla hastened toward the door, which Mr. Pelham closed behind them.

Upon breathing the fresh air again, she was greeted by the sound of giggles, sweet as chimes swaying in the breeze. Indeed, the Pelham children were frolicking in the courtyard. Priscilla laughed at the sight, which was pleasant to her eyes. She glanced back toward the cell from which she had come. To her astonishment, Charlie's rosy cherubic face filled the window, and he waved. She returned his gesture.

As she followed Dr. Guildford back to his chaise, Priscilla reflected upon her mentor with growing tenderness. Under his guidance, she had already achieved more than ever before in her life, and, though his manners were peculiar and his convictions eccentric, she was persuaded that his heart was a thing more likely to rule him than any other entity.

"Roger!" Priscilla called to him as he reached the vehicle. "I feel compelled to thank you for your willingness to instruct me in your skills. You are a wise physician and a man of many talents. I am honored to labor at your side—and to count you as a friend."

The expression of deep surprise, superseded by a tooth-baring grin, that came upon his features gladdened Priscilla. Though he said little else during the ride back to Mrs. Laurence's home, she felt certain that he was gratified by her praise.

Priscilla returned to the Gaol two days later with a basket of choice victuals for Charlie. To her delight, she was told that, having been sentenced to a sizeable fine instead of the expected flogging as punishment for his offense, he was no longer an inmate and had been sent back by armed guard to rejoin his regiment.

Chapter 47

The Intrigue

Priscilla's responsibilities as Dr. Guildford's assistant began to infuse her days with growing satisfaction. Still, sleep had long eluded Priscilla. Her restlessness was particularly intense one night two weeks after receiving Frances's letter regarding her father's inheritance. The weight of broken dreams was unbearable in the darkness. Grief and anger were allied to provoke her. She longed for the forgetfulness that accompanies slumber.

As she tossed on her side, her eyes fell upon an object beneath the window. She thus recognized the old chest that Phillip Parr had given her before the family's departure. Priscilla recollected his words concerning the chest: *It is full to capacity of useless, silly, sentimental old things that would be of no use to anyone else.*

Even as she was enraged to recall her father's bitter words, her curiosity was stirred. What had been useless, silly, or sentimental in his eyes might be highly valuable to her. What did the chest contain?

With ever-increasing interest, she threw back her covers, crept out of bed, lit a candle, and walked over quietly to the worn chest. She blew voluminous layers of dust off the trunk, sneezing as the dust billowed in her face. Priscilla fingered the antique golden clasp. The lid of the chest fell open without much effort. The only items housed there included a small batch of letters. She carefully lifted this batch out of the chest.

Using great care, she unfolded the first letter, which read:

March 10, 1746

My dearest Elizabeth,

I write to you with a humble, yet hopeful, heart. Perhaps I should call you as is proper, "Miss Stanley." Yet, you are ever "Elizabeth" to me—enchanting Elizabeth.

I hope to call upon you next Wednesday at your home. Would you have me come, dearest Bess? Might I dare to entertain these expectations? When I saw you at the assembly last month, I loved you. In my eyes, you were no longer a child—but a vision. Perhaps you remember our conversation last spring. You may not recall, but I have certainly not forgotten. You laugh at men, and yet, how I wish your fiery eyes would but turn upon me again. Laugh at me if you will. Only do not deny me your smiles.

If you would be merciful enough to bestow a word from your excellent pen, I shall be content. Your most humble and devoted servant—Phillip Parr.

Priscilla smiled to herself. These were love letters her father had written to her mother thirty years ago! Amused, Priscilla flipped through several other letters, all authored by her father. She came to the first in the final few of the cluster.

May 20, 1746

Dearest Bess,

Words can express neither the fullness of my heart nor the flight of my soul. I have courted your most excellent person for so brief a time, yet I feel as if nothing could ever erase the memory of it. Every laugh, every look, every smile have I taken as encouragement. I shall come to your father's house next Tuesday. I desire, above all things on this earth, to receive his consent for my happiness. Have I your own consent for the venture? In truth, although I have imagined otherwise, I have not received the slightest intimation of your feelings for me. Why cannot you show them? You are cruel to tease me.

Therefore, darling, write with haste once more to communicate my fate. Whether or not I receive your hand, I shall always live in joy at the memory of our conversations and in agony at the realization of lost hopes. I am Faithfully, Devotedly, Lovingly, and Forever Yours to command—Phillip Parr.

Priscilla sighed as she folded the letter. Her eyes had grown heavy, and she decided to return to bed. Nevertheless, she closed the chest

Cadence to Glory

with a touch of unwillingness, for she had taken pleasure in reading the letters. Priscilla promised herself to continue the following day with the remaining letters in the batch.

She awoke the next morning with a great desire to resume her perusal of the letters. After breakfasting with her aunt, she climbed the stairs energetically and entered her room. She opened the chest once more and quickly reached for the letters. As she lifted the letters, her fingers brushed against the base of the chest. Strangely, she detected hollowness there! Tapping the chest base again, she reached the same conclusion.

The chest had a false bottom!

Priscilla was suddenly torn between confusion and curiosity. The latter emotion, however, soon gained mastery as she realized that something worthy of concealment must be hidden therein. She applied pressure to one side of the base until it gave way. Breathlessly removing the square division, she beheld two crisp envelopes that were not yellowed with age like the love letters. Both envelopes were addressed to her father in a strange hand and dated 1774. Philadelphia was their origin. Impatiently, she clutched the two envelopes, opened the first of the two, and withdrew the enclosed letter.

With shock and consternation, she read the following words:
Dear Sir:

If you recall the contents of my last letter, you also remember the caution I then urged.

You will be amazed, therefore, that I have lately abandoned such reserve. The recent disorder in Boston has forced the Society into action once again. I formerly instructed you to be prepared for our notice at the proper time. That hour has unequivocally arrived.

Boston is the center of treason, but the Virginia Colony, particularly its capital, is its chief outpost. Funds for the rebellion, along with other forms of support, pour into Boston from that quarter. I am certain that the authors of such collaboration are amongst your exalted and broad acquaintance. We need names and information which you can furnish. It is essential that we begin to collect evidence against them and have them monitored. Search your acquaintance, sir, for the defenders of the revolution. By doing so, you would perform an invaluable service to the Society, to the empire, and to yourself.

My nephew J. has written to inform me that he has conferred with you and related many details regarding plans of the Society. He has attempted to make inquiries—to no avail. They do not trust him as they trust you. If he did not state the fact clearly enough, I must declare your aid essential in this matter. The shipping lanes must reopen with full exchange of goods, or else we are all ruined.—G.S.

Priscilla hardly paused to think before opening the second envelope, which also hailed from Philadelphia and was dated 1774. The letter housed therein was briefer than the first.

Dear Sir:

I have received your information.

The list you have provided is even more useful than the Society could have hoped. I have forwarded duplicates to both J. and E., as well as various other members.

If fresh information comes to you, send it immediately. Indolence will neither strangle the rebellion nor hang the traitors who support it. It will certainly hinder our Society for the Preservation of the Empire.

I shall write more as circumstances require.

Having delivered this note by my most trusted courier, I may confidently sign my name as—George Seymour, Esq.

Priscilla gasped!

Memories, suddenly illuminated by the letters, came in quick succession. Rachel's threat of secret knowledge, potentially ruinous to the Parr family, was instantly clarified. Priscilla recalled John Seymour's pointed inquiries regarding Thomas's affiliation with the rebellion. The younger Mr. Seymour had intended to use Priscilla, since she was then sister-in-law to Thomas, as a means of acquiring information to incriminate him! When she refused to betray Thomas, perhaps John Seymour had courted Frances in hopes of finding a more naïve informant. In Priscilla's mind, the actions of "J.," as he was identified in the letter, deserved even greater suspicion than before.

Other realizations dawned. Priscilla wondered if Anne Seymour had received Thomas's attentions in order to conduct espionage for her brother. She also remembered shadowy conversations between Phillip Parr and John Seymour, perhaps during a ball or following church, which signified little to her at the time but now assumed a sinister importance. Her father's debates might have been an instrument of intelligence in order to measure the extent of financial and political support for the revolution within the Williamsburg gentry. Most curiously of all, it now seemed likely that he had tolerated his children's own matrimonial ambitions in order to unearth the enemy's most intimate secrets. Priscilla particularly remembered his cryptic justification for supporting Ben's marriage to Rachel: *I have my reasons.*

Still, mysteries remained. How had Rachel, certainly no confidante of Phillip Parr, uncovered his intrigue? Why had he abandoned the highly sensitive letters to Priscilla's keeping by leaving the chest with her? After all, she had discovered the hidden compartment without much difficulty. In addition, why had John Seymour carried the farce so far as to propose marriage to both Priscilla and Frances? How had George Seymour's assets been salvaged? Furthermore, who was the infamous "E." who was also mentioned in the second letter as a member of the Society?

The answers to these questions, Priscilla deduced, might never be known. The mystery that distressed her most, however, involved her father's deceit.

How had a man respected by all who knew him for so many years stooped to personal treachery? Surely he realized that his list of names would probably be used to hang his nearest acquaintances—and even relations—if the rebellion crumbled! What spite had motivated him to betray his dearest friends? Richard Eton and his sons, along with George and Henry Adams, had undoubtedly been included on the list.

Priscilla recalled her father's past investments in George Seymour's shipping enterprises. The rebellion and the consequent closure of the Boston port had unquestionably posed financial losses for them both—as referenced in the first letter—even though George Seymour had evidently written the letters shortly before his death. How would the patriots of Williamsburg react if they knew that Phillip Parr had intrigued against them for greed alone? A notion rose up in her mind as she relished the latter thought.

Revenge upon her father was within her grasp! A presentation of the letter would make his treachery public, and his name would be ruined. He would be labeled a traitor until the day he died. The esteem in which he was still held in the Virginia Colony, even following his return to England, would vanish. His good name would die forever in these parts!

One part of Priscilla rejoiced in the prospect of vengeance. She would reward him for his abandonment of her! Still, her heart ached, and she hesitated.

Why did it ache so acutely? Nothing more than love—love for the father who had loved her once—restrained her. In her mind flashed all the years of her childhood. She could never bring herself to wound her family in any way, which such a declaration would surely accomplish. Phillip Parr could have forced her to desert Thomas, but strangely, he had not. The wrenching choice he had given her, by this estimation, had been a kindness.

It was unusually cold for a June morning, and a fire had consequently been lit in her chamber. She fingered the two letters and strode over to the fireplace. With a trembling hand, she hurled them into the flames.

Priscilla began to weep, for she had cast her anger and resentment toward her father into the fire as well.

Chapter 48

The Declaration

Murmurs of anticipation percolated through the throngs that had assembled around the Williamsburg Courthouse. The day was crisp and cloudless, and a fair sun poured its full brilliance upon their heads. Priscilla, who had ventured forth to join them, drew a deep breath in order to still the flight of her own heart on this momentous day, for she, along with countless others who had gathered, awaited the emergence of Benjamin Waller, the clerk of courts. He was expected to proclaim the Declaration of Independence of the Colonies from Great Britain, which had been issued three weeks before by the Continental Congress in Philadelphia.

As she awaited the appearance of Mr. Waller, Priscilla pondered all that had transpired in the month of June. Patrick Henry had been appointed the first governor of Virginia under the new order. Following the Virginia Convention's recommendation, rumors of an imminent Declaration of Independence had pervaded the troubled parlors of Williamsburg. Confirmation of the event had finally arrived a week prior to the present day.

Priscilla's reverie was curtailed by the emergence of Mr. Waller from the courthouse. A strange hush settled over the crowd. Clearing his throat beneath the white portico, he commenced to read the document in his eloquent lawyerly voice, and Priscilla closed her eyes in awe.

She was astounded by the risks undertaken by the signers. Where her father had secretly submitted a list of suspected revolutionaries, these men had abolished doubt as to their own guilt by boldly sending their names to the king. If the colonies proved unable to wrest their independence from Britain in battle, the king would have no peace until he signed their death warrants. The signers risked their fortunes, their lives, and their families for an ideal. Considering their sacrifice, Priscilla was ashamed to remember her own past dedication to neutrality. How sharply these men contrasted with Phillip Parr and the Seymours, who had condemned their friends and neighbors to future prosecution in order to preserve their own wealth!

As celebratory cannon fire roared across the Palace Green following this proclamation, she suddenly understood why Thomas had always referenced his affinity with the colonies. Together, they had chosen a path of extremes that boasted both peril and glory. All support had been withdrawn. Only the strength of conviction could sustain them. She had broken with her father's house to pursue an impossible hope. As the innocence of childhood had ebbed and discernment had risen in its stead, the urge for independence—ancient as the mountains—had forged its own destiny. Liberty, it seemed, was as natural and inevitable as the coming of age.

A nation had been born—and must fight for survival.

※

A few days after the Declaration of Independence had been proclaimed from the courthouse steps, Priscilla and her aunt Laurence were invited to dinner by the Guildfords. The shock was still fresh, and the conversation repeatedly returned to the Declaration.

"I never thought it possible." Mrs. Guildford sighed as the maidservant placed the roast duck before her.

"Neither did I," her husband said. "I never supposed the Congress would take such drastic measures."

"They will all swing from the gallows before Christmas, I daresay," Dr. Guildford scoffed.

Priscilla nearly dropped her glass in astonishment. "They exhibit great courage in what they have done. This is the stuff of heroism!"

"I would rather be a living coward than a dead hero." Dr. Guildford howled with laughter. "Let them have their monuments—I would rather have life!"

Mrs. Laurence, drawing her handkerchief to her mouth quickly, appeared to cringe at the physician's remark. "It was not unexpected that we should fight the redcoats in our Congress as well as on the battlefield."

Priscilla idly fingered the green damask tablecloth. "Still, the greatest battle rages in the heart of man."

"What do you mean, Miss Parr?" old Mr. Guildford asked.

Priscilla spoke slowly while her thoughts took shape. "Liberty cannot be removed from a heart once it has entered. Trials and hardships, such as we now experience, cannot hinder its growth."

"Yes, this war imposes *great* burdens upon the ordinary citizen," Dr. Guildford sneered. "After all, British goods are lost to us!"

"You are spoiled, Roger," his mother laughed as she sampled the veal. "Our bereavements are small compared to those of others. Only consider poor young Mrs. Adams—"

Priscilla glanced upward anxiously. ""Has some evil befallen Katherine?"

Mr. and Mrs. Guildford exchanged glances.

"Forgive me, Miss Parr, but we thought you had already learned of her loss." Mrs. Guildford wore an apologetic expression.

"What is it?" Her fingers tightening around the silverware, Priscilla braced for a blow.

"The news came yesterday." Mrs. Guildford drew a deep breath. "Her husband has been killed in battle."

The tidings struck Priscilla forcibly. Her spirits, recently elevated by the Declaration, stumbled again as she stared into the horrors of war. Death, its footstep final and unmistakable, could not be reasoned into oblivion. The loss of a childhood acquaintance, such as Henry had surely been, also killed a part of her innocence that still remained.

The ideal had survived, but the man had perished.

Following dinner, Priscilla departed the Guildfords' home in a state of absentminded distress. Hardly knowing what to expect, she hurried to the Adams home. Priscilla finally decided that, since Katherine had never manifested a resentful temper, the call could only be perceived as an act of kindness.

Priscilla was received by Katherine in the parlor.

What an altered creature greeted her!

The moment Priscilla entered the room, Katherine fell into forceful weeping upon the sofa. Tears splashed onto her trembling palms, which covered her pale countenance. She shook violently for some moments. Priscilla was unnerved by such a display of grief from one who had always checked her emotions. Endeavoring to recover her composure, Katherine, shrouded in mourning black, finally spoke.

"I have done very well until I saw you, Priscilla!" Katherine gasped, her voice wracked by sobs. "Henry and I spent so many wonderful evenings with your family. Can I not erase the time? How can I continue without him?"

"Your son shall be a comfort to you!" Priscilla rushed to her side. "He is the part of Henry which shall always be yours, Kate."

"David is ill. I may lose him also!"

Priscilla sensed that her words fell upon deaf ears. "Nonsense! David will live. Thus you must persevere."

"Senseless bloodshed!" Katherine suddenly lifted her hands in bitter rage. "My son shall never look upon his father—shall never hear his voice. Was Britain so harsh a taskmaster as to warrant *this*?"

Priscilla could not speak. Instead, she watched one of the strongest individuals she had ever known sink into desperation before her very eyes.

Cadence to Glory

Following her painful visit with Katherine, Priscilla was not long in returning to the Adams home.

George Adams, sick with grief, took to his bed soon after news of his only son's death reached Williamsburg. Dr. Guildford and Priscilla were called upon to attend his needs. His heart had not been strong in recent years, and this new calamity further diminished its fitness. Thus was Priscilla summoned to the house of sorrow.

More than ever, she feared for the life of him she loved most—the elusive Thomas Eton.

Chapter 49

The Accident

In the midst of her sadness, Priscilla received a letter from Frances. This letter, the contents of which could not have surprised her more, read as follows:

Dearest sister Priscilla,

What news! We have suffered a terrible fright.

At the time of my last letter, our brother's gambling debts had mounted and Father, upon receiving his inheritance, was better able to discharge them. This burden was a source of fierce quarrels between them, and they were barely speaking.

The disunity which had arisen was abruptly ended by an alarming event.

We have been in Buckinghamshire since the season concluded in London. Ben had derived great pleasure from riding about the grounds after Father took possession of the house. A month ago, however, he did not return from his afternoon ride in the park. One of the gardeners soon discovered that our brother had been thrown from his horse. Ben was carried into the house, where he lay unconscious for a little over two hours. Our family, noting the force dealt to his head by the accident, prepared for his death. I cannot express the agonies which I myself endured. They are still much too painful to bear contemplation.

Ben revived at last to behold the face of his wife, who kept vigil nearest him. He awoke shaken and pale, as if he had seen death. Our physician, Dr. Humphrey, pronounced him fortunate to have survived the blow. Our gratitude to God knows no bounds.

At first, his speech and gait faltered. We wondered if he might suffer ill effects from the incident for the rest of his life. Rosamund, however, has aided him in his recovery by constant supervision and care. She walks with him through the gardens so that he may return to his usual pace. She constantly converses with him so that his tongue may find its rhythm again. Several weeks of careful attention and practice have largely restored his former capabilities. Indeed, she has refused to leave his side.

His character, not his health, has sustained the most decided change. He is conscience-stricken. Ben awoke with the full impression that God had spared him, and, in his own words, he refused to abuse the mercy of his Creator. Death had hovered so near—yet had not touched him. The realization made him wild with remorse. A fortnight ago, as I walked ahead of Ben and Rosamund in the gardens, I overheard the following discourse between them:

"You—of all people—have shown more kindness than I deserve," he said quietly.

"I have taken a vow to care for you in sickness. Is that not sufficient?" Rosamund asked.

"I saw your face first...as I awoke. I had never known it to be so beautiful...so pure."

"It is not I who has changed."

"I was plunging into my own...my own destruction!" He struggled to speak. "I spurned the love of a child—and the love of such a woman as yourself—for the idleness of youth...for a memory."

"You talk as if you were dead! God has offered life and hope, as you well know."

"Forgive me for my offenses against you." He then turned to her with some effort. "If you cannot forgive me, little wife, then test my devotion. Humbled as I am, lend me the prize to which I have been blind these many months—your excellent heart."

"It is already yours!"

I can attest to his sincerity, Priscilla. He has begun to visit the nursery in earnest. It seems that he is determined to match his former coldness with an equal measure of affection. He has dropped his former friends, who once led him into corruption. His gambling, as far as I know, has ceased, and I have yet to see him accept strong drink following the accident. My hopes, although not entirely secure, are improved.

I noted previously that his speech and walk have now returned for the most part. The fall itself, however, has afflicted him with headaches which, although infrequent, are severe. We all hope that this particular effect will abate with time.

I almost forgot to mention that Richard Carey has graduated from Cambridge. You must imagine my delight when he sent me a well-bound book of geography a week ago. In the note which arrived with it, he praised my "fine mind and natural curiosity" and insisted that "such gifts as these must be nurtured." I hope that he feels welcome to visit Kennet Hall soon, which now, upon his graduation, he is at liberty to do. He has not forgotten our lessons—or so his letter declares.

Praying that you are cheered by these tidings, I am your faithful sister—Frances.

Upon reading Frances's epistle, a smile overspread Priscilla's features, for Rachel Eton Parr had been laid to rest at last.

※

George Adams suffered a sudden bout of breathlessness, and the young physician's summons for Priscilla's assistance was particularly urgent. Once Mr. Adams's condition stabilized, dusk had settled over Williamsburg. Dr. Guildford was consequently obliged to walk Priscilla home.

Gloomy thoughts preyed upon her as they walked together. "It pains me to see Mr. Adams waste away thus. Still, one cannot be amazed by his grief. His son, you know, was a fine young man. I am fortunate to have known him."

Dr. Guildford said nothing. She noticed that he was unusually quiet this evening. The silence occasioned her much discomfort. She fancied that he was often glancing sideways at her in the darkness. She flinched at the thought.

She became anxious to induce him into conversation. "Young Adams's widow is my dearest friend in the world. Henry's death, compounded with her child's sickness and old Mr. Adams's decline, must tax her strength exceedingly. How can she bear it?"

She turned to measure Dr. Guildford's reaction and instead found his dark eyes resting upon her face with an intensity of feeling that unnerved her. The passion she glimpsed there was reminiscent of one from whom she was divided by blood and toil. Within moments, Dr. Guildford grasped her hand.

In her panic, a thousand revelations burst upon her at once.

Two years ago, her mind had been the very equal of Roger Guildford. All had changed. For the first time, she marveled at how fundamentally Thomas's influence had shaped her character. Thoughts of Thomas, however, drove her to desperate anger—and stoked thwarted desires. These yearnings, so long denied, languished in the wilderness of her soul.

The appearance of the young physician upon this barren landscape offered hope. She could once again derive comfort from a well-informed, rational mind. He was by no means heartless, and, despite his political apathy, she found him to be the second most amusing man she had ever met. The first, she thought bitterly, was as good as lost to her. For an instant, she wondered if she had erred in discouraging Dr. Guildford's more serious intentions early in their acquaintance—and if their revival signified her last opportunity for some semblance of happiness. These sensations, however, died swiftly, and, as memories of Thomas inflicted darker pains, she held her head in shame.

Before Thomas, she—like Roger Guildford—had never been inclined to consider mighty notions of good and evil. Thomas had stirred her soul from its great slumber and inspired new life in an intellect long poisoned by skepticism. In all this, she had clung to him like a final hope—as he would ever be.

All other hopes—and affections—shrank before his glory.

Priscilla withdrew her hand. "No man looks at me in that manner—save one."

"I look as I feel!" Dr. Guildford drew her so closely to him that, for some moments, she could not escape. "How can I strangle my own desires? I shall not! Since I first met you—"

"Stop! I beg you would not—"

"I *will* say it! I have concealed my hopes long enough—at your wish. My heart has thundered so violently in secret. Now, you must hear its beat as well!"

Priscilla, overpowered by his grip and her own confusion, began to feel ill, and she was powerless to speak.

"I love you, Priscilla Parr." His eyes glittered in the darkness of the evening. "Yes, I love you. Do not look surprised. Surely you have beheld the truth before…in my eyes, my words, the tone of my voice!"

"I thought that, after that first brief episode, you came to view me only as a friend. Was that not our agreement?"

"A friend?" Dr. Guildford laughed mockingly. "I wanted you to think of me as something else—a man who wants to marry you! Yes, Priscilla. I want you for my wife. Let us be married today—tomorrow—as soon as may be!"

"I have received great fulfillment in serving as your assistant, for I have been useful in that capacity." She finally freed herself from his embrace. "I have no wish to give you pain. Please do not force me to do so!"

"We could journey to Paris—to London. I would have you adorned more grandly than Marie-Antoinette herself!"

"No!" Priscilla hardened her expression. "I am promised to another. You know that."

"Ha!" Dr. Guildford's outburst reeked with scorn. "He is a mere lad."

"He is twenty!"

"A lad!"

Priscilla's heart altered toward Dr. Guildford in an instant. He had ridiculed Thomas, an offense she was ill prepared to forgive. No longer did she pity the rejection he was to receive. No longer did their friendship check the rebuke that rose to her lips. "He is more a man than you. At least he is not devoid of principles."

"And what is he, pray? I know his kind—impractical dreamer. Are not you and I more equal in temper and values? *We* are not prisoners to ideology."

"A man who professes no convictions is not to be trusted, for he does not know his own mind. He has no conscience."

"Your Thomas's conscience is tender, is it not?"

"That will do, Roger!"

"I am not finished!" Then, in a more sorrowful tone, he said, "You have played me false all these months. I expected you, to whom love has been so cruel, to be sincere."

His accusation stung her, and Priscilla lowered her gaze. "Your imagination mistook friendship for passion. You saw only what you wished to see."

"Can you tell me that your heart has never warmed at my presence? Look at me, Priscilla." He raised her chin. "I want to see your eyes."

"Yes, my heart did warm. My heart warmed at the presence of a teacher—and a friend—in whose company I took pleasure. Nothing more!"

"You told me once that you initially regarded the Eton boy as merely your friend." Dr. Guildford trembled with a sort of desperation rarely found in a man of his temperament. "Can you not learn to love me as you loved him?"

"No. I can never love anyone half so much as I love him." Torn with compassion by the forlorn look that seized his features, she attempted a smile. "Let us forget this audience. *I* am prepared to forget—and to carry on as before! I should like to continue as your assistant, if you will have me."

His eyes narrowed—and gleamed with spite. "You will regret this. I have offered you everything. Perhaps one day you shall marry him! Oh, yes. You are resolved, I see. You have relinquished your family, your prestige, and your dignity for that dreamer whose head is forever in the clouds!"

She struck him with all the strength she possessed, so heartily that, for a moment, he lost his footing. "Evil man! How dare you! Leave me! I never wish to see your face again, you wicked creature!"

"Good evening, Miss Parr." With a resentful smirk, Roger saluted Priscilla with a tip of his hat and deserted her on the street before she could even gather her thoughts.

As she watched his shadow retreat into the night, she was overtaken by remorse for slapping the young physician. Perhaps she had spoken too harshly. Yet, how could she pardon his words to her? With the greatest disregard for the sorrows she had borne, he had thrown all her shame into her face and had abused Thomas's honor. She would have pitied his misfortune more had he not been so vindictive. It seemed as if, after she refused him, he wished to inflict as much pain upon her as possible. This physician had reopened old wounds that had begun to heal. Dormant sensations of hopelessness returned, and she struggled to tame them again.

She supposed that her tenure as Dr. Guildford's assistant had ended. She was sorry for its conclusion. Such an employment had eased her soul, occupied her mind, and endowed her life with purpose again. Most of all, she mourned the loss of his intelligent company, which had furnished much solace and diversion in the preceding months.

She stood not far from her aunt's home. Eager to give way to her distress within the privacy of her chamber, Priscilla crossed the street and hurried toward the threshold.

Chapter 50

The Englishmen

Scarcely a month after Priscilla refused Dr. Guildford's proposal, her spirits were bolstered upon receiving the following letter from Frances:

Dearest sister,

So little time has elapsed since I wrote you last, but events of a most intriguing nature have transpired.

We are presently in London. Sir Henry and Lady Blount are also in town. Last night, they hosted a ball at Hanover Square, and our family was invited. It was a grand occasion, the like of which I have never beheld. Nobles were present, Priscilla. Only think of it!

We had just taken our places in the ballroom and formed many new acquaintances when a certain ripple of interest served as a mild interruption. An arrival was eagerly anticipated by those who were better informed than myself. A few moments later, a tall dark-haired young man strode into the room with a party of friends. His presence was imposing. All eyes were drawn to his fair figure. (I confess that my own heart fluttered a little when I first saw him!) His features were chiseled in perfect proportion. He carried himself with great decorum but mostly conferred with his own set. It was clear that he did not wish to mingle with the broader assembly.

I thought little more of him for some time that evening though I still marveled at the interest his appearance had excited among those gathered. My next notice of the young man occurred later once the dance had begun. I was sitting to the side, but my view of the couples was obscured by onlookers. Two women, both of them fashionably arrayed, were standing near me as they scrutinized the dance.

"That young upstart is determined to have him," one woman sneered.

"I hear that her father has come into some money," the other said. "Still, one can scarcely forget that they are colonials. Pray, look how awkwardly she dances!"

The women burst into laughter. Although it was mockingly done, I thought it delightful that they referenced my fellow colonists. I felt a great curiosity to see someone who had also tread the colonial shores. Amused and eager, I followed the gaze of the women. To my surprise, their eyes rested upon the dark-haired young man whom I had noticed earlier as well as his dancing partner—none other than our sister, Ivy!

Surely you feel my astonishment at that moment. I had never seen the man prior to that evening. Hoping to learn more, I turned and searched for the remainder of our family within the great crowd. Catching sight of them at the far end of the same room, I approached them. Ben, whose health is not yet equal to dancing, stood with Rosamund and our parents. The object of their interest matched mine.

"Who is he, Father?" I asked upon joining them.

"Sir Geoffrey King," Father beamed. "He has just returned from a year on the Continent."

"I once gambled with his younger brother and thus have some knowledge of the man's reputation." Ben colored with shame as he referenced his past behavior. "Sir Geoffrey's character, I understand, is not without blemish."

Father wheeled upon him angrily. "What do you mean?"

"I remember hearing something about an elopement, from which no marriage resulted." Ben shuddered. "He is suspected of having fathered half a dozen love children."

"Shameful!" Rosamund cried. "We must counsel Ivy to guard her affections."

"Nonsense." Father straightened his waistcoat. "Such tales always follow any man of means. It is often a ploy to claim inheritances."

"As to the elopement, any young woman who gives herself over to passion deserves her fate!" Mother fanned herself with energy.

Cadence to Glory

"It would be a fine match for Ivy," Father said. "In fact, she could not marry more to my liking. Sir Geoffrey boasts both fortune and connections."

I could not resist. "He has not proposed to her yet, Father!" I giggled.

Anxious to contemplate the incident in solitude, I moved away from them shortly. The dance ended, and the couples dispersed. I continued to observe Ivy and Sir Geoffrey from a distance. He appeared to speak quite courteously to her. I watched him draw her hand to his lips, whereupon she rewarded the gesture with smiles and laughter. He whispered something into her ear, and I noticed the blush which spread upwards to her brow.

"My eyes deceive me!" A voice behind me arrested my attention. "Can this be my young pupil?"

I turned—and beheld Richard Carey standing before me!

It had been many months since I last saw him, and I naturally searched for any change in his appearance. His golden-brown hair still frames an earnest countenance. His green eyes still glitter with energy. His brow is still creased with much study, and, as before, it is his lively manner, not his face, which renders him pleasing to the eye.

I hastened toward him. "I received your geography text! It has consumed me—for the better. Yet, mathematics must remain my favorite. Where have you been these months?"

"Since my graduation, I have been studying the law at Lincoln's Inn here in London. I still wish to be a great statesman, you know."

"Of course!"

He tilted his head to one side. "What do you wish to be, Miss Parr?"

Call it lack of brilliance or ambition, Priscilla, but I had never thought of it before!

"What is there for me to do?" I sighed bitterly. "I dearly love to learn, as you have shown me. The science of numbers—mathematics—fascinates me. What can I do?"

"From the moment I met you, Miss Parr, I sensed a bright mind, pristine and untested. Why else did I take the time to help develop that intellect? One must seize circumstances, not be ruled by them. You hail from the colonies—the revolutionaries will not be satisfied with continuity! They are determined to be free."

"Hush!" I glanced around to ascertain that none had overheard his remark. "Those words could be construed as treason."

He laughed. "If it is so, then men more glorious than I shall lose their heads!"

I was awed by him, Priscilla. His wit excited mine. I realized that he openly acknowledged thoughts which I had long stifled within my own breast!

"I am indebted to you, Richard," I said. "You have opened my mind to discernment. Confusion has given way to clarity. I cherish the memory of our lessons, you see. I begin to know myself—and yearn for more from the world!"

"That hope is the seed of greatness, Frances." He smiled. "I am honored by your gratitude, but if indeed you feel indebted, repay me with your hand in the next dance."

"I shall be delighted!" In truth, I was flattered beyond belief.

Following the dance, Father approached us. After greeting Richard, he noted that a headache—the remaining symptom of the accident—had afflicted Ben and that we were all consequently obliged to return home. After Father had disappeared, Richard inquired for our London address. When I gave him the information, he whispered, "I shall see you again soon. I will call upon your family Monday next." I was inestimably sad to leave him. He has awakened aspirations within me—humble little Frances!

My heart shall burst if I write another word. Be happy again for my sake, dearest Priscilla! Your devoted sister—Frances.

Part V

Chapter 51

The Widow

Roger Guildford was destined to be consoled in his loss. A few months following his fruitless interview with the woman he loved, his downcast eye fell upon someone who had, of late, irrevocably lost her own happiness. He was initially astounded by her forbearance, although her pain was impressed upon each line of her mild face. Yet, he felt only astonishment, not attachment of any kind. At that particular hour, his heart had been fixated by Priscilla Parr. Still, following his tempestuous interview with Priscilla, his mind wandered back to the grief-stricken young woman who had been one of his patients. He envisioned her smooth brow, steady gray eyes, and the melancholy expression that now haunted them. The saintly composure with which she bore her loss, so foreign to Dr. Guildford, drew him.

Astonishment led to admiration, and admiration turned to passion. The young physician yearned to be comforted by her. What solace his broken heart might find in those gentle arms! When all reflection had been exhausted and when his devotion had peaked, he traveled to the young woman's abode. He confessed everything, including the tangled progression of his feelings, and did not leave until he had extracted her promise to marry him.

Priscilla's surprise could well be imagined when Mrs. George Adams arrived with her two daughters to acquaint Mrs. Laurence and her young niece with these intimate details—and the fact that Katherine Lee Adams had consented to become the wife of Dr. Roger Guildford!

Upon hearing the news, Priscilla descended into confusion. Why would Katherine marry so rashly? She was the last widow in the world Priscilla expected to wed so soon after her husband's death.

Surely Dr. Guildford had deceived Katherine! How could his affections have discovered a new object in so short a time? Katherine knew Roger merely as her physician! Priscilla even feared that he had sought Katherine's hand out of spite in order to avenge himself upon Priscilla for spurning his proposal. After all, Priscilla knew his flexible conscience well. Plagued by such doubts, she decided to ease them by calling on Katherine.

Upon entering the Adams home, Priscilla found Katherine in the parlor, clutching a tear-streaked lace handkerchief. As soon as Priscilla was announced, Katherine met her gaze.

Although Katherine's eyes were red with weeping, she forced a cheerful smile. "Good morning, Priscilla. Do sit down."

Priscilla hastened to the sofa and turned to Katherine with a stern countenance. "What are you doing, Kate?"

"I beg your pardon?" asked Katherine, shocked.

Priscilla's voice rose. "What do you mean marrying him whom you cannot love—and so soon after Henry's death?"

The question delivered its blow to Katherine. Her lips twitched, and Priscilla feared for a moment that Katherine would burst into tears.

Katherine's eyes returned to the floor. "I have no other alternative."

"You have done as you should before now. You live quite comfortably beneath your father-in-law's roof. George Adams will never cast his son's widow, not to mention his grandson, into the street!"

"Those are ignorant assumptions, Priscilla." Something like fury crackled in her tone. "Mr. Adams may not survive the month. His heart has weakened since we received news of Henry's death. You know very well that Dr. Guildford has paid more than one visit to this house in the past month—and for professional reasons! *You* have accompanied him. Yet that is not all! Mr. Adams's finances are not as they once were."

Priscilla could say nothing. The rarity of Katherine's anger rendered it all the more forceful once provoked. Priscilla was a little ashamed to have incorrectly assessed Mr. Adams's estate.

"Once the poor man is gone, Jane and Harriet shall also be forced into matrimony." A sort of subtle desperation crept into Katherine's voice. "I cannot bear desertion *and* poverty. Any aid which my parents, so far away, might have offered is lost to me."

"A loveless marriage is the greatest poverty of all!"

"If only my own welfare hung in the balance, I would feel as you do. But my son, sickly as he is, must be supported. A father is required in his case."

"Kate, you always have a refuge in my Aunt Laurence's home! She is a charitable woman."

"I shall accept no charity. Kind as you are, Priscilla, my son and I will never burden your aunt. No, I must marry Dr. Guildford." Katherine studied her warily. "He told me of his former affection for you, Priscilla. Could it be that, once you thought him beyond your grasp, his former proposal grew more attractive?"

Priscilla drew back in horror. "Do you truly think me so base as that?"

After some moments of hesitation, Katherine closed her eyes and sighed. "Of course not. You must pardon me for placing such poor faith in your character."

"Do you love Dr. Guildford?"

"No. I hardly know him. However, he saved my life once before—remember? I also cannot forget his services for David."

"Gratitude alone cannot anchor a marriage." Priscilla scoffed. "If you cannot love him, do not marry him."

"I must."

"You have always insisted that you would only marry for love. Why compromise your ideals now?"

"Time erodes our silly little girlish notions, doesn't it?" Katherine laughed bitterly. "Like flowers withering in the parched earth, we die in parts with the changing season. It was natural, even proper, to dream from the safety of our secure childhoods. But life! We have met the savage wilderness. Survival must guide us, and the heart must be slain."

Tears flooded Priscilla's eyes to hear Katherine trample upon their girlhood ideals. It rattled her sentimentality. The lofty standards she had long cultivated had been scorned by her closest friend, one who had cherished such convictions herself for so many years.

Priscilla struggled to suppress resentment. "You married Henry for love."

"Yes, I did love Henry…and always shall." Katherine's eyes brimmed with tears. "Yet, when I married him, I was naïve and sheltered, surrounded by family. I bore no obligations and was therefore at perfect liberty to marry for love."

"Roger is not like Henry. He is amusing and lively, but he is also vindictive and, in many respects, unprincipled. Since you have been married once before to an upright man, I fear the comparison will find Dr. Guildford wanting. You can fare better than him."

Katherine shook her head. "There is no one else. I cannot continue with my son alone. I am not strong like you, Priscilla."

"You are the strongest person I know!"

"No, I am not. I am the shadow of my former self. Until you hear a babe's cry pierce the night, touch his fevered head to match your own, and awake to an empty heart, *do not judge me!*"

Katherine was immovable. Priscilla trembled to encounter her impenetrable gaze, which, like a stone wall, forbade dissent. Protest, Priscilla decided, was futile. She could not alter Katherine's mind. The battle, it seemed, was lost.

With these sentiments, Priscilla quietly rose to leave. "I see now that I cannot dissuade you. Yet, remember that you shall always have a friend in which to confide."

"I will not forget." Katherine attempted a smile.

Priscilla returned home in dejection. Her thoughts revolved around pity for Katherine. She truly mourned her friend's fate. Katherine's goodwill, despite an assurance to the contrary, appeared lost. Priscilla searched for any action she could have taken to prevent this debacle of a marriage. She realized that she deserved partial blame since her refusal of Dr. Guildford had resulted in his pursuit of Katherine. *Yet,* Priscilla thought, *I could not have destroyed my own chances for happiness merely for Katherine's sake!*

"Are you well, Priscilla?" Mrs. Laurence asked as they lingered in the sitting room following dinner that evening.

Priscilla, overcome by qualms, was in no temper for discretion. She related every detail of Dr. Guildford's doomed proposal to herself, as well as her painful audience with Katherine. Mrs. Laurence, removing her spectacles and fingering her needlework, listened in deep thought.

"I am glad you struck the physician," Mrs. Laurence said once Priscilla had concluded her account. "I never liked him!"

Priscilla laughed in spite of herself. "Why is that, Aunt? I myself was fond of his company, although he provoked me beyond all restraint at our last meeting."

"I suppose his humor was never to my taste." Mrs. Laurence leaned forward in a more somber manner. "Do not fret. We are independent creatures whether or not we choose to acknowledge it. We are rarely compelled by anything! Guard your own doings, Priscilla, and leave Katherine to God."

Katherine was true to her word.

On an October morning, she became Mrs. Roger Guildford in a small ceremony hosted within the Guildford home. Once again, Katherine was a comely bride, but the blush of her cheek was no more. It was infrequent to glimpse her smile, or even a single sparkle in her gray eyes. The man to whom she was wed often glanced at her profile with reverence—as if she were his superior, not his equal.

Priscilla could not resist thoughts of Henry. He had been a righteous man who had captured the devotion of the woman he loved. Even his death was heroic, his blood mixed in the mortar that would form the foundation of a nation. In the end, his life was extinguished in the pursuit of liberty. Yet, in his brief existence, he had been blessed with great happiness such as some men never know. And his memory would live on in the form of his son, in the heart of the woman whose love for him still burned, and in the spirit of the country for which he strove and died.

Chapter 52

The Revolutionary

The winter of 1776 ushered in fresh trials.

The dining tables of Williamsburg were bereft of British delicacies, the more privileged sector of the populace having finally exhausted its previous surplus. In addition, the severe weather of that season exacerbated Mrs. Laurence's rheumatism. Both Priscilla and her great aunt suffered harrowing colds.

The arrival of spring heralded relief for the latter two complaints. Mrs. Laurence, however, did not appear to have escaped unscathed. Priscilla noticed a fragility about her aunt that she had never before observed. The elderly woman ceased to take daily walks in her garden, as had long been her practice. It was evident that a weakening had occurred. When confronted by an anxious Priscilla, however, Mrs. Laurence adamantly denied any such decline.

In March, their spirits were brightened by a visit from Katherine, who was accompanied by her young son. The child's health had lately improved under the perpetual care of his stepfather. David Adams was dark haired like his mother, but his deep green eyes yet gleamed with the lively wit of his late father. Priscilla detected a keen intellect there since she deemed the boy's vocabulary remarkable for his extreme youth.

Katherine herself did not escape Priscilla's scrutiny. Young Mrs. Guildford had learned to smile again, particularly as she gazed upon her son's newly rose-hued complexion and dimpled grins. She never mentioned her husband in the course of the conversation. Katherine spoke only of her son's progress, concern for Mrs. Laurence's health, joy to see Priscilla, and relief regarding winter's conclusion. Katherine, by her warmth and ease, appeared eager to quell any resentment between herself and her friend. Priscilla, always sensitive to intimation, was only pleased to oblige.

April brought few additional visits from Katherine but marked the demise of one of Williamsburg's most prominent citizens. The death of George Adams had been long anticipated, and such expectations softened the blow. He had never recovered from the shock of his son's death, and, in the end, his heart failed him. The good man had been in the grave less than a week, however, when rumors concerning his near bankruptcy began to proliferate. Before the month was out, Mrs. Adams and her daughters sold the house and threw themselves upon the mercy of her brother in Richmond, who was kind enough to extend his hospitality.

Priscilla knew something of their fate from Katherine, who received the occasional letter from her former mother-in-law. Both Jane and Harriet Adams married soon following their arrival in Richmond, just as Katherine had foreseen. The girls were fortunate enough to marry into the same genteel comforts with which they had been born. Their respective husbands, who had escaped service in the militia by virtue of advanced age, thus relieved most of their father's debts.

In coming years, old Mrs. Adams would travel to Williamsburg for sojourns in the Guildford home in order to visit her grandson, David. Her stay was never long, however, since she always feared that her late husband's remaining creditors would discover her presence in town.

May eventually arrived—along with the following missive from Frances:
Dear Priscilla,

My pen falters to write this note. Hope has fled, and the news which I must now relate cannot be framed in any possible context to lessen its devastation.

Our dearest father was buried yesterday.

I can only imagine your shock at this moment. It could not be more severe than my own at this dreadful hour. We had only recently returned to Kennet

Hall from London. Father was walking the grounds with Ben, who has almost completely recovered from his accident, as well as his steward. The steward was giving his weekly report when Father collapsed.

Within half an hour, the physician was summoned, Father was moved into the house, and we were all alerted as to his condition. Before I could even reach the room where he lay, he passed from this life. Upon arriving, Dr. Humphrey confirmed his death. He also concluded that a heart seizure was responsible. Mother has shut herself up in her chamber.

Words fail, words fail!

I could not even bid him farewell or look into his eyes for a parting glance. Please pardon the brevity of this note. My feelings are too keen for expression! I am your devoted sister—Frances.

Priscilla nearly fainted to read the letter.

What cruel joke had fate played upon her? The crushing pain of loss seared her instantly. The sensations of a lost child quickly supplanted the initial shock. Delusions of her own strength crumbled. The bedrock of her youth was split, her point of reference erased. She longed to cower once more beneath Phillip Parr's shadow and to recover the security she had scorned. For once, she despised Thomas—him whom she loved so deeply that she had defied her father and protector.

"My dear, you have paled!" Mrs. Laurence flung her book aside.

Priscilla could only pass the letter to her aunt with a trembling hand.

Upon reading the letter, Mrs. Laurence unleashed a sharp cry.

"Any hope of reconciliation I might have cherished is gone forever!" Priscilla crumpled upon the sofa as sobs wracked her frame. "You must condemn me now. I, the child whom he loved, gave him the most grief!"

"Were you not the same Priscilla when you defied him as you were as a child?" Mrs. Laurence said with a fierceness that startled her niece. "The spectrum of his feelings—his anger, his affection, his sorrow—ran so deeply against the child in whom he most beheld his own faults and strengths. *You* were that child, Priscilla! When he came to me asking that I offer you shelter, he wept. I remember his lamentation to this day: 'The child I have nurtured is strong enough to stand against me. Thus my blood has sired a noble stock—a rebellious progeny!' His pride was in you, Priscilla. Else, he would never have permitted you to choose your own fate!"

These revelations sent a shiver of warmth through Priscilla. As long as her father had lived, she had drawn her courage from him. Now she stood alone, and all support was removed. The memory of her entire existence flashed within her heart. She slowly realized that, while he had given her life, she must decide its course. This conviction, and none other, honored his memory—as well as the confidence he had invested in her. This epiphany reopened the door to hope.

In moments when emotion could discover no relief in words, Priscilla retrieved her paints. A tribute assumed a shape in her mind, and she plunged headlong into its pursuit. For days afterward, she strove for its completion in addition to the transformation of her sorrow thereby excited. A single object consumed her mind in an anguish-laden creative frenzy. Hours disappeared in an instant as she wove her dream. On the morning of its perfection, Priscilla unveiled her painting to her great aunt.

"Oh my!" Mrs. Laurence's hands covered her throat.

The content of the work was highly unusual and apt to disturb the artistic elite of the day. Still, its bizarre charm drew the eye. It depicted a young girl riding against the wind on a well-muscled stallion. Her shining hair mingled with the sharp breeze as she raced through a field of emerald green hue, which rippled like the ocean beneath a cloudless sky. Observers might draw their own conclusions, but Priscilla recognized her own form riding toward Tom and a radical destiny—exactly three years before.

Mrs. Laurence, donning her spectacles, moved closer to examine the work. "Why, it is *you* in the painting, Priscilla! What is its title?"

"Merely, *The Revolutionary.*"

"Priscilla!" Mrs. Laurence flinched with surprise. "Are you now a devoted child of the revolution?"

The words initially hesitated upon Priscilla's lips. The plight of the colonies had, for some time, mirrored her own. To publicly pledge thoughts that had lurked only within her heart occasioned some doubt. Then, her father's words to Mary Laurence emerged like a fiery beacon. Clarity ensued, and Priscilla uttered the resolute answer:

"*Yes!*"

Chapter 53

The Passing

Priscilla's friendship with both Roger and Katherine Guildford was gradually restored.

This renewal was chiefly precipitated when the Guildfords invited Priscilla and Mrs. Laurence to dinner. Although Katherine had taken pains to assure Priscilla of her goodwill, the latter still approached the evening with trepidation. The memory of her last conversation with Dr. Guildford occasioned Priscilla some discomfort. She also hesitated to observe the very marriage from which she had attempted to dissuade Katherine. She found instead an unusual surprise.

The evening commenced as Dr. Guildford paraded his young stepson before the company. Everyone delighted in the child's gestures and expressions, which even Priscilla admitted were precocious. His wide eyes shone upon them all, and none praised little David with more energy than his stepfather.

"Tell me if our David does not look through us!" Dr. Guildford bounced the child on his knee. "The boy has a brilliance in the eye. Can you not see it, my bonny Kate? Ah, how he laughs! How can he reserve merriment to behold such a mother? She anchors me—and bids me to silence when I should hold my tongue."

Priscilla's gaze shifted to Katherine, whose cheeks burned with embarrassment. Still, Priscilla fancied she detected a pink tinge in her friend's countenance that betrayed something like pleasure.

"You know your own tongue—its limitations *and* its merits." Katherine struggled to suppress a smile. "Your heart knows right from wrong—acknowledge it, and do likewise."

"So speaks my lady, my better self. She always chides me, and I well deserve it!" Dr. Guildford turned to address the child in puerile tones. "Will your musket fire upon a redcoat someday, young lad? Capture hundreds, dear boy. Shall you pause to wonder, 'Is he friend or foe?'"

"Roger!" Katherine's eyes flashed a gentle reprimand. "We must teach our son the distinction."

Her gaze softened him, and he replied in a calmer voice. "I cannot bear *your* reproach, Kate. I suppose our David has the eyes of a patriot!" Glancing toward his wife meaningfully, he smiled and half-whispered, "After all, what is love without liberty? Indeed, what is love without truth?"

Following this brief interlude, which Priscilla would contemplate for many days afterward, the child was lovingly whisked off to bed. As the party subsequently proceeded to dinner, Katherine paused to assist Mrs. Laurence to the table.

Dr. Guildford lingered behind in order to address Priscilla. "Have you lately noticed a frailty about your aunt?"

The question filled Priscilla with alarm. "I have often feared that she never completely recovered from the cold which vexed her this past winter."

Dr. Guildford's grave expression, particularly coming from one so often given to joviality, particularly distressed and perplexed her.

"Her breath is shallow tonight." He gestured toward Mrs. Laurence, who, leaning upon Katherine's arm, shuffled toward the dining room. "She walks with greater difficulty than when I first knew her."

Priscilla entered the dining room and was anxious for her aunt throughout most of the evening. The thought of losing Mrs. Laurence struck her with numb dread. She observed her aunt during the meal and was troubled to affirm Dr. Guildford's evaluation. An ashen pallor drained the elderly woman's cheeks, which appeared strangely gaunt by the glow of the Guildfords' candelabra.

Priscilla's thoughts were briefly disrupted by Katherine, next to whom she sat at dinner. "You must be surprised that I, who denounced the war in my hour of grief, should revoke my own sentiments this evening."

Relieved by her friend's sudden candor, Priscilla nodded. "I am astonished indeed."

"I scorned Henry by mocking the very principles for which he gave his life. Sorrow cannot alter facts—it blinded my judgment then."

"Pardon you, I shall!" Priscilla laughed.

"And you?" Katherine smiled as she raised her glass. "Where do *you* stand? Do you scoff at freedom now as you once did?"

"No," Priscilla said firmly. "I shall never turn my back on the revolution."

Amazement followed Priscilla's return home. The strange affection that had arisen between Dr. and Mrs. Guildford puzzled—and intrigued—her. That Roger Guildford's vociferous cynicism would be conquered by the quiet clear-mindedness of his bride was a spectacle to be marveled at in the eyes of many. In a sharp reversal of opinion, Priscilla rejoiced that Katherine had ignored her own prophecies of doom regarding the match. Indeed, Priscilla now recalled her former objections with no small amount of shame.

Still, pressing worries eclipsed Priscilla's fascination with the Guildford marriage. The words of the physician regarding her aunt haunted Priscilla. As she sat across from Mrs. Laurence in the carriage on the return home, she again noted that her aunt was indeed pale. The elderly woman's hand, thin and gnarled as ever, trembled anew as they both entered the house.

After Priscilla retired to her chamber that evening, such anxieties persisted. Before she extinguished her candles for the night, however, a forceful rap on the door quickly interrupted her thoughts.

To her dismay, she opened the door to a maidservant, who stood quivering from head to foot. "Please, come quickly, miss!"

Panic froze Priscilla's heart. "What is the matter?"

"It is Mrs. Laurence! She is ill—and asking for you."

"Please fetch Dr. Guildford at once." Priscilla, clothed in her nightgown, rushed down the hall to her aunt's chamber and threw open the door.

There she beheld Mrs. Laurence. The woman's eyes were fixed upon the ceiling, and her chest heaved in distress as she gasped for breath. The sight sickened Priscilla to the heart.

She hurried to Mrs. Laurence's side and clasped the frail hand. "I have come, Aunt! Dr. Guildford has been summoned. You will soon be well again. I am certain of it."

"It is no use, Priscilla," Mrs. Laurence murmured between breaths. "My heart is weak."

Priscilla kept vigil at the bedside as they both awaited the physician. In the dreary silence, punctuated only by Mrs. Laurence's laborious respiration, Priscilla sensed the sting of impending loss. The aunt who had taken her in had become like a second mother. When all the world had forsaken her, Aunt Laurence had protected and nurtured her. *There* Priscilla was sure to find a sympathetic soul in which to confide. In her fragility, Mary Laurence was strong.

Dr. Guildford's arrival halted Priscilla's desperate musings. He was followed by Katherine, who immediately went to Priscilla and extended a hand of consolation. Dr. Guildford's expectations were grave by the indication of his countenance.

Still, as he rushed to Mrs. Laurence's bedside, he forced a smile. "How are you feeling, Mrs. Laurence?"

"I am unwell—I cannot breathe!"

Dr. Guildford fingered her pulse. Priscilla heard his sharp intake of breath as he uncurled Mrs. Laurence's bent fingers, the tips of which had acquired that blue tinge so characteristic of poor circulation. After several moments of calculation, evaluation, and further examination, he gestured for Priscilla to follow him.

Once Priscilla, Dr. Guildford, and Katherine had moved into the hall, his expression turned somber again. "Mrs. Laurence shall not survive the night. There is nothing I can do."

Katherine's features twisted in sympathy. "Oh, Priscilla, I am so sorry to hear it!"

The grim prognosis left Priscilla with none of the demonstrative woe that had accompanied knowledge of her father's passing. Instead, a silent hopelessness stilled the words upon her tongue. She felt like a figure in a dream as she entered the room again and took her aunt's hand once more.

To Priscilla's surprise, Mrs. Laurence spoke first, albeit in faltering tones. "You have been as a daughter to me, and a more faithful one I could never have found. I always say this…do I not?"

Priscilla strove to steady her voice. "Indeed."

"I do not say it idly. You see, I did once bear a daughter. Her name was Elizabeth—Elizabeth Laurence, my only child. Her hair was golden as the sun, her eyes blue like a clear sky. The very image of my husband John! Elizabeth was the sort of fragile yet determined soul that you are, Priscilla. Plagued by a weak constitution since birth, she died of consumption at nineteen. Such brilliance…such goodness…to be enclosed by the grave when its fragrance has only begun to enrich the world!" Mrs. Laurence then gave a painful sigh.

Priscilla blinked with shock. "Why did you never speak of this daughter, Aunt?"

Mrs. Laurence failed to acknowledge the question, yet resumed her speech. "Your father placed you under my care when you were nineteen—the age of…Elizabeth! I could scarcely believe it. It was as if God had entrusted me with another daughter. Only do not fail me, Priscilla! May the painting be one of many. You have chosen liberty—*chase it!* You have been given life."

"I promise." Priscilla wiped away the tears that now ran down her cheeks. "I could never deserve your great kindness to me!"

The end was serene. Pausing only to pray or read Psalms aloud, Priscilla stroked her aunt's hand. Roger and Katherine Guildford, speaking to the suffering woman in soothing tones, also tarried at the bedside.

Five minutes past midnight, the labored breathing ceased, and Mary Laurence slipped away.

Chapter 54

The Spy

The death of Mrs. Laurence removed Priscilla's greatest support. The future, now devoid of her aunt's love and encouragement, appeared bleak. She wondered if her own loneliness was not unlike that which Mary Laurence had endured following Elizabeth's untimely death. Priscilla could only feel ashamed of her own pain when she contemplated the anguish Mrs. Laurence had suffered beneath a cheerful countenance for so many long years.

It nevertheless astounded Priscilla that her aunt Laurence ensured her provision from the grave. Since Mrs. Laurence had no direct descendants living, the reading of the old woman's will was awaited with no small measure of curiosity by her acquaintances. Their astonishment and disappointment upon learning that the entirety of her fortune and estate passed to Priscilla Parr can scarcely be imagined. This fiery scion of the Parr bloodline had become an affluent, and thus independent, young woman. At last she was free, yet Priscilla mourned that this taste of liberty had come as a consequence of her beloved aunt's passing.

In such a state of mind, Priscilla greeted the following letter from Frances at the first of August:

Mary Beth Dearmon, MD

Dearest sister,

Our spirits, so forlorn after Father's death, have been lately lifted by a certain event.

Ivy was married to Sir Geoffrey this morning. They shall spend the wedding night at Redmond Park, Sir Geoffrey's estate in Sussex, from whence they shall set off for the Continent for their wedding tour.

You may recall that, as I related in an earlier letter, our brother suspected Sir Geoffrey's character. Those doubts, as far as I know, were never resolved. Still, Ben had no heart to oppose a match so fully approved by our late father. I hope that love exists there. I can assure you of Ivy's affection for him. In addition, I believe the title of "Lady King" pleases her very much.

Richard Carey was among the guests at the wedding, which took place in the chapel at Kennet Hall. I espied him during the ceremony, and our eyes met. He had fulfilled his promise to call upon our family following the London ball. We had pored over the geography book together, and he had brought me a more advanced volume on mathematics, my favorite pursuit. Ben has learned to like him well—thus his invitation to our sister's wedding.

Richard approached me following the ceremony. He spoke of his progress at Lincoln's Inn and his future plans. "I intend to pursue a seat in the House of Commons when it next becomes vacant."

"Which seat?" I asked.

"My eye is fixed upon one of the Cambridge seats."

"It has been a lifelong ambition for you, has it not? I remember! You shall be a fine statesman someday. I know of no heart half so devoted to Britain—and the liberty of her people."

He gazed at my face intently. "What is your ambition, Frances?"

"I should like to pen my own mathematical theories."

"Excellent!" He beamed. "You are more than capable of such a feat."

"I did not think so myself before—" My voice trailed off as I became fearful of betraying the strength of my own feelings toward him. "—before discovering the merit of scholarly pursuits."

"It opens one's door to the world," he said. "And to other things as well! It introduced me to a particular marvel over a year ago…in Sir Henry Blount's library. Do you remember that day also, Frances? I shall never forget. A young lady was there who possessed promise which she herself had yet to unlock—brilliance *and grace beyond compare. I know her better now, and she is dearer to me at this moment than anything else on earth."*

Priscilla, my heart nearly ceased to beat! Happiness was mine to command. I had nurtured hopes of such a declaration since Sir Henry's ball in London. Anticipation, uncertainty, and hope culminated in a joyous outcome. That such a man could love me—awkward little me!

"I remember, Richard." I sensed a fevered blush rise to my cheeks. "I am honored by your sentiments."

"Have I permission to write to you while I am in London?"

I suddenly felt giddy. "You have it."

Thus was a particular understanding established between Richard Carey and myself today. He departed for London this afternoon. The sooner he arrives, the sooner I shall receive a letter from his hand.

I can scarcely write for glee. How ignorant a girl I must be to have once considered Seymour! Your affectionate sister—Frances.

Despite Priscilla's previous refusal of Dr. Guildford's proposal, she was still highly regarded by his elderly parents, so much so that her former aversion to old Mrs. Guildford had subsided. She surmised that the physician's passion for his new wife erased any resentment his kindred might have otherwise nursed on his behalf. Instead, the elderly Guildfords often called upon Priscilla, but one such occasion in late August was to occupy her attention for weeks. The dismayed expressions of the pair as they entered Priscilla's parlor frightened her.

She rose to her feet in alarm. "Your faces betray evil tidings!"

"The tidings are intriguing, but not quite evil," Mrs. Guildford said.

Mr. Guildford made himself comfortable on the settee. "James, our manservant, has overheard a rumor on the street."

Priscilla's interest was enticed. "Which rumor?"

"It shall be a *great* scandal!" Mrs. Guildford laughed.

"Please tell me," Priscilla said as gently as possible.

Mrs. Guildford smiled and wrinkled her nose as if suppressing her delight to bear such news. "William Eton has deserted the Continental Army!"

Priscilla stood quite still with amazement. "Surely this is a mistake," she gasped. "I heard him pronounce a soaring defense of the rebels at the Governor's Ball—nearly four years ago. In fact, he pledged aid for their cause!"

"Perhaps he disguised his motives." Mr. Guildford shrugged. "We have details. It seems that he has acted as a spy for the redcoats since entering the war. Encrypted letters from his British contacts were uncovered among his possessions and held as proof of his guilt."

Priscilla sensed herself grow pale with shock. "How did he escape hanging?"

Mrs. Guildford sighed as she righted a stray white hair that fell from her cap across her brow. "He learned that some of the officers suspected the truth, and he was thus able to flee before they had his things searched."

"Where is he now?"

"No one seems to know his whereabouts." Learning forward, Mr. Guildford fingered the gilt handle of his cane. "He is believed, however, to have reached the British ranks."

Priscilla's thoughts churned. "If this report is true, then he is no longer effective as a spy now that his intrigues have been discovered. What shall the redcoats do with him?"

Mrs. Guildford waved her hands nonchalantly. "I suppose he will fight with them."

Priscilla was secretly disgusted by the Guildfords' indifference to William Eton's alleged offense. After the couple left that afternoon, Priscilla paced the floor. The deception William had practiced upon all his friends and acquaintances was unparalleled. She still could scarcely grasp the evil that had lurked beneath that quiet brow for so many seasons past. His infamous reserve had long been an instrument of duplicity. *Indeed, he is so unlike Tom*, she thought with a shudder.

Memory and conjecture followed fast behind one another. She recalled Thomas's assertion of four years ago that Mr. Eton moved the family to Williamsburg in hopes of severing his eldest son's friendships with noted British sympathizers in Richmond. William's supposed pursuit of a wife had come to nothing, and, in light of recent revelations, Priscilla was convinced that it had been merely a screen to conceal his intention to conduct espionage in the capital of Virginia.

A bolt of realization struck Priscilla. Could William Eton be the mysterious "E." in George Seymour's correspondence with Phillip Parr? The possibility coincided with logic. Perhaps the seeds of William's treason had been sown as a young lad, when visits to his uncle's plantation would have thrown him into company with the Loyalist Seymours. The thought brought to mind Thomas's odd remark concerning Anne Seymour: *My brother thinks marvelously well of her!* Priscilla wondered if Thomas had even then suspected a conspiracy.

In the silence of that lonely evening, anger spilled over into the realm of action. She pondered her own abilities and how they might aid the very revolution that William had betrayed. Paintings, she quickly decided, would never win battles, but medical knowledge might. Her experience as Dr. Guildford's assistant would hold some value for the beleaguered Continental Army.

The hour to pledge her support had arrived.

Such a trek to join the forces of freedom would pose many dangers with which Priscilla was not equipped to contend alone. In this dilemma, she thought at once of her Aunt and Uncle Wallace, who had proven resourceful on many past occasions. After all, they were old acquaintances of General and Mrs. Washington. The Wallaces' connections within the movement were extensive, and Priscilla determined that their assistance might be of most use. In this spirit, she resolved to write them.

The following morning, Priscilla called upon Dr. Guildford in order to solicit a letter of commendation, which would confirm the soundness of her character and the sufficiency of her skills. Such a request required a full disclosure of her plans. Although her announcement elicited surprise, the physician proved obliging. After composing the letter in her presence, Roger Guildford sealed it and wished Priscilla a good day. Having procured the letter, she rushed home and penned her own epistle to her uncle. She enclosed her lines with those of Dr. Guildford and dispatched both letters.

Chapter 55

The Journey

Priscilla received a response from her uncle in early October.

My dear niece,

Your letter was most welcome, and I am honored that you should apply to me for assistance in this worthy endeavor you have proposed.

I have already taken the liberty to make the necessary arrangements. Your guide will be a certain Abraham Wright, an informant for the Continental Army and a Virginian for whose character I can vouch. He is aware of troop movements and is therefore well suited to convey you hence. You are to meet him at the Market Square in Williamsburg at half past nine on the morning of October 25th. He will take you north.

Your aunt sends her love. With many prayers for your safety and prosperity in these perilous times, I am affectionately—J. Wallace.

Priscilla was delighted, yet surprised, to receive such a satisfactory reply. She had half-expected her uncle to remonstrate with her concerning the great dangers implicit in the scheme. Nevertheless, she rejoiced in his understanding. As she had awaited his response, her fervor to participate in the revolution had attained such a zenith that she had almost been prepared to depart Williamsburg alone. Her uncle's letter ensured a less vulnerable exit.

With her journey thus confirmed, Priscilla commenced to plan for her own absence. She furnished her servants with wages for the foreseeable future as well as detailed instructions for the preservation of her belongings. In addition to retaining their own quarters, they were to maintain the house in good order until her return. Priscilla also arranged to carry a large sum for her own sustenance. An evaluation of her possessions in order of importance was also required. Although the decision was wrenching, she finally decided to pack only her worn Bible, a second pair of shoes, two cloaks, a change of gown, clean bandages, and an extensive collection of medical notes she had taken during her months as Dr. Guildford's assistant. She also resolved to include a pair of Mr. Laurence's shoes, which her great aunt had always cherished in his memory. Priscilla pondered the value of those sentimental articles to some bedraggled soldier.

Weeks elapsed at this level of preparation and activity. Despite her eagerness to proceed with her plans, however, Priscilla could not escape pangs of remembrance and nostalgia the day prior to her departure. She braved the bustling streets alone to walk toward the churchyard of Bruton Parish. For some time that morning, she stood before her Aunt Laurence's grave in quiet reflection. Fond memories of the kinswoman who had shown her such kindness drew tears to Priscilla's eyes. She sincerely believed that her aunt would have sanctioned her present course. Priscilla even wondered if the old woman's death had not wounded her more deeply than that of her father.

Upon leaving the churchyard, Priscilla walked home in silence. She saw Thomas upon every street corner. As she passed the Palace Green, she remembered the fresh-faced young boy with whom she had capered there so many years ago. For once, however, she did not long for the days of childhood. Although she had been innocent, she had also floundered in ignorance. She rejoiced in the demise of her naïveté.

Priscilla paused upon reaching the Eton house. The drapes were heavily drawn as if to conceal the shame of William's treachery from the world. Her heart leapt at the sight of the house where she had first glimpsed Thomas four years ago after such an extended separation. She still remembered how his eyes had so inexplicably arrested her. In retrospect, she was certain that she had loved him even then. The memory of Mr. Eton's attempt to divide them, however, accompanied these tender recollections. This knowledge did not render her desperate as in former times. Priscilla was now a woman of independent means. As such, *she* was no longer at the mercy of that capricious patriarch, and, consequently, neither was Thomas.

Upon returning home at last, she was surprised to discover that a letter from Frances had arrived during her walk. With rising anticipation, she broke the seal of the missive and read the following words:

Dearest Priscilla,

Many hopes which I had begun to cherish at the time of my last letter have since seen fruition.

Ivy and her new husband are due to return from the Continent any day now. I am a little surprised that she has written no letter to the family since her marriage. Still, I suppose we should not expect communication from Ivy. It is likely that wedded bliss forbids the composition of letters and other such mundane affairs.

Our brother has a son at last. His wife was delivered of the child yesterday. Young Charles, named for our brother who was lost, must become a great personage indeed to justify the ambitious expectations which have already been affixed to him. He is a healthy child with a bounty of dimples, and his arrival can only portend prosperity.

The birth of Ben's second child, instead of eclipsing his first, has produced the opposite effect. The fulfillment of his longings for a son inflicted shame for his past conduct during a period when such a desire was thwarted. Guilt, along with a natural inclination, has compelled him to shower affection upon the child he once spurned as a symbol of her mother's death—our niece, Sarah, whose antics at this tender age portend a brilliant mind. In addition, although the birth of Charles has drawn Ben and Rosamund closer together, I believe it is a credit to our brother's character that he learned to love her before their son was even conceived.

The remainder of this letter is devoted to my own good fortune.

I am to be married within the month. Richard and I had not exchanged three letters before we were engaged. Ben and Mother have come to respect him highly, and our proposed marriage therefore received little protest from that quarter. Richard shall soon conclude his studies at Lincoln's Inn, after which he intends to pursue one of the Cambridge seats in Parliament. I am confident of his success. His fiery eloquence and incisive wit cannot fail to capture support wherever he goes. My judgment, as well as my great love for him, declares this to be so.

You will be gratified to know that I have begun to pen my mathematical theories. Hopes of success in this regard are yet premature, but I will not shun the attempt.

I wish you as much happiness with Thomas as Richard and I are destined to know. Never fear for me henceforth, Priscilla. I have found myself at last. Your loving sister—Frances.

The engagement of Frances heralded a new season. Priscilla contemplated the years and circumstances that had shaped them both. Frances's newly awakened intellectual aspirations could only be viewed as additional evidence of these changes. Old hopes had perished, and new expectations had taken flight. As God directs the affairs of man, so had His hand wrought their respective destinies. Priscilla communicated these sentiments and more in a congratulatory note to her younger sister, which she left in the care of the manservant with instructions to mail it following her departure.

Priscilla awoke the next morning in a state of readiness tempered by uncertainty. Her spirits were eager, although her reason urged apprehension. Following a light breakfast, she collected her previously determined traveling items. Placing these possessions within her bag and bidding goodbye to the servants, she ventured forth from the house. Passing the buildings that had dominated the landscape of her childhood, she nevertheless refused to succumb to the fit of sentimentality that had seized her the previous day. With a mind that would not be swayed, she reached the Market Square at the appointed time.

The chants of merchants, although less strident and numerous than before the revolution, burst forth around her. She was accosted by tradesmen who mistook her for a potential buyer. Having courteously shunned their efforts to flaunt their wares before her, she stood apart gazing at the lively spectacle. The clamor briefly relieved her mind of fears regarding the future. She was thus startled to perceive a light touch upon her shoulder.

"Miss Parr?" an urgent voice whispered.

She quickly turned and beheld a stocky man wearing a seasoned green coat. The tilted angle of his hat obscured his countenance.

Her heart swelled with expectation. "Sir?"

"My name is Wright—Abraham Wright," the man quietly replied. "Come with me."

Chapter 56

The Soldier

Priscilla could not suppress horror at the sight before her.

In the two months since she had left Williamsburg, she had endured more perils and hardships than she cared to remember. The onset of winter had particularly crippled and hindered her journey, but her travels had been somewhat eased by her purchase of a horse in one of the small towns along the way.

Priscilla, along with her loyal guide, had reached Pennsylvania at last. Still, none of her sufferings could equal the scene she presently beheld.

"The Continental Army?" she asked Mr. Wright, who rode his own steed beside hers.

"The very same," Mr. Wright replied.

Men, young and old, trudged wearily in the distance. She first espied their haggard forms through the trees. As her horse repeated their steps, she noticed the freshly spilled blood lining the path the soldiers had tread into the snow only moments before. Where she had expected a shining military force, a raggedly clothed multitude of half-starved men greeted her instead. She suddenly despaired for the revolution.

"Where are they going?"

"Making their way to Valley Forge, where they will spend the winter," Mr. Wright said.

Priscilla, accompanied by Mr. Wright, followed the soldiers deeper and deeper into the forest. The freezing cold of the morning was almost intolerable. Her breath became a chilled plume that billowed before her eyes. Her hands became numb as they gripped the reins. Thick clouds brooded overhead as if to blot out the sun at war's decree. The winter air stung her face until she reached the rear of the army.

The stench of disease and death swiftly clung to her senses. As she pulled up her horse beside the men on either side, Priscilla realized that they barely regarded her presence. Their eyes were instead fixed upon the unseen road before them. Many of the weather-beaten revolutionaries were wracked by harrowing coughs, which pierced the uneasy silence. Seemingly unmoved by the snow beneath their feet, they limped forward. Officers on horseback somberly surveyed the scene from atop the hill as the soldiers ascended. She concluded that her own sacrifices on behalf of liberty were nothing in comparison with those who surrounded her at that moment.

As Priscilla rode forward slowly, her gaze fell upon the trail of suffering that littered the roadside in the marchers' wake. Young men, swathed in gory bandages, collapsed—only to stand again as they leaned upon their muskets for support. Some, however, failed to rise. Priscilla could no longer remain oblivious to this great struggle for life. Dismounting her steed, she clutched her bag and rushed to aid the soldier nearest to her.

She placed a hand upon his arm and shook him gently. "Sir!"

At her light touch, the man's gaunt frame tumbled toward her. She recoiled swiftly.

Open-mouthed and pale-faced, death stared back at her.

After feeling for his pulse and detecting none, she covered her face in desperation. For a moment, she considered lying down in the snow and embracing the fate to which the poor soldier had succumbed. Why had she come at all? How indeed could a sheltered young woman who had never before tasted the bitterness of physical hardship sway the fate of nations and remedy human misery? Her own futility struck a vicious blow.

A sudden irregular movement arrested her attention. Another soldier, grasping his shoulder, dropped out of the cavalcade.

She hastened toward him and knelt in the snow without a second thought. "Sir, I have labored beside a physician—and can help you."

The man grimaced with a jolt. "My shoulder…it has tortured me for days…since the action at White Marsh."

Without seeking his permission, she immediately palpated his shoulder joint. A square aspect, as opposed to the standard rounded contour, greeted her fingertips. "A dislocation." She reached for a small broken branch that lay in the snow beside her. "Clench your teeth upon this."

Following the example set by Dr. Guildford, she proceeded to rotate the man's bent arm until range of motion at the shoulder was restored. After the deed was done, the man's muted cries subsided.

She assisted him to his feet. "Your condition should improve."

He turned to her slowly. "Thank you, miss." His weary eyes wandered past her face. "Only likewise help my brother-in-arms. The boy fell a few paces back. He saved my life at Saratoga. There he lies…next to yonder tree."

She instantly spied the young man as he lay limply in the December snow, destined to perish. Searing pity drew her to his side. As the grim march continued around her, she unclasped her cloak and draped it across his thin shoulders. Reopening her bag, she withdrew the sturdy shoes that had once belonged to Mr. Laurence. Priscilla thus clothed the soldier's naked feet. She then invested all her strength in a successful attempt to help him stand once more. As he rose to his full height, which was considerable, his eyes—though partially shaded by the blood-soaked bandage that ringed his head like the laurels of victory—suddenly entered her view.

Priscilla initially averted her gaze, but something quickened her heart like fire.

Those eyes!

They met her own with so familiar an expression that she trembled forcefully. The power of recognition drew a bitter sigh. The love born in her girlhood could not wither, even in the icy forests of Pennsylvania.

She leaned her head upon his breast as her tears moistened his threadbare uniform. The agony of separation vanished in a mere moment—as if it had never been. So violent was her joy that she believed herself incapable of releasing him.

Strength gradually returned to his limbs, and his long fingers stroked her hair. "Oh, my love," he whispered in a broken voice.

Her tears gushed with even greater volume than before. "Can you not hear the cadence to glory? It has already begun. We heard it long ago, you and I! Lean upon my shoulder. Let us live... *and take our liberty!*"

Retrieving the musket that had fallen to his side, Thomas plodded onward. Priscilla strode with the fierce will she had always known, determined that nothing would ever wrench her from him again. With liberty and love in their youthful hearts, the pair continued forward, side by side, in their faithful march toward the revolution.

Chapter 57

The Nation

The skies over Williamsburg were brilliantly blue the day that Thomas and Priscilla became man and wife.

Priscilla was now twenty-seven years old. Her countenance remained lively as ever. Nevertheless, her fondness for petty disputes over form and fashion had given way to a penchant for more selective battles as well as an unswerving resolve. Her years as a nurse for the Continental Army had sharpened her will and heightened her compassion. She had come to feel that her fate was bound to that of the revolution. Such a conclusion was confirmed by her own marriage.

Little of the impetuous youth remained in the man beside her. His tender white hands had been hardened by the musket he had clutched for so long. Battle had also inflicted a scar above his left eye, which still echoed pain from the blow. The desolation of war, however, had inflamed—rather than tempered—his ideals. Priscilla still recognized the fierce gleam in his gaze that had first so deeply moved her ten years ago.

The four witnesses to their union, who lined the front pew of Bruton Parish throughout the ceremony, had also changed.

The awkward affection that had sprung up between Roger and Katherine Guildford prior to Priscilla's departure from Williamsburg six years ago had since deepened. Roger had learned to rely heavily upon his wife's fortitude and patience, qualities in which he himself was deficient but which had first drawn him to the young widow of

Henry Adams. On her side, Katherine was still occasionally embarrassed by her husband's boisterous antics. These sensations, however, were nearly always eclipsed by abiding gratitude for his love and care for her son David, whose present robust health she attributed to the medical expertise of his stepfather.

In addition, the physician's persistent devotion to her could not be long resisted by a heart so warm as hers. She had borne him three children of his own, which had cemented their bond. Katherine had also come to take pride in her husband's professional accomplishments, for his willingness to incorporate smallpox inoculation into his medical practice had earned him great prosperity and renown in Virginia.

Nevertheless, they had known adversity as well. Their second child, a daughter, had perished shortly after birth, and Dr. Guildford had lost his elderly parents the previous year. In all these trials, the physician's steadfast support had almost made Katherine forget his many faults, and, despite the difference in taste and temperament that still remained between them, she had learned to love him.

The second couple to witness the union of Thomas and Priscilla had also suffered the testing of time. Shame had primarily afflicted Richard and Augusta Eton. Mr. Eton's threats of financial ruin toward his younger son had been withdrawn upon being informed of the elder's treason. In the eyes of his aged parents, William's political betrayal was deemed a personal betrayal as well. The contrast between the two brothers was as stark as that between self-interest and sacrifice.

In the first months following the discovery of his espionage, William had sent his father many letters in quick succession stating his situation with the British army and his need for funds. Not only had the elder Mr. Eton refused each application for his aid, but he had also forwarded his son's letters to the proper authorities in hopes that the young man might be found and made to suffer the punishment prescribed by law for traitors.

Thus did Mr. and Mrs. Eton disown William. The crimes of the elder son dwarfed the fancies of the younger, including his choice of bride. For this reason and since Priscilla had demonstrated support for the revolution, the consent of Richard Eton for the marriage was awarded to Thomas when he returned to Williamsburg after the war. Mr. Eton, although now enfeebled by severe rheumatism, gazed with undisguised pride upon Thomas—a faithful son of the revolution.

The ceremony also invited thoughts of those near to Priscilla who were absent from the occasion. Immediately following the British defeat at Yorktown, she had written to her sister Frances for the first time in four years. Several months afterward, she had received the following reply:

Dearest Priscilla,

I rejoice to hear your voice again—if only on paper!

Much has changed since we last exchanged letters.

I have been the wife of Richard Carey for four years. In this period, I have also become the mother of sons. The elder is named Joseph after Richard's late father. The younger is named Phillip, for reasons which you will surely deduce.

My husband was unable to obtain one of the vacant Cambridge seats in the House of Commons, but he recently captured one of the Kent positions. His lifelong objective is partially fulfilled. In fact, his latest speech on the floor of Parliament drew much admiration from prominent newspapers. I am utterly convinced that he shall be a great man someday.

As for my own ambitions, I am delighted to inform you of the completion of my treatise on mathematics. It was published under the pseudonym "Frederick Carlisle" and has been received to significant acclaim in Britain. Perhaps you will hear of it also—on the American side of the Atlantic. I long for the day when I can freely identify myself as its author. Alas, the times are not yet ripe for that revelation. I shall always be prepared for such a transformation.

Our brother and his wife yet live. He is still plagued by severe headaches, the last remaining symptom from his accident. It is likely that they shall afflict him for the remainder of his life. As the father of a growing household, however, his mind is distracted from this weakness. In addition, he recently purchased Pennington & Co., an enterprise which operates from Bristol and sends merchant vessels into the Indies. Ben's new venture is not without risk, but successful voyages often yield magnificent profits. Of all his children, young Sarah is particularly fascinated by the entire business. I must confess myself amazed by her wit. Although she is flighty, she has not the cold and troubled heart of her late mother.

Before giving an account of our sister's fate, I shall relate news of a scandal which has erupted upon these shores. A month ago, word of a fierce duel surfaced in London and the surrounding counties. The case involved a once-secret Loyalist society which had maintained a vast espionage ring in the colonies prior to and during the war. The conflict existed between two members of the society and concerned a broken engagement. Rumors came in fragments, and I soon heard that both men hailed from Virginia. Names and facts succeeded hints. A certain William Eton had challenged a man named John Seymour to a duel—and had slain him!

Details crept into the public realm. It seems that William and Anne had long been secretly engaged. You communicated in your letter that the discovery of William's treasonous activities had resulted in his disinheritance. Following the British defeat, William, desperate for money, fled to England, sought out the Seymours, and claimed Anne's hand. When Mr. Seymour, suspecting William's motives, refused to allow the marriage after all, the duel was arranged. (Mercifully, it appears that our friend Margaret Lee Seymour was well provided for by her husband's will.) The next day, William and Anne were married. As far as I know, he has still not resumed his profession, but they are sustained in London by the fortune left to Anne upon her father's death. They are not received by decent society. Their names have been tainted by this tragic affair.

The remainder of this letter concerns our sister Ivy and the events which preceded her death over three years ago.

Although she married Sir Geoffrey in good faith, his character was soon exposed. Their wedding tour was scarcely a month old when he expressed the truth to Ivy. He declared the existence of numerous mistresses, particularly in France. He also revealed that a sizeable debt incurred during an earlier stay upon the Continent had induced him to marry her and thus claim the fortune of fifteen thousand pounds she received upon our father's inheritance of Kennet Hall. In short, he had sought an heiress—and had found one. She had served her purpose, Sir Geoffrey informed our poor sister, and might now return to Redmond Park or do as she pleased. (I tremble to write his vile words, Priscilla.)

Ivy returned to England alone, carrying the child of her faithless husband. Upon reaching Redmond Park, she confessed the ugly particulars to our mother in a letter. Richard and I, then newly married, visited Ivy shortly before the birth of her son, and I have never beheld a pride more thoroughly crushed than hers. She had plunged beyond the reach of solace. Her labor was difficult and, coupled with her despair, proved too much for our sister. She died the following morning.

Ben discovered Sir Geoffrey's whereabouts through the latter's brother and then promptly wrote to the villain. Sir Geoffrey's letter of reply expressed irritation regarding the child's birth and indifference concerning his wife's death. He refused to leave the Continent at that moment and instead suggested that Ben serve as the infant's guardian until he returned. The child, named Isaac, remains in our brother's care to this day.

I pray that I have communicated these events as clearly and truthfully as possible.

Our mother and brother are aware of this letter and bid that I suggest you come to England following your marriage, a prospect for which they joyfully hope. I am instructed to convey their deep affection for you.

Richard also hopes to meet you soon, for I speak of you constantly.

God bless you, dearest Priscilla. I wish you utter happiness, for you have richly earned it. I am ever your affectionate sister—Frances Parr Carey.

The griefs and joys contained within the letter had been considered and experienced by Priscilla in full measure. Still, thoughts of Britain—and intimations of future excursions there—shrank before the burning light of her love for the man to whom she was joined before God. Their lives would continue where the war had disrupted them. Thomas would receive his degree from the College of William and Mary as he had originally planned. They desired to then relocate to Richmond, which had supplanted Williamsburg as the capital of Virginia in 1780. There Thomas, after studying the law under a distinguished attorney of his former acquaintance named Robert Locke, hoped to establish his own firm and enter the political realm. Priscilla expected to continue her artistry with greater courage than before as well as to nurse suffering humanity wherever her compassion and skill were needed.

Britain never emerged upon the horizon bordering their dreams. The children had broken free to seize liberty. Reaching toward the uncertain, they had attained it—and reaped glory. As they would later tell their children and grandchildren by the light of many a glowing fire, they were heirs to the revolution.

It was therefore only appropriate that Thomas and Priscilla, their commitment to one another indomitable as the towering oak beneath which they had once pledged their troth, were married three weeks after the Peace of Paris was signed—and on the soil of the new nation.

CPSIA information can be obtained at www.ICGtesting.com
Printed in the USA
LVOW04s1951190215

427562LV00034B/1294/P

9 781502 768612